THE CROW ROAD

Kerry McGinnis was born in Adelaide but has spent most of her life in the Australian bush. She started writing at the age of nine and has published seventeen books. These include two volumes of autobiograpy and twelve Outback mysteries with Penguin Random House; the first book of her trilogy 'Far Seeker' was published by Elliot Mackenzie Ltd UK and the next two by Keypress Publications. Kerry's hobbies are reading, music (she's learning the harp), gardening and travel. She currently lives in Bundaberg, Qld.

ALSO BY THE AUTHOR

Pieces of Blue
Heart Country
The Waddi Tree
Wildhorse Creek
Mallee Sky
Tracking North
Out of Alice
Secrets of The Springs
The Heartwood Hotel
The Roadhouse
Croc Country

The Far Seeker Trilogy

Far Seeker
The Burning Mountain

THE CROW ROAD

KERRY McGINNIS

THE CROW ROAD

KERRY McGINNIS

© 2021 KERRY McGINNIS

All rights reserved

Apart from any fair dealing for the purposes of private study, research or review, as permitted under the Copyright Act, no part of this book may be reproduced by any process without permission.

Paperback

ISBN

978-0-646-83370-5

Designed and Typeset by Keypress Connections
Palmwoods Queensland

DEDICATION

To the memory of Jill Slack. Poet, writer, mentor, friend.

THE STORY SO FAR

When the Great King Cyrus expanded his empire into the Lower Land to subjugate the kingdom of Rhuta he set in chain a string of events that eventually brought about his death. Leona, princess of Rhuta and sworn to celibacy as the god's Oracle, broke her oath and fell pregnant to Cyrus's son Smerdis. Twin boys were the result, the eldest smuggled from the birthing room to be raised in secret as the rightful heir to the crown. The younger, Prince Marric, whom Cyrus had anointed as his successor, to live in obscurity until he became a fugitive hunted by his uncle Temes, Cyrus's youngest son. Temes arranges Cyrus's murder along with the rest of his family (including, he believes, Marric) then seizes the throne of empire where he reigns as a sadistic tyrant.

Despite the dangers besetting them the brothers reach adulthood, each assuming the mantle of his calling, Darien as a warrior prince, Marric as a prophet. The people of Rhuta rise behind Darien to fight for their freedom. The kingdom of Barat, a free country to the west of Rhuta, joins them along with the resistance fighters of subjugated Ansham. Temes's cause is hampered by disaffection in his army and by being permanently at war with the tribes from the Seas-of-Grass, a vast prairie land adjoining Appella's eastern borders.

Rhuta wins the war and Temes's death brings peace: freedom, courts of justice, and religious practice are restored but Temes is not the only ambitious Appellan in that militaristic country. And fifteen years on when a new generation looks to old grievances and past glory, trouble looms once more for the brothers and the people of Rhuta.

KERRY McGINNIS

1

It was, Burran thought in a mixture of fury and terror, a bloody stupid way to die. His arm muscles cracked and he tightened his grip on the branch, unable to tear his gaze from the snake's deadly form. The dark head was reared to strike a mere hand's length from his fingers. He could see the scales across its throat the colour of green bone, and the way they gradually darkened to an olive-y brown over the upper parts of its body. It was a big one, not quite as thick through as his own wrist but damn near and, he estimated, as long as he was tall. Not that this mattered. A bite from even a baby tanda would kill, and this specimen was plainly full grown.

He dared not move but unless he did and soon, his hands would open of their own accord. It was a fair drop but survivable — if the snake didn't get him first. Which it would. Tanda strikes were known to be faster than the eye could follow. He could drop but he'd never get clear for it would strike the moment he moved. Pampasans apart, they were the deadliest creatures in the Seas-of-Grass.

The air above his head suddenly divided and he ducked involuntarily, the movement causing his aching hands to slip on the tree branch. He felt himself plunge earthwards, but the snake followed him down; its coils were on top of him, heavy, writhing across his shoulders. He gave an inarticulate yell of horror and flung out an arm to fend it off, as his body crashed into a sturdy lateral branch as hard and solid as rock. The momentary halt in his descent separated them. He bounced off the tree and the earth caught him, smashing the air from his lungs. Wide-eyed, he struggled to rise, to find and distance himself from his enemy, but pain was an iron grip holding him fast. He could neither breathe nor move. His last thought before blackness took him was that the tanda had got him and he hadn't even felt its bite.

Consciousness returned as a sea of red shot through with fire. He heard himself give a sharp cry as his right arm was ripped upwards, then his breath went out on a gasp that dragged his eyes wide to the sight of the barbarian crouching above him.

'Bel's balls!' This was worse than the snake. He grabbed frantically for his sword and a flood of liquid fire froze his arm. 'Haah!' he roared and the woman — for it was a woman, he belatedly realised, leaned heavily on his chest.

'Pr-risoner,' she said in accented Appellan. 'You, pr-risoner.'

She looked calmly fierce — or fiercely calm — he thought. At any rate, quite sure of her ability to constrain him. Her long dark hair was plaited into a tail and her chin carried the swirled ink of a tattoo. She was small, measured by Appellan standards, but lithe and wiry with well toned musculature, as the weight behind her body showed. Barbarian eyes, Burran knew, were slightly slanted and invariably dark, and hers were no exception. She was young too, more girl than woman, dressed in pants, boots and some sort of soft tunic divided between her small breasts by the strap of a quiver. He could see the arrow tips above her right shoulder. A knife handle protruded from one boot and a short, curved blade hung from the belt cinching her waist.

'Merciful Mother,' Burran muttered. And he'd thought

the tanda was trouble! Where was the bloody thing anyway? He lifted his head, saw his captors face darken and spoke quickly in Appellan, 'Snake. Where —?'

'I kill,' she said firmly. 'You. I fix.' She scowled, lifting the deadly Pampasan bow in her right hand and jerked her head at him. 'Come,' and warningly, 'I kill.'

The threat seemed one very likely to be carried out. Burran lifted his arms, the right one more slowly testing the limits of the damage. He'd put his shoulder out in the fall, he realised. It ached fiercely enough but the crippling blaze of agony he'd experienced on waking had thankfully passed. Once on his feet he saw the body of the tanda looped about itself in the trodden grass, an arrow skewered cleanly through its head. He swallowed and the girl noticing, gave a satisfied little smile as she jerked her head at his mount.

'Run — I kill.'

He nodded his understanding, careful to move slowly because she seemed rather fond of the idea and certainly looked ready enough to carry it out. Besides although the danger was no less, he had achieved his goal after a ten-day of sneaking about dodging Appellan patrols in the hope of somehow making contact with the tribes from the Seas-of-Grass. He had always been hazy as to how exactly he was going to manage this without being summarily killed, but it seemed that he had. Which wasn't to say that his execution didn't wait around the next bend.

The snake might have proved an easier ending after all. They said the venom was quick while the Pampasans were a byword for savagery. The tribes lived in a permanent state of warfare and were known to have a short way with outsiders. Burran's pulse raced at the thought. He was no soldier, he reminded himself, just a blameless independent trader from Rhuta, which country had no quarrel at all with the tribes. If he could just convince them of the fact.

His captor tied his hands together with a leather thong then jerked her chin at his horse. Both packhorses had pulled loose from their ties, possibly at the sight of their master hurtling out of the tree, but they had stuck around to feed. The woman scooped up the lead ropes and affixed them to Burran's saddle, then gestured again for him to mount.

Bigger and stronger, if not much taller than his captor, he meekly obeyed. Only a fool would not. The endless pattern of waist high meadow that stretched to the horizon on three sides of him, broken only by the very occasional tree, was not he knew, as empty as it looked. This woman, girl, was no lone hunter. Her clothes looked serviceable but they were of good quality, her quiver-fringe was tipped with silver and from the chunky gold chain about her neck hung a globe of amber. She was somebody of consequence in the tribe, which meant that she had an escort.

He saw them on the thought. One moment the land was empty, and the next six men had risen from the grass. Lithe, and dangerous looking, as darkhaired as the girl, and armed to the teeth with identical weapons. Keeping his face still Burran looked them over. Young, save for an older man who nodded impassively to the girl's quickly flashed look of triumph. He said something, it sounded like a word of affirmation and she nodded, obviously pleased. One of the others jeered and then they were crowding him, shoving and shouting in their outlandish tongue until the older man spoke again, and they moved back. Then came an upheaval in the grass from which six of their sturdy mounts suddenly appeared, as though wished into being. Trained to lie down, he realised, hidden by the grass. They all mounted and with the girl at the head and the rest jostling about him rode deeper into the verdant meadows from which few, if any, outsiders ever returned.

It required an effort to keep his shoulders slack and the tenseness from his hands, to remember that he was here by choice. Eyes and ears alert, however useless that should prove to be, Burran rode docilely to his fate, thinking of a room in the palace at Ripa, and a man's narrow, dark, clever face laying out this crazy plan that was like to get him killed. The Lady protect me, Prince Marric, I must've been mad, Burran thought glumly.

They stopped for a meal when the sun stood halfway down the western sky. The older man said something and the little party halted and swung down. They had ridden for perhaps three hours, Burran calculated, and there was nothing in sight but grass. Oceans of the stuff, head heavy with seed, the gold slowly overlaying the green. Tiny birds swayed here and there on the seed-heavy tops, and myriads of spiderwebs were strung between the stems. They seemed to be following a narrow trail through it, marked only by the pad worn by the passage of hooves. A stranger would have little chance of escape even if he were free, for lacking water or direction he was as likely to run unwittingly towards danger as from it.

One of the Pampasan, the long haired one, who had been the first to jeer and threaten, grabbed his bound hands and heaved him from the saddle. Burran hit the ground hard and lay still, offering no resistance. A boot took him painfully in the hip then the girl shouted something and his tormenter scowled but desisted.

'Bastard,' Burran muttered and if the word was unknown to the man the sentiment wasn't, for his eyes flashed balefully. Stupid, the trader berated himself. Long Locks wasn't likely to forget. He sat up, bound hands resting on his thighs and waited. They gave him a few mouthfuls of water before the skin bag was snatched away, but no food though they made their own meal seated cross-legged around him, chattering away in their incomprehensible language.

He had a little of the tongue for he had spent seven years now travelling the continent of Balusia first as an apprentice for the house of Trader Ramie and then on his own account as a small trader/agent for the king's twin brother Prince Marric, statesman and royal advisor to the throne. Like all traders Burran had a quick ear and a facility for the half dozen languages spoken across the continent; the ability had stood both him and the throne in good stead since the kingdom had regained its rightful ruler.

Burran had been a boy when the royal brothers had overthrown the tyrant Temes, King Darien's uncle, who had hacked a bloody path through the nobility of Ansham and Rhuta to seize his illegal prize. For almost two decades he had held wanton murderous reign over the two countries, pillaging, looting, killing as he chose until the economy of Rhuta and Ripa, its principal trading hub, had been decimated. Its citizens, taxed and flogged and tortured beyond bearing, had finally risen under the brothers' leadership and when the battle was done and the tyrant dead, life had begun again for Rhuta's embattled citizens.

Now, listening as his second trade demanded, Burran heard the girl speak several times of someone called Leris. The older man in the company was Yerb, but he could catch no other names. Yerb seemed to be in charge even if it was nominally the girl's show. He wondered if he himself was the prize in some kind of test set young warriors where they led a raid or captured an enemy to prove themselves worthy of leadership. In which case, if the girl was as important as he suspected, then Yerb's purpose could be to see that she succeeded, or at least came to no harm.

Regrettably, from Prince Marric's point of view, very little was known in Rhuta about the politics, quarrels, and economy of the volatile people of the Seas-of-Grass. And his agent's knowledge wouldn't improve it Burran thought, until his (Burran's) grasp of the language expanded. The trouble was the clansmen spoke quickly, slurring their consonants in a way that made it hard to distinguish between words. His ear needed a lot more practice. Burran, straining to attain it, kept his face blank and wished that his hands hadn't been tied quite so efficiently. To distract himself from the throbbing ache he studied the faces around him, catching the eye of Long Locks, presently using his dagger to cut off a section of what looked like dried or smoked meat. The man grinned nastily at him, fed the chunk into his mouth then mimed a slash of the knife across his own throat. Burran yawned and looked away.

When they were ready the girl came to stand above him, her face fierce. 'Up.' The accented Appellan mangled the word but the gesture that accompanied it conveyed her meaning. 'You — ride.'

'I know sweeting, or you'll kill me,' Burran said whimsically with a tired grin. 'A bit of dinner would've been nice, too.' His tone must have provoked for the fist in his ribs didn't, this time, come from Long Locks. He was hauled roughly back into the saddle, his reins taken up by one of his captors and they jolted off again through the interminable ocean of grass.

It grew dark and still they rode. Burran's head as well as his hands ached by then and he had a raging thirst. He was jostled along more quickly as the night fell, the man leading him having shortened the reins, so that their knees frequently bumped. It was quite difficult, he was discovering, to balance in the saddle without the benefit of either reins or light. There was no moon and the star sprinkled sky was dizzying in its enormity. He looked up once and almost fell as the world tilted, thereafter he kept his gaze down. Then Yerb spoke and he sensed a sudden eagerness in those around him, a shifting, a perceptible creaking of saddles as the riders straightened in their seats. Lights burst suddenly out of the blackness ahead as the smothering grass dwindled about them, and in the shadowed dimness he discerned a wide clearing. They had arrived — if not at their final destination then at least somewhere. Burran let out a cautious breath of relief, and readied himself for the next move in the play.

As far as he could see in the leaping light occasioned by a series of fires the place to which they had come was more camp than permanent village, or town — if these people had such a thing. The tales told of them were of a houseless, nomadic society perpetually on the move across the vast swathe of grasslands they inhabited, and fiercely defended. But they must, Burran reasoned, have settlements or how else did they raise their food, and administer whatever laws bound and controlled them? Certainly the hut he was thrust into through a round doorway had the settled look of a much used building. Walls and floor were of clay, the latter a hardened glaze darker than the ochre-coloured bricks of which it was constructed. The roof was thatched with long bundles of tightly strapped grass, weathered into greyness in the fitful firelight, and, he guessed, annually renewed. It was supported by thin lathes of timber and the only window opening was set small and high in the wall. The door was a circle of stiff hide lashed to what looked like a willow frame that had been bent to shape.

Pushed into its dim interior, his hands still secured, Burran looked his prison over, shrugged and lowered himself to the floor. The door closed behind him and a chatter of voices arose without. Somebody called what sounded like a greeting and he heard the girl reply and her excited, triumphant laugh. Light from the fires flickered unevenly through the window. He could kick the pitiful door open he supposed but to what end? Escape, save as a last resort, was not part of the plan. *It will be dangerous*, the prince had said, *understand that. But I do not think you will be harmed.*

'And it's important?' Burran shook his head at the memory. Dumb, he'd been dumb even to ask, knowing what he did about the slender, dark eyed man he served.

'Of course. There is some vital purpose. I cannot see the end. Only that it matters.'

'You'd better be bloody right, Prince,' Burran muttered now under his breath. His stomach growled hungrily and he had the mordant thought that death by starvation mightn't be entirely improbable either.

Time passed, voices came faintly to him and presently the sound of music. Some sort of reed instrument accompanied by a regular beat not quite deep enough for drums. The occasional shout echoed along with raucous laughter. It sounded very convivial to Burran and did nothing for his parched throat and empty belly. He spent a little time trying to stretch the leather that bound his hands and failing rolled over onto the floor, to husband his resources in sleep.

He was sleeping when they came but some vestigial awareness roused him a second before the attack. There were two of them, the handheld torch, a branch thrust into the coals of the fires now sunk to embers, providing a flickering, inadequate lighting in the murk of the hut. The first kick landed before Burran got his feet properly under him and the next felled him again. Long Locks rasped something and swung a hard fist and his companion joined in with relish, their grunted incomprehensible words an accompaniment to the beating.

Burran, smothering his more tender parts with his tied wrists, dodged and rolled as best he could as the blows rained down. He got in only one riposte when the second man brought his gloating face too close to his own. Pain and fury momentarily over-riding caution Burran whipped his head forward, smashing the weight of his skull into the other's unguarded nose. It brought a howl of protest from his assailant and, by the instant warm spatter across his own cheek and throbbing head, a rush of blood from the broken nose. There was little time to savour his victory however, for an instant later the world exploded and everything went black.

Burran woke, moments or it could have been hours later, to find himself alone, in considerable agony and total darkness. Gasping with pain he got himself to his feet, every inch of his body protesting. His lips were split, he had a pounding headache, an extremely tender face and the sight of only one eye. The other, he discovered, had swelled shut. A faint paleness showed where the window was and he shuffled towards it, to view what stars he could see. No light or sound broke the darkness save the soft sough of the wind. The door rattled and he wondered what would happen if he managed to open it. But escape was not only not possible, it was out of the question. With his hands tied, and the horses guarded, as of course they would be, his captors didn't even need the poor security of the hut. They could just have left him alone by one of the fires and he must perforce still be there in the morning.

It will be hard... The prince's words. Yeah, well — Burran spat the salty taste of blood from a gashed inner cheek — if a single beating was to be the worst of it he'd got off lightly enough. All the same let him survive this situation and Long Locks was going to regret his night's work. That, his battered body slumping back to the floor where he groaned and lay still, he promised himself.

The rattle of the door opening woke him. He made to sit up, was hurtfully reminded, and satisfied himself with squinting through his one good eye. It showed him a grey light beyond the day space where the camp was stirring, and the girl, dressed and armed as before, entering with Yerb watchfully at her back. She called something to him, a command and then, eyes adjusting to the dimness let out an exclamation that conveyed both anger and alarm. Burran struggled into a sitting position. Pride be damned he thought, if they wanted him ambulant they could untie his hands. These members were now quite numb and an awesome shade of purple. Taken together with how his face felt he was probably not a pretty sight.

The girl whirled on the older man, rapping out a question which he repudiated curtly. Lifting his hands, shaking his head he plainly knew nothing of the night attack — or if he did wasn't about to admit it. Snarling, the girl dragged the dagger from her belt and came forward to cut his hands free. It wasn't a simple task for the flesh was so swollen about the thongs that she had to ease the tip of the blade between his wrists with some care to avoid cutting him.

She barked a question at him, plainly 'Who?' but if he could, or had wanted and been able to name the culprits, he was too parched to speak. He managed a croak and she spat out something angry and curt to her minder. Yerb demurred and she wheeled on him with a rapid fire string of either instructions or curses, and gauging by the high colour in her face and her snapping eyes Burran wouldn't have bet it wasn't the latter. It was enough. The man flung up his hands and went, to return presently with a flask of water.

Burran's hands were useless, throbbing great hams on the ends of his arms. She crouched beside him and held the vessel to his lips, pulling it away whenever he choked from drinking too greedily. He closed his single eye at the bliss of the cool nectar irrigating his throat.

When then was no more she stood, considered him for a moment, then bowed stiffly and made a short speech of which the only word that stuck was what sounded like a name: Sonj.

Burran repeated it in an interrogative tone and she tossed her black plait and struck a slim hand against her breast, saying again curtly, 'Sonj.'

Understanding dawned. He struggled stiffly to his feet and stood before her, finding himself only half a hand taller. He bowed in return as he repeated the name.

'Sonj.' Then pressing a hand to his own bruised front enunciated slowly, 'Burran.'

She nodded, mouthing the strange sound, making of it 'Berhan.' It was near enough and taking the opportunity while it presented, the unfamiliar words awkward on his tongue, he asked for food. Half a day and a night had passed since the honey from the tree where she had captured him, had been supposed to supply his last meal. His own rations had been finished the day before that and his hunting had met with little success. He was very hungry and worse, knew his body to be weakening from the effects of that hunger.

Outside the hut the grey he had seen proved to be mist. It veiled the grasslands beyond the cluster of rude buildings from which the dew dripped, and half hid the horses someone had brought up. The flames of a fire cast a dull aura from which men's voices sounded, their shapes half visible in the cloaking moisture. Burran followed the quick striding girl — Sonj, he repeated silently — Yerb watchful at his back, and absorbed as much as he could of his surroundings. There seemed to be no regular inhabitants, which made the centre no more than a camp. But the fire had been lit on their arrival, which argued that the patrol led by Sonj had divided, those who hadn't ridden out waiting here for their friends' return.

Burran wondered why. When they reached the fire he counted a dozen men standing and squatting about it as they took their morning meal. One, he was happy to recognise as the man whose nose he had broken the previous night. Long Locks standing beside him said something that made Broken Nose scowl, then wince. The organ was red and swollen and both his eyes had blackened in sympathy.

Sonj, walking straight up to the pair, snarled something and before Long Locks could reply delivered a stinging open-handed blow to his face, followed up by an angry tirade she punctuated with a stabbing finger. The rest of the group stared in silence but the struck man made no attempt to retaliate or deny his deed.

Face crimsoned from more than the blow, he stood enduring the dressing down until finished, she smacked the food from his hand. He accepted that too, without demur. Turning then to Broken Nose Sonj did the same with his breakfast. Yerb watched impassively as with a jerk of her head she sent Long Locks from the fire while a snapped order had Broken Nose scurrying to procure and deliver food to Burran. Face carefully blank the latter took it in his swollen hands and squatted to eat.

The meal consisted of dried meat strips and some sort of flat cake, oaten, he thought, so presumably somewhere within the vastness of their plains the Pampasans farmed. Too hungry to be critical he ate with concentration and drank the hot liquid of some stewed herb his unwilling servant also produced. By then the mist was thinning with the sunrise. Large numbers of crows flew in to strut along the huts' roofs cawing noisily, white ringed eyes inquisitive and knowing. Then Long Locks led the girl's, and Yerb's and Burran's, saddled mounts forward. He also brought the loaded packhorses, along with two other saddled mounts, which turned out to be his and Broken Nose's.

The reins of these and the packhorses' lead ropes were scooped up by the riders, and the girl led out, Yerb at her shoulder and Burran following, his aching hands still unbound. Glancing back at the deserted ring of huts he saw his previous night's assailants following the cavalcade on foot. Neither looked happy. Burran was heartened. It was partly the food, partly the fact that he held his own reins however clumsily, but also the knowledge that whatever the final outcome, nobody was going to kill him today.

He was of a sanguine disposition and told himself that the initial contact had always been the trickiest bit. He'd managed that and still breathed; he'd manage the rest too.

2

That day mirrored the previous one in that the grass ocean rolled endlessly before them under the blue bowl of the sky. It was warm, but not unbearably so for summer was new. There was nothing to see beyond the grass and the sky, nothing to hear save the moving horses, the sough of the wind that made undulating waves of the grass tops, and the cawing of crows. There must, Burran thought, be other birds in these wide expanses besides them and the little wren like ones he had seen the day before, but if so they were hidden away in the dominating feature of the landscape. The two men following them on foot had fallen behind, too far back now for footfall, or complaint, if they made it, to be heard.

Today, Burran saw, each rider carried the belongings previously left in the camp. The slim sleeping rolls were tied behind the saddles while the rest was carried either in soft pouches balanced over their mounts' withers, or rolled into skins and attached to a saddleflap with the rider's leg over the top. A hardy people, they travelled light and were in no way hampered by their baggage.

At noon they halted to eat, which allowed the laggards to catch up. The girl interrupted a conversation at their arrival to snap something at them. Both bowed meekly and sat without partaking of either food or water, but when they moved on she had relented enough to permit them their saddles again. He'd been right then, Burran saw; someone with authority. Surveying the shoulder high growth beyond the little circle they had trampled flat for their resting spot, he wondered how hunting worked here. Could you even see the game? And how would hare or coney manage to move in it? Or fox to catch them? Then Yerb stood up and they resumed their saddles and rode on.

At sunset, just when Burran suspected they meant to keep riding until they hit the shores of the Eastern Sea, they arrived at their destination. The country had changed by gradual degrees, the first scattered trees appearing as the sun westered, their frequency gradually increasing, along with a slight elevation in the land. When they finally ascended the last gentle slope and reached its top Burran looked down on a shallow, well wooded valley with a stream running through it, the water shining pewter in the dying light. Smoke rose from the cook fires of many houses where lamps had begun to wink on. Green lines of agriculture showed on the slopes and there was stock at pasture and the faint tinkle of bells overlaid by a heavy pounding such as a working smithy might produce.

All Burran's trading instincts roared back, subsuming the prince's agent, and he sat eagerly forward on his mount. Here was new country, the heart of a strange and different culture with many needs and who knew what goods — either useful, strange or wonderful — to exchange for them. And he, the first outsider, was here in their midst and about to discover it all.

It was quite a large settlement spread along the length of the valley. Fishing boats were drawn up on the river bank, above a mill by the water with a large storehouse nearby; the probable source of the grain in the oat cakes. Further downstream were pens and yards and a tannery, judging by the stink and the many hides hung over poles to dry. There was a timber yard holding the trunks of felled trees, either rafted or towed there, he supposed, with piles of split timber.

Paths rather than roads ran through the town and Burran could see no sign of wheeled traffic but railed shelters, where horses might be held, stood at the back of most buildings. He saw artisans' workshops, closed now their workers had gone home. A smithy whose forge still glowed with embers. A bowyers workshop, its front wall lined with drying lathes for future bows. A pottery with a vast, mud plastered kiln beside it. There were few people about, most would be at their evening meal, but those he saw who stopped to watch their column come, carried no arms. And why not, deep as they were here in home territory?

When the girl finally pulled up they were among the houses. Swinging down she spoke to the men leading Burran's packhorses. The rest dispersed, Yerb taking the girl's reins which left her free to walk across to Burran.

'Come.' She jerked her head and obediently he dismounted and followed; Yerb, watchful as ever and leading their three mounts, trailed behind.

She was really quite pretty, Burran thought dispassionately. Oh yes, and deadly. A fact not to be forgotten. Her people had raided and killed their neighbours for past-time, and had held their own against the Appellan forces sent against them, which included killing Cyrus, one time Great King of all Belusia. They were a practised and murderous foe, cunning and quick, never meeting in open battle but appearing and vanishing out of their grass like demons from the Appellan's Abyss. Ambush, and lightning raids upon unprotected farms or unwary trade caravans, were their specialty.

Once, the old tales had it, the youthful Cyrus, then little more than a hill chieftain, had followed a raiding party deep into the Grass and fought hand to hand with a Pampasan queen whom he had killed. It had been the beginning of his rise towards greatness. Until the same people had eventually taken their revenge on him and thus loosed upon the land his son, Temes, to bring long years of terror ended only by the uprising in Rhuta.

And now Cyrus's grandson Darien ruled in Ripa, and Burran, here at his brother's instigation, had to somehow change the mindset of this murderous nation, into becoming the friend and trading partner of his own. It will be hard ... Indeed it would, he thought sardonically, if not impossible. And let's not forget that to achieve it I must first survive.

Yerb, with a brief whistle brought a young lad running. He gaped at the three travellers, eyes widening at Burran, but took the reins and led the horses away into the darkness. Then silently the other man stepped up beside the Rhutan and Burran felt something slip over his head. He stiffened as the noose fell about his throat and with a great effort of command didn't raise his hands to fling it off. Yerb handed the trailing end to the girl who snapped something at him, then tugged lightly on the rope. For a single instant Burran's heels refused to lift, then flushing he forced his feet to move and allowed himself to be led off.

They didn't travel far. The dwellings which at first glance appeared haphazard in their placement, were actually Burran saw ringed concentrically about a large central hall. A place for feasting, or meetings, he thought as they entered. No guards stood before it though it was obviously an important structure, its tall timber supports heaving the roof trestles twice the height of a man. Here was no mud brick but a lavish use of stone and wood with a dais at one end, and a chair of state. The floor was flagged and the light came from cressets in holders against the walls.

It also served it seemed, as somebody's dwelling. The long table before the dais contained dishes from a meal recently served and a clutter of weapons and other gear, while a saddle, bridle and an elaborate horse cloth were stacked to one side. Bows and quivers and the short and deadly curved blades hung or lay amid mundane household articles. He saw a child's toy, a spindle, a half-knotted rug. At the rear of the dais behind the high chair of state a door hinted at living quarters of which this was the overflow.

Sonj called, 'Leris,' the name Burran had heard before, followed by a rattle of words, then the door he had just noticed opened and a woman came through, her face lightening from repose to register satisfaction. She clapped her hands together once and nodded and the girl cast a triumphant glance back at him, pleased, he could see, by the reception his presence had wrought. The golden tones of her skin, part suntan, part native colouring, bore a slight flush as she led him to the table and pointed at a chair. 'You — sit.' With a twist of her wrist the shaming noose flipped over his head, freeing his movements.

He sighed, 'I know. Or you'll kill. It grows a wee tiresome all these threats.' The hairs on his nape lifted as he spoke. He stilled, suddenly aware of an unseen presence somewhere behind him. Lifting a hand to rub his neck, he twisted his head as if relieving stiffness but could spy nothing in the shadows.

The woman Leris said in painstaking Appellan, 'Guest. Not kill. Be welcome please. Sit, eat.'

He bowed, the action hiding his relief. It was all right then. The prince's sight had not, in this instance misled him. 'I cannot always read the meaning of the Seeing aright,' he had warned. 'It is only fair that you should know; I have been wrong before.'

'Greetings, lady,' Burran bowed. 'You speak Appellan then?'

'Little. Words only.' She was perhaps ten years older

than the girl, to whom she bore a certain resemblance, the same dark hair and eyes, though her face was broader, and there were fine lines about her lips and eyes. And the same swirls of tattoo marring her chin. She wore command like a cloak and he intuited that here was a leader, perhaps even a ruler. They said that women led and fought like men in the Grass. She approached him, right hand forward and not knowing what else to do Burran received it into his and bent to kiss it. She snatched it back and equally startled he raised his eyes to meet her frowning gaze. Nonplussed he spread his hands in apology.

'Your pardon, lady. What?'

'Sonj.' A rapid word and the girl came forward extending her hand in turn to the woman who clasped the offered arm, receiving in return a grip about her own forearm. He understood then. It was a warrior's form of greeting and of course these women were warriors. There was no place in this world for court courtesies.

'Ah,' he nodded, and when Leris offered her hand again he responded correctly.

'So.' Her eyes bright with satisfaction Leris placed a hand on the closest chair, repeating, 'Sit. You, we teach — talk, living yes?'

'We learn to speak together, and know each other?' Burran hazarded slowly, unsure how far her understanding of the language went. 'Me you,' he gestured between them, 'make friends?' She was nodding, brow creased with the effort of following his meaning. He tried to simplify the message, wondering if she could read and write, and how long it would take for him to become fluent in their tongue. A season or two? And, more pertinently, whether this was a one leader crusade or if the whole nation desired rapprochement with their neighbours. Judging by Long Locks's antipathy the latter seemed unlikely, which might make his personal situation rather precarious.

The food was good; meat, mutton he thought, a strong cheese, goat perhaps, a platter of what looked like assorted weeds that Leris pushed towards him. He helped himself and tried them, finding the fresh crunch and herby taste a perfect foil for the fatty meat. There was more of the oat cakes and a fermented drink that tasted like no beer he had ever drunk, served in wooden cups, and to finish a handful of early berries. He knew them from home and exclaimed with pleasure. 'Ha! boysa. Good, yes?'

'Good,' Leris agreed and Sonj who had shared their meal said, 'Eulth.' She held up a berry, 'eulth.'

'Ah,' he nodded, repeating the word, then inspired, made writing motions with his hand and raised an interrogative brow.

'Yes, yes.' Leris was nodding but Sonj had already risen and hurried across the dais to the room behind to return with a scroll of coarse paper, a stoppered inkhorn and quill. Burran smiled as he took it, and caught up in the satisfaction of the moment, she permitted herself a brief smile in return. Flattening the coarse paper and in the smallest hand possible, for there were going to be many new words to learn, Burran wrote *boysa* and then its counterpart in Pampasan. It was a small start, but it was a start.

Neither of the women however would leave it at that. He must write until the entire contents of the room and even the scraps left on the table had been catalogued before he finally dropped his pen, pushing the paper away. 'Finish,' he said, and cradling his whiskery jaw on both hands mimed sleep. 'Rest now.'

The hour was late; only silence and blackness under a sky of stars lay beyond the hall. Taking a cresset from its stand Leris led him from the building and on a winding path through the darkness to the door of a small house of clay brick. Stepping inside she used the flame of her own light to kindle the lamp waiting on a shelf.

Then with a word she turned and left. He called, 'Wait,' without thinking but when she stopped he realised the impossibility of learning more from her. It would all have to wait until they could converse more freely. Her reasons for allowing his presence here, her exact position in the town/tribe/nation that made such a thing possible. How the patrol had known where to find him, and most intriguing of all, by what means his own master had been informed that Burran's presence would be welcome in the Grass. It was too involved, too chancy a message to try to convey. Instead he reached to tap the cresset and say the word for it. She nodded and he waited brow raised, until she fumblingly repeated it.

'Good,' he smiled, then bowed satisfied, and let her go. The toil awaiting him shouldn't, he thought, be one-sided. If he must learn their tongue they could also learn his. Language, the prince had said, was a tool that fostered understanding. And without that peace could not exist.

Left alone he lifted the lamp and explored the little house finding the amenities basic but acceptable. There was a table, two sturdy chairs, a cupboard, a clay lined hearth for cooking, a bed, a basin for washing. Utensils for eating and cooking had also been supplied and, he discovered, his own belongings returned to him. His clothes and bedding lay atop the grass stuffed mattress on the bed with his weapons disposed beside it. That argued trust and good intentions, he thought, before logic intervened with a more cynical reasoning. He was just meant to think so, for it would be death to use them. If they really trusted him returning his horses and gifting him with a map would more nearly prove it.

***

In the palace in Ripa where it was almost as late, Prince Marric pushed aside the papers he was reading, and delicately touched his forehead where the pain had flared, sudden as a stab from the dark.

'What?' The king looked up. The brothers were not alike, Darien's red hair in sharp contrast to Marric's black. Separated at birth and reared apart they had since learned each other very well, and if his brother's strange gift still sat uneasily with the king, he was not so foolish as to refuse the advantages it could bring his reign. With sudden sharpness he said, 'Fenny? My mother?'

'No,' Marric replied tranquilly. 'A brief seeing from the Grass, that is all. My man is there, and safe for the present. I own it is a relief. It has been some moons since he went and had he died we could never have known the manner of it. We should call it a night, Darien.'

'Aye,' the king yawned. 'You have a headache and my bed has been waiting this last hour. When do you return to the Lakes?'

'Tomorrow. Tarris will burst if I delay longer.'

'No doubt', the king said dryly. 'Don't encourage the brat, Marric. It would do my son no harm to learn control.'

'True, but it will come. And it is never too soon for him to become known to the people. How better than to share for a little their way of life? He will learn it is not all palaces and ease, and that will benefit his training as nothing else could.'

'Of course you are right.' Darien rose and stretched, pushing his own papers aside. 'No, leave them, Jerrod will put them away. I'm for bed.'

The party left Ripa early next morning while the mist still lay above the smooth roil of the Great River, and the palace gardens dripped with dew. It was a small party: Marric and his secretary and the young princeling Tarris, with an escort of attendants and soldiers. Protection of their persons was unnecessary for the peace attained at such price fifteen years before remained unbroken, but the army, Darien maintained, needed to earn their keep.

It was a long climb back for the nation, Marric knew, to the heights of prosperity their maternal grandfather's reign had once enjoyed. Temes had undone and squandered so much in his twenty-year tenure. He had ruined lives, outlawed worship, taxed trade to the hilt; there had been torture and theft and rape and murder, all done in his name. Ripa, the golden city, had been brought to its knees and the economy beggered, but slowly and steadily, under his brother's competent hands, it was regaining its former mantle.

The Mother's sacred spring had been cleared and the shrine rebuilt. The once powerful Temple of Bel, a hotbed of sedition before the war, had been cleansed of recalcitrant priests and the bulk of its income diverted to the treasury. Nowadays the priests kept the feast days, and prayed before the image of the god, but the high-priest had no seat at the council table among those who advised the king.

Tarris, an athletic thirteen-year-old whose half Appellan heritage showed through in both his height and auburn hair, fairly bounced with impatience to leave.

'You could try helping,' his uncle suggested, 'there are boxes to be ferried to the packs.'

The boy looked scandalised. 'The servants will do it. Is it true Uncle that once you were a Trader? Rel says you have been everywhere. To the Black Country and Meddia and have even gone on ships — which my father, the king, hasn't. Is it true?'

'I was an apprentice,' Marric said. 'And yes, I have visited those places. And packed camels, and lit campfires and carried water at need. Work is not demeaning. It built this city, this palace, and it has done me no harm.'

Affronted the boy said, 'But I am a prince!'

'So, they tell me, am I,' his uncle replied, adding

thoughtfully, 'We do not care so much for consequence in the Lakes. Can you swim, nephew?'

'Swim? No. What has that to do —'

'Ah, I believe we are ready.' Marric swung into the saddle, calling as he reined away from the boy to take his place at the column's head, 'I think perhaps it is something you had best learn.'

They travelled at a good pace though there was no hurry that Tarris could see. Proud of the bow he carried he had wished to divert from the straight cross-country route to hunt, only to have the request denied by his uncle.

'You will find sport enough on the Lakes. The birds there fill the skies, indeed the skilful seldom return without a full bag.'

'Birds,' the young prince curled his lip. 'I was thinking rather of deer.'

'Another time perhaps. We have victuals enough for the journey.'

Tarris sulked but it had no effect on his uncle and riding stubbornly silent beside him, he cast surreptitious glances at his father's twin whose face never showed what he was thinking. His father was, on occasion, given to royal rages, but Tarris had never seen this quiet man beside him less than equable, and wondered how the two could be so different and yet so closely related.

He knew that the palace servants held his uncle in great awe. Marric's mother, Tarris' grandmother, who had been killed by a plot of the high-priest, and who in turn, so Rel swore, had been slain by Uncle Marric, had been an Oracle of Bel. The wishes of the god had come to her in visions, and it was whispered that Prince Marric had inherited his mother's gift. If so he had never spoken of it. Only the way men looked at him, their respect tempered with awe, showed that it could be true if even soldiers were a little afraid of him. But he never wore a sword and Tarris doubted that the story of him killing the high-priest was anything more than a tale.

He had asked his father about it once but his timing had been wrong in that he had been in trouble earlier that day. He'd been rude to one of his father's councillors who was only a common trader anyway, and had unfortunately, been overheard. The king was still angry with him as his curt dismissal of the question had shown.

'When you have learned enough courtesy to behave as you should, you may ask me again.'

So of course he couldn't, but it was possible he thought suddenly, that if he asked her, his Aunt Fenny would tell him. Women mostly did what he asked. His nurse had always been easy to get around, and his mother, the queen, doted on him. It was no secret in the palace that his two sisters, Saffon and Rosel held second place in Ling's heart. It was natural after all, he was heir to the throne. The most important person, after his father, in the whole of Rhuta.

They made camp just before sundown. The animals were unloaded in an orderly line and the campfires readied while the tents were raised. Tarris shared with his uncle but the cook of the party had a tent all of his own, even though the captain and his soldiers he saw, had nothing over them but the sky.

'It is good practice,' his uncle said when asked. 'Men on campaign must be able to hear without hindrance.'

'But there is no danger here,' the boy protested.

'So it would appear,' his companion agreed affably. 'Let us suppose then that they are accustoming themselves for when there may be.'

Tarris stared at him. 'So did you sleep uncovered when you were trading?'

'Yes, in fact we did. And sometimes owed our lives to it. Now, everyone is busy and we will need water for washing. Why don't you take the pail there and bring some from the stream? Tomorrow the way is dry and we must rely on what we carry.'

Tarris would have liked very much to point out again that he was a prince, but something in Marric's dark, steady gaze changed his mind. Taking up the handle he did as he was bidden. His uncle behaved properly in the palace, he thought, just like he belonged there, but really the man was not very royal at all.

3

The province of the Lake Country, which his uncle governed, was a revelation to Tarris. In theory he knew it to be a watery wilderness on which its inhabitants built their homes, but the reality was both astonishing and strangely beautiful. The party came upon the fringe of the lakes out of dry, scrubby land across which they'd been riding seemingly forever, into the fresh green sight of willows fringing a vast shore. Not a great deal could be seen of the actual water because of the myriad islands of man-high floating reeds which, moved gently by wind and current, drifted across the face of the lakes. The province was roughly two thirds the size of Rhuta, his uncle informed him, but with half its population, nearly all of whom lived in floating dwellings.

When they had unpacked and turned the horses into a fenced field a fleet of little boats were located by the soldiers and they all embarked, Tarris and his uncle in the one light craft, his secretary and an attendant in another, and the rest two by two until all had been accommodated, with the baggage piled on two large flat raft affairs, towed by four of the boats. The captain of the escort led off and his uncle, picking up the paddles, sent their vessel shooting after them so fast that Tarris was forced to clutch at the sides. They were reed boats, sealed with pitch and seemed very unstable.

'Sit still,' his uncle advised. 'You will soon find the way of it.'

They paddled a long way, swooping around the really quite enormous islands of reeds, startling waterfowl into flight, their wake setting the reeds rocking. He saw a furry shape his uncle said was an otter and then completely lost his bearings. With the shore out of sight it was all water, towering growth, and bird flecked sky; a fish jumped and one of the soldiers started to sing, the chorus soon taken up by the others. His uncle joined in and Tarris, sitting behind him, listening and watching the rhythmic swing of his shoulders, thought it just as well that his father, and not this man who behaved like a common soldier, was king.

They came eventually to Lake Town, a bustling hive of floating homes and businesses, linked together on massive reed platforms, either side of watery streets. All were a universal grey, the colour of the dried reeds from which they were constructed. Dozens of the little boats crossed and traversed the spaces between the buildings, smoke rose from cooking fires and a cheerful clangor filled the air: children at play on the platforms, women's voices, men calling greetings and questions, and the hammering of industry.

Tarris was astonished. 'Does everyone live here?'

'Here in Lake Town and in the other settlements. The lake system is a vast one. The Lady's shrine is on the shore, and some few families graze animals, but we are a people of the water, Tarris. The lakes give us sustenance and are a defence as well. This is home. Up you go.'

He had spun the boat around bringing it to rest at the foot of a ladder leading to the platform above. The painter was looped with a practised flick and Tarris, wobbling unsteadily, lurched sideways to grab the ladder and pull himself up. Marric followed and looking behind him the boy saw that the raft with their luggage was already at the foot of the platform while the men responsible for it, standing as insouciantly as if the moving boat were solid ground, tossed it up to the servants who received it. To one of them Marric put a question. 'My lady is at home?'

'She is with a guest, sir,' he responded. 'Shall I arrange refreshments?'

'That would be appreciated. Come nephew. It has been a while but you will remember your aunt Fenny?'

'Of course,' the boy said. It had been several years since he saw her last for his girl cousin was sickly, and rarely travelled. Uncle Marric had no sons, which was a pity. Girls, particularly sick ones, weren't much use for games, or sport, or anything really. He followed his uncle into the dwelling noting that all the rooms, their reed lined walls woven into patterns, were smaller than the palace's, and comfortable rather than grand. Instead of woven rugs the floor covers were skins, and save for the tabletops even the furniture was made from reeds plaited and worked together. In an airy inner room furnished with padded couches and chairs, two women were sitting over a serving of wine and cakes. One, he saw was his aunt, fair-haired and as pretty as he remembered, the other an older woman with a grey head and a grave, somewhat forbidding face, though she smiled at him kindly enough.

Aunt Fenny came forward at once to kiss his uncle and return his greeting. She stretched a welcoming hand to Tarris. 'I am so glad to see you,' she smiled. 'Be welcome, Tarris. Perilla will enjoy your company. This is the Lady Ananda, high-priestess of the Goddess's shrine. Make your bow, Tarris.'

He was too old to be told, but he did it anyway, offering the correct words of greeting and was amazed to see his uncle bow deeply before her, because after all, even though a person of importance, she was still only a priestess.

'My Lady. You are welcome as always. A family call?'

'No, Marric. Linna has awaited your coming. I am here at her command.'

He stiffened then and Tarris saw his aunt move suddenly and then stand very still.

'I am sorry,' Ananda said compassionately. 'So sorry, my dears. She said to tell you that it will be soon. We have been praying that you would return in time.'

Tarris saw the blood drain from his uncle's face then, and the blind way his hand went out to seek and grasp his aunt's reaching to meet it. He said, 'No,' in a low grating tone that made the boy swallow and step back.

Alarmed, he cried shrilly, 'What? What's wrong?' but was ignored. And found that he had been mistaken in thinking his uncle had no temper.

'How can this happen?' Marric roared. His face darkened below the frowning brows as the blood rushed back. 'She has had everything of me! In blood and pain and exile, I have obeyed. My service has been true. How can She now take my child?'

'Our lives are spun at Her command, Marric,' the priestess rebuked sternly. 'This you know. We serve, we do not command. Compose yourself. It is my loss as well.'

Aunt Fenny was crying silently, her hand still gripping her husband's but at this she sobbed, 'Oh, Mother,' and flew into the priestess's arm, making strange strangling sounds of grief. Tarris, embarrassed and annoyed by such unseemly adult behaviour, left the room unnoticed. It must be the sickly cousin they meant, but if she was going to die how could the priestess know in advance of the fact? Bel's priests hadn't come to the palace last year to warn them when Ling's father had choked to death at table. He wished the strange stern woman hadn't been there to upset everybody. He would've quite liked something to eat after his long ride but, he supposed kicking gloomily at a door frame, there wasn't much chance of it now. Certainly not immediately anyway.

It was the following morning before Tarris encountered his cousin. Perilla was resting, his aunt had said the previous evening. She herself seemed back to normal he decided, over a long delayed dinner. She made the proper enquiries about his journey, and what he liked, and there was no sign of the wild passion of grief he had witnessed. His uncle was calm again too, he was thankful to see, with an occasional word for him, and for the big, fair-headed man called Osram whose function seemed to fall somewhere between friend and servant. He was an Appellan, though he spoke good Rhutan as well, slipping as easily as his uncle did between the two tongues.

It was Osram who suggested that his son Leu show Tarris around and teach him boat craft.

'An excellent idea,' his uncle said. 'And to swim. He will need both skills.'

'Leu will see to it, my lord,' the big man said comfortably. 'They can hunt together and if you wish Tarris, join my son and the other boys at their weapon work.'

Tarris had brightened immediately. This was more like it, though he would have preferred a little more formality from the man in his form of address. Then, at breakfast Perilla had been present, a thin waif of a child in her tenth year with her mother's clear gray eyes and a mop of brown curls. She was listless, and so pale there was a faint blue tinge about her mouth, but there seemed nothing else amiss and watching her pick at her food he suspected she acted that way on purpose, like his sisters when they wanted attention. His uncle was certainly fooled. He stroked the brown curls and when they rose from the table he picked her up in his arms and carried her to a chair on the sunny deck and sat beside her there, completely ignoring Tarris. In the end it was Osram who came to bear him off to a long open platform where the young boys came each morning to be instructed in weapon craft.

Tarris nodded his thanks though it wasn't really necessary, the man was there to serve after all. 'Is he any good with a sword, your son?'

'He works hard with it,' the big man said. Which meant of course that he was no better than average. Tarris who had been praised for his own blade work, instantly felt better. He did not relish having to learn the water skills the boys here would have practised from birth.

He said, 'I would like to hunt while I am here.'

'When you can swim I'm sure Leu will be glad to accompany you,' Oswald said. 'And here we are.' They stepped across the narrow reed bridge linking the platforms to find a dozen boys both sides of his own age either talking in pairs or groups or battering at each other with practice swords.

Leu, called over by his father, was plainly of Appellan stock. He was taller than Tarris with his father's fair hair and a hint already of his size. His face was square and pleasant with a scatter of freckles across the nose, and friendly blue eyes. He wore, as everyone here seemed to, the plain tunic, slim breeches, and the soft soled shoes of the Lakes with no ornamentation save a dagger and pouch on his belt.

'My son, Leu,' Osram said briefly. And to Leu, 'Son, Prince Marric's guest, Tarris. He will be staying a while and you and your friends should make him welcome. Teach him to swim and use the boats,' he grinned then, 'and bring him home for meals. I leave him in your hands.'

'Yes Father.' Leu smiled blindingly at his new acquaintance. 'Be welcome Tarris. You will join us for weapon drill?'

'It is why I am here,' the young prince replied, nettled by the lack of formality from both of them. 'My father is the king.'

'Mine is a soldier,' Leu said. 'Do you use a bow at all? We could go birding — when you can swim.'

The drill master was a Laker, competent enough, Tarris thought, watching him, but without the skill of his own instructor back in Rhuta. Because the boys were almost of a height, and Tarris but a year younger, he paired him with Leu and the two fenced together, Tarris pushing hard against the careful defence of his new acquaintance who managed to hold his own, more from a sort of plodding strength of arm, Tarris thought, than natural skill. Well, his father was of oxlike stature and big men were rarely quick.

His pride smoothed the boy was prepared to be generous and putting away the practice weapon when the drill was over, said, 'You have good defence. Shall we go birding now? Only I will have to get my bow first.'

'Not before you learn to swim.'

'Why? We are not going to swim to the birds, are we? Just get a boat,' he ordered, irritated by the way they all harped on his lack of prowess in the water.

Leu's blue eyes widened. 'You cannot be serious. If it overturned or you fell out you would drown.'

'Then you could save me. In fact it would be your duty to do so,' Tarris snapped.

'But I might be too busy saving myself,' Leu pointed out good-humouredly. 'I must obey my father, Tarris and he bade me teach you to swim. Do you not also obey yours?'

And so the next few days passed in the shallows of the lake where, once he recovered from the petulance of having his wishes ignored or circumvented, Tarris's body achieved buoyancy and the ability to move through the watery medium, and he even began to enjoy the exercise.

On the third afternoon Osram came to find them, oaring swiftly into the shallows to spring from the craft onto the willow shore. He stood watching both boys stroke towards him and nodded a grave greeting.

'So, your skills progress, Tarris. That is good. Tonight, my wife and I will be pleased to house you as our guest. And perhaps tomorrow also. Leu will bring you. Anything you need for your comfort you may borrow from him.'

'Why?' Tarris baldly.

'The prince and his lady have been called away,' the soldier replied uninformatively. 'You will be very welcome with us.' He said no more but stepped back into the boat, thrusting it off with a powerful push of the oar.

'Called where?' Tarris asked blankly staring after the departing boat. 'My uncle said nothing of it this morning.'

'It will be his little flower,' Leu looked solemn. 'That is what my father calls Perilla. They will have taken her to the shrine. You knew she was dying, did you not?'

Tarris stared at him. 'There was a woman, my aunt's mother, when I first came — she said — But I didn't believe... Besides, how can anyone know such a thing? My cousin is sickly yes, but half of it is surely put on for the attention it brings. I have sisters,' he explained, adding scornfully. 'Girls! It is what they do.'

Leu was frowning then his face cleared. 'Ah, because you follow Bel in the city. I had forgotten. Here we worship the Mother. Our high-priestess sometimes receives Her messages. It will have been that the Lady Ananda carried to Prince Marric and his wife.' Struck by a thought he asked curiously, 'Then your god has no oracle to make plain his wishes?'

'Not since my grandmother,' Tarris admitted, adding curiously, 'You mean my aunt's mother can tell what is to happen? Really?'

'No. It is the Lady Linna who is very old, and blind now they say, so she never leaves the Shrine. But when her life ends, then yes, perhaps the Lady Ananda will receive the goddess's word. Or not. There is Prince Marric after all.'

Tarris's nape tingled. 'My uncle tells the future too?'

'You did not know? It is a hard task, my father says, requiring great courage.' His face was unwontedly grave as he moved to collect his discarded clothing. 'Come, we should go back. Sport is not seemly now. All Laketown will be in mourning tomorrow.'

At the Shrine the boat carrying the body of Perilla and her parents was met by the white robed sisters of the Mother but Marric, voiceless and frozen faced, picked up his child and bore her into the cool, white room where the bier had been prepared. He laid her gently upon it then bent to kiss the pale forehead. His daughter's lashes lay in dark half moons upon her pallid cheeks, the blueish tinge of her lips matching the hue of her nails. She would never smile at him again, never laugh, or grow to marry and bear a child and learn the joys and terrors of parenthood. She, who had never owned the energy to swim or drive a boat through the water, now lay with a twist of willow catkins in her brown curls and had left him far behind on a shore of sorrow from which there was no escape.

Ananda was comforting Fenny whose tears spilled without conscious volition down cheeks as pale as her daughters. 'I cannot stop them,' she said weeping.

'Then let them come,' her mother said. 'It is the lot of women to weep, my dearest. They will help you bear the pain. Ah, Marric,' she lifted a hand but at sight of his rigid face stopped short of touching him. 'Go to the Shrine, and may it ease your heart.'

It would not, but neither would standing here, hearing his wife grieve. Besides, if he stayed his tongue might betray him into saying something he would later regret. The new shrine, rebuilt since the war, was an elegant structure with fluted pillars, a domed roof and a marble altar, having also stone seats where worshippers could linger with the peaceful sounds of the birds and the trickle of the spring to encourage contemplation.

Today the Lady Linna, doyenne of the shrine, grey and blind and shrunken by great age, occupied one of these, the bench softened by bright cushions against the hardness of the stone. Seeing her Marric halted, bowing stiffly. 'Your pardon, Lady, I had thought the place unoccupied.'

'There is only me and the Mother,' she said kindly. 'Make your offering in peace, my son.'

'I had not thought to do so today,' he said harshly, 'having little to be thankful for.'

Without moving the milky eyes staring straight ahead she said sharply, 'Have you not, Prince Marric? Put anger from your heart.'

'You tell me so? My daughter is dead,' he said bitterly, and could have howled for the pain of it.

'And you were gifted with her for ten years of laughter and loving. Is that such a small thing? We of the sisterhood knew, and even your wife, though her heart would not let her admit it, that the child's life was always on loan to you. And now she has been taken, in compassion, to avoid further suffering. Be glad for her release and let your anger go. All our lives are in Her keeping Marric, as you know full well.'

He would have roared at her then, told over his tally of losses and toil in the Mother's service, except for the truth behind her words. The Mother measured the days of them all. As well rail against the fact as against the falling rain because one became wet. And it was true, his daughter had been sickly from birth and knowing it to be so he had pretended, for Fenny's sake, that she would strengthen as she grew. The signs had always been there, in the blueness that came to her lips as her life beat faltered, in the strength that ran from her like water from a holed bucket. She, the only living child of their union was gone to join the souls of the two half formed children that had slipped too early from their mother's keeping, and with a flash of insight like a punishing blow from the goddess herself, Marric knew there would be no more.

The old priestess must have known it too. She said gently, 'Life is not over, Prince Marric. You have your wife, and your brother's children. And the work which only you can accomplish. It is natural to grieve, and the goddess takes no offence by it. Stay awhile until your spirit calms and I will leave you in peace.'

As if silently summoned a young novitiate appeared and the two departed. There was nothing magical about it, Marric realised. Linna had the enhanced hearing of the blind and his own inner turmoil had failed to let him hear the girl's step on the path. Slowly, absorbing the truth of the old woman's words, he let his anger go and opened his mind to memories of his daughter. To the wound of love he had felt at first sight of her tiny face and the miniscule finger that clutched his own. To the echo of gurgling laughter, like sun on running water, and the weight of her in his arms when she had run to him, breath gasping, and he had caught her up to spare her further effort.

Linna was right. He too had if not known, then had always feared to lose her. And then from nowhere came a sudden sense of comfort, like a blanket of warmth that enfolded his spirit, and a voice that spoke within his mind, 'Mourn, and be strong again. For you will be needed.' He had the briefest glimpse of a woman's face, old, seamed, with a cloud of white hair, and shrewd dark eyes.

It was there and it was gone. He felt it like a support removed and gazed dazedly about, but the shrine was bare and silent save for the song of a lark, and the sound of trickling water. Presently he got up and left to return to his wife.

***

Long Locks's name was Rost and now he had thrown Burran for the third time. The Rhutan landed hard, struggling for wind and rolled just in time to avoid receiving the other's knees in his belly. Gasping for breath he got to his own knees, squinting through a half-closed eye and snuffed blood as he searched for his opponent.

The fight had been building for days, Rost pushing it ill-temperedly with jibes his victim couldn't understand and jostlings meant to be accidental. And now, on the bank of the river where Burran had wandered to clear his head after a morning of intensive and frustrating study, he had made his move. Usually, Yerb was somewhere in the background, but not today. He wondered if that was by design, like Rost's and his three friends' sudden appearance. At least, Burran thought mordantly, it was still one on one.

Rost called something. But all he could translate of it was the word for pig. Speaking carefully in the same language Burran said, 'I like mine roasted.' Or at least he hoped that was what he said, as he flung himself at his opponent, grappling him about the waist and at the same time thrusting his leg behind the other's. A trick that Rost, for all his quickness and dirty tricks, didn't seem to know. They both crashed to the ground, Burran uppermost, and using fists and feet and even teeth, each tried to damage the other, Burran attempting to break the fingers squeezing his throat, then yelling as Rost's teeth sunk into his wrist. With a heave the other flung him over, his weight compressing his chest, just as Burran put all his remaining strength into a punch at his head.

Because Rost had at that moment got both hands around Burran's neck and was lowering his head into his shoulders for the extra purchase it gave him, the blow caught Rost flush on the jaw. His body went instantly limp and he fell backwards, leaving his opponent to roll slowly onto his front before rising to his hands and knees, the breath whooping through his tortured throat.

'Bugger this, for a game of soldiers,' he wheezed painfully then looked up, readying himself to meet the rush of the other three.

It didn't happen, the excited yelling had ceased and two of the young men were bending over Rost whose slack lips leaked blood from a bitten tongue. The third man jabbered a question, of which Burran caught only the word 'dead'.

'No,' he rasped, then remembering, repeated it in Pampasan. As if to prove it Rost opened his eyes, which when they cleared and alighted on Burran, lit with fury. Thrusting off his helpers he rose to his feet, but his balance was gone and he staggered. One of his comrades reached for him and Rost snarled something, flailing like a drunk at the proffered hand. The movement had him floundering backwards and, unaware of its proximity to his feet, straight over the riverbank to vanish from sight in the rushing water.

All three of his comrades seemed vastly alarmed. Burran, waiting for the man's head to reappear, watched them rush at the bank and yell at each other as the body rose then vanished again. Though obviously concerned they made no effort to follow him in. When at length it dawned on Burran that none of them could swim, he said, 'Oh, Bel's bloody balls!' ripped off his boots and dove straight from the bank.

Fortunately it was deep water, and with quite a current, but of course it would need to be to turn a mill. He swam rapidly downstream, pursued by frantic cries, took a breath and dived, and the first thing his hands touched was hair. He got an armlock around Rost's neck, turned him right side up and kicked for the surface.

The men were there to help when he hauled the semi-conscious body ashore. Burran punched it hard in the chest area and Rost coughed, choked, and discharged a huge amount of river water. His eyes opened and he stared vaguely at the men surrounding him. A large lump showed through the wet strands plastered to his head; his hand rose gingerly to explore it and he groaned and swore feebly.

'Rock?' Burran asked. His feet squelched in his wet boots and his hair dripped onto his soaked shirt. He made swimming motions with his arms speaking slowly, to be understood. 'You should learn, yes?'

Rost nodded, grimacing as the movement hurt and answered one syllable at a time, 'Your tongue is very bad, Outlander dog.' He added something to his friends that Burran didn't catch and they laughed and hauled the man to his feet where he stood swaying a little. For a moment the two ex-combatants stared at each other then Rost said, 'Ro-asted.' His mouth twitched and he suddenly grinned and whacked his enemy on the shoulder but his eyes remained wary and the Rhutan couldn't read their message. Was the man offering a truce, or simply pretending? He'd go with pretence, he thought and keep his knife handy. Killing or injuring a member of the tribe wouldn't help his mission, but neither would his own murder.

'Roasted,' he agreed, which set everybody laughing again. Obviously his reply to the earlier insult had been wildly inappropriate. Let the joke be on him then, it would lower their expectations of his abilities. Nobody feared a fellow they could scorn, and condescension was preferable to antagonism.

Bark was the name of the man whose nose Burran had broken on their first encounter. Both he and Rost as far as he could work out, were cousins of Sonj who was the youngest, and only surviving sister of Leris. Who in turn, Burran came to realise as time flowed by and his knowledge of both language and the intricacies of tribal custom increased, was the principal leader and law-giver of her district under the king. She was the Errol of Carj, the name of both the town, the river, and the area it was set within.

The title, he thought was the equivalent of an earl in Rhuta. Neither blood nor gender mattered in the selection of errols, he gathered. Those with the ability were appointed by the king and governed the people under their care until injury or death removed them. Few saw old age. Leris had, as was the customn, inherited the position on the death of her mate. (Husband was not a word he had yet encountered in their tongue.) The Pampasans were more a confederation of states than a nation, and when the separate clans were not either protecting their borders from, or raiding outlanders' farms and caravans, they squabbled amongst themselves, often with fatal results.

Burran had as yet been unable to form an understanding of their religion, save that the god they worshipped was something to do with a horse spirit. They valued their horses above all other possessions and the grass rich land ran vast herds of them. The tribes counted their wealth in horseflesh. Before their young people could ride with a warrior band they must first catch and break-in their own mount, and their subsequent place in the band depended, as he had already guessed, on completing a challenge set them by their elders.

Sonj's had indeed been his own capture, though much remained unclear about the manner of this. How had they known for instance where he would be? Or, more worryingly, had they guessed and if so how, that he was expressly there to be taken by them? He hadn't language enough yet for difficult discussions and instinct warned him that acquiring the answers to this one called for caution. Whatever Leris's plan for him, his presence here was resented by some as the frequent sneers or dark looks cast his way attested. Rost however was the only one so far to make his displeasure physical.

Something else Burran had yet to discover was whether the king shared his errol's enthusiasm for trade and discourse to occur between their two nations. Given the fact that three moons after his arrival he was still in Carj and had not been taken to the monarch's seat, the answer he decided, was probably not.

4

On a morning with a touch of autumnal chill to it Rost hallooed at Burran's door before he had finished breaking his fast. The Pampasan was horsed and held the reins of a second animal which he tossed to the Rhutan. Since Burran's own mount had vanished into the local herd along with his packhorses, it was the first time he had been offered a horse.

'Come,' Rost commanded briskly. 'The errol has sent me to take you to the tumuli. There is one would meet with you there. What, you were still abed?' he asked, taking in Burran's bare feet.

'On the contrary I was eating. Will you join me?' Then as the Pampasan shook an impatient head. 'Well, let me get my boots on, and my gear.' Abandoning the meal he pulled on footwear and collected the pouch of writing implements that went everywhere with him. Amused by his constant collecting of words Bark had called him Scribe in the Rhutan tongue, for the cross fertilisation of language that Marric had envisaged was happening. Now Rost and his friends could insult one another in both languages, and Burran mostly understood what was (slowly) said to him.

Once astride the chestnut mare, though she lacked the height of his own brown Swift, Burran was struck by the difference that being in the saddle made to his vision. The grass, though not as tall in the valley, still limited a man's sightline. The sun hung low still above the eastern horizon, which he could now see, touching the heavy dew that clung to the heads of the grass stems with beads of glittering colour. The spider silk was hung with them. The air smoked with cold and the fallen leaves cushioned the sound of the horses' feet. Burran had pulled a cloak over his tunic but Rost rode bare-armed, the muscles sliding under his golden skin, and the bow that he was rarely without, riding across his shoulder.

'Where do we go, is it far?'

'Not so much,' Rost said. 'Ulfa has sent for you.' He hesitated, eyeing his companion as if wondering how much information to impart. 'She is a wise woman, a shaman. She knows of your arrival and would see for herself if you,' he sought for the words and settled for, 'make a danger to the clan. If you mean evil by us,' his eyes flashed suddenly showing the warrior, 'she will know. She has great power. You would do well to fear her.'

'Of course I don't mean your people harm,' Burran protested in exasperation. 'I am here for peaceful trade. My country lives by trade and why would we not wish to do so with yours? Even Barat trades with us now, to our mutual benefit.'

The name had caught the other's interest. 'What is this Barat?'

'We call it the Black Country' — Burran went on to explain the geography, politics and military capability of their ally. Naturally their fighting ability interested the Pampasan most though he plainly disbelieved the part about mountains spewing fire.

'You have seen this yourself?'

'No,' Burran admitted. 'But I have spoken with men who have. The Baratans claim it to be the home of their god.' He shrugged. 'It may be so. Every land is different. Appella has the Light and we the river god, so why not one of fire?'

Rost made no answer but rode in a thoughtful silence for a while which he broke to say grudgingly, 'I envy you, Scribe. You have travelled much. Here, we do not leave our land.'

Burran shrugged. 'Trade does that. It brings not just goods but new ideas and news. A king may rule the better for knowing what his neighbours are doing. It brings opportunities that may never have been thought of. The closed country is like a closed mind; if nothing new gets in then nothing can be learned, and much may be lost through ignorance. What are those mounds?'

They had come suddenly into view, humping up out of the grass that stretched endlessly save for a few sparse clumps of trees, always rare away from the vale in which Carj lay. On the semi open plain the tumuli seemed to grow out of the very ground: enormous, turf covered humps like small rounded houses, or very even low hills. They had ridden for at least an hour since leaving Carj and Burran was suddenly aware of the isolation of the spot. The land ran away forever before him under the endless arch of the sky, with only the silent mounds to break the line of the horizon. He counted seven but there seemed to be more still behind them.

Rost drew rein and turned his mount as Burran also stopped. 'They are the Mounds, or barrows, the home of our dead,' he said. 'Yonder,' with an inclination of his head he indicated a distant skein of smoke, 'lies Ulfa's place. I will await you here.'

Burran stared hard at him then shifted his gaze to the silent mounds. A breeze blew over them and somewhere a crow cawed but otherwise all was still and a little shiver went through him at the strangeness of it all. In Rhuta the dead went into the soil, in Appella they burned their corpses and in Ansham, it was said, they preserved the bodies in caves until they were slowly turned to stone... It was a tale, most likely, but all these methods suddenly seemed preferable to the looming menace of the silent hillocks before him.

He wondered if it was a trap of some sort. Rost's face was carefully blank but he held his shoulders tensely and his eyes shifted constantly to the tumuli. Drawing a breath Burran said, 'Very well.' He lifted his reins and rode towards the smoke. He had no idea what to expect from this woman, a priestess, he assumed, and a powerful one to make her home so close to the place of the dead. The many dead, if the size of the grave mounds were a measure of their number.

The hut he eventually came to was a low huddle of stone, with a stone chimney at the back, a roof thatched with grass and a rough looking table and chair set before it. It looked not unlike a barrow itself, humping out of the ground, and Burran wondered what she did for water, then had his answer when he rode to the nearest tree, a poor scrubby affair bent sideways by the perpetual wind of the plains, to tie his horse, for nearby was a stone coping about a natural spring. He secured his mount and turned to find that the priestess or shaman had come out of her dwelling and was silently regarding him.

'So,' she said, her voice surprisingly deep for one of her wizened stature, 'you are the one.'

Burran stared, so surprised he almost forgot to bow. She stood little higher than a child of eight summers, and was so slight he thought he could raise her in one hand. Her hair was a wild white corona over a deeply seamed face in which the eyes seemed pools of jet. They held his own as if they were chained and when he would have torn them away, he found he couldn't. Then her own gaze moved and his could too.

'Come,' she said, in that deep man's voice, 'sit, and tell me of your master.'

It never occurred to him to employ the first instinct of an agent and lie. She would know. He said simply, 'Lady, he is a prince who wishes nothing but good to come of my visit.'

The dark eyes, hooded by their deep sockets studied him, then she cackled unnervingly. 'You think it a visit, Outlander. Did he tell you that?'

'I — what do you mean?' She had flustered him. Burran recalled the prince's steady gaze, his voice warning, *it will be hard*, but surely he hadn't meant… It was a task, that was all, and when it was done he would return as he had from Meddia and the cities of Appella. He said boldly with more assurance than he felt, 'When my task is accomplished I shall leave. Why should I not?'

'Ah, but why should the rain fall here and not there, or this mare bear and that one be barren? Who can say?' The song of a lark lofting above them fell into the silence as she finished speaking and Burran turned his head slightly, tensing up at the faint sound of drumming hooves.

The old woman leaned forward, her own head cocked. 'You hear them? The spirit horses of the dead, carrying their riders to battle. They lie together beneath the barrows we raise for them, the women and men and the brave mounts slain with them.' The black eyes glittered with malice as he paled at her words. 'You have something of mine?'

It was the wind, Burran thought, repressing a shudder, only the wind. The hairs on his nape had lifted and he clenched his left hand which lay hidden from sight down beside his leg. Remembering then, he fumbled at his belt withdrawing the dagger the prince had given him. It was an inoffensive weapon, sharp enough to kill but mainly used to cut meat, though it had initially been taken from him at his capture. Taken and returned, the thin stripping of leather wound about the hilt untampered with.

He palmed it now and taking his time stripped the covering off to reveal the pair of silver lions, stylised but recognisable, their forms reversed on either side to form the hilt. He presented it to Ulfa. 'My Lady, I was to say that this gift comes with the goodwill of my people who were never the enemies of yours.'

She took it up, her fingers trembling a little until they firmed about the grip. 'Ah, my grandmother's drinker of blood,' she crooned. 'So you are back, and thirsty I warrant.' Her hand flashed with a speed he could never have imagined her age could produce, and Burran starting back, stared stupidly at his slashed wrist.

'Blood,' Ulfa ran a finger across the reddened tip of the blade and licked it. 'So, we will take you now to your mistress. Come,' she commanded, then tsked scornfully at the sight of him holding the wound. 'You bother at a tiny scratch? Well for you then that, as you say, your people are no enemies of mine.'

Cursing under his breath Burran removed his grip on the wound. Apparently whatever had occasioned the attack was over. She was heading for the barrows and he followed reluctantly, with the blood leaking over his hand.

Ulfa led him to one of the smaller mounds that had grown into the landscape in a way suggestive of age, which if it was the tomb of her grandmother, wasn't to be wondered at. The old witch looked to be ninety herself, and for a moment he wondered, given her size and oddities, how she had survived childhood. The Pampasans did not strike him as a race that tolerated weakness or diversity. But perhaps her peculiar talents had manifested themselves early enough to save her. He thanked Bel that his own prince was outwardly normal. Then the faint sound of hoofbeats thrummed again against his inner ear and he inhaled audibly.

'Ha,' Ulfa cackled, 'They know. They sense the blood.' She paused before the mound that was far taller than her and pointed at the closed end. 'Here, lift the lintel, yes, and now the end block.' He did her bidding, shoulder muscles cracking, and as he heaved at the heavy stone slab, staining it and a tiny flowering daisy growing in the crevice beside it with his blood, a narrow hole appeared.

Ulfa kicked a toehold in the turf wall and clutching at his body to steady herself as she climbed, rose painfully up on tiptoes to thrust the knife into the space. It disappeared but he heard no tinkle of its fall as she half collapsed against him to regain the ground. He replaced what he had moved and lowered his arms as the drumming hooves faded until it could have been no more than the thunder of his pulse in his ears.

'They acknowledge your master's intent,' the old woman said then and cocked her head. 'Charge, my lovelies!' she screamed suddenly, her cry loud and harsh as a carrion bird. 'Drive them forth along the Crow Road! Let not our enemies bide in the land.'

She was mad, Burran thought, but the intense intelligence in her dark eyes belied the assumption. 'We are not your enemies, Lady,' he said. 'We would join our hand to yours in friendship. What is this crow road you speak of?'

'Friendship, hah! Was it not your master's own grandfather that shed the blood of my line? On this very spot.' She stamped her foot like a petulant child. 'But we harried him and his murderous men and many we killed.' She nodded fiercely, speaking with immense satisfaction. 'And thus we named it, as they fled with our warriors in pursuit, and so it remains, Outlander. Ah, they feast well our feathered friends, and the bones of our enemies are proof of that.' She cackled again, her black eyes narrowed on Burran's face and abruptly his uneasiness in her strangeness was replaced by anger.

'Why?' he demanded harshly. 'You mock me and speak in riddles of acts long gone and forgotten. Why send for me today? You saw me, did you not, that first night? I felt you there behind the wall. What are you — shaman, witch? Then you know I speak the truth when I tell you that I come only to establish a trading relationship with your people.'

'Oh, and not to spy?' she spat virulently. 'Be careful trader! Our little friends are never far off.' She waved one skinny arm in the air, the act immediately answered by a raucous caw. Burran jerked his gaze up in time to see a lone crow come gliding down to the roof of the mound. Its head tilted to eye him before the bird stabbed its beak repeatedly into the rubble like a man whetting a blade. It was a natural action, he assured himself, he had seen these birds do it a dozen times but there was something malevolent in the gloating way it watched him.

He shook the fancy off, but the old woman had noticed and cackled again at his discomfiture. He said thinly to disguise his own unease, 'The world is changing, old woman. Appella grows again in strength. One day she may tire of the wasp that constantly stings her flanks and move to crush it. A trading alliance can offer a people more than commerce. The Grass will not always protect you.'

'You think not?' Ulfa snorted in dismissal of his words. 'And yet here we have lived since the Great Mare birthed Her first foal. And here we will stay till the last hooves leave the earth.'

'Easy to say,' Burran scoffed. 'And if drought were to take the land and the horses die? If your enemies were to burn the Grass — what then?'

Ulfa darted her head towards him, showing her teeth like a cat, and hissed, 'Do you threaten me, trader?' From nowhere a knife had appeared in her hand, she darted it at his groin and he leapt back in alarm. Then, his mind catching up with his reflexes Burran steeled himself to stand.

'No,' he said stolidly, one eye on the dirtied tip of the blade hovering beside his tightened scrotum, 'I give you possibilities to consider, that is all.' He swallowed. If the old crone chose she could unman him in a heartbeat and there was nothing he could do to prevent it. To lay a hand on her would be to invite his own death.

'Hah!' The threat slowly withdrew and Burran drew a steadying breath and followed her as she stumped her slow way back to her hut.

'She saw you?' Rost asked when Burran, his wrist roughly bandaged, appeared from behind the mounds to rejoin him. The old sorceress had scooped moss from the spring's edge and bound it in place before dismissing him. He had no idea what she had taken from the meeting or why, apart from delivering the dagger as he had been charged to do, it had been called. Mounting again he had felt nothing but relief to be escaping from her presence. His companion's eyes flicked to his bandaged arm but he didn't ask and Burran made no effort to explain. Instead he asked, 'Did you hear riders?'

'No.' Rost hipped about in the saddle, one hand reaching reflexively for his bow. 'When? Where?'

'Perhaps I was mistaken and it was the wind,' Burran said. 'Does the old one advise Errol Leris, do you know?'

Rost relaxing again, lifted his shoulders. 'Who can say?' He stared at Burran then smirked. 'Scribe, she has frightened you.'

'But it was you who stayed back and I who rode through the barrows and heard the hooves,' Burran retorted bristling. 'There are some things it is wise to fear, and the gifts of the gods is one of them. There is a man so gifted in my country.' Then curiosity overcoming his ruffled feelings, he asked, 'Do you still bury the horses of the warriors you lose in raids?'

'No. It was done in the old days, for those slain in the land's defence. Nor do we still raise the barrows. It is not practicable when one is raiding.'

'I see.' For a small group to carry a horse's carcass any distance, or to undertake on the spot the major effort a barrow would require with no tools and perhaps wounded to deal with... Burran let the thought go. 'Where now?'

Rost's lips lifted in a grin. 'We hunt. I have arranged for Bark to meet us with a bow for you. You have hunted before?'

'No,' Burran admitted. 'In the city one buys one's meat. I have used snares for small game when travelling. There is no point in killing deer, for instance, if the meat rots before it is used.'

'Then we shall teach you how it is done,' Rost promised. 'When you travel in the Grass you hunt or starve.'

It was a chance to show him up, Burran deduced resignedly, catching the glint in the other's eye, something he should be getting used to by now.

5

The boat, with two paddles working, wove between the reed islands ahead of its rivals. Leu, keeping his voice low, warned, 'You make too much noise. Angle the blade cleanly.'

'I am,' Tarris protested.

'No, you aren't,' his companion replied patiently. 'Hear that splash? Well so can the birds. We must be like a leaf on the water.'

'So you say,' Tarris grumbled. It seemed at times as if Leu lived only to correct him. Gritting his teeth in annoyance he slowed his paddling, but only briefly for that would let the other boys catch them and he was determined to have the first shot at the water fowl.

'There they are,' he breathed, sighting between the reed islands, fifteen or so ducks at rest on the bobbing wavelets. They had not seen the boat and ignoring Leu's instructions about waiting until they were all in position, Tarris dropped his paddle, grabbed his bow and rose, wobbling slightly, to his feet.

He heard his name hissed behind him but drew and loosed anyway, and to his chagrin saw the arrow whistle harmlessly beneath the bird he had chosen. It let out an alarmed squawk and its wings beat the air. The sound was echoed by the rest and Tarris had time to see that the flock was vaster than the handful of birds he had glimpsed, far vaster in fact, as with a great clatter of wings hundreds upon hundreds of them took quacking flight. Then, while he stood gaping at their numbers, unable to believe he had missed, the boat whipped about beneath him until it was facing in the opposite direction, and he fell out.

Tarris's yell was cut off by the water closing over his head. He dropped his bow and surfaced coughing up Lake water to see Leu sitting calmly in the craft a dozen paces off watching him, his mouth a straight line of displeasure.

'You did that on purpose!' Tarris's nose and gullet burned, igniting his temper. 'You've lost me my bow.'

'You lost it,' the other boy said. 'And you have ruined the hunt. Every bird on the lake will have taken flight. I told you to wait.' With a thrust of his paddle he sent the boat skimming backwards another dozen paces.

'Come back!' Tarris shouted. The other boys had caught them up and had halted their boats and were watching. Face burning with fury he put down his head to thrash his way through the water, because there was no other choice. He would kill Leu. He would punch him black and blue for his own satisfaction and any other boy that dared to snigger. None did, they stared like wooden dummies but neither did they move to help him. He knew what sort of a figure he must cut, and cursed the hasty shot that had caused the trouble.

He was a prince, he raged silently. He had a right to claim their duty, to shoot first if he wished to, and once he was in that boat they would learn it. But Leu kept edging his craft back a little at a time, and only when tiredness slowed the other boy's arms did he glide up alongside the head now bobbing lower in the water, to say briefly, 'Get in.'

Tarris tried and couldn't. The final indignity for him was having Leu help him inboard where he lay spent and sullen recovering breath and strength, too weary to even sit up. Neither spoke on the way home and when he was able Tarris, nursing his wounded pride, made no effort to help paddle. So Leu thought he knew everything about swimming, hunting, and boats? Fine then, let him do the work.

Still without speaking Leu pulled the craft in to the landing platform at the royal house and Tarris, dripping water, climbed the steps and stalked from sight. He scowled at his aunt's servant met in the hallway, snapped, 'I need dry clothes,' and vanished into his room. Raising his brows a trifle the man followed him and found what he needed. He added a towel to the bundle which he delivered wordlessly to the boy, saving his comment for the ears of a fellow servant.

'The brat's got his nose out of joint. Had a ducking by the look of things.'

'Boys,' his companion said tolerantly. 'They'll sort him out eventually.'

Tarris meanwhile, drying and dressing himself while vowing vengeance, came to see as he cooled down that he had placed himself in an untenable position. He couldn't complain of Leu's conduct without admitting to his own. There was no way he was going to apologise, but if he didn't, given the peculiar independence of mind that the Lakers seemed to practice, he would cut himself off from the other boy's company and be stuck on his own. Back in Ripa no comrade would have dared to act as Leu had done. The companion would have meekly accepted blame for the lost bow, apologised, offered his own in return, and Tarris would eventually have forgiven him. The episode would've been over and forgotten with his own dignity intact. And at some stage he would probably have found another bow for the boy, who would've been becomingly grateful.

But that was the city. It was he saw dimly, different here, and he had no idea how to handle the problem he had brought about.

He still hadn't solved it when it was time to join the adults for the evening meal. The Lady Ananda was present and some other old woman, introduced as the Lady Khat whom he vaguely remembered meeting before. She asked him how he was enjoying his visit, and how old his sisters were now, and similar irritating enquiries. Aunt Fenny was shrouded in melancholy as she had been since her daughter's death, and Uncle Marric was so abstracted that Jerrod the secretary had to speak to him twice before he paid attention.

He apologised, listened and answered in his measured way, and then as if reminded of his social obligations, asked Tarris how his day had been.

'Like Bel cursed it,' the boy muttered, but Marric's attention had already wandered.

'That's good,' he replied, his mind obviously elsewhere. Mourning his sickly brat, Tarris thought furiously. He remembered the tales the servants told about his uncle and wished they could see him now. They talked in hushed tones of his mysterious powers but all he could discern was a man moping around like a sick cat. And it wasn't even as if it was a healthy son that had died. As soon as he could Tarris muttered an excuse to his aunt and took himself off to his room. The night, and the days that would follow, stretched endlessly before him. Forgetting how eager he had been to leave the sameness of his life in Ripa he heartily wished himself back there. At least there those in the palace showed him proper respect and nobody in their right mind ever set foot in a stupid boat.

In the morning Tarris breakfasted and instead of waiting as he usually did for Leu to pick him up, climbed carefully down into the tied craft at the foot of the pontoon and paddled along the waterway to the training area. And it was as well he had done so, he saw, for Leu and most of the other boys were already there. His sense of ill-usage swelled at the knowledge that they dared ignore him. Leu nodded an unsmiling welcome and got a flat stare in return.

'Ooh,' a young voice somewhere in the loose group announced, 'somebody's upset. I reckon he needs another swim.'

Tarris's choler rose to choke him. He lunged at the group with no clear idea of his intent beyond killing whoever had laughed at him, and found himself thrust suddenly backwards by the boy blocking his path. It was Leu. Without turning he said flatly, 'Shut up, Sor!' And to Tarris, 'Let him be. I'm the one you're angry with. Just apologise and we'll forget it.'

'To you!' Strangled by temper and incredulity his voice came out high-pitched as a girl. 'Princes don't apologise you — you mud-crawler! You're the one who tipped me out of the boat and lost my bow. You had no right. I could have you flogged. I could —'

Leu, arms folded across his chest, looked at him in disbelief. 'You're such a child,' he said witheringly. 'We're not your servants. Grow up, Prince.' Disdaining the other's fury he turned away as if Tarris were in truth the child he had called him and his tantrums had wearied him beyond bearing.

It was too much. With a howl of rage Tarris flung himself at the other boy and bore him to the deck in a flurry of punches. Leu's initial astonishment quickly passed and the rapid battering that split his lip and marked his cheek saw his own temper break through the placid surface of his nature.

'Idiot!' he yelled. 'I'm bigger and stronger than you.' His fist hit Tarris flush on the nose loosing a stream of scarlet. The prince yipped in pain and kicked wildly, connecting with the other boy's shin. Leu swore and hit him again, in the eye this time, then wrapped his sturdy arms around Tarris's body and squeezed. Struggle and wrench to free himself as he might Tarris could not break the grip and found himself staring into implacable blue eyes only a hand's breadth from his own.

'Control yourself,' Leu gritted. 'What's the matter with you? You expect us to run after you because you were born in a palace? Well, it doesn't work like that.'

'I am your prince!' Tarris shouted. 'And you have no right to touch me.'

'No, you're not.' Leu's grip tightened. 'This is the Lake Country. Your uncle is our prince. You are the spoilt son of his brother and your actions bring shame upon them both.' His teeth bared in a mirthless grin. 'My little sister has more sense than you. And far better manners.'

'You — you — I'll kill you!' Tarris struggled wildly but without avail until a man's hand suddenly grabbed the pair of them and pulled them apart.

'Enough.' The drill master cuffed Tarris when he swung blindly at him, then shook him like a terrier with a rat. 'You are here to learn, not to brawl,' he said dourly and without pausing swept the boy sideways. Tarris felt himself falling and gave a strangled yell that ended as the water closed over his head. He went down into cold, inky darkness before his shocked mind understood what had happened, then instinct had him kicking his legs, as Leu had taught him, and he rose coughing to the surface. Leu's wet head was the first thing he saw. Amazingly the boy grinned at him.

'He has a quick way with him, Harla,' he said as if he had forgotten all about their fight. 'No, you can't go back today.' This as Tarris, ignoring his friendly overture stroked towards the ladder. 'We'll have to leave.'

Tarris paused scowling, one hand on the ladder. 'Why?'

'Because he'll just throw you back in. No brawling, no horseplay on the weapons ground. Army discipline. Come on.' He swam to the nearest boat, caught the support that anchored piling to roof above it, and hoisted himself from the water into the craft. Tarris hesitated.

'You can't,' Leu insisted. 'On the drill ground Harla's word is law. If another dunking doesn't work then a beating will.'

The thought was insupportable. Grudgingly Tarris swam across to the piling but his arms weren't up to the task of lifting his body that high. Furious with himself and his companion for being witness to his weakness, he swam back to the ladder, climbed it and embarked that way. It was humiliating to know that Leu had spoken the truth. He was indeed the stronger of the two. Wet and disgruntled he huddled in the boat while Leu paddled them away, the sounds of the practice swords echoing dully behind them.

Tarris had paid no attention to where they headed until they neared the shore.

'Where are you going?'

'We,' Leu corrected. 'We're going to our tasks. It's the rule. If you're banished from drill you have a day's work as punishment. We'll be stockpiling wood for the town's use.' He ran the boat into the shallows and hopped out, steadying the craft for the other boy. 'Come on. It's this way.'

Tarris thought of protesting his status but knew it would avail him nothing. Scowling he followed his companion quite a long way, first through the fringe of willows and then up the gravelly swell of the ridge to find a wheeled track through the low scrubby bushes.

'What wood?' he asked crankily.

'Why the stuff every household burns,' Leu explained patiently. 'Those who work in the trade harvest it from the scrub. It takes a lot of wood to cook all the dinners that Lake Town eats. We will be given a cart to fill and if we do not work willingly we could find ourselves back here again tomorrow.' He turned to face Tarris. 'My father says that letting your temper lead you is the best way to lose at anything — an argument, a swordfight — and he is right. See where it has led us?'

'It was your fault!' Tarris said hotly.

'No, it wasn't, but it doesn't matter now. Here we are so you had best get over your grievance and work with me,' Leu said calmly. 'It is not so hard. Just take the axe they give you and pull the cart. A child could do it. This way.'

He strode off without waiting for an answer and shortly Tarris found himself confronting an enormous mound of wood, piled across an area as large as the drill pontoon. There was a hut beside it and a row of barrows such as he'd seen the palace gardeners use, a sort of tub on wheels with two shaft-like handles protruding from the front. A man came out of the dimness on the windowless hut to eye them and sniffed.

'Punishment detail, huh?'

Leu nodded cheerfully. 'Harla. Fighting on the drill ground.'

'Right then.' The man stepped into the hut and returned with two short-handled axes. 'Get yourselves a coupla carts and get started. I'll be keepin' an eye on you, mind.'

'Of course.' Leu inclined his head and pointed at the stationary barrows. 'Let's go Tarris.'

A child may have been able to pull the empty carts but first filling and then towing them back was hard, sweaty work, particularly as the day heated up. Nor was it an easy matter to find acceptable wood, for the country had been well fossicked over and they were obliged to go long distances to reach an unharvested area. When they had twice filled them the man gave them water and a hunk of bread and sausage for their noon meal. They ate it squatting outside the hut where a thin overlap of roof supplied shade. Tarris's nose was tender and the eye he'd been hit in had swelled almost shut. The skin about it felt taut and sore and the man chuckled as he noticed the boy fingering it.

'Fair old shiner you've got yourself there, lad. Hope it was worth it.'

Tarris scowled at him and the man shook his head and winked at Leu. 'Youth. Hot and hasty, eh?'

'A piece of foolishness,' the boy dismissed the incident and the implied question to take another drink. 'It is time we got back to work.'

'Hey,' the man's eye's narrowed, 'you're the big fellow's lad, aren't you? The one that guards our prince? Thought I seen yer before.'

'Yes.' Leu stood up. 'Come on, Tarris.'

And because he too wanted to be away from their host's inquisitiveness Tarris obeyed and soon they were trudging back over the heated ground, the empty hand carts bouncing behind them.

'Is your father truly my uncle's bodyguard?' Tarris asked as they loaded the wood they had chopped. He paused to wipe his face. 'Why does he need one anyway?'

'It is more custom than need now,' Leu said. 'They are old friends. But during the Uprising,' he gave the word the significance of a title, 'your father tasked him to protect the Prince when they travelled to the Black Country.'

'To Barat? Why would he go there?'

'It is a long story. Briefly the king of that country's grand-daughter had been stolen. My father and his companion found her and it was your uncle who travelled there to return her to her home. My father went along to guard him.'

'From what?'

Leu stared at the young prince. 'From the Baratans, from bandits, from King Temes's men. Has nobody ever spoken to you about our history? King Darien wasn't given his throne, you know. Our people fought a bloody war for it. Do men not tell of such things still in Ripa?'

'My father is always busy,' Tarris said defensively. 'Of course I know about the war! Everybody does. But the servants spin such wild tales of that time that I don't believe half of them.'

'Well, you should. Hundreds of Laker men died in the battle and many more would have perished if Prince Marric had not brought the archers of Ansham to our aid, and the cavalry from the Black Country. He went there willingly to die, you know, that his brother might take the throne, but the Goddess saved him. It is true,' he said simply seeing the other's incredulous expression. 'My father was at his side. He said your uncle is the bravest man he has ever met. And he has fought many times, my father, in Appella's wars, and Rhuta's, so he would know.'

'But —' Tarris thought of the mild mannered man he knew who lived as simply as any other Laker, and was in every way as ordinary and unremarkable as his subjects. 'He's not a soldier, just my father's adviser — the same as any of the merchants on the King's Council. They talk about tariffs and whether to build another dock, and how much grain to store. Twice I have had to sit and listen through a full half day of it. I thought I would go mad from boredom! It is more about book-keeping than statesmanship.'

'And if there were no docks for trade, or tariffs to pay for the docks, how does a country operate?' Leu asked. 'Or would you have us ruled by the sword as in King Temes's day? Ask your uncle, or any man who fought to free Ripa and our people from the tyrant's grasp. Ask about the day they stormed the old tower to free the prisoners. Our prince was there for that, and my father at his side.'

Tarris frowned. 'What tower? I know of none in Ripa.'

'Because your father ordered it razed.' Leu dropped the last chunk of wood into his cart and stowed his axe safely. 'A full load,' he said with satisfaction. 'One more should do it.'

Trudging back, arms aching from the weight of the cart he drew behind him Tarris said grudgingly, 'How do you know all this stuff?'

Leu shrugged. 'I listen. My father's army friends visit; sometimes one or two come hunting with us. I hear their talk. It is how one learns. Harla too, if he is in a good mood will tell stories about famous bladesmen he has known. The old king, Cyrus, the father of Temes, had a champion called Rissak. He was the best, Harla says. He guarded your uncle when he was a child.'

Tarris was so surprised he stopped in his tracks. 'Rissak?' he said. 'That one-eyed old soldier that hangs around the palace? Him — the best? Why, get on his blind side and he wouldn't even know you were there.'

'Maybe you should ask your uncle about him too,' Leu suggested over his shoulder. 'Come on! Do you want to be doing this tomorrow too?'

The day finally ended but it had left Tarris with much to think about and somewhere, in the midst of his ruminations and sweaty toil his sense of ill-usage along with his quarrel with Leu, was forgotten.

Flexing his aching arms as he lifted the paddle that would help take him home he said, 'I shan't risk that again.' Blisters from the axe handle had formed on his palms. He said, 'I never thought where the wood came from before.' It had always just been there to warm him or cook his meals. Appearing at need without any effort on his part.

'It's better than a beating,' Leu said cheerfully, and then as if he had seen the look this produced on his companion's face, added over his shoulder, 'Yes, he would beat you too. Army discipline. Men must be trained to obey or battles would never be won.'

'I suppose your father told you so?' Tarris asked sourly.

'Uh huh.' Leu, oblivious to his tone, plied his paddle. 'I'm starving. I wonder what's for dinner?'

6

A few days after the hunting trip Errol Leris sent for Burran. He was sitting on the ground leaning back against the tree that shaded the side of his house when a dark-haired youngster brought the written message. The boy approached him warily, a hand on the hilt of his dagger. His eyes flickered nervously and he held himself tensely as if expecting an attack.

Keeping his hands still Burran nodded a greeting to him but the lad ignored the overture. He thrust a folded note from his hand; it fell at Burran's feet and as he leaned forward to pick it up, the boy backed up, then turned and stepped carefully away, the arch of his spine indicative of his desire to run. Pride, Burran guessed, was all that stopped him.

The note, written in Pampasan, bade him come to the hall. He read it twice to be sure he had the message correctly, then rose, dusted himself off and went to see what was required of him. It would be the first time since his arrival that he had approached the errol's dwelling. All his and Leris's interactions had previously occurred in the open, within sight of whichever members of the community were about at the time.

This, obviously, was different. Burran wondered if it augured a greater or lesser degree of trust. He was aware that his presence in Carj wasn't universally approved and he suspected that some among the locals, Rost possibly, or Bark, even both perhaps, befriended him the better to spy on his actions. He had long thought there had been something manufactured about the former's quick conversion from outright hatred to tolerance. Yes, he had saved Rost's life — or had he? Might he not just have pretended to drown? The whole thing could have been a set up. It didn't pay to forget that he was dealing with a ruthless and cunning people, as their long history of raids and atrocities against Appella showed. And he was all too aware that he could not as yet begin to guess at the hidden currents in Pampasan society.

At the hall he knocked and when bidden to enter found Leris seated at the table where they had shared food that first night. Sonj was present in the background, hands busy at something on the dais. She appeared to be weaving some article, a rope he thought. One end was fixed to the wall and she continually jerked on and twisted the bit she held, feeding more of the tough grass stems into the lengthening body of her work. He had seen no cattle since his arrival, he remembered, and guessed that for the tribes the grass must replace hide for the hundreds of items needed for their horses: ropes and halters, girth straps and reins to name a few.

Burran dragged his attention back to Leris who greeted him and bade him be seated. She said bluntly in her own tongue, eschewing small talk, 'We have a problem, Scribe.' The words were calmly spoken and initially it surprised him that she knew of his nick-name, but then remembering his earlier thoughts on the subject of spies, it didn't.

He said, 'Yes? Why is that?' So long as she spoke slowly and used plain words he was now practised enough in their tongue to follow her speech.

'A rider has come from the east,' she said. 'From Glam. The king bids me bring you to him. It is a summons that cannot be ignored. We leave at daybreak.'

'Yes? Why is that bad?' For it was plain from her very stolidness that it was.

She inhaled and he glimpsed the anger behind her studied indifference.

'Because someone had betrayed me — us. Your presence here was not meant to get out. Not yet, until my people had grown accustomed to the idea that trading could benefit us. We have stagnated for years behind walls of hatred for all those who live beyond the Grass and there are many who wish this state to continue. They do not care about the cost of maintaining it, for the loss of our young folk. It is no longer freedom we defend,' she said bitterly, 'but a prison of our own making. And until the fighting ends so it will remain.'

'And your king is of another opinion?' Burran asked carefully.

'Hardfar is a man,' she said contemptuously, 'and thinks only of the glory of battle. He has birthed no child for slaughter. But he has power and the young men follow him. It will be one of them who has sent word you are here.' She looked broodingly at him. 'It may be, Scribe, that you ride to your death tomorrow.'

Burran felt cold fingers touch his spine and swallowed. 'What of the trade goods I brought? Perhaps if he saw what dealing with us could bring him...?' There had been silk, and jade from Meddia, fine glassware made in Deems, fantastically coloured sea-shells over-landed in lamb's wool from the distant Appellan port of Quade; small, expensive goods. And surely items that a barbarian king would find both novel and enticing. All men wanted what was rare — every trader knew that! Leris had kept the pack of trade goods but if he could persuade her to present them to the king...

'Yes,' she nodded. 'I had hoped to — but needs must. Though I think weapons would appeal to him more.

Besides, why trade for what he believes his warriors can take at will? No, he will see no need for you or what you bring.'

'But you do?' Burran pushed gently, knowing even as he spoke that her opinion would not be enough to sway a monarch already set on his path.

The flat stare she turned on him was laden with a grief he glimpsed momentarily before it vanished again behind the blank facade of her race. 'I have lost two sons, my mate, my mother, and both my other sisters in raiding parties,' she said. 'Sonj is all that is left to me, and even she I risked to bring you here. A chance I had no choice but to take. So Ulfa said. She believes the Great Mare herself would have peace in the Grass, but wishing for it will not make it happen. No, nor curb the pride of a leader who courts no personal risks by his decrees.'

Burran, remembering the old seer, suppressed a shudder. Mad or not she had sent shivers of warning through him. 'He does not listen to her — your wise woman?'

Leris snorted. 'He is a man. Oh, yes, he fears her, but he cannot bring himself to believe that a mere woman should decide on matters of war. For all they have done little battle to earn it his clan style themselves as the Blood-drinkers, as if they alone had ever fought for the Grass!' She snorted. 'It sounds well to a certain type of man, those who think farming beneath them, a task for women and boys.'

'But I thought — I mean, you are the errol. Women have prominence in your society, they are war chiefs, they govern as you do here —'

'Yes, and there are some who would have it otherwise,' she said shortly. She stood abruptly. 'We leave at first light. It will take three days and I would advise you to use the time to think on how to save yourself, if indeed it can be done.'

One desperate plan occurred to him then and that a slim enough chance, entirely dependent upon the old woman who might think his fate none of her concern. He watched Sonj jerk and twist at the rope she built and said hesitantly, 'If the one you call Ulfa could accompany us? Somehow she knew of the knife I carried. Might she not have other knowledge that could help me — us?' He wondered if Leris herself was aware of the significance of the dagger he had returned. His prince was, and thought it important, which the old woman's subsequent actions had shown it to be.

The question made Leris pause an instant. Her black eyes stared at him then the smooth lids lowered and she gave an infinitesimal nod but all she said was, 'I cannot command her. If she wills it — then perhaps. But it is a long ride and she is old.'

Burran felt his one hope, which had never been great, slipping away. Trying not to plead he said, 'But you will ask — for the sake of the peace you desire between our races?'

The errol's answer came sourly. 'Your race is not the problem, Scribe. Rhuta can only ever be a lever against the curst Appellans. But to Hardfar you are all outlanders, and therefore enemies of the Grass.'

Burran spent the rest of the day and half a wakeful night flogging his brains for some strategem that might work in his favour when he was brought before the king. However when he woke at dawn from a fitful sleep no plan had occurred to him. He could not flee and his chances of winning over a hostile monarch were slight to non-existent. If the old sorceress were to accompany them and confront the king — But realistically what could she do? Seers were widely respected, even feared, but their murder was not unknown. Temes had caused the death of the Oracle of Bel and Appellan soldiers had once killed a Meddian prophet during an attempt on Prince Marric's life. If Ulfa tried to forestall Hardfar's plans for Burran might not she suffer the same fate?

Gloomily Burran checked over his preparations: sleeping roll, cloak, writing implements, weapon, then Sonj appeared at his door with the first lark song, leading a spare mount. He saddled it swiftly, packing his gear into the roomy set of bags slung over the saddle seat.

'Food?' he asked, and she nodded at the heel of a loaf left over from his breakfast.

'Bring what you have, Scribe. We will hunt as we go. And here,' she handed him a tightly rolled scroll of paper. 'For the words.'

'Thanks,' he said wryly. 'Like capture and death, you mean? What does your king do with those he wants rid of?'

'Cuts off their head,' she said composedly, 'or tears them apart between the horses. But you will be safe. The old one comes with us. She will save you.'

Burran swallowed. 'I see. Well, drinkers of blood — Makes sense I suppose.' And a frail old woman was going to save him? He judged she'd be lucky to survive the journey let alone have vigour left to defend him against Hardfar. And why would she even want to?

It was a slow journey. Ulfa travelled in a litter which dictated their pace, and besides the errol and himself ten others accompanied them. It made for a cumbersome party when you included the pack horses. Sonj attended her sister, another young female warrior saw to Ulfa's comfort, while Rost and his seven companions were responsible for the hunting and the camp. Well, six of them were for the seventh was Bryn, Leris's messenger. Burran guessed he had possibly eleven summers, and wasn't entirely certain that the silent lad could speak. It was he who had brought the summons to the hall and wherever the errol was, seemed always to be somewhere in the background, earnest young gaze fixed on her face.

They travelled east and how they found their way across the rolling plains with no landmarks to guide them, was beyond Burran. There were tracks around the settlement but a day's ride distant these petered out into the occasional single bridle path or horse pad where the wild herds had converged upon watering points. Burran glimpsed his first such herd on the evening of the first day, a forest of tossing heads and muscular shoulders, black silhouettes above grass stained gold by the dying sun. The rolling thunder of their hooves as they wheeled into a gallop carried clearly to them.

'How many?' Burran asked Sonj who had reined up beside him.

Face glowing with pleasure at the sight she said, 'Oh, three sets of hands perhaps. Look, there is a foal at the back, you can just see his head when he leaps.'

'It's a wonder he can get through the grass at all,' Burran commented.

'His dam keeps him behind, so the others flatten it for him. Is there no grass in your country?'

'Well of course. But knee-high maybe, not like this. And we have no wild herds, our horses are bred in paddocks and stables.'

She tossed her head disdainfully. 'Servitude. Ours are free as the Great Mare wills they be.'

'And yet you ride them. Is that not a form of servitude?'

Her eyes flashed scorn at him. 'The Great Mare Epona is the mother of us all. She grants us the right. It is a partnership, a bond not — not slavery,' she said forcefully. 'You understand nothing, Scribe. When we die our bodies and spirits both go into the Grass and return to Epona's children. They are us and we are them and so it has always been.' The tattoos on her chin striped her face giving it the aspect of a furious wildcat — kitten he corrected himself — as the dark eyes glared at him before she wheeled her mount away to take up a position beside her sister.

They raised a felted tent for the women that night but the rest of them slept around the fire. The old seer, who had scarcely spoken a word, save to grumble at the food, vanished early into the tent followed by her attendant, who shortly reappeared, a spate of angry words following her out.

'She — I think she is in pain,' the girl, Rana said excusingly. Her face was flushed. She sat down with lowered eyes and as Leris made to rise and go to the old woman, quickly shook her head.

'It will be hard on her, the travelling,' the errol replied, subsiding again. 'We are fortunate indeed she consented to come. It is many years since she last left the Mounds.'

So, this was an unusual event. Burran clutched at the idea. Did it mean she could save him and his mission? He ran a surreptitious eye over his lounging companions. All save the errol, who wore a preoccupied crease between her brows, seemed at ease, their limbs relaxed and the firelight lending a coppery cast to their features. His gaze dwelt longest on Sonj whose downcast eyes watched the flames. The delicate tattoos added an alluring mystery to the perfect oval of her face, becomingly framed by the tiny ridges of her braided hair. She wore the amber amulet, and like the others, the arms that never seemed to leave her person. A kitten, he smiled a little at his earlier thought, but one with claws. Something to remember.

He felt another's gaze upon him and glancing casually about encountered a hot glare from Rost that was instantly veiled, but not before Burran glimpsed the threat it carried. Casually he yawned and looked away to conceal his shock. Was that jealousy he had seen? Did the man have an interest in the errol's sister and sense a rival in Burran? It was true they were often together and perhaps he did feel a mild attraction — she was pretty and unintentionally funny in her attempts to master the new language. He had been blind, he thought disgustedly, but at least he no longer harboured any doubt as to who had reported Leris's plans to the king.

The morning was a repeat of the previous day, with the horses saddled, the litter prepared and the camp packed up. Rost ranged his mount beside Burran's in the unbroken expanse of grass and dug a booted toe into the haunch of a passing packhorse to hurry it out of its leisurely amble.

'So do you know where you are, Scribe?' There was a hint of disdain in his tone which Burran chose to ignore.

'East of where we were yesterday,' he replied peacefully. 'Why? Are you lost?'

'There's about as much chance of that as there is of you finding your way to anywhere alone. So if you're thinking of trying it one night, I wouldn't.'

Burran widened his eyes. 'Now why would I do that?'

Rost shrugged. 'The summons to court, perhaps? Few outlanders survive a meeting with King Hardfar. His clan is the Blood-drinkers; he has little use for those from a nation of traders.'

'My people fight when they must. Or did you not know that we won a war against Appella? Something I believe you Pampasans have still to do.' Rost scowled at that but Burran, affecting not to notice, added thoughtfully, 'Trade of course is better than war. It brings with it strong allies that serve as a deterrent against enemies. Something I would have thought any king would be glad to have. The world is wider than the Grass, my friend, and Appella grows again in strength.'

Rost snorted disdainfully. 'We have beaten them before when they were a more powerful race.'

'And spread more thinly then to hold down their empire,' Burran agreed affably. 'Now Ansham is a free country and Rhuta and Meddia have thrown off the Appellan yoke, which means your enemy is free to concentrate his forces wholly upon your borders. If General Morrik should choose to again enlarge Appella at your expense, well...'

'By Epona's tits I should like to see them try!' Rost's face darkened with angry blood.

'It is as the Lady wills,' Burran said piously, 'but you yet may get your wish.' Then Sonj reined her mount in beside him with a question and Rost scowling, dropped back to ride beside Rana.

7

Later when the day was ending and he found himself for the moment beside Leris the errol abruptly asked, 'What is your quarrel with Rost, Scribe?'

'I have none,' he said. 'I sense he doesn't like me, but few of your people care for outlanders. And I suspect it was he who informed on my presence here. Would that be possible?'

'Rost?' The woman's brow contracted but after a moment she nodded reluctantly. 'He is one of several who may have done so. He thinks my position should be his. My mate fostered him when his father was slain and he has his followers. He is a leader, a good fighting man, but it is all he knows.'

'I think,' Burran said, 'that he likes your sister.'

Leris looked startled then frowned as if the thought did not please her. He waited but she was studying the area and suddenly raised her hand. 'Here, we will make camp here.' She reined her mare in and dismounted to stride across to the litter from which Ulfa's head suddenly thrust, like an aged and ugly turtle from its shell. The two confered but Burran, strain how he might, couldn't hear what was said. Shrugging his failure aside he dismounted to help set up camp.

Two days later and the country had changed from the endless vista of grass into farmland where sheep and some cattle grazed. They glimpsed no more of the wild herds but saw instead lightly timbered country, and then areas of crops, and grazing ground and even closely planted ranks of trees though whether they produced fruit or nuts or were grown for their timber, Burran couldn't tell. The arable ground being worked far surpassed the fields of Carj, but then as they made their way through it to the edge of the sprawling city of Glam he saw that the population here was much larger than Errol Leris's domain.

Glam was nothing like Ripa. Here and there a stone building hinted at permanence, but most of the dwellings were of mud brick with thatched and felted roofs, as if their inhabitants' hearts hankered still for the tents of their forebears. It was late in the day when they arrived, their cavalcade winding between the streets, amid the smoke and smells of urbanisation. Industry was on display in the bake houses and meat vendors, in the smithies where furnaces roared, and the sprawling brickworks where slabs of baked clay were piled. The men they passed in the streets went weaponless save for the customary dagger on their belts, but occasionally Burran saw some carrying the deadly bows of the Grasslands. Hunters, perhaps? Or some sort of town militia? There were dye shops with gaily patterned garments drying on racks, a pie shop giving off enticing smells and a man hammering pots by a window to take advantage of the failing light.

When they finally stopped it was at an inn with an extensive stable area where they unsaddled and pulled the gear from the weary packhorses. Ulfa was helped from the litter and stood complaining in the straw littered yard, while her mode of transport was dismantled and piled with the pack goods.

'You and you,' Leris pointed to Bark and another of the escort, 'will sleep here with the prisoner and guard the gear. Bryn will stay too; he will bring messages to me at need. I will have food and ale sent out for you.'

Sonj said something quickly in an undertone, glancing at Burran as she did so, but the older woman shook her head.

'Would you flout the king's direct order? Bring the prisoner, he said. He would not be pleased to hear of him free to wander at will.' To Burran she added, 'You won't be bound but consider these two as your gaolers.'

'As you wish,' Burran said stiffly. Was she expecting him to attempt an escape? What messages was the boy there to convey? And how, as he seemed touched in the head if not downright stupid. Burran assumed they were all lettered but he had seen no sign of it beyond Leris and her sister. The town dwellers among them would read and write, but the nomadic warriors? It seemed unlikely. Burran swore mildly to himself, he had been looking forward to a proper bed and the odour of roasting meat drifting from the kitchen was enticing. He hoped they remembered to feed him and that Bark wasn't tempted to exert his authority as gaoler.

He entered the stable and Bark, investigating ahead of him, jerked his head at an empty stall. 'In there,' he said. 'Wait, take the gear with you, you'll all be locked up safe together.'

Burran dragged the packbags and camp gear in without complaint. The stall at least had been mucked out and fresh straw laid. He had, he supposed, slept in worst places. He made himself comfortable while Bark, from the sound of things, pulled a chain across the door. He could he saw, easily climb the stall's walls but to what end? Even if he managed to get a horse out of the stables he'd be without provisions or directions, and lost in a wilderness as formless as the wide ocean into which the Great River of Rhuta emptied. Besides, here was where the Prince wanted him. His stomach twisted nervously at the reminder, and he hoped by all the gods that tomorrow wasn't part of the events that Marric had admitted he couldn't always see.

The meal eventually arrived, hot and filling. Roast pork with root vegetables and a hunk of chewy but satisfying bread. A pot of ale accompanied it, sour and thick with sediment. Ripa could teach them something of brewing, Burran thought pulling a face, but he drank it anyway. Bark had unlocked the stall door and the four of them ate together, the boy Bryn watching everything with sharp bright eyes. For the first time Burran wondered if he really couldn't speak, for surely he was too young to maintain such a subterfuge? But what a weapon for the errol if it were so. Everyone ignored the lad, and if, as he'd recently learned, others coveted her position, he would be an invaluable window into any conspirator's world. Time then to do a little probing of his own.

'Why does the old sorceress accompany us?' He spat out the dregs of the drink and wiped a wrist across his mouth.

'To advise the king,' Bark said. 'She reads the future and tells what is to come.'

'Truly?' Burran widened his eyes. 'Why then does she not stay at his side?'

'Because she lives with the dead. Her power comes from our ancestors in the Mounds, or so it is said. And there she is closest to Epona, the Mother of Mares.'

Ranj, the second guard leaned into the circle of lamplight and dropped his voice, 'They say if you pass by the grave mounds you will hear the Goddess leading Her children as they gallop. The ground shakes they say with their passing, like a thunder roll — only the skies are clear. I myself have not experienced this, but others have. They only whisper of it though, least they offend Epona.'

'What could she do?' Burran wondered and both men looked shocked.

'Do? She is a goddess, man! She could wither the

grass, or blind the mares or stop them breeding. Her hand is over all Her children but who would knowingly risk Her anger?'

'Then she approves of what you do — the constant raids — even though it must lead to the death of many horses?'

'Not so many,' Ranj objected.

'We but defend the Grass for Her. And without it how could Her herds prosper?' Bark scowled warningly at him. 'Do not try to trick us up with words, Scribe.'

'Where is the trickery? I but ask,' Burran shrugged. 'In my land we have Bel, god of the Great River. And in Appella there is the Asher whom they call the Light — and I never was clear on who or what the Meddians follow; but they are a strange people and theirs is a grim country.'

'Why strange?' Ranj took the bait. 'And where is this land — you have been there?'

'Yes.' Leaning forward Burran adopted his persuasive trader's voice and spoke of the grim citadel now ruled again by a priest king known as the Medic, and the practices of that austere, inward looking race. It was a ploy that seldom failed. All men loved stories that told of the wonders, or curiosities, of distant lands. The telling soothed an adversary's suspicion and made him, or them, more likely to talk in return and anything he could gain in this fashion might help him on the morrow. So stories of the Medic's successful ousting of their overlords from Appella led naturally into return tales of raids fought against the same foe, and from there to exploits of Hardfar and his clan the Blood-drinkers.

There was however, little of comfort for Burran in the telling. It painted a picture of a savage king who counted his success in the number of dead enemies he could boast. Of a man with no interest beyond protecting his own position as leader which included the occasional internecine struggle with neighbouring clans that objected to his iron hand. With a sinking heart Burran wondered what the prince had been thinking, sending him hence. This was not a man to interest himself in trade or alliances with other lands. He would tear Burran limb from limb — or rather his horses would, this apparently being a favoured method of the Blood-drinkers for ending their victims lives by tying their limbs to mounts which were then urged in opposite directions.

Burran was silently contemplating this when Bark rose and stretched. 'Right,' he said, 'I'm for bed. Into your stall, Scribe. We'll be right here and just so you know they keep a guard on the horses.'

'Really? In Ripa we're more trusting of our citizens. But then we live a freer life.' He left them with that thought and strolled back into his makeshift prison to unstrap his bedroll and settle down for the night. For a time he lay and worried, cudgelling his brain for some way to placate the king for the simple crime of entering the Grass, before finally admitted there was none. Or none that he could articulate. He was here because a seer in his own country thought it essential that he should be.

He didn't know the reason for it and the unfortunate and awkward truth was that neither did the seer. What sort of message was that to give an already suspicious ruler? He would be seen as a spy, come to work treason among the Pampasans and be summarily killed for his pains. He wondered gloomily if Prince Marric would ever know his fate or even learn the reason the Goddess had required his presence here among the blood drenched oceans of the Grass.

He must have slept in the end for it was the homely sound of a dunghill cock greeting the morning from the entrance yard to the stable that woke him to the dawn. He stretched at ease for a moment, snuffing the odours of stables and wood smoke then recalled where he was and dread rose in him as he stirred himself woodenly to rise and shake out his bedding, and call for his gaolers to release him in time to relieve himself and wash, and prepare for what might be his last day alive.

Breakfast over the horses were resaddled and the pack animal carrying the trade goods was pressed back into service. The rest of the gear was transferred to the inn rooms, then the whole party rode through the streets to present themselves at the door of the king's meeting hall, where they were halted by a brace of guards demanding their business.

Errol Leris pressed her mount forward imperiously demanding that they make way. 'For we have business with the king, and are here at his request.'

'That so?' the first guard inquired insolently eyeing her. 'Well, his majesty don't see every stray mare as comes along. Got plenty of his own. Might make an exception for the filly 'ere though.' He leered at Sonj and Rost bristling began to push forward just as Ulfa stuck her head through the litter curtains and made an impatient gesture to the nearest rider. It was Bark and he tumbled rapidly from the saddle to go to her side.

'Get me out,' she hissed. When her bowed body was upright she paced up to the astonished guard and glared at his chest. 'I am Ulfa,' she snarled, 'the Keeper of the Mounds and the voice of the Great Mare. Would you like to tell me, oaf, why I am kept waiting to have speech with Her child, Hardfar?'

The last few words were all but drowned by the sudden raucous crying of crows. Burran glanced up to see a host of them winging in to alight on the roof of the hall. They strutted along the ridge capping, peering sideways through beady eyes and one, bolder than the rest, fluttered down to land on the old woman's shoulder. She turned her head to croon at it and the guard swallowed and took a hasty step back. Guards and party alike were staring while figures in the street pointed and called to one another, and the crows set up a constant maddening cawing.

'Your pardon, Mistress.' The guard gulped, cast an agonised look at his mate and then, bowing to the pressure of Ulfa's inimical gaze pushed open the door. 'Please, come. I will tell the king.'

And so the hour had come. Fatalistically Burran allowed himself to be shepherded into the high roofed hall with its stone floor and dais at one end where the king's high seat loomed. It was a large room with a huge hearth, unlit now, and rows of empty bench seats pushed back hard against the side walls. They, and the tables to accompany them, would be brought out at need for dinners and public feasting, he assumed, but for now the room's occupants stood in loose groups before the dais where the distant figure on the high seat leaned a little sideways on his chair, listening to some plea or discussion being conducted before him.

Whole tree trunks supported the lofty roof of the hall and the wall cladding, Burran noticed, bore some resemblance to the art of the Lake Country where they used reeds rather than grass, as was the case here, to weave decorative patterns into their buildings. The city of Glam had not, from the brief acquaintance accorded him by the ride from hostelry to hall, impressed Burran. Ripa's art and sophistication were centuries ahead of the place, but then the Rhutans had literally had centuries in which to build and refine their tastes. Conversely Glam with its rutted streets and unpaved walkways had the air of the makeshift beginnings of a frontier town. Like a new and untried experiment born of a burst of enthusiasm that might not last.

The door guard had pushed his way through the throng about the king and interrupted the talk. Burran saw Hardfar's head swivel towards them just as the crow lifted from Ulfa's shoulder where it had ridden as they entered the hall, and fly towards him. It circled the chair while faces lifted to observe it, then perched on the high back, over which a bear skin was draped, and cawed as the king twisted about to stare at it. He said something, lost in the sudden outburst of talk, and swatted at the bird with a meaty arm. The crow lifted, easily avoiding the blow, and flew back to its place on Ulfa's shoulder. Its call as it landed sounded like derisive laughter and the king surged angrily to his feet to glare at the approaching Carjans.

'What is this?' he bellowed. 'Guard, who are these people?'

'Errol Leris of the Crow Clan from Carj, my lord.' Leris strode forward. 'You sent for me to bring the outlander to you. He is here. A harmless trader, my lord king, who has brought gifts into the Grass, and wishes only to promote commerce between our peoples.'

'So he tells you, woman,' Hardfar said contemptuously. 'Since when has it been wise or even necessary, to believe the smooth talk of those our enemies send to spy on us?'

The guard was making agitated gestures, seeking to draw Hardfar's or his advisor's attention to Ulfa, but was silenced with a peremptory wave of the hand.

'He is not a spy,' Leris refused to back down. Burran admired her at that moment. Hardfar he could see, was a bully, a squatly built brute of a man with a long reach to his arms and a well muscled body. His hair showed traces of grey but old age still waited for him a good way into the future. 'He came to us with gifts to learn our ways and our tongue, and find what goods we might exchange to our countries' mutual benefit.'

'Aye, and if you were not just a brainless woman, you would see the holes in that coat,' Hardfar shot back, 'for a score of arrows could scarcely make more. Of course a spy must learn our tongue or what knowledge can he carry back to his masters? By Epona's tits, are you as witless in all your dealings, errol? Or does it take just a trinket or two to addle your sense? He has our tongue you say — well spy, let us hear it. Who is your lord?'

Burran drew a breath and marshalled his words. He had one chance — and a very slender one at that. Gazing across at the heavy, self-satisfied face with its fierce nose and cold eyes he suddenly knew the king was toying with him. Hardfar had no intention of letting him live. He had probably mentally ordered the horses and ropes prepared from the moment he learned of Burran's existence.

He spoke slowly ensuring that each word was correct. 'I am a trader from Rhuta lord, where King Darien reigns. I come of my own accord to further my business and if you permit it, I would establish trade with your own merchants. We Rhutan traders deal with all the world. I have brought a few poor samples with me,' he said humbly, and from the corner of his eye he saw Leris murmur something to Ranj and the man slip away, presumably to produce them.

'And doubtless you hope to return with a report for your master,' Hardfar nodded affably, 'of conditions in the Grass? The lay of the land, where the water runs, how many warriors the country can field. And all for the cost of a few worthless trinkets.' He wagged his head in mock admiration. 'A cunning trade indeed.'

'My lord, it is not like that —'

'Silence!' Hardfar roared. 'Your lies may satisfy a stupid woman from a small clan but it is I who rule here. You will die, spy. And your paltry bribes,' he said casting a scornful eye over the wares Ranj was spreading out even as he spoke, 'will recompense those involved in the effort of your death.' Stooping he yanked a swathe of silk from the goods displayed and tossed it disdainfully at the group before him. 'You think this the price of our wits? Or this?' A booted foot swung at the delicate handblown vessel painted with river scenes, scattering shards of glass across the floor. 'Such trumpery may fool a stupid woman with her brains between her legs, but it is a man you are dealing with now. Take him.'

Before he could comprehend what was happening Burran felt his arms seized from behind by a brace of guards who had come up to him unseen. He struggled until a vicious fist in his stomach doubled him over, fighting for the breath that had been driven from his body. He never saw the noose coming. It settled over his head and was yanked tight and suddenly he was arched backwards against the grip on either arm, choking for the air denied him.

Of course! The thought was a faint glimmer in his fading mind. It was thus the Pampasans caught new mounts from the wild herds, by stealth and the noose. Sonj had roped him too, but as a sign of subjugation, not intending to kill. Dimly he heard a woman's faint cry of protest, then his knees buckled and there was only a thin awareness shrinking into blackness split by the harsh cawing of a bird. The Crow Road, he was on it now and his prince would never learn his fate... Darkness took him and his captors, feeling the change, released their grip letting his slack body collapse onto the stone floor of the hall.

8

Consciousness returned fitfully. Instinct brought the young trader's hands to his neck to pull at the loosened but still tight cord. Sweet breath rasped in his throat driving the air down into his starved body; he coughed, feeling the flame of outraged tissue in his throat, and finally managed to plant his hands beneath him and thrust upwards, lifting his head enough to take in what was happening.

It seemed to consist of a great deal of harsh cawing. It took him a moment to realise it wasn't the crow but Ulfa who was making it, though her voice was as harsh as the beady-eyed bird on her shoulder. '... and you think your muscle makes you special, or is it what dangles between your legs? Then listen, King Hardfar, for if you value your position, Blood-drinker, if you would hold what you have, then take fair warning as it is sent you from Epona Herself.'

She paused — for effect, Burran guessed. It should have been a ludicrous sight, the tiny bowed sorceress with the bird, half as big as her head, riding her shoulder, her slight form almost hidden by the crowd of men surrounding her. But none save the king were actually looking at her. The rest stood rigid, their eyes averted and now that his senses were coming back he was himself aware as he had been at their first meeting, of something uncanny about her. The hair at his nape stirred and he was suddenly glad that her attention was focused on another. Atavistic fears tightened his flesh into goosepimples and caused him to swallow.

'Well,' much of the bluster had vanished from the king's voice. 'I am listening, mage. Give me the message.'

'Open the door,' Ulfa said, and when nobody moved, gave a vicious poke to the nearest ribcage and snarled. 'Are you deaf? Open it!'

The man hurried to obey and Burran groped through the hammering of blood in his ears, for the strength to stand. He made it on the second effort but the pulsing beat in his ears continued, and then he realised the sound was outside himself and that every head in the room was cocked to listen to the approaching thunder. A man cried out in amazement, another swore, and those nearest the door turned of one accord in an attempt locate the source of the stampede. Ulfa raised her hands commandingly, her voice an eldritch screech.

'Hear me sweet Mistress, Great Mare, Mother of thousands. I your servant call to you. Show him Epona, show this king what disobedience to Your will means.'

Instantly the thundering hooves ceased. They didn't fade into the distance, they simply stopped between one hoof-fall and the next, and a silence that blanketed even the noises of the city settled like a pall over the streets outside, the hall, and its thunderstruck inhabitants.

Ulfa raised a bony hand, pointing it at Hardfar's face. 'Behold your future, king. A land barren of horses. No mares, no colts, no mounts for war. Epona will leave the grass and without our Goddess what will hold the clans together? Not you. Not me. Kill this man and you doom us all.' With a swift movement she seized the crow from her shoulder and with a flick of her wrist that was so fast Burran caught only a momentary glimpse of the tiny blade gripped in her fist, cut its throat.

The crow died without a squawk and then the hot

blood was flung at his face. He reeled back in surprise feeling its warmth and tasted on his lips its salty, iron flavour.

'The blood mark of Epona's own creature is upon him,' Ulfa cried over the sudden roar of voices. 'Who harms this man suffers the Goddess's curse. He is the guarantee of our future.'

'Which will be short enough,' Hardfar spat furiously. 'How does he guarantee anything save the spilling of our strength to whoever sent him?'

'Am I a both a man and a short-sighted fool?' Ulfa demanded witheringly. 'He is a hostage, one who will never leave the Grass. Our clan leader is wise beyond a mere man's understanding, but it is ever the mares that lead the herd.'

That was true enough, Burran thought. The stallions were there for protection and procreation, it was the mares that led. He felt utterly numb, and at the same time amazed that his mind could occupy itself with anything beyond his own predicament. So the danger was past. He would live — but never to leave? The sentence had hit him like a blow. Was that then the true meaning of the prince's words? It will be hard. Had Marric known when he said that, that he was sending him into exile, or was his fate simply a part of what the prince had confessed he could not always see? It made little difference he supposed, smearing the blood from his lips. The dead bird lay on its back at his feet, black claws curled into its death spasm, the glossy feathers stained at the neck where the flesh gaped, its fate delivered as swiftly as Burran's own.

The noise around him had died. Burran slowly became aware of the silent regard from those around him. Rost looked — disappointed, he thought, Leris gratified, and Ulfa? He couldn't decide. He saw Sonj's strained smile and Ranj's speculative gaze. The boy Bryn was staring at the dead bird. He made an inarticulate noise in his throat and suddenly darted forward to pick up the body. Ulfa said something in a low tone but he hunched his shoulder and turned away from her, retreating to the errol's side.

As if recalled to her surroundings Leris faced the king again and nodded gravely, 'With your leave, my lord, we should go. It is a far ride home. If you do not find them acceptable should I remove the trader's gifts?'

'There is no need to trouble yourself. My women may find amusement with them.' Hardfar showed his teeth. 'In my experience women are easily distracted by geegaws.'

She bowed her head. 'As it pleases you, lord.' A single look sufficed to gather the party as she turned on her heel and left, the others following.

They rode back to the inn, packed and reassembled the litter, and as the sun reached its full force threaded their way through the noisy streets to reach the peace of the countryside beyond. Burran, smearing a palm across his cheeks to wipe away sweat, noticed the stain on his palm and realised that he still wore the blood of the dead crow. Its brothers lining the roof pole of the hall had taken silent flight when they had emerged and moments later, faint as the tremble of an echo against his inner ear, he had heard the soft drumming of hooves. He had shot a glance at the old shaman only to find her enigmatic gaze upon him. She had been watching him, and seeing him notice her face had briefly worn a smirk — a grimace? He wasn't sure what he had glimpsed, but he felt the coldness on his skin as the hairs pulled erect and had looked quickly aside.

Sonj, riding nearby had seen his expression of disgust as he wiped his stained palm across his thigh and pushed her horse to his side.

'You should be grateful, Scribe,' she said bluntly. 'She saved you. Or would you rather have been ripped apart?'

'I am,' he said, 'grateful for her intervention. But we traders do not deal in blood, or butcher any creature to make a point.'

The girl tilted her chin and her eyes scorned him. 'We are a warrior race. We do not fear blood.'

'Well, I'd rather it was kept within the skin of those that own it,' Burran snapped, nettled by the accusation of cowardice. 'That bird trusted her, it came to her of its own accord, and she killed it.'

'It was Epona's, to do with as the Goddess willed. And She willed that its life end to save yours. You understand nothing, you — you Outlander!' She glared at him, angry beyond any reason he could account for. She ripped her mount's head about and would have ridden off had he not caught and held the rein nearest him.

'Then supposing you explain. I cannot learn what is kept hidden. Who is Ulfa, and what is she to your clan that she would make this long trek to save me, only to bind me here forever? How can trade between our countries benefit yours if I am unable to leave? And what is the meaning of the crows flocking to her that way?'

'Why would they not? They are our clan's totem.' She stared at his incomprehension. 'Do not your own clans possess such a thing?'

'No, why would we? We are a civilised people,' I mean, he added hurriedly not wishing to offend, 'we are not — not tribal, the way your people seem to be. We have a temple and a high-priest, and once, they say though it was before my time, there was a priestess who was our god's Oracle and spoke his messages. But she was the mother of our king and is long dead. There have been no others since.' Well, only the prince but he served the Goddess of the Lake Country. Burran decided not to confuse the issue with that piece of information. 'So who and what exactly is Ulfa?'

'She is the shaman of our clan. The spirits of the dead speak with her and she does the bidding of Epona the Great Mare. She reads the signs the Goddess sends and thus tells the future.'

'So,' Burran nodded. 'She is powerful, the old woman? More powerful than the king? And where was his clan's shaman today?'

'Not all clans have them. In fact it is rare, and growing rarer. Ulfa is why my sister rules our clan,' Sonj admitted in a burst of candour. 'Rost thinks, because he is a man and was fostered by my sister's mate that he should. He is like the king, believing men are somehow superior. But he fears Ulfa. Once, it is said, in my grandmother's time, those chosen by the Goddess were more common, but of late,' she frowned, nibbling at her lip, 'that has changed. Many men now think like Rost that only they should rule, that women should not even be warriors, let alone errols.'

'But the king respects your shaman? Though it seemed to me he didn't like that errol Leris had brought her along.'

Sonj treated him to another hard stare. 'Ulfa goes where she pleases. My sister does not control her. And say rather that our king fears her — as he should.' Burran saw her shoulders twitch to the shiver that ran through her. 'You heard the horses, Scribe. They come to her call, as do the crows. Would you not fear someone with that sort of power?'

He replied honestly, 'Yes. But I do not see why she would pen me here. King's sons are hostages, or other nobly born men. I am a simple trader who matters to no-one. Where is my value to her, or the king?'

'Perhaps she has other plans for you,' Rost said, heeling his horse between the two of them. 'You should listen more closely, Scribe. Never leaving the Grass could simply mean you will die. A shaman's words seldom carry but one meaning.'

Burran felt a little frisson of disquiet. Of course Rost was right. Malice might have prompted the remark but that made it no less true. He had heard enough whispers about the prophecies of both the prince, and his mother, one time Oracle of Bel, to know how words could be either deliberately twisted or misinterpreted. *He will never leave,* she had said, not *He will live in exile.*

Viewed dispassionately it even made a twisted sort of sense. Ulfa had enabled Leris to defy the king but if the latter had no intention of allowing trade then it was a hollow victory and his continued presence could only be an embarrassment to the people of Carj. It might even weaken Leris's rule. Prince Marric had assured him that women carried the same status as men in the Grass, but that, however true it may once have been, had seemingly changed, or was in the process of doing so. Weighing his scraps of information, one against the other, in proper trader fashion, Burran came to the gloomy conclusion that Rost might have winkled out the truth of it. Where is my value? Burran himself had asked the girl, and the plain fact was that he had none.

***

In Ripa as soon as the news of his brother's arrival reached the palace the king hurried to the forecourt where the party was dismounting in a bustle of servants and stablemen come to take charge of the luggage and horses. Because he was the biggest man there Darien's gaze found Osram first, and beside him the smaller figure of Marric accompanied by Tarris and another fairhaired boy.

'Marric.' The king flung an arm about his brother's shoulders. 'I only heard a few days ago. I am so sorry! You should have let us know.'

Marric shook his head tiredly. 'What could you have done?'

'We — Ling and I — we would have come. Bels balls! We are family, Marric! It is our loss too, we could have grieved together.'

'And still she would be dead.' Marric's face was closed to him, grief had thinned it, Darien saw and hollowed his eyes. His brother had always been self contained and there were parts of him that he still did not know and doubted he ever would. He nodded abstractedly at his son hovering in the background and let his arm fall.

'How is Fenny?'

'With her mother. She will forgive sooner than I for it seems she knew, but hid from the knowledge, that Perilla was doomed. From birth apparently, though no-one saw fit to tell me.'

'Forgive?' Darien asked at sea.

'The Goddess.' Abruptly he changed the subject. 'Tarris has made a friend who has come on a visit. Osram's boy. He is good for the lad, a useful sparring partner but more importantly he affords his rank no consideration.'

'Ah, that is rare indeed. I am obliged to you for the thought brother. Now, come away in. There is wine and food and any quantity of matters to discuss, though,' he added suddenly remembering, 'that can wait until you are rested. If you would like time alone — or would wish to visit the shrine...?'

'No.' Marric's jaw set. 'I would rather work.'

'Very well.' Sighing, Darien let him walk away and turned to his son.

'Welcome home, my boy. I swear you have grown taller. Did you enjoy the Lakes?'

'Yes, Father.' The boy bobbed a brief bow. 'I learned to swim. This is my friend Leu.'

The fairhaired boy flushed in confusion and made his obeisance. 'My lord king. I am very happy to be here. Tarris has been telling me of life here in the city.'

'Your first visit?' Darien asked kindly. 'You must enjoy it then, there is much to see. Tarris, run along now, your mother and sisters will be waiting.' He turned to clasp arms with Osram, an old comrade in arms. The latter's gaze watched the boys run after Marric's upright figure and shook his head.

'The sorrow is on your brother, my lord,' he observed quietly. 'His little flower — gone in an instant they told me. If ever a man had deserved better of the fates —'

'I know. I could wish a bird had been sent with the news. I understand it is two months and more since her death. My heart grieves for his loss, Fenny's too. How is she?'

'She mourns as women do, and is the better for it I think,' Osram said slowly. 'It would help mayhap if he — but it is all work with him.' He shrugged, 'I have tried my lord, with words, with drink and hunting, but he will have none of it.'

'I thank you for that,' the king said. 'You are a good friend to him.'

'He is my prince,' the simple words held the finality of cause and effect.

"Well at least if it is work he wants there will be ample, with the royal visit due almost daily.'

Osram cocked an eyebrow. 'The manat from Barat? It's that time already?'

The king nodded. 'Aye, as Rissak would say.'

A loose confederation of rulers, composed of the heads of states of Barak, Rhuta, Ansham and lately Meddia, met annually for discussions on everything from trade, to a general exchange of news concerning regional events; particularly on matters pertaining to Appella which had begun of late to show alarming signs of hawkish behaviour.

There had been fifteen years of peace since Temes was toppled. His defeated country was led now by one Morrik, who had miraculously survived both his late ruler's purges of the military, and the subsequent battle for Ripa. And the man now styling himself a general seemed intent upon rebuilding the Appellan army. With the loss of the satellite states his late king had ruled he no longer had the pool of manpower that Cyrus had enjoyed but by all accounts, a smaller, leaner force was being forged. A worrying development for those who had suffered under the reign of the tyrant Temes.

Osram jerked his head vaguely south at the distant alps, no more than a faint blue blur on the horizon behind which his erstwhile country ran.

'Trouble?'

Darien grinned wryly and clapped his shoulder. 'Well, back when we planned to retake the throne we never thought it would be easy, did we? Not the taking nor the holding, but it hasn't come to that yet, thank the Lady. And now I must go to my brother. You'll find Rissak in the barracks.'

Tarris saw little of either his father or uncle during Leu's visit for the following day first the royal visitor from Barak with his entourage of courtiers, clerks and escort arrived, then in quick succession, the Medic's party from Meddia, and with less consequence and far fewer followers, Slate of the Old Race from Ansham. He had just six in his party, small, dark-haired men with their shepherd's bows slung on their backs.

They said little, glancing aside at the busy streets and the many buildings crowded within the city's walls. Theirs was a mainly pastoral society dotted with small tribal villages for little of their land lent itself to farming. They seemed unimpressed by the wonders of the Temple of Bel but the crops and orchards surrounding Ripa roused an admiring interest in them.

Tarris, from a vantage point in the stable's loft where the two boys had gone to watch unobserved, was able to name the important visitors as they appeared and dismounted in the courtyard.

'The black ones are from Barat. That's way off to the west. He's called the manat. A silly title; it just means king.'

'I know,' Leu murmured, 'my father has been there. He went with the prince before the war started. He says there's a mountain that breathes fire. They fought for us, you know — the Baratans. The manat of the time sent cavalry to help Rhuta.'

'I know that.' A little nettled to find that Leu was more knowledgeable than himself on the subject, Tarris pointed to the grim visaged party presently clattering into sight. 'That lot will be the ones from Meddia. You can tell by the way they dress. They have a law that says it has to be plain. No gold or jewels allowed. Not like the manat.' Even from high in the stables they could see the glint of the gold torc around the big black man's throat.

'I heard Rissak tell my father that the Meddii are all priests, and famous healers too.'

'How would he know?' Tarris asked.

His friend shrugged. 'Maybe he's visited their country? He was King Cyrus's man before he became your uncle's bodyguard, and Meddia belonged to Appella back then. Don't you learn this stuff, Tarris?'

The young prince waved the question aside. 'That's all years back, before I was born — before my father was born, even. What can it matter now. Rissak is as old as the hills.'

The blue eyes regarded him in faint astonishment. 'No he isn't. He and my father were soldiers together under King Cyrus. They're probably about the same age and my father isn't old.'

'He's older than mine,' Tarris pointed out.

'So?'

'So, nothing.' Tarris shrugged. 'The one in the grey tunic there is Slate. He's head of the council in Ansham. They don't have a king since the old man called Arn died. Apparently their goddess chose Slate to follow him, though I don't know how.'

Leu watched the bustle below him as the horses were led off, the escorts directed to what would be their quarters for the ensuing days, and the dignitaries and their advisors ushered indoors. 'What will they do now?'

'Talk,' Tarris said dismissively, 'for days, very likely.' He jumped up. 'Come on, I'll show you the temple, and afterwards we can go to the markets. They have performers there some days with dancing dogs and all sorts. And there is a stall that sells sweet tarts. Hurry up, sluggard!'

9

As Tarris had said for the duration of their stay in Ripa the visitors' talked. With Doku, the manat of Barat, there was an old friendship for Marric and Darien to renew. Doku was newer come to his throne than the latter, his grandfather the old manat having died but three years since. They had been busy careful years for him, he said, as he strove to abolish some of the stricter traditions of his people for their own good, though many of the older men in government resisted the change.

'I want a more open society, one in which our women too, can play a part. Though you would think,' he said wryly, 'that I was asking for the blood of their youngest. It has always been this way, Sire, they tell me. Besides, the women themselves would not want it. When I ask how they know, did their wives and daughters tell them so, they look at me as if I were mazed. Ask a woman? they say. If I were my grandfather I would have had them all strangled by this.'

'Replace them, appoint younger men,' Darien suggested.

'You make it sound so simple,' Doku grumbled. 'Your reign is new remember, I on the other hand follow in the footsteps of a tradition set when the world was young. Sooner the sacred mountain should fall that a woman's opinion be heard among men.'

'How does your sister Amtee?' Marric asked. 'She is well?'

Doku sighed. 'Yes, I thank you. But she is the biggest argument against my reforms. They use her, the old men, as reason enough to keep women secluded from general society.'

Marric nodded understandingly. As a child Doku's sister had been stolen away, raped and left to die on Rhutan land. 'Don't lose heart my friend. It is a worthwhile project. And please give Amtee my best wishes when you return, and my wife's — she was fond of Fenny.'

Darien rose to refresh their wine glasses and Doku, settling back with the light from the window glancing across the broad planes of his face lighting his skin like polished ebony, said, 'So how goes it with Appella? Is Morrik still running things there?'

Darien sipped and grimaced. 'Yes, and the traders tell us, still recruiting. Of course, a country is entitled to defend itself but they have ever been a martial race, the Appellans, and one quick to avenge themselves.' They fell into talk then on matters they would bring up in Council the following day until a servant came to murmur that it was time for the noon meal. In the large dining room they found Darien's wife, Ling, entertaining the rest of the party under the disapproving eye of Lukt, chief Medic and healer-king of Meddia.

Marric, observing the martyred look she cast her husband sighed. The austere outlook of the Meddii court made heavy going for their hosts, but he supposed it was something that they continued to come to the annual get-togethers. Pre-war no Medic healer had ever left their homeland. They were an inward-looking people and it had taken the uprising that had thrown off a weakened Appella's shackles to bring them out of their self-imposed isolation. He turned from the austere leader with relief to fall into conversation with Slate, his tongue easily finding again the language of the land where he had been raised.

***

The two boys wandered through the temple precinct past the giant tiled murals of the god Bel, and the huge tapestries adorning the walls. The floors were of polished slate, and the inner sanctum, which they could not enter, was screened by a dark timber finely carved with scenes of Rhutan life being carried on beneath the benignant gaze of the great fish-tailed deity. Somewhere a group of girls was singing, their voices rising pure and sweet through air tinged with incense.

'It is very grand,' Leu said, following him back down the curved steps to the courtyard. 'Our shrine to the Lady is simple — nothing like that. Do you also have lessons here?'

'Nah, it's just for girls. They learn to read and their letters, and the hymns of praise for the processions. And to sew the tapestries. It takes years to finish one — so Saffon says. She hates sewing. I have a tutor, and an arms-master of course.'

'Shouldn't you also have a guard — when you're out like this?'

Tarris hunched a mulish shoulder. 'Oh, don't you start! I'm perfectly safe in the city. And Rel is such a bore. I give him the slip whenever I can. Well, what of it?' he demanded catching the other boy's look.

'Just that it's not very fair,' Leu observed. 'If it's his task to accompany you — your father wouldn't just be angry with you, would he?'

Tarris smirked. 'I expect Rel's used to it by now. Come on, we'll go this way, by the main square where the fountain is.'

The market was noisy and crowded and full of people. It seemed to Leu threading his way behind the prince through the narrow alleys left between the myriad stalls, that most of Ripa's population must have been present. Nimble footed boys bearing trays on their heads and shouting their wares added to the din, and he had to step lively around the thrusting, bartering throng to avoid being jostled off his feet. There were produce stalls, and water vendors carts, and tinkers plying their trade amid a mound of kettles and pots and groups of gossiping housewives blocking the path as they waited on utensils being mended. Nearby a barber was shaving his customers with a dangerous looking blade. Leu's mouth watered at the sight of plums and apricots piled beside heaping mounds of corn, their silken tassels shining in the light. There were stalls of leatherwork and cheap jewellery, and clothing, and sandals, and many of potted edibles and herbs, either bunched or dried, and other, to him unidentifiable objects that gave off a strange odour.

He looked around to ask Tarris what they were, just in time to see the man lunge at his friend's back with a naked knife in his hand. The assassin wore a robe with the hood pulled up, despite the warmth of the day, and must have kept the weapon within its folds for nobody within the crowd seemed to have noticed until Leu himself shouted.

He yelled, 'Hey!' and 'Tarris! Watch out!' even as he flung himself at the man. The boy was tall for his age and strong, and the killer, startled, snatched a quick look in his direction. Tarris alerted spun aside just as Leu, still yelling, propelled himself between them snatching at the dark robe, and when the blade stabbed down it entered his flesh rather than the young prince's.

There was an instant uproar. Leu sprawled onto the flagstones with a ribbon of blood trailing from his upper arm, feeling the cloth he'd seized twitched from his grasp as the man fled. The quicker witted stall holders shouted and attempted to grab the hooded one. One man was knifed for his pains, another bowled over, and then a white-faced Tarris blocked his view. The prince shouted, 'What — who? You're bleeding,' his voice shrill as a girl's with shock.

'Call a guard,' Leu gritted his teeth against the pain beginning to make itself felt. It had been like a heavy blow on his upper arm at first but the sight of his blood made it real and brought the pain to his attention. He felt sick and dizzy. 'They must catch him! He was going to kill you, Tarris!'

'Well, he's gone now.' Squatting beside him Tarris craned his neck to look but the man had vanished into the throng, some of whom had now recognised him. 'You saved me. You there,' he pointed imperiously at the closest apparel stall. 'Bring me a cloth for my friend's arm. And have someone run to the nearest guard post.' A woman's sudden scream whipped everyone's head her way as she fell to her knees at the side of a man who had just collapsed. It was the stall holder who had tried to intervene.

'Arri! Oh, Bel save us, he's dead,' she sobbed. Then an important looking man was there, helping Tarris up.

'Are you well, Prince? This is intolerable! In broad daylight! I have sent a man for my carriage. Come, it is but a step. I will take you back to the palace.'

'My friend is hurt.'

'And a man is dead,' Leu said faintly. 'Somebody should send for the guard.'

'All will be attended to. Come now.' Leu was hauled to his feet and a way cleared through the crowd. The woman's sobs diminished behind them, drowned in a furious wave of shocked exclamations and talk and in no time Leu found himself bundled into a vehicle; his arm had been bound in some piece of clothing that was soaking up his blood, and his head felt light enough to float off his neck.

Half fainting, he heard Tarris say querulously, 'Why would anybody want to kill me?'

At the palace their arrival disturbed the council sitting and brought the queen rushing to her son's side. Amid the babble of questions and the boy's rescuer's account of what had occurred it was Prince Marric who came first to Leu to unwrap the bloodied cloth and inspect the deep wound below it.

'Send for a healer,' Darien, holding up a hand to still the man's windy explanation, glanced briefly across at his brother.

'I'll get one of the Meddii,' Marric said, rewinding the makeshift bandage. 'Hang on lad. We'll have that seen to in a moment.' He returned with one of Lukt's party who demanded a quiet space and the satchel from his room. A servant was sent after the latter and while they waited the boy had a moment alone with the prince.

'Will you inform my father, sir?' he asked. 'It's just a cut but he'll worry.'

'Yes of course. And you must tell me all you can remember. What happened and where and how. Did he say anything, the man who attacked you?'

'No. It was Tarris he was after, not me. I shouted a warning and jumped at him to — I don't know, stop him somehow. I thought I could push Tarris aside, but the man was already striking down and he got me instead. I grabbed his robe. He was in a hooded robe — but he pulled free. And he knifed a stall holder to escape when the man tried to stop him. A woman screamed and — and said he was dead.' Whitefaced he stared at the prince, adding artlessly, 'Tarris can be annoying but why would anyone want to kill him?'

'Well, that we must find out,' Marric said gravely as the door opened. 'Your part was bravely done, by the by.

Now I'll leave you to the healer. You couldn't be in better hands for he is a Medic of Meddia.'

Back with Darien Marric said worriedly, 'This I do not like. The would-be assassin was hooded and the lad didn't get a good look at him. It seems the fact that he failed is only down to young Leu who noticed the knife in time to spoil his stroke. Where was the boy's guard?'

Darien breathed out, his lips a thin line. 'I've been into that with my son. He sneaked away without him — and not the first time either. Perhaps this will teach him a lesson. He could've been killed.'

'Osram's lad almost was,' Marric said mildly. 'I hope you've impressed that on him. A handspan to one side and it could have taken him through the lung. But to return to my point: why the attack now? And who is behind it?'

'If not some madman with an imagined grievance it must be Appella,' Darien said forcefully. His brow was creased with worry. 'I cannot believe a Ripan responsible. We have an excellent relationship with the people — the traders, the temple, the shipmasters — none of them report discontent. Whenever some matter is brought before council it receives immediate attention. No,' he shook his head. 'It can't be a local.'

'Whether or not,' Marric murmured for Ling was approaching, 'he is still out there and just as likely to try again. Guard the boy, brother — and yourself. I have no wish to become king by default.'

'I have Rissak, but I will have him choose another soldier for myself, as well as one for Tarris. And they shall be Appellans. To show we trust them, because word of this is already out there and I don't want the city turning against Appellans who are citizens.'

'A good thought. And regarding Tarris, Darien, he owes his life to young Leu. I should encourage that connection were I his father. I imagine he makes an abrasive companion for I notice that he cares little for rank and speaks his mind. In truth he's very like Osram, and with that in mind I have no doubt he will make an ideal bodyguard when the two are grown.'

'And meanwhile he'll keep Tarris from making too much of a tit of himself?' Darien said wryly. 'I know my son. He thinks the court his world and has no idea of life beyond it. His mother spoils him but it is my fault too. It has been refreshing to hear someone other than myself disagree with him. I must say he takes it rather well, too. I was surprised.'

'Practice. The two had a falling out over something at the Lakes. He sulked for a day while Leu ignored him and they patched it up. They've been tight as brothers ever since. Well, if you want time to speak to young Leu, I'll get back to our guests.'

Darien shot him a look together with a wry grin. 'Ever the diplomat, brother. Of course I was going to thank the boy. Though safeguarding the succession deserves more than mere words.'

10

The man selected by his father as Tarris's bodyguard was a tall Appellan called Sandos. He appeared the day after Leu's stabbing, sauntering casually through the palace garden to find the two boys seated on the coping about the fountain. The prince, chastened and hatless, was urging his companion to return to his room.

'It's not as if you can do anything,' he pointed out, 'so you should rest.'

'Don't fuss,' Leu snapped. 'I'm perfectly fine.' The injured arm throbbed in its sling, but it wouldn't hurt any less wherever he was. He caught sight of the approaching guardsman and rose warily. 'Who's that?'

'From the barracks.' Tarris stood too. 'Hi fellow! What are you doing here?'

'Looking for the brat whose life I'm going to be responsible for,' the man replied. He was fair haired with a leathery looking skin from a life spent outdoors. He looked stern and not best pleased with the task he'd been given. His mouth was a hard line, his grey eyes severe. 'I'm Sandos. Are you Prince Tarris?'

'I — yes,' the boy replied, taken aback by the man's attitude and words. 'This is my friend Leu. He saved my life yesterday.'

'Which wouldn't have been necessary if you'd had the mother wit to listen to your elders,' Sandos replied sternly. 'Let's get one thing straight, Prince Tarris. I serve the king; he says guard you, I guard you. You do not move without me and you never try sneaking off. Where you go I go. Is that clear?'

Tarris's mouth opened in shock at being thus spoken to. He reddened and said, 'How dare you? I —'

'You,' Sandos cut him off ruthlessly, 'were responsible for getting a good man dismissed from his post and suffering a royal bollocking into the bargain. Did you even give it a thought, that's he's lost his living through no fault of his own? And that your friend there could've been killed as a result? Just so you could show what a big man you are.'

Scarlet with fury Tarris said, 'I'll report you. You can't speak to me like that!'

'No time like the present,' Sandos sounded bored. 'Though I think your father's a bit occupied with his visitors at the moment. Tell Rissak instead. He can pass it on.'

Leu was frowning at his friend. 'Was he really dismissed, your servant? That's not fair, Tarris. It wasn't his fault.'

'Well, the king did it, not me,' Tarris ground his teeth. 'Why is everything suddenly my fault?'

'Because you're responsible. You have to apologise to the man, help him to find another position. He mightn't even have a place to live if the palace was his home.'

'So?' Tarris said, 'Is that my fault too? Servants get turned off all the time, and they seem to manage.'

'They shouldn't have to,' Leu said quietly, 'if they've done nothing wrong. It was men like him, servants and — and bakers and watermen — just ordinary people, who fought for Ripa and put your father on the throne.' Abruptly he stood, his good arm unconsciously cradling the slinged one. 'I think I will go and rest,' he said and walked away.

Scowling, Tarris stared after him. Sandos nodded to himself. 'There's a lad with a decent sense of justice. Well prince, if my life's to be at risk preserving yours I need to know you'll do as you're told. Is that clear?'

The boy blustered. 'The assassin was a madman. It'll never happen again.'

'Or it will,' Sandos said remorselessly, 'and better planned next time once they see you're guarded.'

'But,' he stammered, feeling a clutch of fear. 'Who are they? Why would anyone want me dead?'

'Apart from you being an annoying little turd?' Sandos grinned mirthlessly. 'Any quantity of reasons. Start with you, the easiest target, go on to the king and then your uncle. Then you've got civil uproar and a leaderless country, ripe for the plucking by any attacker with an army. You need to take the long view, boy. Yours is a rich country, so the prize is worth a few year's of effort.'

Tarris frowned. 'But that's rubbish! Rhuta has no enemies. We won the war, didn't we?'

'And you don't think that mightn't have made you some? Time you started using your head, prince. There's more to royal life than sneaking off to the markets. And more to ruling than having everyone bow and scrape just because you've a title. Bel's scales! I'da thought history woulda shown you that, or are you too dull to learn? Now if you're going to complain, trot off and do it. Otherwise you don't leave the grounds without telling me.'

Tarris had never been so thoroughly handled in his life. His fury swelled as the guardsman sauntered casually off and for a wild moment he considered either flouting his dictum or going, as Sandos had advised, to Rissak. But he was a little scared of the scarred man who was his father's shadow. His single eye had a disconcerting way of measuring the king's son that hinted at an unfavourable comparison with another. Of course he was nobody, a used up soldier who should have been turned off long since, but his father seemingly had a fondness for him. Tarris abandoned the idea. In any case Rissak wouldn't go against the king's wishes and they, it seemed, included having his only son guarded by a loud mouth commoner who'd never learned his place.

In the end he took his wounded dignity to Leu's room in search of support and found his friend struggling one armed to force his spare clothing into a workmanlike roll.

'What are you doing?'

Leu lifted calm eyes to meet his. 'Moving to the barracks. I'm heading home with the first messenger. While the Prince is here my father must stay, but I needn't. I don't wish to disturb the queen so please give her my thanks for her hospitality.'

'But — but you can't!' Tarris blurted. 'What is wrong with you? You're supposed to stay — Is it because you were attacked? It won't happen again you know, there's no need to fear.'

With a snap in his voice Leu said, 'I am not afraid! Though you should be! You ride roughshod over people Tarris and care for nothing but your own dignity. Ordinary people don't matter to you. They're useful, or they're turned off. Well, I'm not waiting around for that to happen to me. I have my own friends back home. I don't need you to add to them.' He shouldered the roll, grimacing at the movement and stepped towards the door but Tarris, face red and furious, got in his way.

'This is about Rel, isn't it? For Bel's sake he's just a servant! We hardly spoke. Why should I care what happens to him. Anyway he's a man, he can look after himself.'

Leu regarded him levelly. 'Sandos was right, you are a brat, a spoiled one. Everything must go your way, nothing is ever your fault. Did you never think, as you are royal that this man you don't care about, is part of your people, whom it is your duty to protect? The Prince your uncle would tell you so. That is why there are kings.'

He pushed past the boy and Tarris, shaking with fury, shouted down the hallway after him. 'Go then! Run back to your stupid little village. I don't need you.' He remembered then that Leu had saved his life but the words were said and he couldn't, or wouldn't, take them back. In any case Leu was gone. Tarris slammed the guest room door hard and stalked off.

On the morning of the third day after Leu's departure and the first time he had left the palace's environs, Tarris sought out Sandos and gruffly informed him that he was going to the barracks. The man, who had been lounging against a wall in the forecourt immediately straightened, his right hand from long habit, reaching to touch the blade at his side as he fell into step with his young charge.

'Planning to ride?' he asked.

Tarris stared straight ahead. 'No.' He was nervous, angry with himself, and afraid that he was too late. Why had he waited so long? Leu was probably gone. Tarris had no idea how often messengers travelled between Ripa and the Lakes. There were birds for short messages, but there could be a dozen reasons why a man should be sent instead — in which case Leu would have left with him. It would almost be a relief if that were the case — but no, he admitted to himself, it would only be easier, and still solve nothing. He had to fix this.

He found Leu on the practice ground clashing swords with a young trooper. Instead of interrupting as he would normally have done Tarris waited in the background clenching and unclenching his fists until the bout ended, then Leu, who had been peripherally aware of him since his arrival said something to the trooper. The man nodded put up his sword and left. Tarris swallowed and waited as his erstwhile companion walked slowly across and nodded to him, unsmiling.

'Tarris.'

'Leu,' he cleared his throat, 'I was afraid you'd be gone.'

'This afternoon.' It was a man's sword he held, the hilt fitting easily into his right hand. His injured arm still rested in a sling. 'A trader's leaving for the Lakes. I'm travelling with him.'

'Don't go,' Tarris said. 'Please. I'm sorry. I went to my uncle — he's found a place for Rel.' Sandos had retired a sword's length or two but he was fiercely conscious of his presence behind him. 'I would like you to stay and — and,' it almost killed him to get the words out, but he did, 'to tell me when I am wrong.' He waited in an agony of spirit. Leu would laugh or would say something he would never be able to forget... It didn't happen.

'Then of course I will,' the other boy said calmly. He hefted the weapon, the muscles in his forearm swelling. 'You want to try a bout? We'd better get the practice blade though — I don't want to cut you.'

'Ha!' Grateful for the reprieve Tarris managed a snort. 'Except it'd be me cutting you. Where are they kept?'

***

The Leaders' Conference ran for a ten day with a break in the middle for some hunting which Lukt and his brother Medics declined. Slate and his two companions however enjoyed themselves and even Marric shook off his introspection long enough to join in — and made the best shot of the day, according to what Osram later told his son. He himself hadn't hunted. His task, like Rissak's and Wendo's, the king's new second bodyguard, was to ensure their own principals didn't themselves become prey of the unknown assassin.

'Perhaps after all it was an isolated attack,' Darien said privately to his brother that evening. 'Someone with a grudge grabbing an opportunity because the boy was there.'

'And having the forethought to do it cloaked and hooded?' Marric shook his head. 'You must be vigilant. The country needs stability, especially with the treasury all but empty, so a regent coming in over your dead body won't help.' Temes's reign had been ruinous and though fifteen years had passed since he was deposed, the economy burdened with war debts was still fragile.

'Then you should look also to your own safety, brother.'

'I am, or Osram is. And,' Marric added soberly, 'I've had more experience at dodging death than you have.' He stretched his neck and grimaced. 'How much longer do you think, before we've covered everything? I would be back with Fenny as soon as possible.'

'A day or three. Unless the wine runs out sooner,' Darien added dryly. 'For all they don't make or import it the party from Meddia can certainly put it away.'

A brief smile lit his brother's face. 'It's the only chance they get at a decent vintage. The ale they serve back home would stun a goat.'

'That explains it then,' the king said gravely and went off to change for dinner which would lead to another long night of wine and diplomacy, and a headache on the morrow.

Three days later as the king had predicted, the council of nations had all but wound up, defensive alliances renewed, and trading talks concluded amid a general consensus that despite the growth of their military, it was too soon yet for Appella to present a viable threat to their neighbours. It was impossible, given the shape in which Temes had left Rhuta, for Darien to maintain the army he had scraped together to oust his uncle. The country simply hadn't the means to pay for its upkeep.

Meddia, insular in outlook, was much the same, and while in Ansham every man kept his weapons they were in effect a collection of farmers and shepherds scattered widely across their small, hilly country, needing time to muster were they needed. Barat alone had a standing defensive force with a powerful cavalry arm, but it was a wealthy country and had besides already beaten back one Appellan army.

'So we will be looking to you, my friend,' Darien told Doku as the large black king stood with the reins looped over his arm, preparatory to departure, 'if General Morrik loses his head in the next year or two. Bel grant he doesn't! And I think it is too soon yet. But for a leader whose gold supply can be little better than mine to spend so much of it arming his nation —'

'Aye,' Doku agreed. 'Well, we'll be with you should it come to that. Maybe you should have taken that country over at war's end, made it all the one. Your grandfather managed it, after all.'

'So he did,' Darien said wryly, 'and him the best general ever known. But even if I'd wanted to it wouldn't have worked. Too much hatred, too many of them, too few of us. We'd all have starved together, until the inevitable riots led us to civil war. All we wanted was to recover our own, and having done so, all we — I — want now, is to hold it.'

'Well,' the king of Barat enfolded his counterpart in a hug, thumping his back, the black head incongruous against the bright flame of Darien's hair, 'we'll see that you do. Your god be with you.' He turned to Marric to repeat the gesture with the slighter, smaller prince. 'My respects to the Lady Fenny. I am sorry not to have seen her. You should both come west soon for a visit. I am sure my sister would be delighted.'

He swung into the saddle and his escort that had waited patiently hoisted his standard and closed around him preparatory to moving off. Darien stepped back raising his arm just as the arrow winged out of the morning light and slammed with an air-splitting thwok into the flank of the horse immediately behind him.

The animal reared and screamed then bolted down the street. Rissak shouted, 'Ware!' knocking Darien to his knees as he did so, then yelled furiously at his younger counterpart. 'Well, get after the bastard! The roof there! Look, he's running.'

Marric, wrestling Osram aside, caught a glimpse of a cloaked figure legging it across the flat roof of the barracks but before he could move Doku had spurred his horse into a gallop. His escort after a moment's frozen indecision raced after him with cries and shouts in their own language, begging him, Marric guessed, to stop or come back. The Baratan king however was a cavalry man and his mount well trained. The two came level with the building across which the would-be assassin fled, then Doku rising in his stirrups with the blade of his dagger between his fingers arched his back and threw.

Marric saw a glitter of light streak across the space then the running man threw up his hands and fell. He was out of sight from the men on the ground but Wendo had scaled the barracks wall and a final leap had landed him on all fours on the roof. He ran forward then slowed and pulled his blade before falling into a crouch. A few moments later he stood again and drew his hand across his throat. Rissak grunted.

'He's dead then. Pity.'

'So we still don't know who's behind it?' Darien brushed himself off. 'Think he was aiming at me, or Doku?'

'Bloody bad shot if it was your black mate,' Rissak said. 'It was you right enough. Musta been prone up there, waiting his chance. Saw his shot, rose up and — Archer. That's interesting.'

'A poor one though by Ansham standards if that's what you're thinking.' Marric eyed the distance. 'No wind, so an easy shot. But you stepped back just as he loosed.' By tradition the bow was neither an Appellan nor a Rhutan weapon, but anybody could learn its use, and the dead man had plainly been less than proficient. 'But it proves nothing, either way. Might be that nerves made him hurry the shot.'

'Yes.' The king was frowning as Doku clattered back. 'It does however, show they're serious, whoever they are. We'll see in a moment.' He nodded at the roof where Wendo, sword once again sheathed was hauling the body to the edge. There he tipped it unceremoniously over and the dead man crashed to the ground. Rissak strode forward and turned it face up as Doku's shadow fell across it.

'Anyone you know?' The manat bent to drag the corpse up by one arm and retrieve his knife.

'A nice throw,' Darien said, and 'No. Stranger to me. Anyone?'

Marric said, 'Appellan, you think?'

'Could be,' his brother replied staring down at the dusty face as he rubbed his own cheek, 'but who's to say? Going on looks alone I could be too. Tallish, brown hair, he's certainly not Rhutan.' His people were a small statured, dark haired race. 'Doesn't mean he isn't half, or half Meddii for that matter.'

'Well, he's not one of mine,' Doku said, which brought a smile to the king's preoccupied face.

'Hardly. Could be up from Deems, I suppose.' The port town hosted a polyglot population with islanders thrown into the mix and even some overseas visitors.

'Might he be from this Grassland place you speak of?' Doku asked. 'They are your enemies, are they not?'

'They're everybody's enemies,' Rissak grunted. 'That said they're raiders though, not assassins. And physically he's nothing like 'em. Besides they never leave the Grass, you wouldn't find 'em in a city.'

'You're sure of that?' Darien raised a brow at his bodyguard.

'Be a first if you did, my lord. Besides what purpose would it serve?' Frowning Rissak fingered the scar on his face. 'Morrik now — I can see 'em wanting him dead. Might make an exception for him,' he conceded.

'Hmn. So, a damned mystery. But it does prove whoever's behind the attempt is serious,' the king repeated.

'We're forewarned then. I'll set some enquiries going,' Marric said. 'If there's a whisper of anything afoot the traders are the ones most likely to have heard it. Leave it in my hands for the present.' But he felt less than hopeful of the outcome; he had ears enough in the city for his men to have already reported on it, and none of them had.

Doku, mounted again, turned his horse. 'Keep a sharp eye and a good guard, my friend,' the large black king said, 'and live till we meet again.' He raised a hand in farewell and the Rhutan contingent watched his party trot towards the gates, the light dust of their going settling like a shroud over the dead man at their feet.

11

Three days after the last of the visitors had left Marric came to the breakfast board dressed for travelling. 'I must go,' he said. 'The Lady Linna passed in the night.'

'Ah,' Darien nodded. 'Well, she was old, ancient in fact. It will change life for my mother,' for so he still regarded the woman who had fostered him.

'Yes,' Marric agreed soberly. 'I must be there for the funeral and ceremony both. And for Fenny who will need to take on Ananda's work.'

'Sir?' Leu said diffidently, unsure whether he should interrupt the two.

'Yes, Leu? It is a great loss for the Lakes.'

'Yes sir,' he agreed. 'Only I wondered — am I to return with you and my father today?'

'You must ask your father that,' the king replied for his brother. 'If he permits and you wish to remain here then you are very welcome.'

'Thank you, my lord.' The two boys conferred in urgent undertones until Leu nodded. 'Then if he agrees, I will stay. Thank you, my lord, my lady.' The two boys left as soon as they could, hastening from the room bound, Marric knew, for the barracks where Osram could be found.

He nodded after them. 'He's a good lad and time in the city can only benefit him. Osram will agree.'

'I hope so,' the king said. 'However it's happened his presence has changed Tarris. Or maybe he's just finally starting to grow up. This last ten day he's been a different boy. Well, that's the least of our worries — you will take care on the journey? It was a dream I suppose, the message?'

'I'll have Osram,' Marric answered. 'And yes, a dream.' He seldom spoke of his visions. In this he had seen a funeral barge on the lake with the white robed sisters of the shrine headed by his mother-in-law, singing the elegy. A great sadness had entered him and then the scene had faded to be replaced by the face of a younger Linna, eyes wise and all-knowing in their deep network of wrinkles, for she had been old when first they had met. *It is time and I am weary, my son.* The words had trickled into his mind like faint whispers. *Guard what is yours for trouble comes.* He said nothing of this, however, to Darien. A warning he must heed, but against what and when? Time alone would tell and until he had firmer knowledge there was no point in unnecessary alarm. The Lady knew, he thought mordantly, that years meant nothing to the Great Ones. A decade to them could be no more than a blink of the eye. Responsibility for the warning conveyed in the message, whether it manifested in five years, or ten, or two, was his, not Darien's

Marric wasted no time. They were gone by midmorning, the big man riding at his side and a small escort following with the pack mules. Osram, shifting his buttocks in the saddle, said, 'Well, that's over for another year. It'll be good to be home again.'

'You don't mind your boy staying behind? Because it wasn't a royal order, you know. Darien left it up to Leu.'

''Course not! At his age I'da given my eye teeth for the opportunity to be quit of my parents and see a bit of life,' Osram said cheerfully. 'He's a bit older than the prince, maybe a bit steadier too. The cubs'll be good for each other.'

'That was my thought also.' Abruptly Marric added, 'The Shrine's lady passed in the night.'

'Ah. Wondered what the hurry was. Well,' he rubbed his jaw, his suddenly uneasy eyes continuing to quarter the ground around them, 'I take it the Lady Ananda'll be stepping up? Or did your goddess tell you different?'

'No, it will be Ananda. And Osram, keep your ear to the ground. Yes, even in Lake Town. Any word of unrest or disquiet, anything at all. There's something brewing. I don't know what and I think it might be some time coming — but that's just a guess. Still, anything you learn — I need to know it at once.'

'Aye. Like a warning, was it?' Any mention of his visions always unsettled the big man, Marric knew.

'Something like that. And taken with the two attempts in Ripa — well, it pays to be cautious.'

'Aye,' he repeated stolidly. 'You can rely on me.'

Marric threw him a grateful look. 'I know it.'

The trip was uneventful; they travelled as fast as the laden mules allowed and on the last day Marric and Osram left camp at sunrise to ride ahead of their escort.

'You're sure about this?' Osram asked and when Marric nodded, said only, 'Right. Bring your bow then.'

They reached the Lakes in mid-afternoon and left their mounts for the escorts to deal with before taking to the water.

'You'll have missed the funeral,' Osram observed as they paddled, his broad shoulders making nothing of the toil, despite his weight in the boat.

'Yes.'

'The Lady Ananda might expect Darien to have come too.'

'No.'

Osram, shrugging mentally, gave up and plied his oar.

A grave faced Fenny came to greet her husband. 'I have been waiting,' she said releasing herself from his embrace. 'We sent a bird but you're too early for that. Ananda told you?'

'It was Linna. She came to me with a warning, and I saw the funeral barge.'

Fenny's brow creased and with a pang Marric noticed the faint lines about her beautiful eyes. The first harbinger of departing youth. He smoothed them with his thumb. 'What sort of warning?' she asked.

'Oh, a very general one.' He sighed, and turned from her looking about his home. 'I'm hungry love, we had no lunch. I grow weary,' he said with sudden force, 'of the Goddess's cryptic ways. Trouble is in the air but I am given no hint of its cause, nor from which direction to expect it. Burran has been gone these eight moons now and I have heard nothing from him and been vouchsafed no glimpse of him. I am a blind man, stumbling in the dark, surrounded by dangers I cannot see.'

'The snow is still in the pass,' she said sensibly. 'It will soon be gone though so a message may come then. Now come, you will feel better when you have eaten. Sit, and forget work for a little. Tell me about the others. They are all well? What of the girls? Ling will have been busy with the heads of state there. No wives came with them to Ripa, I suppose?'

'No,' Marric let his worries be diverted. 'I scarcely saw the girls save at table. Saffon is a pretty child, her sister is all teeth at present. And Ling seems well. She sent her love. Both she and Darien have grieved our loss. I was to tell you that.'

Fenny sighed, her face creasing up. She looked aside then shook her head determinedly. 'That's good, that they're well. Yes, Saffie will be a beauty. A year or two and Darien will be looking about him for a son-in-law.'

'She is just a child,' Marric protested. 'And he has more important things on his mind.'

'She's only a year younger than Tarris and he will be fourteen in a ten-day. So, two years say — fifteen is none to soon for handfasting given it will take a year to organise the wedding. And what could be more important than your daughter's happiness?'

They both fell silent then as a servant brought food and wine. Fenny reached for her husband's hand and they clung together for a moment, caught by grief, remembering afresh that they had no daughter so the worry and joy of seeing her settled would never be theirs.

Over the meal Marric told her of the two attempts on the royal lives. 'Darien has an extra bodyguard now,' he said. 'And the servant that escorted Tarris about, when the boy let him, that is, has been replaced by a soldier. All are on their guard and the man that made the attempts — assuming it was the same one — is dead. But it worries me that nobody recognised him. All we can know for sure is that he wasn't a Baratan.'

Fenny stated the obvious. 'Not black then?'

'No. And Rissak, who has fought the barbarian race, says he isn't from the Grass. A dead stranger — yet he sought to kill them both. It means something; but what?'

The question, and the lack of an answer, would continue to plague him. The weeks slipped away into the new moon, and then another, and then a third. The pass to the Upper Land was open again and the traders' caravans going forth but still no word filtered through from Burran. He had left on his mission a year ago, and save for the one glimpse Marric had had of him riding with a long haired Pampasan toward what had looked like turf covered mounds, there had been nothing since. He might well be dead or a prisoner of the Grass; but strain how Marric might for a vision the Goddess seemingly had nothing more to impart on the subject.

In high summer there came an urgent summons from the palace. It arrived not by messenger but the speedier method of flight. The miniscule writing on the brief message gave no details but the urgency of its sending was plain. Marric's fingers tightened on the scrap of paper as he glanced up at Osram.

'Horses,' he said. 'We leave for Ripa immediately.' He called back the servant who had brought the tiny reed capsule from the pigeon cote. 'Where is my lady?'

'At the Shrine, my lord. Should I send for her?'

'There is no time. A quill and paper, please. Tell the kitchen to pack travelling food, no more than I can carry on a horse. And bring my cloak, and bow.'

He penned a quick note to Fenny, *Darien needs my help. I must go, my love. Stay safe for me.* He handed it to the returning servant saying, 'See she has this the moment she returns. I will have them send a bird when we arrive there.'

'Yes, my lord. Uh — where, my lord?' asked the bewildered man.

'The city.' He folded the cloak over his arm and as a boy rushed in from the kitchen with a packed saddle bag said peremptorily, 'Do you know if the cook has anything I can hold and eat now?'

The boy grinned. 'She's made some smashing pies sir.'

'That will do. Bring me two, will you?' He took them with a word of thanks, laid them carefully on the empty bench in the boat, tied as always at the foot of the house platform, and rowed himself rapidly shorewards.

They ate the pies before leaving. Osram had saddled two horses and had two more on lead reins. His wife had also filled a saddlebag for him and a travelling cloak was tied behind his cantle.

'You sure this is necessary?' he said, swinging into the saddle. 'Man's getting a bit old for sleeping on the ground.'

'We could ride all night if you'd rather,' Marric replied.

'Yeah,' the bodyguard scoffed, then catching sight of his principal's face, instantly sobered. 'Bel's balls! You mean it. What's happened?'

'I don't know,' Marric replied grimly.

The simple admission jolted the big man. 'But —' He bit off the protest. It was uncanny, and it unsettled the hairs on his nape but for as long as he'd known him the king's brother had been able to read the future. To hear him admit now that he couldn't was as big a shock as their present unexpected activity.

They travelled fast. A niggling anxiety that ran deeper than seemed called for by Darien's brief message: *I need you here urgently*, tugged at Marric's nerves. Not the least of it concerned the sheer frustration of not knowing its source. Surely, if something were badly wrong the Mother would warn him. Yet She hadn't, unless this anxiety that pressed him forward, making the idea of rest insupportable, was from Her.

In the end Osram said bluntly, 'Look Marric, we'll be walking if you keep up this pace.'

Conscious that his mount was flagging, even as he had continued to press it, Marric reined in with a sigh. The night was black with the thin edge of a new moon riding high behind them. 'How far do you think we've come?'

'Damn near halfway, the pace you've been setting,' his bodyguard grumbled with the ease of familiarity. 'For Light's sake, what's it all about?'

'I don't know,' Marric said irritable in return, 'that's the problem. But you're right. We'll rest them. I make it past midnight.'

'Well past.' Osram dropped heavily from his horse and led it towards some low shrubbery. 'Fire and food, hmn? It'll let them recover and a slower pace after will help more.'

Marric, doing his best to ignore nerves that craved movement, could only agree.

In the end they rolled themselves in their cloaks and slept briefly while their small fire died and the horses stood hipshot amid the bushes where they were tied, occasionally rattling their bridle rings. Night birds called and a little wind blew the scents of dust and dried grass over the sleeping figures, and inexplicably, the smell of a stormy sea. Brine spray whipped cold against Marric's face as he hauled on the rope, and the sky above him tore apart with a fierce white slash. The ship was tossed like a leaf on the raging water and somewhere a man cried out in fear as the sails cracked like thunder and the rain came torrenting down.

'We're all gonna die!' the man pulling behind him on the same rope screeched, abandoning his task as the ship rode up and up until it seemed to teeter on the point of balance. Marric's heart slowed then raced, waiting for the end, then a rope's end lashed past him and a deep and brutal voice, roared, 'Get back to your post you snivelling ape, or by the Light I'll make sure of it.' Next moment the deck plummeted, fast as a falling horse and a loose barrel all but took Marric's legs from under him. He gave an involuntary shout and jerked awake to Osram's hand on his shoulder.

'It's near enough daylight, my lord. We should get going.'

12

When the late afternoon sun blazed gold on the temple roof the pair reached the city. Their mounts shuffled wearily through the gate, heads low, their flanks and shoulders white with the rime of dried sweat. They went directly to the palace stables where Marric dismounted with a stifled groan of relief.

'Get yourself a meal, then rest,' he said to Osram as the stable boy came to take the four horses. The backs of the ridden pair steamed as the saddles were lifted off. Marric shook his head and patted his mare's neck. 'Sorry,' he murmured softly. She deserved better treatment. 'Grain her well,' he told the boy, 'and see she goes into her stall dry.'

'Yes, my lord.' He led them off and both men stood for a moment too tired to move.

Osram smothered a yawn. 'I could eat a buck, hooves and all. What's next?'

'I'll let you know. When I find out.' Straightening his clothing Marric headed for the palace.

'I didn't expect you so soon,' Darien exclaimed, greeting his brother. 'When did you leave the Lakes?'

'Noon yesterday. Rode through the night.' Marric yawned mightily and slumped into the closest chair. His eyes felt grainy and his clothes, he noted vaguely, were layered with dust. 'What's the problem?'

'It can wait until you've eaten and rested.' Darien strode over to pull a bellrope. 'It's urgent yes, but I didn't mean for you to kill yourself getting here. Where's your escort?'

Marric yawned again. 'Only Osram. I've sent him off to eat and sleep.' His eyes drifted closed and the thought he had been trying to formulate suddenly caused him to jerk them open. 'There hasn't been another attempt on you or the boy?'

'No, nothing like that. But come, food, then rest. And while you're sleeping there's some people I have to gather. Always best to get the news direct from the source.'

'You're right. But food later.' Heaving himself to his feet Marric passed a hand across his face. 'I'm too tired to think just now, let alone eat. Leave that till later.'

The sun had westered and less than an hour of daylight remained when Marric woke. Still tired he would have relished longer in the bed but anxiety had gnawed at his sleep and it was almost a relief to roll to his feet and splash his face with water. Darien had thoughtfully supplied him with a change of clothes — not his own, they would never have fitted. Pulling the borrowed tunic over his head Marric blessed whichever palace member had donated them. He would need a further change, he supposed if his stay was to be protracted. And that would depend upon the nature of the emergency for which he'd been summoned.

In the council chambers where generations of Rhutan kings had met with their advisors, Darien and half a dozen turbanned men were waiting for him. He recognised them as they rose and bowed, rehearsing their names as he returned their greeting. They were the heads of the various guilds within Ripa, all the men of influence in the city, in whose hands the country's economy rested. Once the high-priest had attended too, but that office no longer had a place at this table. And the army chief was missing. So, Marric silently noted, taking his seat beside his brother, it wasn't a military matter, but one affecting the city's fortunes for gathered here were the principal players in that sphere. He was suddenly starving and as if it had taken only that realisation to call him, a servant appeared with a cloth-covered tray and set it before him.

'Eat,' Darien urged. 'Normally we would wait on your meal but the matter is pressing, the news already a ten-day old. It took that long for the messenger to reach us.'

'I am here and listening,' Marric said inhaling the rich smells of meat and gravy as he reached for his knife. It was Guildmaster Ferga of the merchant's guild, who replied. 'It was I who brought the news to the king, Prince Marric. You remember Trader Ramie? He is Merchant Ramie now, in partnership with your old master Luka, but he still travels. Aye, well it was he and his men who stumbled on the caravan. One of their own. Every man of 'em dead, and the animals too. Slaughtered where they stood. The beasts were hobbled you see so they must've been loading up — at daybreak I'd guess. Perfect time for an ambush: men half asleep, caught with their hands full. The goods all taken of course, though how they managed that without transport...' He broke off, grimaced and continued. 'Sorry, my lord king. It's just — The thing is Prince, the killers came from Ansham.'

Marric paused the food halfway to his mouth. 'And you know this how?'

Darien said gravely. 'Every man died from an arrow wound. An Ansham army arrow. Ramie collected a handful as proof.'

'I see.' He completed the movement, chewed and swallowed thinking about what he'd just heard. 'Thieves from elsewhere shifting the blame? Taking advantage of the fact Ansham are well known as a nation of bowmen? Whoever is behind it wanting us to believe that Ansham is responsible? Though it is harder to think of a reason why Slate would order such a thing.'

'He wouldn't.' Darien said positively.

'I don't believe it either,' Marric sipped at his wine. 'To what end? It doesn't make sense. They are our allies. So why undertake something that must inevitably place them between two enemies? For though peace may reign now the bulk of Appella holds no love for them.'

'Well, putting that question aside for the present,' Darien said, 'There is more. Someone is targeting our merchants. Ships are missing, and since the beginning of summer four warehouses have been burned to the ground, not to mention a section of the docks. Men are out of work as a result, and trade is badly affected.'

'And it's not just warehouses,' Guildmaster Trent said. The big smith scowled, 'There's a wagonload of sheet metal just up an' vanished 'tween here an' the border. Wagon, men, horses — gorn into thin air. Not to mention a load of dressed timber. Though the bastards just burned that, wagon an' all. Two men dead an' one of 'em the principal so the business is crippled.'

Marric pushed his half-eaten meal away. 'You said ships were missing.' A vivid impression of the dream ship tilted at a crazy angle against the raging sea filled his head. 'Might it not just be the hazards of the sea — storms, running aground?'

Ferga nodded. 'Aye. Once, twice even, in a season but four are missing, Marric. All captained by experienced men. Taken with the losses we have already sustained it is too big a coincidence. The first to go missing should have docked last summer, the last not to return was an early winter sailing. That is a lot of truly terrible storms. Or sabotage. Or pirates. I incline towards the last. The cargoes of all four were valuable.'

Darien looked hopefully at his brother. 'I thought perhaps that you —?'

Marric shook his head. 'No. There's been no warning,' he murmured. To the table at large he said, 'Well, plainly we must take precautions until we learn who is behind the attacks, and then —'

'Then we take action.' Darien's hard blue gaze swept over his counsellors. 'In the meantime soldiers will accompany the next big caravan. And I will send a contingent also with Wave Dancer, when she sails. We must get to the bottom of this. We must! The losses are already in the thousands of silvers — and that's just the cargo, never mind the value of the ships, the wagons, the animals, and men's lives.'

Marric's thoughts had ranged further. 'A distraction?' he murmured. 'But what is it for? Do they seek just to weaken us or is it to keep us from seeing something we ought? First the attacks on you and the prince, and now this. It smacks of a deep laid plan. I think I must go to Ansham. There is a man there I need to speak with.'

Darien's mouth opened then closed again firmly as he swallowed whatever objection he had been about to make. Marric, appreciating his restraint, said softly. 'Of course I will be careful, and Osram will be with me. But it is not a matter another can do. And this needs sorting, Darien. Rats in the storeroom can lay low any house, including yours.'

'You will take an escort of soldiers then, at least?'

'No. How will that look to Slate? That you send to blame him or his people for something I am certain they weren't responsible for. The two of us will be fine. You forget, I was raised there and Osram knows the backways better than he ought.'

Despite the pressing sense of urgency upon him it was two days before Marric was ready to leave. The bird that had been despatched to Fenny on his arrival was followed by a long letter sent by horseback telling her of his plans to the extent that he went to consult with Cran. She would understand the reference. He was circumspect with the reason for the king's summons, alluding only to the damage done to the warehouses. He assured her of his health, knowing she would read the word as safety, and adding that Tarris had begged to accompany him. He is a different boy, he wrote, both Sandos and Leu have been good for him. The extra day was partly to meet with the half dozen agents in the city that regularly reported back to him on matters that might later need to be brought to the king's attention. But it was also to give Osram time with his son.

Ling, who was a little in awe of her brother-in-law, made him welcome as always, though a certain accustomed wariness in her manner showed her not to be entirely comfortable in his presence. She had managed to put it aside for his last visit, whilst grieving for her husband's niece, but now her awe was back. Marric was used to it. Others who knew of it found his ability unchancy, even among those who followed the Mother. Ling's daughters however had no such reservations and openly envied him his freedom.

'It's not fair,' Rosel, the younger one with the teeth, said rebelliously. 'I hate being a girl, and a princess. Mother won't let me do anything.'

'It would be worse to be a poor boy,' Saffon pointed out smugly from the elevation of her three years. 'You'd have no shoes and nothing nice to eat.'

'I could be a prince, with shoes and food, and go where I wanted. So there!'

'That's not quite true, you know,' Marric said, smiling on her. 'Your brother wants to come with me and he can't, so you see even princes don't always have things their own way.'

'Never mind that. Tell us a story Uncle,' Saffon coaxed. 'How did you meet Aunt Fenny? Was it very romantic?

Did you fall right in love?' Surprised he noted that Fenny was right, apparently the child was old enough to be interested in courtship. 'I asked Mother,' she continued, 'but she didn't know. You were married before she was, she said.'

'Ah, now that is a tale.' He smiled at the girl whose light voice so achingly reminded him of his own lost child, and patted the open weave of the chair beside him on the terrace. 'Sit down then and I'll tell you about a little girl who was stolen from her people —'

'But we want to hear about Aunty Fenny,' Saffon objected.

'No, about the little girl. Who stole her? Did you find him and fight him?' Rosel demanded.

Mentally rearranging the facts to suit his young listeners' ears, Marric said, 'You shall hear both. It was like this...'

When he had finished a vastly expurgated tale he looked up to find his twin, shoulder propped against the trellis, watching them. Darien smiled at his daughters. 'Run along girls, Mega is looking for you.'

They obeyed, calling their thanks to Marric as their father came forward to take the seat Saffon had vacated. 'You are very patient with them.'

'I find them delightful.' Marric smiled, 'There is something about little girls. Rosel would plainly change her sex if she could. Though I think that would be a shame.'

'She will grow out of it.' Darien hesitated. 'You might have another child, you know. Fenny could —'

'No.' Marric breathed out, added quietly, 'The sisters at the shrine said it was a miracle she carried Perilla. She had already lost two babes by then. There will be no more. Lady Linna told us so herself.'

Darien sighed. 'I am sorry.'

'It is how things are,' Marric said, stolidly turning aside from pity.

The other recognised the withdrawal; his twin had given him much of himself in his service but the one thing he would not allow was a glimpse of his own pain. Accepting that he said only, 'When will you leave for the Upper Land?'

'Tomorrow.' Marric stood and stretched. 'It may not help but if nothing else I can apprise Slate of the situation. The last thing we need is for our allies to begin to mistrust us, which now I think of it could be part of the design behind these acts.'

'The God's curse on all meddlers and ill wishes,' Darien suddenly exploded. 'I tell you brother, sometimes I wonder if the throne is worth the struggle. We have rebuilt and repaired and put down dissent, and got the people to accept our Appellan allies... And now this — there seems no end to the problems we face.'

Marric nodded. 'We always knew that winning it was the easy part. It is harder to build than destroy. I will do what I can, and we must hope it is enough.'

13

They left at daybreak before the city was astir, trotting through the gates with the pack mules on a lead string and only the city watch and the water carriers abroad. Osram was dressed in his guardsman's uniform but Marric had aimed for anonymity with a plain tunic over long trousers and a serviceable cloak tied behind the saddle. Darien had wished him to take a bird but he had vetoed the idea.

'Whatever I discover will be more complicated than a dozen words can describe. And knowing that we have arrived at Valleyford tells you nothing more than you would expect.'

'But if you were attacked and needed help?' the king fretted.

'We would either be dead or have managed to save ourselves long before the bird could be loosed,' Marric pointed out. 'Relax brother. We will go quietly by the back ways Osram knows. If there is news that can't wait I will find a messenger.'

Defeated, Darien stepped back. 'Then may the Lady's hand be over you.'

'It always is.'

They had mounted then and left, Osram snuffing as they crossed the bridge as if he could already smell the thinner, cooler air of the Upper Land. Marric, divining this asked, 'Have you ever been back — since joining Darien, I mean?'

The big man shook his head. 'No, well, wasn't any reason right after the war. We had our hands full here anyway.' In the aftermath of victory Darien had set his army to the municipal works in Ripa neglected throughout Temes's long reign. Everything from dredging the river to dismantling the blood-stained tower where the final battle for the city had raged had fallen to them. 'And I don't reckon I'da been any too welcome — I daresay they saw us as traitors, them as supported the Pretty Boy.'

Marric smiled to hear the old appellation once given to his vanity driven uncle. 'It mightn't be much different now. Another good reason for using the smuggler's way. The traders report that the authorities are becoming quite militant in their handling of outsiders.'

'Best we dodge 'em then,' Osram said practically. 'Not likely to be a problem 'less they've settled the border country since I was last there.'

That had been a good sixteen seasons ago, Marric reflected but where they planned to cross into Appella the land was fit only for pasturage, so an increase in population seemed unlikely.

Long days in the saddle saw the mountains come nearer as the distance behind them grew. They fell easily into the camp routine, and as their packs were heavy with food they bypassed the towns along their route, coming at length to the foot of the climb that marked the smuggler's way into Appella.

'Asher's balls, I hope I can remember it,' Osram muttered, stroking his growth of new beard. 'It's a bloody long time since I scouted this way for Cyrus.'

'I haven't forgotten how steep it was.' Marric stood in his stirrups, searching the upper reaches of the cliff before them. 'Look, there to the right of that boulder where the crooked tree is — isn't that a path of sorts?'

'I'll check.' The big man dismounted and pushed his way through a thicket of scrub oak that not been there the last time they had come this way before the war. Waiting in the stillness of a sundrenched morning Marric heard the rattle of falling pebbles and then a thump followed by a hearty curse. Overhead a skylark sang then folded its wings and vanished as it coasted back to earth. The scent of fading blossom came to him along with a whiff of fox, and the saddle creaked as his mount moved his weight to the other hip. Then the bushes parted and Osram was back, beads of blood along a scratched forearm.

'You were right. The scrub's blocking it so we'll have to lead the nags through. Watch your footing, it's rough going for the first little bit.'

The rest wasn't any easier either. Last time, Marric remembered, only the mules had been happy and the track hadn't noticeably improved since. They climbed and climbed, his weak leg trembling from effort after the first hour or two, but there was no room to even stand level, let alone set a camp, until they reached the top. Pebbles and small falls of scree on the chanciest sections rattled down the cliff from their progress, and the horses snorted and trembled, rolling white eyes as they were coaxed and dragged upwards. Their noon meal was eaten standing, Marric watching with envy as a mountain goat, eyeing them from higher up, suddenly snorted and bounded away, floating from ledge to stone to a crack in the rock as if blown upwards.

'Dead easy,' Osram said sourly, wiping a hand across his mouth. He stepped forward to relieve himself into the emptiness below them, then picked up the mules' lead rope again. 'Ready?'

'Yes,' Marric sighed. 'Let's get it done.'

They rested once the climb was over then rose reluctantly, their leg muscles already stiffening, to move on. 'No point marking the trail for others,' Osram said. 'Man never knows when he might need it again.'

'Not in a hurry, I hope,' Marric quipped. He rubbed his arm for now the sweat had dried on him the air had a bite to it. 'Feels like autumn's already come.' He glanced around at the once familiar terrain seeing conifers and scrub oak, and patches of holly. In winter the snow lay deep over the thin soil of the Upper Land. The people, particularly the Old Race of Ansham were hardy and frugal, hunters and shepherds for the most part, for wool and mutton were staple products of the area. Their liberation from the Appellan yoke had been the price of joining Darien's forces and though the big estates, established during the years of Ansham's subjugation, still remained in Appellan hands they were now subject to heavy taxes and local laws. There could be no doubt however where their owners' loyalties lay so avoiding contact, Marric thought, was imperative.

He said as much to Osram, who nodded brusquely. 'Well I wasn't heading for the main track, Prince.'

'Now I have offended you,' Marric observed mildly. 'I only get my title when you're out of sorts.'

He got a glare and then a reluctant grin from his companion. 'Let's just leave it that I'm not a fool. You want to go on or find a camp? Not much daylight left?'

'Camp, I think, as soon as we find water.'

Shortly afterwards they came to a collection of rocks that hosted a spring, just a trickle of water, enough to spill into a narrow gutter, plainly the origin of a small creek. They filled the collapsible leather water bucket and moved a bow shot or two away from the source to allow the wild creatures access during the night. They hobbled the mules and their mounts, and kept their cooking fire small, allowing it to die when the meal was ready. They ate quickly as darkness fell, then sought their blankets, Marric stifling a groan of relief as the weight came off his weak leg.

As if he had heard him Osram rumbled, 'By the Black Apes! It don't get any easier as you get older.' The day had obviously tired him too.

The clicking of a cricket next to his ear woke Marric. He turned his head irritably and opened reluctant eyes to see that the sky in the east had greyed to dawn. Time to be moving. He sat up, noticing as he did so the swish of a horse's tail on the edge of the scrub. The night had been cool, the animals would have sought shelter from the wind. He sat up then froze at the sound of a distant yell.

'Osram!'

'I hear it.' The big man had started from his blankets and was pulling on his boots, all he had removed for the night. Marric grabbed his and then his bow, slinging the quiver over his shoulder. Another cry sounded and the sudden rush of hooves, the noise coming from further down the creek.

Osram's glance was grim. 'Sounds like a fight. Horses?'

'Quieter on foot. Come on.' Running, they set off, Osram with his blade in his hand. Ten minutes later they stopped panting within the shelter of the creek whose course they had followed. It had become a little stream, continually fed by the spring, with a lush growth of willows and aspen screening the banks. They halted among them and Marric caught his breath on a gasp of dismay.

'Lady of mercy! It's a caravan.' They were getting the worst of it too, with at least eight mounted raiders racing their mounts about the rudely interrupted camp, shooting arrows into the handlers as they scrambled to reach and hold the half-loaded camels down. The peculiar bellowing of the beasts, and the dust raised as they fought the men added to the confusion of the melee.

'Bandits,' Osram said, about to charge forth. 'They're in for a bloody surprise.'

'Wait!' Marric said. 'They've bows. Let's lower the odds a little first.' He nocked an arrow, pulled back and centred on his target then loosed. The man flew forward a pace and fell. Marric reached for another arrow and then another. Three of the raiders died before the rest noticed what was happening. One shouted and pointed at the solitary bowmen which was when Osram bellowed and raced forward. Probably taking it as a sign he was leading a charge the man whipped his mount about shouting at his followers as he fled. They heeled their mounts after him, but not before Marric had put an arrow in the last man's back. Osram, skidding to a halt at the camp's edge, and finding nobody left to challenge, swore.

There were dead men, dead animals, spilled baggage and shocked survivors, and a group of disturbed and bellowing beasts, so it took a little while for Marric to get the story. Trader Tonic told it tersely. A wiry Rhutan of middle years, with a grey beard and the squinty eyes of a man whose life's work had involved looking at distance, he thanked his rescuers distractedly, while directing the salvage of his caravan.

'Almighty Bel!' he swore. 'They came out of nowhere. Appellans — with bows! Since when have those bloody murderers used bows?' He couldn't seem to get past the wrongness of it. 'They shot everything in sight — men, horses, camels. We'd just started packing the beasts and — what in the name of their own damned Abyss were they going to do with the goods once they'd killed off the transport? It doesn't make sense! Six of my men dead, the bastards, and Harro'll be lucky to make it.'

Harro, Marric gathered, was the unconscious body with air leaking from the hole in his chest and pushing frothy red bubbles from his slack lips. 'Lung shot,' he agreed. 'And I rather think they weren't here to rob. This has happened before. To one of Merchant Ramie's caravans. They killed everything that time too.'

Tonic frowned in confusion. 'You say? Why?' Then, as another question occurred. 'Where'd you spring from, anyhow?'

'We were camped at the head of the creek. Didn't know you were here until the yelling started. Look, my friend and I will help. If he lives get your cook to organise a meal, it will put heart into the men before we deal with your dead.' The caravanners he knew packed all their beasts save the one carrying the food, before they broke their morning fast. 'And should he make it,' instinctively he lowered his voice though there was little chance the man could hear, 'we need to rig a sling for Harro.'

'Yes, of course. I —' Tonic tucked up the end of his turban. 'Who — are you a local?'

'I was,' Marric said uninformatively 'Round these parts they call me Matto.' It seemed prudent to keep his identity quiet and was glad of the evasion as Osram came up to him, his expression grim.

'Take a look. One of 'em dropped a bow.' He nodded at Marric's own and showed also a fistful of gathered arrows. 'Recognise them?'

Marric did. He fingered the plates of ram's horn that strengthened the belly of the bow. The arrows too were familiar, fletched with quill feathers of the wild goose, a favourite with the Ansham bowyers. 'Where did you find it?' he asked.

'By the body. Looks like one of your men got lucky,' he told Tonic. 'He's the only one they lost to your lot. Throat's cut. Pretty good going,' he said approvingly, 'getting that close with a knife to a killer with a bow.'

Tonic frowned again. 'Show me,' he said and they picked their way through the carnage to the outer reaches of the camp.

Osram had rolled the dead man over. He was short and dark, dead face snarling and his throat gaping like a second mouth below his chin. He was poorly dressed in tunic and worn woollen pants, his feet in the hide sandals the shepherds wore, but despite the horrific slash across his throat there was very little blood where he lay. His tunic however was soaked with it.

'He wasn't one of them,' Marric said.

'Not? — Well he's not mine,' Tonic retorted. 'Old Race by the look of him. Bastard!' He kicked the body. 'What do you mean, not one of them? Next you'll be telling me he's not dead, or half my bloody team either!'

'You're meant to think that,' Marric said patiently. 'Look at him. Where's the blood? On him, but none on the ground where he was supposedly killed. No — he was dead when his body was flung here and the bow tossed down beside him. Before the killing started I'd wager. Look, he's not even wearing boots — and where are his quiver and arrows? Then ask yourself how a competent bowmen gets his throat cut with a loaded bow to hand. Yes, he's Old Race, a shepherd at a guess. That's the idea. Whoever found the massacred caravan was supposed to think that Ansham was responsible.'

Tonic stared then nodded. 'They were Appellans,' he affirmed, 'the attackers, the ones that rode off.' He strode across to the first man that Marric had shot and stared at his corpse. 'Him too. And nobody's gonna tell me different.'

'I'm not arguing,' Marric agreed. 'And when you reach Ripa I want you to go to the palace and report it — the whole of this morning's work. It's important. Will you do that?'

The trader studied him a moment then nodded. 'Aye. I will. I'll warn the guild too. Who exactly did you say you were?'

'They call me Matto. I work for King Darien. Tell him my name and where we met. I don't think it will happen again this side of the pass, but keep a sharp eye, just in case.'

'Aye,' The man said, adding vehemently, 'you can be bloody sure of that.'

14

When they eventually left Tonic's shattered caravan, Marric collected the bows and blades of the three dead Appellans. 'I'd take the bodies if we were closer,' he explained. 'Not that I think Slate will doubt our word.'

Osram nodded. The dead men would be well and truly ripe before they reached their destination. 'He can always send someone to check the corpses, if the animals have left anything of 'em. So who's this friend of yours we're visiting?'

'A smith called Cran. You've met him — that night their leaders signed the accord that forged the alliance between us and Ansham. But that'll have to wait now. It's more important for Slate to know the mischief Appella's brewing.'

'Right.' Osram, leaned over to smack his palm against a mule's flank. 'Move, you lump of lard or you're dog's meat.' The beast jumped forward and its two companions quickened their pace also. 'What do you think Darien'll do about the caravan?'

Marric sighed. 'What can he do? Send soldiers with them. Complain to Morrick. Who will be outraged and say that he's not responsible for the actions of bandits, and anyway there's no proof they were Appellans.'

'Bugger that!' The big man's colour rose with his ire. 'What about witnesses? I'd call dead men proof enough.'

'They'll be scattered bones by then. That you and

I and Tonic have seen. I doubt his surviving men will recall if they were green or tailed, let alone their physical attributes.'

'Aye,' Osram nodded despondently. 'I've seen that myself with new recruits when it comes to battle. Terror seems to wipe their minds clear.'

They made good time that day even riding at the mules' pace under a clear sky that offered nothing to their gaze but the flight of an eagle. Osram rode warily but it was Marric who said quietly as night approached, 'Don't look around but I think we're being followed.'

'Yeah?' The Appellan's right hand rose to scratch his cheek then dropped to hang by his thigh, close to his blade. 'What — you saw something, heard it?'

'No,' the other admitted. 'It is more a feeling, for a little while now. It might be a wolf I suppose. Or I could be imagining it. Whatever it is it's put the hairs up on my neck. Let's just see what happens.'

Osram grunted, thinking of arrows. He dropped back a little to cover his principal's back with his body, not that that would help, he thought, if the watcher had ill intent and was paralleling their course with his own. He had neither felt nor sensed anything, which both annoyed and alarmed him, as did Marric's words. The man had an uncanny gift that he might fear but would never ignore. Unconsciously the fingers of his free hand spoked out in the sun sign that warded evil from the followers of the Light.

A little later with the sun westering fast, they made camp, Osram choosing a spot with a nest of large boulders they could put at their backs. It would also provide cover for an attack, but the possible refuge it offered seemed worth the risk. He put the horses on a short hobble to restrict their movement while Marric lit a cook fire, tossing their bedrolls carelessly towards the stones. They ate by its light, then fed it with one of the large logs Osram had dragged in, before withdrawing to their rest. Their bedrolls were indistinguishable in the half light from the smaller boulders as they moved them further into the rocks. Osram draped a blanket over his shoulders and settled his back against stone.

'I'll watch. Leave your boots on.'

'Call me at moonrise,' Marric said. He stared into the night then gave a little shrug. 'I don't feel him now though. Perhaps it was just a wolf.'

'Better to be sure than wake to find your throat cut,' Osram replied.

However the night passed uneventfully and they rose to a cool morning with a light mist wound like a gauzy scarf through the timber. Osram, scouting the area for tracks found nothing beyond the scratchings of some small rodent, and the tracks of a wild dog.

'Too small to be wolf unless it was a cub, and then it wouldn't have been alone,' he told Marric. He gave a last careful look around before admitting, 'It don't mean you were wrong though.'

Sometime around noon Marric broke into the lulling sound of hoofbeats and insect hum to murmur, 'He's back. It's like an itch on my nape. Do you hear anything?'

Cocking his head without turning it Osram listened. 'Nothing. If you're right, he's good. Must be mounted or we'd have lost him by this. What say we drop the mules, turn and charge back? He's behind us, he'll have to shift and we should hear him.'

Marric shook his head slightly. 'He could be off to one side, the trees are thick enough. Then he'd know that we know he's there. Let's wait. Look for a spot to lay an ambush.'

The opportunity came a little further along where the ground dipped between a boulder the size of a small house and a thicket of beech. They rode singly into the narrow space as close to the rock as they could, and halfway through Osram reached up to grab the stone and pull himself onto it. Marric, prepared beforehand, took his mount's reins and continued without a pause creating an unbroken set of tracks for the stranger to follow. He rode on for a short distance, before securing the horses in cover and heading back, ghosting along the way the hunters and shepherds of Ansham did, as quiet as the fall of autumn leaves.

Satisfied that he was close enough to the ambush site he sank to his knees and waited, emptying his mind of all but his surroundings. He heard the twitter of birds in the branches, the stealthy rustle of mouse or vole in last year's dead leaves, and then like a warning pulse on his nape the undeniable presence of the one tracking them. He waited, grasping his bow, remembering another ambush when his frozen hands had loosed an arrow at a man's back for the sake of his horse and the food he carried. Only it had been Rissak then, freezing on the rock above their quarry, not Osram lying in sunshine...

A thump, followed by an equine snort and rapid thud of hooves stopped his train of thought. A broken off cry had him on his feet and running and he rounded the boulder in time to see Osram cock a vindictive fist and slam it into his captive's jaw.

'Wouldja, you little bugger!' he said wringing his hand. 'Well, try that for laughs.'

'Osram!' Marric snapped. 'Enough, I want him able to talk.'

The big man snorted. 'Best of luck with that. It's only one of them heathen bastards from the Grass! What in the name of the Light is he doing here?'

'He's just a boy. What, he bit you?' Marric eyed the toothmarks on Osram's hand. 'Lay off the rough stuff, just secure his hands for now.' Mention of the Grass had kindled a wild hope. 'Treat him gently and let's see what he can tell us.'

'What, you speak their tongue?' His companion asked. He hauled the boy onto his front and tied his wrists. 'Don't look like much,' he added, running his gaze over the slight form, 'but they're all killers.'

'Yes, yes. And Appellans are evil giants and those from the Black Country are cannibals. So we were told as children,' Marric said impatiently. 'He has had ample time to harm us if that was his intention. Look at him, his bow is across his back. Wouldn't he have been carrying it if he meant to murder us?'

They both stared at the boy with the bronzed skin, the slightly tilted dark eyes and blank expression. If he was afraid he didn't show it. A wooden effigy had more expression, Marric thought, but for all that the boy couldn't disguise the nervous swallow, or the rapid beat of his pulse in the vein of his neck. Marric set his weapon aside and sat before his captive breathing slowly. 'Don't loom,' he said mildly to the scowling Osram. The man moved back grudgingly. Marric, remembering Amtee, touched his chest and said his name, repeating it slowly.

The boy's tensed shoulders slackened. He nodded and suddenly grinned, an action so unexpected that Marric stared. The boy opened his mouth to emit a gargling sound, then shook his head.

'That supposed to be his name?' Osram asked. 'Why's he grinning at you?'

Marric said nothing and the boy, leaning urgently towards him repeated the action, the gargling and the head shaking and suddenly Marric got it.

'He's telling us he can't talk. Burran,' he said clearly, leaning forward in his turn. 'Do. You. Know. Burran?'

The boy nodded, bobbing his head up and down.

'Did - he - send - you?'

The nodding was repeated, and this time Marric spoke normally. 'You carry a message from him?'

Another nod, followed by a wrenching of his bound arms. Marric rose then, pulling his dagger.

'What are you doing?' Osram demanded.

'Cutting him free. He has something for me.'

'Not till I get his knife, you're not.' The boy scowled as he took it and the moment his right hand came free it dived into his tunic. Instantly Osram had gripped it, slamming the lad's back hard against the boulder.

'For the Lady's sake!' Marric said in exasperation. 'Let him be, Osram.'

Reluctantly the big man released his grip, the boy scowled fiercely at him then completed the hand movement, producing a slim length of cane which he handed to Marric.

'Thank you.' His fingers trembled a little as he took it. Burran lived then, the boy's presence as much as the script rolled within the cane told him that. And the fact that his messenger had learned the Rhutan tongue. How he had managed to find him was a mystery unless — Marric's neck prickled. It wasn't impossible he supposed. All people had their gods and it was arrogance to assume that he alone heard from his. He put the thought away for later consideration and gently teased the paper from its nest within the cane.

It was quite short, a note rather than a letter.

Bryn of the Crow clan brings this. I am held as hostage with them but well treated. Bring a caravan to the border next summer. I will watch for you there. The Crow clan would have peace and trade, but the country is divided. Ulfa the sorceress bids you come — for your king's sake, she says.

There was neither signature nor salutation, just the bare message. Marric reread it, conscious of the dark boy's unwinking stare. When he had done he looked across at Osram. 'Will you find his horse? He's probably not far, and bring ours too. We'll eat while I work out a reply.' He had no ink and only the paper Burran had sent him, so the back of the sheet must suffice. Or he could send a verbal message. He cocked his head considering the young barbarian. The lad must have some way of communicating with those he knew.

'Can you speak with your hands, Bryn?'

Eyes bright with intelligence the boy nodded, fingers flashing readily.

'Good. We will eat. Then I'll give you a message to carry to Burran. Yes?'

His silent interlocutor nodded again.

'How many days since you left the Grass?' Marric held up several fingers, aiming an interrogative look as he added to the tally, when he had both hands extended Bryn nodded and held up one of his own. Fifteen days then. The boy nodded confirmation as he fingered his jaw and Marric remembered Osram's punch.

He grimaced. 'I am sorry about that.'

The boy shrugged and they sat in silence regarding each other until Osram returned with their animals and began unloading the ration pack.

15

Two days later Marric and his companion reached Valleyford.

They approached it from the opposite side of the river to the road, looking down upon the sprawled palace and the hamlet clustered at its foot from the shallow hills where Marric had once followed behind the old shepherd Arn. He remembered the boar he had shot that final day, the day his uncle's killers came, and he and Rissak had fled for their lives into the winter snows that had almost taken his.

'Well, there it is,' Osram said unnecessarily, pulling him out of his reverie. 'Wonder how the little savage is getting on?'

Bryn had left them immediately after the shared meal, simply rising and bowing to Marric before springing to his saddle and riding off, ignoring the big Appellan as if he didn't exist.

'I doubt you need to worry,' Marric said dryly. 'He crossed a hostile country to find me. I imagine he can get home too.'

'Yeah, and how did he? Find us — you, when he'd never seen you before?'

Marric shrugged. 'If he could speak I'd have asked him.' He picked up the reins and glanced at the mules that had taken the opportunity of their stopping to graze. 'Let's go see if Slate is at home.'

They were challenged at the gate which was manned by two soldiers, grim looking men armed with pikes and blades who blocked the entrance way. One of them demanded their business.

Osram predictably bristled at his tone, leaning forward to say, 'This is Prince Marric of Rhuta, come to call upon your boss, mate, so how about you step out of the way before I make you?'

The man so addressed lifted the point of his pike. 'You don't rule here now, Appellan. So shut it.'

'Osram!' Marric barked and spoke in turn to the guard. 'I greet you in the Mother's name. I am Marric, once of these parts and I come from King Darien with urgent matters to discuss with your master. We will leave our arms with you, if you wish.' He heard a strangled sound from his companion and quelled him with a glance. 'Something has happened,' he guessed. 'Is the smith Cran here? He knows me.'

The guards conferred, shooting sideways looks at the two, then one went off and after an interminable wait returned with the burly smith, unchanged it seemed to Marric save for a sprinkling of grey in his hair. He greeted Marric warmly and nodded to Osram.

'I have seen you before. Ah — when the accord was signed, yes?'

'Aye. And I notice that some of your lot haven't got any friendlier since,' Osram grumbled.

'They have reason,' Cran said shortly, but he waved them through. Marric immediately dismounted, handing his reins to Osram in order to walk beside the smith.

'You are well?' he asked. 'Something has happened — what is it?'

Cran shot him a sideways look. 'Of course you would know. Slate was attacked two days since. Ambush. He is like to die of it. An arrow in the back.'

Marric's heart sank but he knew there was more. 'And?'

'A Laker arrow. The ambusher got away. What, you are not surprised?'

'No. There has been an attempt made on Darien, and his son as well. Only the Mother's hand stayed their deaths. So who is in charge now?'

'Well the council, of which I am one, but the country needs a figurehead so, in the interim until we know if he will recover, Slate's son Jem.'

'Then it is him I must see, but the council should also be present.' In a few words he sketched the attack on the caravan. 'He was one of yours, the murdered man. A shepherd at a guess. We buried him with the Rhutans and I gave him the rites as Arn taught me.' He sighed and said softly, 'I would that the old man was still with us for to speak frankly I fear the future, Cran. There is trouble coming but I cannot see its shape.'

'That is nothing new.' Cran pushed a hand through his hair and halted. 'We have an apartment in the palace, Berta and I. Will you come and refresh yourself first or —'

Marric considered. 'Perhaps you would look after Osram's comfort? For myself I think it best I go first to this Jem. If he is young and uncertain in his leadership he might take it amiss that I not bring my news straight to him. We cannot afford to let misunderstanding or wounded pride come between us.'

'Aye, you are right,' Cran nodded. 'He is a little jealous of his authority at present. We on the council are all so much older. You can find the way?'

'I will manage.' Marric spoke briefly to Osram then strode off, making for the kitchen entrance he had used as a child.

The years fell away before him for the palace, sprawling and ill-designed as it was, had not changed. He glimpsed the little courtyard outside what had been

Taba's rooms, then the heat and bustle of a busy kitchen filled his senses. The endless warren of passages stretched between numerous rooms and in one of these he found a servant to whom he announced himself and his purpose.

The man sniffed and rubbed his nose as he eyed Marric's unpretentious garb, plainly not believing his claim to be a prince.

'Well I don't know. Wait here and I'll go and see.'

While he kicked his heels a cat sidled along the passage towards him. It stopped at arm's length from him and sat, its tail curled neatly about it and Marric dropped to one knee to stretch out a hand, feeling the softness of its fur as it came to butt its head against his palm. He wondered if it was a descendant of Taba's little cat. It didn't seem impossible. An old sense of loss filled him and then the servant was back with a companion, a man Marric knew.

Smiling he regained his feet. 'Pra. It is good to see you again.'

'Prince Marric — it is you! But how — never mind. I regret you have found such a poor welcome.' He glared at the servant who prudently vanished.

'Well,' Marric glanced deprecatingly down at himself, 'an easy mistake. I heard the news from Cran, who got me past the gate; how is Slate?'

Pra shook his head. He was older, balding, with the brown knotted limbs of a hill man. He had made one of the Ansham party at the heads of government meeting in Ripa. 'Not good. There is hope, but the healer says the arrow pierced his lung. But come, I will send for food and wine and find a chamber for your use.'

'Thank you. I have one man with me and we came at haste with news. I would see your heads of council if I may, for I — we — have urgent matters to discuss touching upon the safety of our countries.'

'Yes, of course. I'll send word at once to Jem. This way.'

The council was called in what had been Marric's grandfather's Judgement Hall, a rather grandiose pillared room with a dais at one end where Cyrus, and later his son Smerdis had sat to hear the charges and hand out sentence to wrongdoers. The banners and throne-like chair had long gone and the councillors sat around a plain table with Jem, an intense young man somewhere towards the middle of his second decade, at the head. He had an aggressive manner that reminded Marric of Keelin, Arn's grandson, who had hated all things Appellan. Anger lurked in Jem's speech, and suspicion, for naturally he had learned that Marric's own province was the Lake Country from which the ambusher who had felled his father, had supposedly come.

'Why then should we listen to this man?' Jem had cried with more angry passion than sense. 'Did he plan the raid himself and has he now come to gloat over the results? My father lies dying and you would have me listen to his probable murderer who plots against us?'

'I would have you listen to my words before you start levelling accusations,' Marric said calmly. 'Or should I assume that you ordered the murder of two Rhutan caravans that recently passed your borders?' Osram had brought him the arrows with their rust-coloured tips and broken fletches, and these he now flung onto the table. 'I could not bring your dead countryman with me, but he was there along with the three Appellans I killed driving them off. There are seventeen dead Rhutans and a score or more of slain camels and horses to the account. All killed with arrows made by Ansham fletchers.'

Jem surged to his feet, face scarlet with rage. 'That is a damned lie!'

Marric shrugged. 'See for yourself. I spent my boyhood here. I recognise your weapons when I see them.'

Some of the councillors were examining the arrows and murmuring among themselves. It was Cran who spoke. 'Jem,' he said, 'Prince Marric speaks true. He is a friend, almost a son, of Ansham, and these arrows are ours. There is a plot, but it is not of his making. Nor is it confined to our land. His own king has also been attacked.' Having gained silence for him he sat back with a nod for Marric to continue.

It took time to tell and he unfolded the tale slowly: the attacks on the royal house of Rhuta, the killing of the would-be assassin by Doku, the discovery of the slain caravan with its incriminating arrows and the more recent attack on Tonic's party.

'I do not believe your dead countryman was involved. His body was left for us to draw that conclusion and foster ill-will between us. He didn't even die at the scene but was brought there, his throat already cut. The raid was planned and carried out by Apellans as, I believe, was everything else, including the attack on Slate.'

Cran frowned, idly turning one of the arrows end for end. His thumbnail scratched at the dried blood staining the barbed point. 'But to what end? Surely they cannot want war again so soon?'

'They have had seventeen seasons now to recover and re-arm. And the loss of so much territory must be hard for such a militant people to swallow,' Marric pointed out.

'But against us all — Baratan, the Lakes, Rhuta and possibly, for only the Mother knows what Meddia would do, the priest state too! That is a lot of force ranged against them. None but a fool would even dream it, and Morrik does not present that way.'

Pra looked up. 'That is true but if what Prince Marric says is right it need not fall out that way. First we distrust our neighbour, then we cease to trade, and then it is armed neutrality. And when the Appellans come where then is our pact of mutual support?'

'But even so,' a man across the table argued, 'they cannot be certain the attacks would have that effect. In the face of a greater danger would we not make common cause again? And besides, they would have the Black Country to deal with in either case.'

'Unless they too are suffering from problems they believe generated by say, Rhuta,' somebody else put in. 'It being the closest.'

The discussion went on. Jem, persuaded to the now general viewpoint that Appella was behind it all, volunteered to send a party to Barat to ascertain if they had similar problems, and if not to warn them of what was happening.

'And I will recommend to my king that he send soldiers with future caravans, for we cannot stop trading,' Marric said. 'And that is another thing. An unusually large number of traders' ships have failed to return during the last season. Their owners suspect piracy — which seems too much of a coincidence with all else that is happening. Appella has its own seafarers. I am thinking they may have been encouraged to prey upon the merchants' vessels.'

Land locked as it was Ansham had no ships and relatively few of its population had travelled beyond the country's borders, due to the three generations worth of subjugation they had suffered under successive Appellan kings. This had changed since the war but still few had ventured beyond Rhuta and the Lake Country. Marric's announcement therefore found little interest and the talk returned to more immediate problems.

When the meeting broke up Marric asked Jem if his father was well enough to see him. 'For I know the king would wish to have a firsthand account of how Slate fares. He esteems him highly, as he does all the Old Race, but he and Slate have a particular bond.' He smiled a little,

'One formed over hunting, it is true, but none the worse for that.' It was seldom that he himself hunted for the war had given him a distaste for killing.

Jem's attitude towards him had mellowed. 'Come then, he might be sleeping. The healers drug him for the pain, so he sleeps a lot.'

Slate however, though he lay with his eyes closed, was conscious, for he muttered a query as they entered the room where he lay. It was the one that Smerdis had used, Marric realised. He had been a sick man too, a wheezing invalid with lungs affected by the river fever he had taken in Rhuta. Bel's revenge, it had been whispered in Ripa, for his seduction of the god's own Oracle.

'It's me, Father,' Jem spoke soothingly. 'I have brought Prince Marric to see you. From Ripa, remember?' he added helpfully.

'I am not in my dotage yet.' The words lacked strength, being wheezed rather than snapped, but the irritation behind them was plain. 'What brings you here, my lord?'

'A matter of business, Slate. I am sorry to see you laid low. How is it with you?'

'I've been — better,' the sick man gasped. Marric was shocked to see the way the flesh had fallen from his robust frame. His grey face held the flushed cheeks of fever, and his eyes looked muddy and dull. He lifted a hand but it fell limply back to the covers, which made him swear in a weak thread of a voice.

'No strength,' he whispered haltingly. 'Bastard's — done for — me.'

'No,' Marric said forcefully. 'Ansham needs you. We enter perilous times, Slate, so you must get well. You are tired now and should rest. I will come again before I leave.' He pressed the limp hand and exited the room, letting the door close gently behind him.

'What do the healers say?' he asked the silent Jem.

'That he is strong, he has a chance. But it seems to me that daily he grows weaker.'

'Well only the Meddii have better healers than your priests, so I wouldn't give up hope.'

But later walking with Cran he was less sanguine of Slate's chances. 'It looks bad for him. Should he die will Jem continue to hold the reins? He seems very young.'

'Oh, and Darien was not when he was crowned? And you? Though I think those whom the Great Ones deal through know little of youth.'

'It may be so,' Marric admitted, 'but Darien was trained to rule. Jem is not.'

Cran sighed out a chestful of air. His body kept the bulk and thews of his calling, though Marric doubted he still practised it. 'You are right. It is not an easy job and he lacks his father's foresight, but that may just be his lack of years. If we lose Slate it will be time enough for the council to reach a decision on his successor. Our traditions have never included hereditary rule. So, what next?'

Their unguarded steps had taken them all the way to the drill ground, empty at the moment though the faint bawl of a hectoring voice sounded from the distant barracks. Squinting in the unshaded light Marric nodded reminiscently at the area before them. 'How I hated coming here! Rissak was merciless with his drill. Not his fault it never did me any good.'

'Some of it must've rubbed off, you are still alive,' Cran observed. 'How is he?'

'Guarding the king; with another to help since the failed attack. Cran, was there ever — apart from Arn I mean — anyone else to whom the Goddess speaks? I know you have —'

'A small skill at finding things, that is all.' The smith shook his head. 'There is not, Marric. At least none that I know of. Among the Old Race it is a gift of the priestly line. There is you of course, and Rissak said that your mother also... But she was of Bel. Why do you ask?'

'Damn!' Marric frowned. 'Initially it was in the hope of speaking with such a one that I came. So you have not had — I don't know — visions or dreams, or — or positive feelings...?' He stopped as his companion shook his head.

'If I am lucky and the time is right I find things: water, ore, very occasionally a person. That is all. What do you seek?'

'Knowledge. There is something —' He frowned, started again. 'That is to say of late I have felt — overlooked. Arn said, years ago, when I was with the traders that he watched me sometimes in the fire? No, well I don't understand that either. For me fire has not... Anyway, I never felt his presence. But this is different, like eyes on my back, but I cannot reach whoever... And then there was the boy.'

He sketched a quick account for Cran of the meeting with Bryn and the message he had brought him. 'How could he have known where I would be? To come so far, so accurately. How could he know me?'

'A barbarian?' Cran's brows shot up. 'What sort of message. From whom?'

Marric waved his hand. 'I have a man there. We need to make allies of the people of the Grass. It is important; this I know. And so I have an agent in place. The message was from him.'

'He is a brave man to go into the Grass. They are savages,' Cran expostulated.

'They are people,' Marric corrected. 'Different perhaps, but underneath they must want the same things we do: safety for their families, stability in their society, peace.'

'Ha! Tell that to the Appellans. They have fought them since my grandfather's grandfather's time, and possibly longer.'

'But have they ever tried talk, or trade? Mutual understanding does not come in a season or two but already Burran's work bears fruit. The boy was a mute but he understood me, so there will be others also by now who speak our tongue. And we have a meeting arranged for next year. He writes that their sorceress will come too. Think of how friendship has blossomed between ourselves and Baratan, Cran. And that despite Temes's attempt at conquest! If men can meet and talk as equals then no barrier of race or custom is so high that it cannot be surmounted.'

'In theory,' the smith temporised. 'A meeting you say? Do you mean that you will hazard yourself again?' All the world, Marric thought with resignation, must have heard of his visit to Barat and its near fatal outcome.

'It is what the Mother requires. Burran writes they will trade, so it is an opportunity for talk and to take their measure. They have no cause to agree unless they want the goods we can supply.'

'Or a chance to ambush you as they did your grandfather.'

Marric grinned. 'That too. Life is risk, my friend.' He turned away. 'I should pay my respects to your wife. It is too long since last we met.'

'Aye, a beardless boy you were then. Come then,' Cran rubbed his hands. 'I am feeling peckish and Berta will enjoy feeding you.'

Marric stayed two days longer at Valleyford. Osram guided Jem and two other councillors to where the caravan had been attacked to view the bird and animal-torn corpses, or what was left of them, of the dead Appellans. Slate, on a second visit seemed, if no stronger, then no worse, and to Marric's surprise, Keelin proved to be one of the healers attending him. It made sense, he reflected. The man had a bitter way with him and his hatred of all foreigners was so deeply engrained as to be habit now, but he was Arn's grandson and must have been taught all the considerable herb lore that the old priest/shepherd had known.

Calling on Cran and Berta to farewell them, he found that the latter knew of his discussion with her husband and had formed her own theory as to how Bryn had located him. 'It will be the tribes' shaman,' she said, 'this sorceress he mentioned? A priest, we would say and possibly a healer too. Somebody of great influence.'

'Like the Medic that leads the Meddia?' Marric asked.

She nodded. 'Exactly like that. Not a ruler as such, but one whose ability protects and guides the people. A bit like you, Marric.'

He was startled. 'I? No, that is Darien's task. I am a servant of the Mother, no more. But to return — you think this woman then has foresight? That it is her regard I have felt? Why then send the boy? He was a child Berta, not as old as my nephew. Why not come herself?'

The little dark woman threw up her hands. 'Men! Just because you can ride off any time you feel like it! A dozen reasons. She is pregnant, or has a babe, or young children to care for. Or she is old. And speaking of boys,' she said darting off the subject in the maddening way that women had, 'What of the king's son and your own family? You had a daughter, had you not. She must be what — ten summers or more now? How old is the king's lad?'

'Sixteen next autumn. He is well, his sisters too. It seems impossible but Fenny talks already of Darien finding the eldest girl a husband.'

'And your own child?'

Marric swallowed, he still found it hard to speak of Perilla. 'We lost her. She was — was never strong. The priestess said she was not meant to live.'

'Oh,' Without another word Berta came round the table and let her arms engulf him in a hug. 'I am so sorry, Marric for the way that sorrow follows you. But perhaps there will be another?'

'No. Fenny lost other babes before Perilla.'

'Ah, that is hard,' she said sympathetically. 'May the Mother hold you close.'

'Thank you.' But his heart still raged against Her decision. He stood, 'I must go. Osram will be waiting. Perhaps I will see you again next summer.'

'Travel well,' Cran clasped his arm.

'Thank you,' he repeated. 'Please send us word if Slate should not recover. And stay alert for trouble.'

Cran answered soberly, a crease between his brows. 'Aye, there is never any shortage of that.'

16

Summer passed in the Grass, the rolling landscape turning from green to yellow to brown as autumn led on into winter. It was a busy time with the harvest to gather and the stock that would become winter meat to kill and preserve. Deer, rabbit and wildfowl were also hunted to add to the store, while autumn berries and roots were gathered by the children to be dried for later use. Then the skins of the animals had to be dealt with and the great bales of grass cut and stored for the many uses to which they were put throughout the snow-bound days of winter. Everything from plaited carry-bags to bundles of thatching material came from the grass. Even the errol worked for the common good and Burran was not excepted from the labour.

He joined in willingly enough. During what amounted to his captivity in this grassy wilderness he had suffered the occasional bout of longing for his own land with its milder climate and pleasant customs, but Carj had effectively become his home. Something that as his second summer there passed was made more palatable by Sonj's company. A season and a half had seen to it that they both now spoke each other's tongue. Haltingly on Sonj's part but well enough to be understood. He did not always read her moods aright and could still be bemused by an unexpected reaction from her, but had long decided that such occasions were as much to do with her being a woman as with her identity as a Pampasan.

The first time he kissed her it had taken them both by surprise and pulling away a little he had waited with some trepidation for her reaction. 'Is this where you kill me?' he had asked harking back to her constant threat at their first meeting. He found he was only half joking — Bel alone knew what taboos his impulsive action had broken.

Instead she had laughed and catching him by both ears, had pulled him back into a deeper, longer kiss. They had made love in the sheltering grass with the sun warm on their naked bodies, while their mounts drowsed nearby, jerking awake to snort at Sonj's exultant cry. Her body was slim and tightly muscled, with small breasts, her skin more gold than brown. The tattoos on her face, so much a part of her that he no longer consciously saw them, were repeated on her breasts, whorls of design radiating out from the nipples and he touched them wonderingly.

'Didn't that hurt a lot?'

'Of course. It is meant to. The shaman does it when first a girl bleeds. To show she is a woman and ready now to contribute to the life of the clan.'

He bent to kiss where his fingers had been. 'I think they are beautiful.'

She knit her brows. 'Do not your women mark the occasion in some fashion?'

'Not on their bodies.' He thought back to the young Ripan girls he had seen with their mothers and maids, saying reflectively, 'They become very giggly and silly, and the highborn ones — the daughters of our nobility — are generally betrothed at that time.'

'Betrothed,' she repeated. 'What is this word meaning, Scribe?'

'A promise to marry, to become the wife of whoever your father chooses.'

Abruptly she sat up. 'So, your women let a man choose their mate for them? Hah! how foolish. Here we choose our own. And if he turns out not to be what we want, we choose another.'

'Then you don't marry?' Thinking she might not know the term he explained. 'Take one partner only, for life, to father your children and provide for you.'

'Why?' She looked puzzled. 'The clan provides, and children come, or not. Does the mare let only one stallion mount her? Why should it be different for us?'

'I see.' He didn't but it seemed more tactful not to push the matter. Plainly language wasn't the major difference between their cultures and for now he was content with matters as they were. Rost, he thought smugly, would be murderous if he knew, but if it was really down to the woman to choose, then there was little the man could do about it.

His conquest of the little barbarian, as he thought of it, took place while they waited for Bryn's return to the Grass. Burran wasn't necessarily convinced that he ever would. To send a boy, and a mute at that, to find in another country, a man he had never seen when there was a high probability that he would be killed by the first stranger he met, seemed the height of foolishness. Or perhaps callousness. He had argued that he should escort him, pointing out that he knew whom he sought, and could at least speak to those he met, but Ulfa wouldn't hear of it.

It was she who had sent for the errol and himself, and in her malodorous little hut that smelled strongly of herbs and old age, had insisted on next summer's meeting. Muttering to herself and snapping at both her visitors' protests, she had overseen the writing of the message and herself selected the boy for the task, demanding that Burran bring him to her the following day. Leris had agreed, they had drunk a strange smelling brew concocted on a smoky fire that further tainted the taste, then ridden home, the errol disinclined for conversation.

Burran had understood none of it. He had tried to elicit from her the type of goods the clan sought to trade, and what they expected the caravan to carry. Then he had asked how the Rhutan traders would find the tribesmen along the vast border between Appella and the Grass, but she had brushed the questions aside. The biggest one of all, how a young boy was to locate Prince Marric, and then approach him without risk of dying on someone's blade, was too difficult even to frame. Burran wondered if the Pampasans had the faintest idea of the size of Ripa (should the Prince be there) or that the population of Marric's own province even existed hidden as it was, among the floating islands of the Lake Country.

'Ulfa will guide him,' was all Leris would say. Burran doubted it. The old woman might be a sorceress but she had never left the Grass. His first excitement at the chance to communicate with his master faded into a fatalistic certainty that Bryn's bones were doomed to lie lost in Appella, while he himself languished forever in exile.

But exile had its compensations, and what had first presented itself as a challenge for a bored young man, changed slowly as summer melted into autumn then firmed into the first cold days of winter when windy gales lashed the standing grass flat, into love.

Burran could not pinpoint the moment when his blood first leapt not just at the idea of bedding Sonj, but at the simple prospect of glimpsing her person. Their love making remained as athletic and joyous as their first coupling, but insensibly he had come to value her glance and the touch of her toughened little fingers, as much as the most intimate embrace. She enchanted him with her grace and forthright ways, with her girlish peals of laughter, like silver beads on a string he thought with fond foolishness, and the sway of her trim body, so warm and welcoming to his. He had found love, he realised with a despair that frightened him because hand in hand with the exultation of the knowledge came the echo of her words about her right to choose another, should she tire of him.

He asked her, over the shared task of picking apart the boiled and twisted horse hair the clan used to make the springy curls that provided the stuffing for their saddles, if he should speak to Leris about their new arrangement.

They were working in the large hall where the folk tended to gather when snow kept them indoors, and he spoke softly in deference to the other dozen present at various tasks. Sonj hoisted puzzled brows at him and it took an effort for him not to reach across and smooth the little wrinkle between them away. 'For why?'

'Well, she is your closest relative and I just thought I should talk to her. Make sure she's not displeased at our being together.'

'Why would she care?' Sonj didn't bother to lower her voice, which held confused overtones. 'I am warrior now. My body is my own, to risk or pleasure as I please. Is this the custom in your land, Scribe? You ask at every step, even in battle?' There was scorn behind the last question.

'Yes — no.' He shook his head. 'Of course not! For battle there must be orders but family is different. Parents, older family members have control and must be consulted. It is — polite,' he said feebly. There was a complicated structure he knew to the clan's social intercourse, but it had practical overtones with none of the overflown etiquette that ruled for instance among the Ripan nobility. People sat where they wished and were served as they came, lacking the stifling pecking order of the court.

'You are funny man,' she blew a strand of escaped hair off her face and the sight of her pursed lips made him ache to kiss them. Rost, seated across the hall with Bark and two other cronies engaged in the fletching of arrows, scowled at him. He grinned back, careless of the other man's smouldering anger. Since their summons by King Hardfar, Rost had ceased to pretend anything but dislike for the outlander. Burran was pretty sure he would harm him if he could, and that saving the man from drowning had probably been a mistake. He wasn't worried. He was under Ulfa's protection and however cavalier the Pampasans' attitude was towards the sexual freedom afforded their young women, taboos abounded about their shaman. It had become obvious to him that no clan member would dare gainsay her. Or disobey her wishes. The boy Bryn had simply bobbed his head and bowed when she gave him his mission, nor had Leris protested at his life being thus arbitrarily thrown away.

And then two days later on a freezing morning that beaded the eaves with icicles, the young mute returned. A sun that lacked any warmth was climbing the milky eastern sky and Burran's breath smoked in the stillness as he crossed to the hall to begin his daily schedule of language lessons for the children. Half of each day was given over to this labour, and save for the very old, of which there were few, most of Carj were now proficient to some degree, in his own tongue. For himself he could swear, make love and conduct a conversation in Pampasan, and even understand the broader points of the clan's religion, though none seemed actually to teach it. If Ulfa was a priestess, she was the only one he had met and religious ceremonies, if they were held, happened without his knowledge.

He saw the saddled mount standing outside the hall and entered in time to witness Leris embracing Bryn's slight figure. The shaggy haired boy was thinner than when he had left, there was a fading bruise on the right side of his face and a half healed scar across the back of one hand, both of which were blue and shaking with cold. He wore only a cloak over his tunic and trousers and Leris led him straight to the firepit burning in the centre of the hall, while calling for Sonj to bring food.

Burran sat with the pair while Bryn ate. The errol waited until his hunger was sated then caught his eye and moved her hands, the fingers flying in voiceless configurations that brought his own into play. Sonj's bright gaze shuttled between the two and Burran wondered if later on, when they were alone, she would tell him what was being said. Then to his surprise the errol nodded and turned to him.

'He brings a message for you, Scribe, from your master.'

'He found him?' Burran's incredulity brought a slight smile to the boy's usually blank expression.

'Of course. It was what he was tasked with. Your master says: The caravan will be there. They will come in good faith even though they be armed for there is much unrest in Appella. They will arrive at the old fort three days after the second moon of summer.'

'Right.' The old fort was the last in the chain that Cyrus had erected along the border, and the first to be built, as a deterrent against the raiding Pampasans. And the mention of unrest, he guessed was to serve as a warning to his hosts that they would come prepared for treachery. That Appellan actions would trouble Rhuta seemed unlikely, but the errol, he judged would be unaware of that. His curiosity winning he asked, 'How did he find him?'

Leris waved the question off. 'It doesn't matter. Would you see to his horse, Scribe? Come, Bryn, you need to sleep.'

She had a point. The boy's eyes were drooping where he sat. Burran left to attend to the abandoned mount and when he returned on the heels of his pupils Bryn, and the remains of his meal, had vanished.

That day which marked mid winter was memorable also to Burran for apart from the boy's return, which had also brought him the first word in almost two years from the prince, it was the day that Sonj moved into his quarters. She came that evening, with her sleeping robe rolled beneath one arm and a small bag of plaited grass holding her possessions. She wrinkled her nose at the sagging strands of hide that underpinned his sleeping platform and tightened them up. 'That is bad for your back,' she scolded, as she matter-of-factly added her robe to the bed.

Burran felt giddy with the joy of her presence. He dared to hope it meant that he was her permanent choice and, remembering what she'd said about her freedom of choice in the matter vowed to himself that he would do everything possible to keep her at his side.

17

Sonj, as Burran had discovered, was a feisty companion, passionate in bed, critical of his efforts to get his tongue around her language, and quick to temper at his assumptions concerning the sexes. She was also playful, affectionate and caring, nursing him through a brief fever at the end of winter, and zealously guarding his diet.

She had no interest in the wider world or his own past. 'You are here now,' she stated unarguably. 'The Grass is your home, you have become barbarian too. Maybe you even learn to shoot one day.' That was a dig at his marksmanship with a bow. He had seen her lodge an arrow in the heart of a fleeing deer while he was lucky to hit any part of the target. But, he pointed out, he could swim, a skill none of the clan seemed to have.

'Because you lived on this so great river,' she had grumbled.

'No, my heart. You cannot swim in the Great River; it is as strong as a—' he sought for a comparison she would understand, 'as a bear.' There were bears in the southern part of Appella and Hardfar's throne, he remembered had been covered with the massive skin of that animal, so they must exist also in Pampasa. 'A man would be pulled under instantly and drown.' He lay back lazily, full of contentment following the evening meal. The room was snug with a fire on the hearth for though spring had arrived with mud and fresh grass, the nights were still cold. 'Tell me,' he said curiously, 'I have always meant to ask. Why does your sister have Bryn live with her? Has he no parents of his own?'

'Leris fostered him. Many of our young are fostered for many of our warriors die. Bryn's father was killed in a raid and his mother left the clan.'

'Why was that then?'

'She said the boy was damaged and put him out to die. So Ulfa banished her.'

'The old woman has that power? If it had been his father who did it — supposing the mother had died, I mean — would Ulfa have banished him?' Burran was curious to know if the shaman's reach extended to the men of the clan. The king had obeyed her through fear of whatever witchcraft she had used to summon and banish the ghost horses, but domestic clan matters were surely different.

'How could it be so?' Sonj demanded. 'Does the stallion rear the foal? The child is the mother's. When there is no mother, then one is provided. We are like the horses, Scribe. The Great Mare leads us and we obey Her will.'

To tease her he objected, 'I thought the stallion led.'

Her unwinking look pitied his ignorance. 'No. He fights the other stallions and,' she thrust her clenched hand forward suggestively, searching for the word she didn't know, 'makes the foals. It is the mare that leads and finds the grass and defends her young. The power is always with the female.'

'And yet,' something suddenly clarified for him, 'your king would change that. I see! So that is why — He thinks the stallion should lead, yes? He would overthrow the clan traditions and what — even your Great Mare?'

'He cannot,' she said positively. 'It is Epona who makes the grass, and gives life and health to Her children.' She dropped back into her own tongue the better to facilitate her urgent words. 'Our lives depend upon Her presence. We are indivisible, Scribe! Without our horses, and Her wisdom to guide us we are nothing. Dead grass clumps that no longer shoot when rain falls. We who oppose Hardfar know it. Such a thing can never be, whatever the king wishes.'

Burran knew his own country's history. He said, 'I'm sure that King Waltu thought the same before Cyrus of Appella decided he wanted Rhuta for his own. Never underestimate the greed of powerful men, my heart. They do not care what fires they start or whose lives they wreck when it comes to fulfilling their desires. We in Rhuta know that. It is why we have allies to call upon, so that it can never happen again.'

She tossed her head proudly. 'We do not need others to fight for us. One greedy man will not change anything.'

But that was all it took, Burran thought. He wondered if his sudden understanding had unveiled what his prince had glimpsed, and was in some way the reason for his being here. Then Sonj, wearying of the discussion, came to nestle beside him displacing his ruminations with the musky reality of her presence and the thought was lost in an upsurge of carnal desire.

Later, spent with lovemaking he said, 'Something else, my love — that first day when you were so fierce, and full of the wish to kill me,' he kissed the point of her tattooed chin. 'Oh yes you were, I saw it in your eyes! I've always wondered — how did you find me?'

'Ulfa knew,' she said simply.

'Knew what? How?'

'That you were coming; and what day you would be at the Honey tree. So I just waited there.'

He reared on his elbow to stare at her and she shook her head, her look accusing. 'You were trying to steal from the Crows' tree! Is it any wonder I wanted to kill you? That was why they beat you, Rost and Bark. Theft is not permitted among the clans.'

Burran flopped back down and she giggled suddenly, her small hands spidering over his chest as she raised herself to kiss his closest nipple. 'I am glad now I did not. Kill you, I mean.'

He drew her body closer. 'Yeah, so am I.'

The following day was the one set for the breaking-in of the colts that had never yet worn a bridle. 'You should train your own mount,' Sonj told him. 'All my people do so, usually long before they pass their warrior's test. So it should be easy — you are older and stronger. And I will help you.' She was so determined that he guessed it was as much to bolster his place within the clan as to show him worthy of her favour. He had ridden all his life but they had been stable horses; he had never caught or trained an unbroken colt.

In the morning he found that it was not as easy as she made it out to be. The bay colt was wild to start with, a snorting, eye-rolling mass of muscle that far outweighed him, and had no desire to stand docilely at the end of a rope while it grew accustomed to his presence. The spectators, which included a sardonic Rost, didn't help. Exhausted from his efforts to prevent the colt's escape Burran wondered how on earth a slip of a girl managed the job — until Sonj, exasperated, slipped between the rails of the yard and with the tail of the greenhide rope he was struggling with, took a couple of turns about a post.

'There. Now he fights the post, not you. When he tires get the headstall on him and then the hobbles. When he realises he cannot escape he will stand and you may handle him.'

She said it as if the accomplishment of her directions were a simple thing, but it took him the rest of the morning to achieve that. When he stopped to give both himself and the trembling youngster a break, his shoulders muscles ached and despite the breeze his body was damp with sweat. He shook his head and blew out a breath. 'Not as easy as you said.'

She clicked her tongue, a sign of irritation. 'You must be confident, Scribe. He is afraid, he knows not what to expect, so you must be calm and sure for him. Then it goes well.'

'Calm? That brute could cripple me with one well-placed kick. I'm too busy ensuring he doesn't to pander to his feelings!'

'You are afraid!'

Stung by the accusation he glared at her. 'I'm sensible, that's all. There's a difference!'

'It is a horse,' she jeered, 'not a bear, not an enemy. You were afraid of the snake too, when I captured you.'

'You'd be bloody mad not to be,' he retorted, angrily aware that Rost could hear every word.

His rival, as he had come to think of him, grinned at his discomfiture. 'Want to see how it's done, Outlander? Watch and learn.'

He vaulted onto the rails and jumped lightly into the yard, causing the colt to shy away and then thrash about in the unaccustomed hobbles. Picking up a rope he caught a loop in his hand and dropped it neatly over the head of a young filly, standing in the next pen, though the area was so small, Burran thought remembering his own half dozen tries at roping in a much larger space, that he could hardly miss. The filly snorted and lunged at the gate which Rost yanked open.

'No!' Sonj called. 'Not in the same yard!' She was over the rails before Burran could stop her, and cursing he followed just as Rost let go of the rope in order to close the gate. It flipped up, curling around the filly's legs as she plunged away causing her to bolt, mad with terror, towards the safety of the other horse who, catching her fear, lunged panic stricken, straight into Sonj's path.

Burran roared her name then flung his body at his colt, reaching desperately for the halter shank. He felt the bay's front legs hit him and bowl him over even as his palm curled about the rope. He clung desperately to it, pulling the colt further off balance than the hobbles already had, and it crashed to the ground beside him, its head thumping like a boulder into his chest. He felt an immense pressure then with a snort and a lunge the horse was back on its legs, both its forefeet landing on his left forearm. He heard Sonj shriek and tried to rise but blacked out instead.

When he came to Sonj's dark eyes, enormous in her white face, swum above him. 'You are idiot!' she shrieked. He screwed his eyes shut, suddenly sick with the pain of his broken arm. The bone hadn't quite pierced the skin but the end of it was pushing the flesh out at an unsettling angle. His chest hurt where the bay's head had thumped down on him and his left knee held a deep, unremitting ache.

'Sorry,' he tried to smile. 'Are you all right?'

'Of course. But now you are broken.' She abandoned Rhutan for her own language to continue scolding only to break off and he was amazed to see a tear track down her cheek. 'I thought you were dead already. I am sorry, Scribe. You tried to save me and now you are hurt instead. Can you stand?'

Teeth gritted he took her arm and managed to lever himself upright fearing an instant collapse, but his head slowly cleared and as long as he didn't put his full weight on his left leg he was able to limp to the support of the rails. 'What about the colt?'

'He is Rost's trouble now,' she said shortly, 'he made it, he can mend it. You cannot climb,' she said seeing him support his bad arm with the good one, 'come to the gate.

I will find a splint then we will go to Ulfa. What is wrong with your leg?'

'Musta wrenched it,' he panted. He wasn't looking forward to the ride to the Mounds, but she obviously expected he could make it so he had no choice. The clansmen, he thought dourly, probably rode with arrows sticking out of them and the odd limb missing. A pulse of pain shot through the arm from fingertip to shoulder, causing him to stagger and he swore at himself, shaking his head when she looked enquiringly at him. 'It's nothing.'

Back at their house she used her own dagger as a splint for his arm, binding it into place before saddling his horse and helping to heave him onto it. For a moment he thought he would pitch straight off the other side but a snatch at the mane saved him and they began the slow trek to Ulfa's hut with Sonj alternating between concern for him and castigating the absent Rost.

'A child knows better,' she fumed. 'You cannot work two colts in the same yard. I cannot see why he does what he knows is wrong!'

'He meant to show me up,' Burran said. His head felt as if it was coming loose from his body and every movement now hurt his chest. 'He's jealous that you're with me. He thinks you should be with him.'

'With him!' She was outraged. 'He stands against all my sister would do, and is the king's toady beside. Huh, I would sooner take a crippled beggar to my bed.'

The knowledge cheered Burran for the rest of the way to the Mounds. There Ulfa emerged from her dark little hut to poke at his injuries then, with a curt jerk of her head bade him enter. She gave him a foul tasting concoction from a none too clean cup, then tugged on his forearm to reset the bone. That done she sheathed it in stiff cloth and bound it firmly with a heavy twine made from plaited grass stems, creating a cover as rigid as wood. He passed out somewhere during the process and woke to find himself naked on her bed while she plastered some herby concoction over his swollen knee and the bright red skin of his chest. She cackled at his discomfiture, said something he didn't catch but which made Sonj blush, then handed her the pot of goo.

'To rub on every day,' the latter explained, helping him back into his clothes. 'How is your arm now?'

'Sore,' he muttered woozily. 'What was in that godawful drink?' The room seemed to be expanding and shrinking by turns about him, and his head was splitting.

'It will pass,' she soothed. She turned to thank the shaman, bowing deeply, then took his lax hand leading him as if he were a child. 'Come. Home now.'

'I hope the horse kicks his damn head off,' Burran said thickly and was disconcerted to hear himself giggle. 'Love it if he did. Love you too, you know. My li'l barbarian. He doesn't. He just don't like losin' —' the thread of it vanished but Sonj wasn't listening anyway.

'Come,' she repeated patiently and led him off.

18

Elsewhere too the seasons turned as they had always done. Stormy days swept across the Lakes, blending the wet grey reed dwellings, and the grey lake water and the falling rain, into an indistinguishable whole. Frogs croaked in a deafening chorus from the reed islands and the cooking fires smoked with damp wood. Wet knots snarled on the ropes that held the little boats to the pontoons, and the rainwater had to be bailed from them each time they were used. At the Shrine Fenny and her sister priestesses were kept busy nursing the usual crop of croup and fevers and chest complaints that winter brought, while the poultry huddled miserably under dripping willows, and little flocks of handfed sheep stank of wet wool.

In Ripa the fields lay fallow, and the fruit trees bare. Men that had found their living working on farms and orchards turned to the riskier business of ferrying firewood into the city, each journey across the Great River a dice with death, for the winter storms raised its level and the strong current occasionally swept down submerged logs and trees torn from its banks. The street sellers worked beneath inadequate shelters, and the traders' ships limped up-river with stained and torn canvas got from battling winter seas.

At the palace Darien conned through the accounts sent by his spies of events in Appella and Marric's own network passed on news from Ansham where Slate was making a slow recovery; from Meddia where the current Medic was ailing (poison was suspected for he was a comparatively young man still) and greetings from Barat, where, 'Thank all gods,' the king, restively striding about the empty council chamber, said to his twin, 'nothing seems to be going wrong.' The royal brow was furrowed with care for two more trading ships had failed to complete their journey, and the last caravan to make it through the pass before the snow closed it for the winter, had been attacked. Without the guard of soldiers, the trader had reported, they wouldn't have survived for arrows had again been used, and as before, those collected as evidence were of the make and style of Ansham.

Marric, in the city for a few days, said worriedly, 'Is it time to call Morrik to account, do you think?'

'How exactly?' Darien asked bitterly. The uncertainty surrounding the loss of the ships weighed on him, his gut told him differently but they just may have been sunk in a storm. 'We have no proof. If I sent an emissary Morrik would laugh in his face, and he might even vanish as well. And, before you even suggest it, you are not going.'

'I wasn't intending to. I'm more concerned about the Meddii. It is a pretty fragile link we have there. If the Medic was poisoned and he dies what's the worst that can happen?'

'I've already thought of that,' the king said gloomily. 'Going on what we know it only needs Appella to somehow point to us as the guilty party and there's an end to Rhutan Meddia relations. If it didn't result in an actual declaration of war. The Medic is holy to them.'

'High priest and king,' Marric agreed. 'They're more likely to cease all trade with us, though. Which would be bad enough.'

'We can't afford it. We would have to raise taxes. God of fishes,' he ran a hand through his bright hair, 'give us a break! Why, for instance, cannot those savages from the Grass mount a full scale war against their damned neighbour? Give them something else to think about.'

'Because it's winter? You can't be serious. Nobody campaigns in the mud.'

In such manner the days went by until spring brought a swelling to the branches in the fruit orchards, and a fervour of nesting awoke in the water birds at the Lake. In time the last of the snow slid into chilly runnels, the pass opened for traffic and in the Upper Land the windflowers and alpine daisies blew brightly among the stone and fresh grass. In the city the traders were hiring men, and shipowners, their vessels refitted during the winter break, began to look about for loading as labour returned to the farms, and crops were sown anew.

Throughout spring and into early summer the king's council sat more often than usual debating the business of government but principally attempting to reach consensus on their first trading venture to Pampasa. The merchant Luka, once responsible for organising the traders' resistance against Temes, was brought out of retirement to help debate the matter, which they canvassed exhaustively. Could the deal be trusted? Was their prince unknowingly abetting an ambush using trade as the simplest lure? If not, then who among the traders should lead the caravan? And most importantly: what manner of goods — should it all be above board — would prove most acceptable to a barbaric people, and what would they offer in return?

So little was known of the Seas-of-Grass, and all of that hearsay that they could only guess. Marric, trying to keep the discussion moving, said, 'Well, they have metal and cloth and horseflesh. That much we know from their raiding. Either they work silver or they import it from across the sea — the king's dagger, which you have all seen, was proof of that. So much we know.'

'Aye,' Rissak, who as the king's bodyguard also attended the councils, interjected, 'and they wear body ornaments. I have fought the tricky bastards and seen armlets of silver and copper.'

'Good,' Marric nodded. 'So there may be mines. And furs perhaps? Appella has bears, wolves, foxes, why should the Grass not have them too? They have a coastline, so shells and pearls, even ivory — if the horned sea beasts of Appella also frequent their shores. I think we may trust that the trade will be worth the risk.'

Trader Ramie who had become Luka's junior partner on Tranche's death and seventeen years later now ran the business, a merchant in his own right, volunteered to lead the caravan. Marric was privately satisfied with his decision knowing that the man had both a cool head and years of experience on the road.

'Do we take an escort of soldiers?' he asked.

Darien opened his mouth to agree then looked at his twin. 'What do you think?'

Marric grimaced. 'It's difficult. We may need protection against Appella, but it won't do to turn up on the border looking like an armed patrol. It's a matter of trust. They're likely to be suspicious of us. After all they have had no dealings with outsiders, or not that we know of.'

'So you would lead unarmed men into what might be an elaborate trap on their part? What if they just fall on the caravan and kill everyone, Prince?' the head of the woodworkers' guild demanded.

Marric shook his head. 'Why then go to so much trouble to arrange it? Sending a boy all the way across Appella to find me. If such was their plan they could attack any caravan that passed within riding distance of their borders. No, I think perhaps an escort that can be dropped off before we reach the old fort. They could wait for us at the closest garrison. Besides we wouldn't be totally weaponless. The men would have their personal arms — that's only normal for any traveller.'

That settled, discussion turned to what items were likely to appeal to the barbarians with each guild member subtly pushing for inclusion of his own workers' goods. Darien, withdrawing a little, signalled Marric and when he joined him murmured, 'What Woda said about it being a trap — Have you thought that the whole set-up might be intended to draw you into an ambush?'

'To what end? My death you mean.' Marric considered briefly then shook his head. 'Why? They know nothing of me. Burran, if he's told them anything, will say that I am a merchant and he my trader. And one merchant is as good as another surely? They don't need to bring any specific one to their doorstep.'

'They might have a spy planted, or have suborned someone who could pass unnoticed in the city, to discover who is important at court,' Darien hazarded.

'An Appellan you mean?'

'Yes, or a disaffected Rhutan.'

'It's not likely is it? Given their history. Besides,' Marric lowered his voice still further, 'you forget the Goddess. It was She who wanted the contact made. I doubt it would be to facilitate my death.'

'And if it is,' Darien said grimly remembering the reports after Barat, 'you would still go.'

His brother eyed him. 'You know I have no choice.'

Darien sighed. 'I do know. Also I have been thinking it over these last few nights and I believe that Tarris should accompany you, which,' he added dryly, 'means Leu also, though Osram may feel differently about that. What?' He caught a fleeting look on his brother's face. 'You don't like it?'

'I didn't speak,' Marric demurred. 'His mother will never agree. Though the boys would see it as a huge adventure, of course. What's your reason?'

'My son is sixteen, or will be by the time you leave. It is time he began to play a man's part.' His mouth twisted wryly, 'At his age you were making your own way in the world, and I was training for war. He knows little of life beyond court. It is time he familiarised himself with it, handled some responsibility and got to know his real subjects, not just the ones that smooth his way. He will be king some day, after all.'

Marric said, 'You are sure? For all I think they will offer us no harm it is still the Grass, and accidents happen. There could be risks I cannot see, Darien.'

'Life is a risk. Who knows that better than you? Osram will be there, and Sandos of course. Tarris actually heeds his counsel.' Darien could still be surprised by the fact. 'Besides I had rather he tried his wings in perhaps helping to stave off war than, Bel forbid! fighting one, however far down the track it comes.'

19

Long before the boys themselves were informed of their inclusion in the upcoming trip, Marric, home once more, mentioned it to Osram, who lifted fair brows in astonishment.

'The king thinks it safe enough?'

'He understands the risks,' Marric said diplomatically knowing that a large part of his twin's reasoning was centred on his belief in Marric's powers. 'I have reminded him however that accidents happen. The prince will have Sandos with him, Leu is to accompany him also. I said I would ask you about that.'

'If the king commands it,' Osram replied stolidly.

'He doesn't — exactly. It's more that he believes he would want to go with Tarris. They are young, and heart friends; it would seem a great adventure to them.'

'Aye.' The big man nodded. He was no fool, Marric knew and must see the advantage of his son's position anent the young prince. If both lived Leu would one day stand beside the throne, boon companion of the monarch. It was a position any man of ambition would strive to afford his son. 'Well then, he must go of course. Extra protection for the prince, the lad is not half bad with a blade, if I say so myself.'

Marric clapped his arm. 'And who better to judge? It was you who taught him.'

Tarris, who had lately been attempting an imperturbable countenance as befitted royalty, couldn't prevent his eyes from widening in pleased surprise at the news that he would accompany his uncle on the journey to the Grass.

'And Leu, Sir,' he pressed glancing across at his friend.

'If his father permits. Though I am sure,' Darien added kindly as the youngster's face stiffened to ward possible disappointment, 'that he will. You will serve as your uncle's aide, Tarris, and learn what you may from the encounter with the tribes. We need to know their ways and something of their culture if we hope to ally them to our cause. Trade is the first step in our plan to achieve this.'

Leu wrinkled his brow. 'But my father's friends, Sir, they say they are nomadic. Would they have industry or — or — What would they have to trade?'

'Many things, I am sure,' Darien said. 'It is a large country after all and its people have metal and ornaments and livestock. That we know. The land must be rich to support them all, for the Appellans consider them numberless, and they have a coastline besides. There could be precious metal, or furs. Smoked fish,' he hazarded, 'or fine horseflesh. Our merchants are ever keen to discover new goods and new markets, and the treasury will benefit from both.'

Leu, whose thoughtful nature always saw the wider picture, asked hesitantly, 'But how will we speak to them, my lord king? If they don't have our tongue and we —'

'Ah, but they do — some anyway. Enough I believe, to make themselves understood.' A secretary entered the room just then with a document and the king sighed, recalled to the tedium of his daily workload. 'Leave us,' he said and grinning excitedly at each other the boys obeyed.

The Lady Fenny, learning of her brother-in-law's decision to let his son accompany her husband was reassured. 'So he must think it safe to permit it. Tarris is his heir after all.'

'It should be,' Marric agreed cautiously. 'But that's not his only reason. He intends the boy to learn his trade. Someday it will be him dealing with allies and enemies alike and nothing will overmatch him like inexperience. Best to make his mistakes now when older heads can mend them. It is no easy task to rule a country, my love.'

'As long as he is safe.' She smoothed a hand over his cheek. 'I don't want the job falling to you by default.'

'As to that,' he said lightly, 'there are the girls. It might go against tradition but I see no reason why Saffon shouldn't succeed Darien if, the Mother forbid! Tarris should die before his father.'

'But Rhuta has never had a reigning queen,' Fenny objected. 'It's nonsense anyway. Nothing will happen to Tarris. And speaking of Saffie — has Darien found a match for her yet?'

'Yes, Ling told me. There's a young duke — well he will be Duke in time, from a province in the north. I've never been there but I believe they breed horses. The engagement ceremony will be held the summer after next.'

'So she'll be fifteen. How old is he?' she asked.

'Born the year before the war, so what — eighteen?' Most of Ripa, Marric thought, dated events by the war. Pre or post or during — you heard it all the time.

Fenny was nodding. 'Not too old for her then. Mother said the saddest marriage she ever saw was your Uncle Swale's. It was his second. His wife died in childbed and he wed again for an heir. The girl was just a vessel to him for he never got over his first love. And then you and your brother were born before she conceived, and Swale was killed. We have been so lucky, Marric!' She came to stand before him and link her arms about his neck saying, 'But you will be going away and who knows when I will see you again?' Her voice was steady but he caught the fear in her blue eyes. 'You will be careful, my love?'

'Of course, I will. It is just another trading trip.' His neck hairs stirred as he spoke but the sensation was gone again on the instant and he almost believed he had imagined it. He thought of the strange boy who had found him across half a continent and a little frisson went through him. The Goddess was involved; he could deny it to Fenny but in his heart he knew there would be nothing ordinary about the planned trip.

When the time came the caravan left from Ripa, a string of slow marching camels with its mounted handlers and an escort of a dozen soldiers. Marric and Osram had arrived the day before and joined their modest baggage to the train. Darien had wanted his brother to take court robes to impress whoever he met but Marric declined.

'They are tribesman and not likely to be moved by fancy clothing. I would rather earn their respect, than their derision.' Tarris, he was pleased to see was plainly, if richly dressed, and he himself was clad in simple trousers and tunic with his travelling robe tied behind the saddle. The caravan was larger than he had anticipated but, as Ramie told him, 'Every damn shopkeeper in the city was mad to be included once they learned what was happening. And none of the guilds would be left out.'

'Well if an alliance, should we make one, is to work it takes both sides,' Marric responded philosophically. 'Better our people come to regard them as customers than as savages.'

The first day they made little distance, but this was normal, Marric knew as the train of beasts, and the men both guarding and guiding it, settled into routine while ironing out the small problems bound to occur at the commencement of any journey. Tarris, accompanied by Sandos and Leu, rode with his uncle. The young prince was in high good humour, fairly bouncing with satisfaction and firing off endless questions. Everything was new and interesting for, Marric realised, until now his nephew had never travelled beyond the Lakes. It was an opportunity too good to miss and he at once set about educating Tarris in the geography, traditions and lifestyle of the peoples of the Upper Land.

The first night a pair of handlers, on Ramie's instructions, raised the young prince's tent. He thanked them and turned to his uncle to enquire where he would have his put.

Marric shook his head. 'I'm an old road hand, remember, I don't need a tent. Unless it rains and I doubt it will tonight.' He slept, like the rest of the men, in the open and thereafter so did Tarris. The weather remained fine as they left the humidity of the plains and the mountains came daily closer. By then the caravan was operating smoothly, every camel knowing its place in the string, the horses herded into camp before daylight each morning and Ramie's calm, be-turbanned presence overseeing it all. Their military escort slept beside them but ate apart from the main camp. And they made no trading stops as they travelled.

'Time enough for that on the way home,' Ramie said to Marric. 'If we've anything left to trade.'

'So you're not worried about the outcome with the Pampasans?'

The wiry, hook-nosed man who had known Marric by another name before he was a prince grinned and shook his head, 'You're here, aintcha? That's good enough for me.'

He grimaced at the trader, saying lightly, 'Such faith,' and went on to speculate about stages and distance once they were through the pass. They needed to time it right as they wished neither to be hanging around without their guards, nor arriving to find that the tribesmen had grown tired of waiting and left. Neither Ramie nor Marric had forgotten the fate of the ambushed caravans. The soldiers' presence made them less likely prey but that would change when those guards had peeled away to kill time at the garrison until the caravan's return.

'Once up there,' Ramie jerked his head at the looming mountains now within a day's ride, 'I figure we'll make our best stages, push 'em along till we're within whistling distance, then slow to a crawl, sorta pace you could walk in a day. We can gauge it better then.'

'Whatever you think,' Marric said. 'I'm not expecting trouble.'

'No?' Ramie's shrewd gaze passed from him to the mountains ahead where the deep cleft they would travel through was now visible. 'Well, keep that bow of yours handy — just in case you're wrong.'

It took a full day for the long train to traverse the pass. The camels moaned and baulked when they encountered the rock underfoot and in the steepest parts Marric felt his mount's hooves skid against stone but patience won the day and by sunset camp had been made by the side of a creek, in the shelter of a copse of scrub oak. The air cooled quickly and Tarris, looking about him with lively interest, rubbed his forearms.

'Cooler, isn't it?'

'We're higher, and near the snow line. Summer's here are shorter too. A fire will be good tonight so why don't you and Leu bring in a bit of wood? Keep your blade,' he said sharply as Tarris made to divest himself of it. 'You're in Appella remember.

A brief look of irritation crossed the boy's face. 'It gets in the way, and Sandos will —'

'I know. But it never hurts to help yourself either.'

Osram who had listened to the exchange watched the two youngsters leave weapons at their sides, followed by the guard and lifted a fair brow at his own principal. 'Something I should know about?'

Marric rolled his shoulders. 'Just ordinary precautions. He shouldn't go anywhere unarmed.'

'And —?'

A look of annoyance skewed his companion. 'You know me too well, dammit! Yes, there's something — or maybe not. I can't be sure and it makes me jumpy. Bear in mind if Appella was behind the attack on the lad then by having him with us we are more or less presenting him to the enemy.'

'If they even know he is.' Osram demurred.

'If they don't then they have fewer, or more inept spies than I fear,' Marric said tartly. 'Of course they know.'

Notwithstanding his caution — and it was no more than that, he told himself — the days passed uneventfully. They met a few travellers but suffered no attacks and the weather continued fine with none of the short lived but fierce thunderstorms that were a feature of the mountains. The further they travelled it seemed, the balmier the golden summer days became. The tension of expectation eased until their military guard took to riding in lackadaisical groups of twos and threes, right at the rear of the marching camels. It took a blistering dressing down of the captain in charge, by Marric, to jerk them out of their lethargy. Thereafter they rode in soldierly formation scattered along the lead, wings and tail of the moving caravan, best positioned to repel the attack that never came.

Then, as Ramie had planned, their progress slowed and they loitered along their way, making their night camp each day soon after the halt for the midday meal. It had the advantage of resting the animals and allowing the men to hunt, which pleased Tarris and his friend though it dismayed Osram when Marric added him to the party.

'Extra precaution,' he said elliptically. 'The itch is still there.'

'The more reason for me to stay with you then,' Osram said.

'If anything happens the soldiers are here.'

'That useless shower!' the big man said with the scorn of one of the King's Own that even Rissak couldn't have bettered. 'I wouldn't trust them to find their own backsides in the dark.'

In the end he had obeyed, however reluctantly, torn between his duty and his son's safety, for a strike at the prince would also endanger Leu, but nothing had happened, which even in the midst of relief put Marric more on edge than ever.

And so the time idled away until they were on the edge of the vast sea of waving grassland and within two day's ride of the appointed meeting place at the abandoned fort. Marric, rethinking the earlier decision to have the soldiers await them at the next garrison, where possible tensions with their Appellan hosts might arise, told the captain to backtrack to their previous night camp and wait for them there until the caravan's return.

'The Pampasans are bound to have scouts out to check us over, and we don't want to alarm them with too great a suggestion of force,' he explained. The captain, still smarting from the dressing down, saluted then, eyeing the endless treeless vista before them, and withdrew with alacrity.

Marric, explaining the change of plans to Ramie, said, 'Until we know just how Appella is involved in the attacks it seems better to keep their soldiers and ours apart. Aside from any bad blood that might cause trouble, we don't want the men spilling what we're doing. It would ruin everything should the Appellans mount an attack on the Grass while we're here. And if they are behind the ambushes they'd never pass up the opportunity. It's what I'd do.'

Ramie grunted. 'Let's hope they don't find out then. You gonna send that bird?'

'Yes.' Marric had already prepared the tiny canister with its message telling Darien that they had arrived and that all was well. Supposing the bird made it back it would be their last communication unless they sidetracked into Ansham on their way home. A royal cote had long been established there, but the suspicion thrown upon Rhuta by the attempted assassination of Slate had prevented Jem from using a bird to report the attempt.

The following morning they moved off, every man's eyes flitting nervously about for they were now within a day's ride of the old fort, situated on the very edge of the Grass, which, as they progressed reached to brush their mount's shoulders. Over the last few days the camels had borne the additional weight of wood for the campfires for living trees were now rarely seen and any dead ones had long been scavenged by the country's inhabitants. At the noon halt Ramie had the handlers begin to collect whatever pats of dried dung they found to eke out the supply. It was very quiet down in the smothering grass which restricted vision and dulled all sound. Only the occasional flight of crows or the tweeting of smaller birds swaying on the grass stems broke into the shuffle of camels' feet and the creak and jingle of harness.

'It seems to stretch forever,' Tarris eyed the grass filled horizon, his voice tight with nerves. 'Has anybody ever entered it?' Sandos had moved both the youngsters up to ride with Marric so that he and Osram flanked their principals.

'Your great-grandfather did once, and nearly died for it,' Marric said. 'He was a young man then. And he did eventually die in the Grass, not far from here actually, in an ambush arranged by your great-uncle. As have many fine soldiers over the years.'

'Some of 'em good mates of mine,' Osram said. 'That bastard Temes sent 'em to their deaths by the hundreds.' He spoke, Marric knew of the Green Devils, Cyrus's elite corps whom his murderer hadn't trusted and wished to be rid of. Both Osram and Rissak had served the old king, though their loyalty now was to his descendants rather than the country Cyrus had reigned over.

Leu asked something then, addressing Marric as he always did as Prince, but his question went unanswered as the latter straightened suddenly in the saddle. Osram's hand dropped in reflex to his blade, his head snapping about. He said tersely, 'What?'

'We are watched.' He could almost feel the eyes drilling into him. 'Don't look back!' he added sharply. 'It's the same feeling I had with the boy. Somebody is aware of our presence.' A crow cawed above him and he tilted his head back to watch three of the creatures pass, their bodies blue-black under the brilliant sky.

'I see nothing,' Tarris leaned elaborately down to fiddle with his saddlebag while casting a glance behind him. 'Are you sure you didn't just sense the birds, Uncle?'

'Keep your eyes front,' Sandos barked, 'you think you're gonna spot what the animals haven't?' Tarris reddened but made no protest at the rebuke.

Leu cleared his throat. 'Father, would the tribesmen's mounts be accustomed to camels do you think?'

'If they're here somewhere in the grass, then yes,' Osram replied. Horses unused to the smell of the ruminants usually bolted from their first meeting. He relaxed his shoulders. 'Lad has a point, Marric. Either they know camels or they're on foot and that don't seem likely.'

'No.' The feeling was still there. Marric watched the crows who had looped around to the west and now seemed to be returning. The little he knew of shamans, for they could be found on some of the islands in the Eastern

Sea, told him that they often bonded with animals that became their totem and infused their magic.

Was it possible that the birds were the shaman's eyes? It seemed absurd but so was using a tongue he didn't know to deliver a message he couldn't recall as he had once found himself doing in Barat. 'I doubt we are in danger,' he said. 'We are invited after all. And we must be close to the meeting point, so act as if nothing is amiss. I would expect a wary people to send out scouts, and we know they are masters of concealment. If spying on us serves to lull their suspicion it can only be good for trade.'

They continued on their way and nothing happened. Some time later Osram cocked a brow at Marric who shook his head slightly. 'I no longer feel it. It's as if eyes were on me and they have looked away for a time. I doubt whoever is watching has gone though. More like his curiosity is satisfied for the moment.'

Osram growled something under his breath and Marric saw the fingers of his left hand surreptitiously make the sun sign for protection. 'We should keep watch tonight.' The soldiers had done guard duty before while the caravan slept.

Marric nodded. 'Not that I think we are in danger, but they will hardly respect us if we take no precautions.'

'Bugger what they think,' Osram said roundly. 'I'm not waking up to find my throat cut.'

For all their wariness they passed a peaceful night amid the tumbledown remains of the abandoned fort. Marric took his turn at an early watch then slept heavily until he needed to rise to urinate. Standing alone under the star filled sky he listened hard with his ears and his mind, but heard only the soft hush of a nightwind ruffling the grass, and the hoot of a distant owl. There was no sense of being overlooked. The night seemed empty of all minds but his own. The meagre campfire, all they could allow themselves, had long since burnt out and the animals on their long tethers were dozing, their bellies full. A nearby camel belched up a mouthful of cud and a snore sounded from within the camp, otherwise all was quiet.

Yawning, he returned to his blankets and fell into a light sleep that lasted until a voice, sharp as a poking stick, shouted in his ear. It brought him to his feet on the instant, snatching at his bow, every sense on a hair trigger as he looked frantically about for the danger. He saw the sleeping forms of his companions shrouded in the greyness of early dawn, the last watchmen standing tree-like in the diffuse light, and behind him, rising out of the grass at the camp's edge the spectral form of the boy Bryn. And with him the figure of Burran.

'You got here, my lord,' he called. 'Welcome to the Grass. This is Bryn and I'd be glad if you'd tell that lot,' for Ramie, and the two bodyguards he belatedly saw had sprung to their feet, blades in their hands, 'that we're friends.'

20

Burran talked while they broke their fast. For Tarris it was strange to hear this foreign looking stranger call his uncle 'my lord' even though his actions spoke, as Osram's did, of a long and easy familiarity that belied the formality of the address. Burran, whose tanned skin almost echoed the shade of his silent companion wore a Pampasan bow across his back and a belt of plaited grass. His tunic was ornamented with seeds and his trousers made of some coarse cloth. He wore his hair in a pigtail and at a quick glance more nearly resembled a tribesman than his own countrymen. Only his worn boots were recognisable, and as if aware of the young prince's covert scrutiny he lifted one, saying, 'I hope your traders have boots in their packs. I've mended the soles of these twice.' The silent boy's feet were encased in a sort of tough hide sandal that would offer little protection to a rider.

Leu tried talking to the boy but received only a blank stare in return.

'He is mute,' Osram said quietly, 'but he understands us.'

Marric, ignoring the interjection said, 'So you're the advance greeter. When do we meet the rest of the clan?' The royal party with their two bodyguards and Ramie sat apart from the rest of the caravan whose curious gazes drifted constantly from their meals to the strangers.

'Tonight. We'll take you to them.' Crows cawed harshly over his words as a pair circled the camp then flapped off to the east. Tarris watched the young stranger's gaze follow them and saw his uncle jerk his head in their direction.

'And the birds? Not too many roosts or nesting trees in these parts, but there seem to be plenty of crows.'

'Yes, Errol Leris heads the Crow Clan. The bird is their totem.' Burran glanced quickly at Bryn then closed his mouth with an infinitesimal shake of his head and Marric took the hint. They would speak of it later when they were alone. Curious he asked, 'You walked here? From where?'

Burran shook his head. 'Our mounts are back there.' He gestured behind him and grinned. 'Ambush tactics. Clan horses are trained to lie down, out of sight.' He drained his mug and got to his feet. 'When you're ready, my lord.'

It wasn't long before they were moving again. Burran and his companion disappeared briefly to fetch their mounts and were back by the time the final camel, the one whose task it was to carry the food, had been packed. Marric took advantage of their absence to warn his companions about speaking too freely before Bryn. 'He may be mute but he understands our tongue and speaks with his fingers. He will be here to forestall any plots we may be tempted to make, and to prevent information they don't want known being passed on by Burran.'

The caravan formed up and followed Burran and his companion. The former, riding beside Ramie asked eagerly after their trip and for news from Ripa. Osram observing at a little distance said, 'He's a brave man to risk coming out here. How is it he survived the first meeting without getting filled with arrows?'

Marric nodded soberly. 'His courage has never been in question. He has risked much. I believe he has the

Goddess's protection but that makes him no less brave. It is because of him that we will be able to speak with the people we meet.'

'True enough.' Osram scraped at his jaw where the beard he hadn't shaved during their travels itched. 'Still doesn't get him past that first sighting when you'd reasonably expect an arrow coming your way.'

'As to that the Pampasans wanted the meeting. It is why I sent him.'

As always, mention of Marric's gift sent prickles up the big man's spine. He didn't ask how the other knew but his fingers made the sign and he rode on in silence.

The crows, or more like them, followed the caravan all day, winging silently past or cawing in the distance.

'Can they sense carrion?' Tarris wondered, hipping in the saddle to study the flight of half a dozen. 'They seem to be flocking the same way we are going.'

'Keep your eyes open Prince.' Sandos was also watching. He hitched fretfully at his blade, his gaze sweeping the grass they brushed through. 'Maybe it's us they're after. They say buzzards do that, track moving things in the hope they'll die.'

'Nobody is going to die,' Marric said forcefully. 'Be alert, yes, but we are invited guests. Do you want our hosts to think us so fearful we find danger in the flight of a bird? That will not accomplish much beyond their rightful derision.'

'Begging your pardon my lord, but these bloody outlanders were killin' my folk afore you were born, and your father before you. You can't trust the buggers no further'n a horse's fart. They ain't like us.'

'They are, Sandos. Exactly like. They have wives and children, they fight for what's theirs. How is that different to either Rhutan or Appellan?' Which last Sandos was. 'When I was a lad in Ansham they called me Outlander too. And before the war which you may remember they helped us win, many a Ripan called the Baratans cannibals — and believed it too.'

'Yessir,' Sandos said dutifully, but his tone implied that his opinion remained unchanged.

By late afternoon the crows had coalesced into a cawing mob that circled ahead of them. Burran deserted the lead to ride back and inform Marric that they had arrived. 'You will deal with the errol. Her name is Leris, a clan leader. She is important.'

'And the shaman your note mentioned?'

Burran cast a quick glance at the approaching Bryn. 'She will send for you when she is ready. Don't ask more.' He raised his voice. 'Follow me, my lord. The errol will be eager to greet you.'

The two of them left, Osram following as a matter of course. Tarris, watching them go hesitated; he wished he'd been included in the meeting but his uncle was the diplomat and hadn't invited him. It was possible that these barbaric people didn't have a royal line, after all Appella no longer did and they were highly civilised. If Marric knew that (and you could never tell what his reclusive uncle did know) then perhaps they set no store by princes and would have regarded his inclusion as an insult on the grounds of his youthfulness.

The crows had settled about the clearing where the clansmen waited. The grass had been flattened in a vast circle and it was strange to see so many of the birds on the ground at once, strutting familiarly between the felted tents and conservative fires. The handlers had halted the camels and the beasts were thumping down on their knees to be unloaded, their low toned grumbling a counterpoint to the men's buzz of conjecture as they eyed off the strangers and were studied most frankly in return.

Tarris as curious as the rest saw that the famed barbarians of death were a slim, not over tall race with a golden-tan sheen to their skin, long black hair and dark eyes slightly tilted at the corners. All wore some sort of facial tattoo which gave them a savage aspect and all were similarly dressed in trousers, sandal like foot coverings and short tunics. Leu nudged him and following his friend's gaze Tarris saw a girl about their own age. Both her arms were raised to fiddle with her hair and the tunic had ridden up enough to display a handspan of her torso. She saw them looking and jerked her arms down with a scowl, staring boldly back at them.

'Pretty,' Leu said. He had lately grown very appreciative of girls.

'With all that ink on her face? She's probably a slave.'

'Father says they don't have slaves, so it's ornamentation.' She had the same chin tattoo they all seemed to wear but in her case it had been carried up into circles on her cheeks. 'I like it, it suits her.'

Tarris sighed, his friend's frequent instant infatuations were wearying. 'Get over it. I daresay she'd gut you as quick as kiss my hand. What is it with you and girls? You used to be more fun, now you want to hump everything in sight.'

Leu, as usual, failed to take offence. 'You're just a bit slow,' he said equably, 'but you'll get there — about the same time as you get your full growth.'

His lack of height was a lingering regret with Tarris. He aimed a punch at his taller friend who laughed and dodged. 'Huh uh, best behaviour remember, the better to impress our new friends.'

Marric meanwhile was feeling his way forward within the errol's tent to which Burran had taken him. Leris, offering him the courtesy of the warrior's clasp, studied him frankly then settled herself crosslegged on the floor. A wave of her hand invited him to do the same. Bryn had already sunk down silently in the background and Burran, with a sensitivity to the situation that Marric could only applaud, eased himself into position midway between his patroness and his master, favouring neither. Osram, unwillingly obeying a slight gesture made as Marric entered the tent, waited outside.

Looking about him Marric noted the grass mats on the floor and a slab of wood like a very low table on which cups and flagons waited and among other things a bowl of very small apples. He waited out the woman's welcome spoken with a slight hesitancy but a fair command of Rhutan, and commented on her fluency when he replied.

'Scribe is a strong teacher. We must obey him.' This close to him she was older than he had first thought. There was the odd grey streak in her hair, and her face was more lined than it had appeared at a distance. 'And he speaks good our tongue.'

'My king will be pleased that we may now converse. Understanding, like friendship, cannot happen between countries if we cannot speak to each other. And it is the dearest wish of his heart that this may be so. He has sent you a small token of goodwill to show you the work of our artisans, and the range of goods we can provide in trade.'

It had taken hours if not days, of thought and discussion, to decide. The gift had to be small and something both unlikely to be found in the Grass, and with enough novelty to arouse interest. The first instinctive choice had been a weapon — a dagger or sword — the next jewellery but Darien had vetoed both. 'We're trying to promote peace, not increase their store of arms! And jewellery I think not. I doubt there are many balls or grand occasions in the Grass. Not from all I have heard of the place.'

In the end they had settled on the silver article Marric now brought forth, together with a handful of almonds. He passed it to Leris who turned it in her hands in some confusion, studying the hinged handles shaped in the same form as the dagger that Burran had returned to Ulfa.

Seeing her lack of comprehension Marric was pleased. She didn't recognise it, so they had guessed correctly.

'It is a nut cracker.' A very fine one, he thought taking it back to fit an almond into its jaws. The silversmith had surpassed himself for the workmanship was superb. He closed the handles, the nut popped and he re-presented Leris with the tool and the kernel. 'It breaks the shell. We call these almonds. Very fine eating. You do not grow them here?'

'Walnuts, but not these.' She sampled it cautiously then nodded. 'Is good.'

He gave her the rest and she spent the next few moments cracking them and sharing them out between the four of them. 'Nut cracker.' She eyed it. 'This will work on the walnut also?'

'On anything you can fit in the jaws.' Marric affirmed. She was pleased, he gave a small sigh of relief. It was a little thing but even little things encouraged liking and from that something more substantive could grow. Then he felt the presence of another, a watchful regard that stirred the hairs on his nape. Glancing casually around he ascertained that only the four of them were there. Leris was offering him a cup and under the guise of leaning to take it he casually shifted his position, as if his legs had cramped, until his back was to the boy. It could only be Bryn, but the gaze that watched him felt inimical, steeped in age and experience as though another saw through the youngster's eyes.

Ignoring it he sampled the strange drink and took his share of the cheeses and the little apples that accompanied them. He was accustomed to the diplomatic dance where protagonists probed one another's interests through the guise of light conversation. Later the serious stuff would begin if, he surmised, the shaman judged it warranted. He sensed no inherent power in Leris, save that of a natural leader. She was the mouthpiece, he thought, and Bryn the eyes — it would be interesting to meet the intelligence behind them both.

He asked about the crows.

'The totem of our clan,' Leris said. 'They follow us for the harvest we bring. In times past raiding was known as 'taking the crow road.' Other clans have different totems. The nearest to us, who I think will in time also wish for peace and trade, have the fox as their totem. The king,' she added, 'has the bear. And like his bond creature he is savage, with no wish for change. Save the removal of women from leadership roles.'

'Ah.' Those few words and the tone they were uttered in told him much. 'But the clans disagree?'

'It is tradition,' she spoke calmly despite the sudden fire in her eyes. 'Always it is the mare who leads the herd. That is the way Epona made us, the power She gave all females, yet in his arrogance Hardfar would go against the Goddess Herself. But we shall not be robbed of our role. He wishes to gain in strength by conquest only the fool cannot see that is an impossible task now. Once perhaps...'

She brooded a moment then sighed, saying frankly, 'We have held the Grass since foals were first born, but we cannot defeat the cursed Appellans. Every season more of our young warriors die in the raids he urges us make but we three clans — the Crow, the Fox and the Coney whose territories march with the border — have said, no more. We bear the brunt of the Appellans' retaliation while he sits safe in the city, protected by the blood we shed. It is time for a change.'

They spoke a little longer but though Marric waited for it no opening to deepen their exchange offered itself. Eventually he ended it by inviting Leris to meet the trader and discuss what goods each could offer the other in trade. And perhaps she and her people would care to join the Rhutans for the evening meal?

'No, no,' she was adamant. 'We have food prepared for all. Besides, we are too many. To feed us all would eat up your supplies.' Her fingers flickered a message as she spoke and Bryn climbed to his feet and left the tent. Marric wondered what his instructions had been. 'Come Scribe,' Leris said brightly, 'let us see what marvels they have brought. You can tell me the meaning of the names I do not know.'

'Scribe?' Marric hoisted a brow at his man.

'It's what they call me, sir. Only the leaders of the clans are literate, but in every generation there are some whose task it is to remember. A living record; before such a one dies his memories are passed on to another.'

'But perhaps now is the time to change that also,' Leris said. She nodded to herself as if surprised by the unexpectedness of the idea. 'Yes, we have little paper but with trade and peace maybe we make time for learning. Your city writes its history, yes?'

Marric thought of the temple library in Ripa where knowledge had been stored since scrolls were invented. There was another in the palace, sadly depleted during Temes's reign but his brother was adding to it as time and finances permitted.

'Yes, we do. It is safer, for men my die unexpectedly or grow old and forget.'

Leris nodded. 'Is more work for you, then Scribe.' She strode out of the tent into the gentle light of dusk, Osram falling in behind them as they made their way across the camp to find Ramie.

21

Initially wary the Rhutans thawed under the influence of food and the avid interest of the score or so of Pampasans making up the errol's party. They would trade on the morrow it was decided but Ramie had selected a small quantity of goods for display around which the men and women of the clan clustered, fingering and exclaiming amongst themselves. Those who had learned a little of the Rhutan tongue asked questions, those without called freely upon Burran to speak for them. He was very much at home among them, Marric saw, particularly with one young woman to whom his eyes often turned. She was lithe and comely save for the disfiguring ink marks on her chin, but it was something they all wore, and Leu at least was not repelled by it judging from the attention he was giving to a slim, sulky looking girl with a tattooed whorl marring her cheeks.

Marric lifted a brow at Osram who was also watching the pair, then searched for his nephew, finding him by the simple expedient of locating the taller Sandos. Savoury smells were coming from the campfire and his stomach rumbled. Osram sniffed deeply.

'Smells good, whatever it is.' He gazed around him at the firelit shadows and the shapes of the clansmen from which the talk and the occasional laugh sounded. It was quite dark now, the bright stars intensifying the blackness of the standing grass. A nightbird called and

Marric fleetingly wondered where all the crows had gone. 'There's a few good mates of mine,' Osram said, 'who'd never bloody believe this. Supposing they were alive to tell.' He spat and turned away. 'And now it's cooking pots and clothes pegs, for Asher's sake!'

'You need to let the past go,' Marric spoke quietly. 'What we're trying to do here, you and I, is to secure the future. It takes time, and effort, and forgiveness, Osram. Don't forget they killed my grandfather and loosed Temes upon us, so I do understand your feelings. But surely it is better to trade in domestic goods rather than death?'

'Aye, sir, I know. It's just — strange, you know? To have 'em this close and not be fighting for your life. You really think a few poxy pots and lengths of cloth will win them over?'

'That of course is up to them. Or, I suspect, to whoever is behind the errol. Somebody is. And apparently there is division among the clans. The king reportedly seeks to abandon traditional values and Leris's people are rebelling, as are her neighbours. Which could augur well for our efforts. It's too early to tell but I am hopeful.'

'And I am hungry,' Osram responded. 'I wish they'd leave off their bloody gawking so we can eat.'

The following morning the traders got down to business. The Pampasans had never minted coins and worked on a system of barter. Leris was intrigued by the notion of money and called Burran to her side for a lengthy discussion on its merits and uses, quickly grasping what the copper and silver tokens represented. In the Grass all contributed their labour, each according to his ability and all benefited by having their needs fulfilled from the common supply. No one clansman had more than another, and if one hungered all did. The land met their needs which were simple enough, while the odd touch of luxury such as Sonj's amber pendant, were either gifted or earned, a symbol of status or prowess. Thus metal weapons could be paid for with charcoal or labour at the smith's forge, and the shaman's medical knowledge by the laborious gathering of ingredients used in the medicine provided.

Barter was time and labour intensive. It worked, but Leris, while quickly grasping the benefit of money, was astute enough to realise that it could have no immediate place in their lives. 'Later, when more of the clans trade,' she said, adding reproachfully, 'You should have told me of this before, Scribe.'

Burran shrugged helplessly. 'If you'd asked...' As a Ripan the idea that money could be a foreign concept had never occurred to him.

At that moment Bryn appeared silently beside the errol, his slim hands flickering into life. She turned at once and caught Marric's eye. 'Ulfa will see you now,' she announced. 'Bryn will take you.'

'Thank you.' He nodded to the boy who turned at once to obey and they headed off through the tents that made up the Pampasans' camp. Marric, when he had finally had the chance to speak alone with Burran had learned next to nothing of the elusive shaman. His spy's knowledge of the weaponry, culture and religion of his hosts had been extensive but he had little of substance to impart about Ulfa.

'She's ancient,' he had said frankly. 'An old, bent up woman, and about the scariest person I've ever seen.' He had shivered remembering. 'She lives with the dead,' he'd confided in a low voice, 'even the king was scared of her.' Briefly he recounted his summons to the city, '...a rough, sprawly unwalled place with a king's hall — more town than city really...' and what had befallen there. 'I tell you, sir, it was uncanny. Every man there heard the horses — like a bloody stampede it was. And then it stopped dead. Everything stopped, even the birds. She did that.'

'No,' Marric shook his head. 'Their Goddess did it through her. She is just a woman, as ordinary as you or me, but she has the power to channel Epona — I have that right? A Goddess of the Grass and the horse herds? Well that is not so different to the Mother. I have sometimes thought,' he had added, 'that under all the names and aspects we grant our deities, that they are but one and present themselves in different guises to meet our many needs.'

Now at last he was about to meet the one who was, he was fairly sure, responsible for his presence here. Her tent stood at the very back of the encampment. The crows of the previous day had been evident since daylight but not obtrusively so, or he had simply grown accustomed to their presence. But her tent was surrounded with black feathered bodies that rose with a great clamour at his approach. Flapping and squawking they settled again on the actual tents, wings out as they found their balance. One landed on Bryn's shoulder, head cocked to study Marric, white ringed eyes bright and pitiless above its sharp, scavenger's beak.

Ignoring its stare Marric lifted the tent flap and entered wondering suddenly how he was supposed to communicate with the shaman. Given her reported age it was extremely unlikely that she would have learned his tongue. He could of course send the boy to fetch Burran, but first he wanted to take the old woman's measure. His eyes skipped over the interior of the tent, almost missing the huddled form in the darkest corner. With the flap fallen behind him the dimness was all encompassing. He could make out the twisted grass stems comprising the floor mat, a small brazier that smoked rather than burned adding to the gloom and making his eyes tear, and one or two domestic items — a basket, a pitcher, and then the humped shadow slumped on what he imagined must be her bedding. There was a strange, acrid smell and for a moment he thought it must be coming from her, and then realised it was carried in the smoke.

The woman cackled something at him, gesturing at the ground, and he folded himself down on the matted floor to sit cross-legged facing her. He wiped the water from his eyes and caught her own dark, hypnotic gaze. She was truly ancient, her face a map of lines and folds, teeth missing, the chin tattoo a wrinkled scrawl without definition. What hair she had was white with crow feathers twisted into the scanty knot atop her head. He recognised her, the face in his vision as she pointed a skeletal hand at him, the flesh of the forearm sagging away from the bone as she did so.

He had never, Marric thought, seen anyone so old in whom the life force was so obviously strong. Power radiated from her, an almost tangible force. It was stronger than anything he had ever sensed in Arn, and she held it with a casualness that stunned him. He coughed in the smoke which seemed all at once to be thicker, and felt his head swim. She must be burning dung. Waving a feeble hand to clear the air, he said courteously, 'Madam, could we — we —' but the words thickened and slurred on his tongue and a moment later he collapsed limply onto the grass mat.

Ulfa called out, the flap lifted and Bryn hurried in to remove the brazier. The shaman filled a mug from the pitcher, fossicked in the basket for a lump of cheese, and brushing off the ash that crusted it sat sipping and chewing noisily her gaze never leaving the unconscious stranger at her feet.

Marric's mind slipped into darkness as deep as night. In fact, he realised blearily, it was night. Night in the Grass with the wide-reaching blackness of the sky spangled with stars beyond counting. He watched fascinated, as they wheeled above him, seeming to spread and multiply like a nest of disturbed ants. No, not ants, people. A golden tan horde of people pouring across a vast undulating space where few trees grew, led by a thousand horses with a great shimmering mare at their head. The picture was so big, and its components moving so rapidly that horse and man flowed into each other. They were one and the same, interdependent, swift and lithe, and wild. Men and stallions, women and mares, youngsters and colts. They bred and spread, and the grass grew and died as the seasons turned, and winter snows blanketed the thatched shelters of the men and thickened the coats of the yearling colts. And the Great Mare led, and Her children, equine and human followed, on and on through countless seasons.

Then a change: a longer winter with deeper snows, a dry summer that shrivelled the grass and winds that blew the dried stalks away. The people were hungry, the horses lean and weak, and from the edge of the grassland, now sere and dry, the strangers came. Tall, fair men raiding and killing, burning the thatch of the dwelling places, plundering what food there was, driving off the horses, butchering and eating the strongest of them. Outrage and desperation fostered hatred and a burning thirst for revenge in the tan horde. To kill what was sacred, a part of their identity. It was not to be borne!

The rains returned and the grass grew and with it, as the seasons passed, a new militancy rose in the people of the horse. Marric's dreaming mind saw the clans ride out, saw the relentless border conflict, and the tumuli raised above the fallen fighters and their mounts. For season after season the shining mare led their actions, but the fair strangers never lessened their resistance. No matter how many of the enemy fell to the Grassland's ambushes there were always more. Gradually the fighting clans thinned, the warriors grew younger, and they no longer raised the tumuli for the fallen. Death had become too common to warrant that much ceremony. While behind the border land, deep in the fastness of the Grass, an easier life and an alternate system of belief was rising. Whilst the mare still shimmered as brightly for the border clans, her reality had dimmed to a shadow for the insular central power of the nation.

Marric twitched and moaned, his head rolling on the grass mat as Ulfa bent towards him. Her fingers with their misshapen joints touched his brow and he fell back into deeper sleep again but now he saw a different landscape, one in which the great herds of wild horses receded further and further across a plain of dying grass from which all sound save the cawing of crows had vanished. Their black shapes were everywhere, flapping and strutting among abandoned thatch, perched on the jutting hipbones of dead horses, and fossicking with bloodied beaks amid the corpses of their riders. A wind keened amid the desolation and the only disturbance was caused by the steady tramp of a conquering army that had finally laid waste to the nation they had fought for so long.

Osram, making desultory conversation with Sandos at the trading ground, glanced restlessly off in the direction that Marric and the mute boy had gone what seemed an age before.

'He's taking his time,' he muttered, 'the prince.'

Sandos shrugged. 'You know what these things are — endless talk in circles, then wine and grub, and more talk. Couldn't thole it meself. My view, you got somethin' to say, get on and say it. None of this beatin' round the bushes the nobs go on with. Who was he meetin' anyway?'

'Some old priestess. Where's your lad?'

Sandos looked around him. 'Somewhere in this mob. Tarris was with your boy and he's prob'ly with that girl he was eyein' off last night. They won't be too far.' He heaved himself to his feet. 'I should find him I suppose, afore he's bartered off for a horse or a roll of felt. Looks to me like Ramie's lot'd sell their own mothers to turn a profit.'

'Well, they're traders,' Osram said absently, his gaze turning again to the path that Marric had taken. He waited. It was well past noon. A little later Sandos returned with Tarris. Shifting restlessly Osram wondered if he should be worried for his principal, but it was reportedly just an old woman he'd gone to see. Sighing, he settled again to wait, rising swiftly when Marric finally re-appeared, looking a little pale and unsteady on his feet.

'Light's sake!' Osram exclaimed. He, Ramie, Tarris and Sandos had been eating a belated meal. 'What happened to you?'

'I'm fine.' Marris squeezed his eyes shut in an effort to ease his thundering head. He felt nauseous and winced from the strong light; the thought of food revolted him. 'Hot,' he said, 'I need to get out of the sun.'

'Use my tent,' Ramie had stopped eating to study him. He inclined his head at the shelter. 'I've got the pricier goods in there, and my bedroll. You look like you should be lying down.'

Marric nodded his thanks and stumbled with darkening vision into the tent. The relief from the searing light was immediate but his head felt as if it would burst. Barely conscious of the wool wrapped bundles of glassware he found the disordered bedroll and collapsed onto it, both hands gripping his skull where the pain pounded with unremitting ferocity. None of his visions had ever brought such agony. His heart thundered in his ears, every beat a pulse of searing pain.

Osram's voice, abnormally loud, came to him out of the darkness. 'What happened? Is there —'

'Go away,' Marric groaned. After a moment he heard his footsteps retreat and then there was just the dark and silence and his pounding head. He lay in a pulsing blackness until presently, despite his agony, he passed into a state of merciful unconsciousness that lasted for most of what remained of the afternoon.

Marric woke to find that the pain had gone and the nausea with it. A soft light filled the tent and when he emerged he saw that the sun lay low in the west, its bottom rim sunk below the grass tops, and that cooking fires had been lit around the camp. He was suddenly ravenous and very thirsty. The animals had been brought in to water at the creek then hobbled to graze and Osram, tunic unlaced and a mug of something in his hand was approaching him from a mingled group of Rhutan and Pampasans around one of the fires.

'There you are. How're you feeling?'

'Better, thanks. Is there food?'

'This way.' He nodded at the fire. 'We're just starting. There's no wine but the beer's drinkable — just — when you get used to the taste.'

Marric nodded. 'How's the trading going?'

'Ramie seems satisfied. Best leatherwork I've seen, and their smithing's not bad either. The bridles are a work of art — they're sparing with the leather and actually use the pith of certain grass for the reins. They treat it somehow and twist it, then plait the twisted stems. A quick look and you'd swear it was leather, just as strong too, apparently.'

'You use what you've got,' Marric said. 'Like our boats and houses made of reeds. So, no problems? Both sides satisfied with the goods offered?'

'I'd say so.' They reached the fire where their own particular group was gathered, serving themselves from the common pot. Somebody handed Marric a plate which he filled, the savoury smell ambrosia in his nostrils.

He settled himself cross-legged and began to eat glancing around at his companions. Burran, he saw had the same young woman with him to whom he was now introduced.

'This is Sonj, sir. The errol's sister. She saved my life the day we met.'

Marric bowed gavely to her. 'Then I thank you for that, Sonj.'

'Is nothing. You are prince, Scribe says, in your own land?'

He nodded. 'Yes. Well, there are two of us here, actu —' He broke off and felt a sudden chill on his nape as a swift look about confirmed what he had already subconsciously noticed. Dismay and a vague memory of some disaster he had been shown and forgotten in the last moments before he woke in the shaman's tent, made him drop the knife he held. The mouthful he had eaten turned to ash in his gullet. 'Where is Tarris?'

'Some of the lads took him hunting,' Osram said unconcernedly.

'When?'

'Some time after the noon meal.' Osram eyed him, there had been a snap to Marric's tone. 'He'll be fine. Sandos is with him.'

'Then where are they? Who took them? Burran, do you know?'

'No, I haven't seen...' He frowned. 'It does seem strange. I mean with the traders here. If they left at noon that's —'

'Far too long.' Marric was on his feet. 'Find whoever was in the party. Where is Leu?' he asked scanning the area. 'Was he with him?'

'No.' Osram also rose, something of the other's alarm rubbing off on him. 'He was with some girl. I heard her refuse for him. She said they had better things to do than chase around in the heat.'

'No doubt,' Marric replied grimly. He glared around at their now worried faces. 'Don't just stand there! This is your prince who is missing. Find him. Now.'

22

A hurried search was immediately undertaken. Marric himself went straight to Leris to ask who had arranged the hunting party but she knew nothing of it, nor had she set eyes on Tarris.

'Not for little while.' She thought back. 'He was here for noon meal, with his tall friend and the grim one who follows him. Far he cannot be.'

But he plainly could for one by one the others returned with no sightings to report, first Ramie, then Burran and Osram, followed quickly by an apprehensive Leu and a girl whom he introduced as Wanna. 'I should have gone with him,' he said guiltily, 'only Sandos was there, Prince Marric and I thought... But I should have gone.'

'He is a baby then, this prince of yours?' Wanna asked scornfully. 'Will he get lost or fall off without you along to see he doesn't?'

Leu, looking suddenly less than enchanted with her, said, 'He is my friend. It was my duty to look out for him.'

She tossed her head. 'In the Grass we look after ourselves.'

'Well, you had better go and do it then,' Leu snapped. 'Sir, shall I saddle the horses? If there was an accident —'

'If there was it could hardly have prevented some member of the party from returning,' Marric said. Dread gripped his nape like a taloned claw. 'This was planned. He is either taken or dead.'

'No!' Leu cried. 'He cannot be. Sandos —'

'Has likely met the same fate. It is no good rushing off, we have no notion where to search. What we need to do is find out who is missing. Who made up the hunting party? I will ask the errol to gather her people and see who doesn't come.'

'And I will take the bastards apart when we find 'em,' Osram promised.

Leris, almost as perturbed as her guests at the turn of events, quickly sent off several runners to muster the clansmen. Marric asked also if she might request the help of the shaman. 'Obviously I cannot speak to her, but if she knows anything that might help find the boy... He is our king's only son and if harm befalls him I cannot speak for what it may do to all we seek to accomplish here.'

'You need not threaten me Prince Marric,' she said coldly. 'I am angry yes, as you. This should not happen. Who has done this will pay. Be sure of that.'

'It was no threat,' Marric said, 'just the simple truth. My brother has the power of armies at his call and should harm befall the boy his grief would be great.' He pulled a hand down his face as if to erase the worry there. 'Goddess! An attempt was made on his life in Ripa but I never thought it would follow him here.'

Leris frowned, 'Then may it not be something my people have done?' It took but a moment for her to shake her head. 'Impossible! No stranger could follow you here unseen. So, one of your own among the traders?'

The idea hadn't occurred to Marric but he immediately rejected it. 'They are simple traders, come along on the trip to improve their businesses. Anyway, none would be a match for Sandos, and Tarris himself is handy with a blade. Our escort who are trained and might have managed it are waiting back beyond the border. Besides, how would it benefit the traders?'

She shrugged, tired and exasperated. 'It does good for us then to lose what we are trying to make?'

'Then who does gain by it?'

Marric saw the knowledge hit her and she swore. 'Hardfar!' She almost spat the word. 'By the Great Mare Herself! This is his doing. I would wager a dozen colts it is his work, and I know his tool too! Rost! Where is he? He spoke against the plan from the start. And if it is him then Bark will be there too. They are as brothers, those two. Wait. I will speak to Ulfa.'

She whirled on the word and hurried off as the clansfolk began to drift together. Sonj, who had gone with Burran to look for Tarris, was with him again, the two asking urgent questions of the gathered people. Sonj on tiptoe for height, seemed to be counting heads. She conferred with the Rhutan when she had completed her tally, then both crossed to Marric, their faces grave.

'Four,' she said, 'are not here. And their horses also are gone.'

'Who?' Marric asked.

Burran grimaced. 'A man called Rost. An enemy of mine. It was him told the king I was here. He wanted me dead — they both did. Hardfar to spite the errol, and Rost because of Sonj here. And his mate Bark is missing. The two are as close as finger and thumb.' He'd been right in his supposition about the young woman then, Marric thought. So it was no surprise that being held hostage sat so lightly on Burran. 'It has to be him that's taken the prince,' the man added. 'Two others as well. But why?'

'I can think of several reasons. To ransom, to force us to leave. Who are the others?'

'Some of his hangers on. He has a bit of a following in the clan. Leris is their errol, but Rost resents being led by a woman. Thinks it's a man's job.'

'Where would he take him?' Marric asked tersely. 'Think man!'

Burran exchanged a look with Sonj who lifted small open-palmed hands. 'What is this he wants to do?' she asked slowly. 'To kill, to hurt, to bring to the king? Only then can one tell. To kill is easiest. Anywhere.' She waved at the Grass beyond the circling dark. 'To hurt — that needs time and is more hard, and for why? To take to the king is a long ride, so Rost, he knows he cannot return, for all here learn what he has done and my sister will punish, yes? And Hardfar will know you come also for your prince, so his warriors are ready. Then the clans fight and it is what he wants.' Her face worked in concentration with the strain of finding the right words until finally growing impatient, she gabbled something in her own tongue.

Nodding his understanding Burran turned a frowning face to Marric. 'It makes sense, my lord, given the current situation. Sonj believes the whole thing to have been orchestrated by Hardfar. He would have the details of our visit from Rost. If he has the prince then the Crows must help to recover him. Their honour is involved, and their deal with you.'

He said something to Sonj in her own tongue that had her nodding vigorously, then turned back to Marric. 'See, the abduction, if that's what it is, will start a clan war that Hardfar would try to use to wipe out opposition to his desire to change Pampasan traditions. Sonj thinks so and it makes sense, sir. It is the excuse he has been looking for. He wants to do away with the women's influence in the clans. Their rights to leadership, to fight in and head the military units. And by doing that he's subtly working at diminishing the power of the Goddess amongst the tribes. If the Crows don't stand against him now they lose any outside alliance they may form with us, then time and the border fighting will do the job for him. In either case he can just slit the prince's throat and take care of the rest of us when we turn up seeking him. If,' he added, 'we even got that far.'

'I see.' It was probably an accurate enough reading, Marric thought. His guts churned with worry because it had occurred to him that the same effect could be had by killing the boy out of hand. Tarris could already be dead. Which would save his captors the problem of dragging him across the Grass land, and would still bring the clan to war before the city of Glam.

Everybody was looking at him but it was Osram who spoke. 'What do we do?' And immediately answered his own question. 'Nothing tonight.'

'No,' Marric agreed. 'A search party at first light. If the clan will help —'

'We will do more,' Leris spoke at his shoulder. 'We will find the ones who tarnish our honour and Epona Herself will look away from what we do to them.' Her voice grated and her breath came hard in her fury. 'He is the son of the brother of the man I took for my own, but he is dead to me. To dishonour his mother's clan just to lick the shoe of that — that —' Words failed her until she burst out again, 'He thinks Hardfar will embrace him and make him great, the poor fool. He will be clanless. Used and discarded — for who makes a renegade one of their own?'

'May I ask what the old — what Ulfa said? Did you speak with her?'

'Yes. She knows nothing of your prince. Only that danger threatens the clan. She wants me to leave warriors enough to defend the camp when we ride for Glam.'

'You think Sonj is right then, that the king is behind this?'

'Who else?' Leris asked bitterly. 'Well, warned he was. Yes. But he is like the stupid bear who sees only the honey he wants and cares nothing for the lives he snuffs out to get it.'

Marric got little sleep that night. Visions of Tarris left for dead in the smothering grass, or dragged bound and helpless on a horse across the grasslands were not, he knew, Goddess inspired, but just his own imagination. He had little hope that Sandos still lived. The blunt Appellan soldier took his duty seriously, and even if he was not prepared to sacrifice himself in the young prince's defence, his nationality was enough to ensure his death. He woke from a troubled doze with this thought in his head, to find Osram stooping above him.

'Are you awake, my lord? They've found Sandos.'

'What?' It was so apposite it took him a moment to process the words. He flung the blanket back. 'Time is it?'

'Dawn. The mute boy went out last night and stumbled across him. They've brought him in. He's in a bad way.'

'He lives? Goddess be praised.' Marric gained his feet and thrust his hair back. 'Take me to him.'

They had brought the injured man to Leris's tent. Sonj met them at the door, her expression grave. 'He dies,' she said. 'Ulfa is with him.'

Marric, pushing past her, wondered if by that she meant that Sandos was dying, or already dead. A lamp threw a small glow over the scene, leaving the corners in shadow and painting harsh lines across the injured man's face. Blood stained his lips and his breathing was wet and heavy. Marric recognised a lung shot even before he saw the stub of the broken off arrow in the right side of his chest. He was conscious barely, his glazed eyes flickering away from the shaman towards the newcomer. A heavily stained bandage bound his right arm, and another covered a leaking scalp wound. His face was grey beneath the tan, pain and loss of blood having taken their toll. But he recognised Marric.

'My fault,' he slurred. 'Failed. Couldn't stop... save...' The words were a husky whisper interrupted by a wet cough and more blood.

'Be at ease,' Marric crouched to press his hand. 'There is no blame. How many men?'

'Five. Headed... south from — from...' He coughed again bringing up a scarlet spatter of blood, shocking in the warm lamp light.

'From where you were found?' Marric asked and received a confirming whisper. 'We'll get him back, don't worry. You have done well, Sandos.' He saw death's approach in the Appellan's face and heard the gentle sigh of the man's last breath. 'Go in peace, my friend.' He leaned back and whispered a prayer to the Mother then folded the dead hands together. 'Thank you,' he said to the old woman hunched across from him. 'He was a good servant to my line.'

He doubted she'd understood his words but she bowed her head and dropped a pinch of leaves into the little clay pot of coals he now noticed beside her. An aromatic smoke arose which, using a handful of plaited grass as a fan, she wafted across the corpse. Sonj who had stood silent throughout the exchange, touched his shoulder and he stood. 'Come,' she said, and led him out.

Osram was waiting. Marric shook his head. 'He's gone. Lung shot. The Mother only knows how he lasted this long.'

'Did he say anything. Where —?'

'Five men, not four. Heading south from where he was found. And how was that?' he asked, turning to Sonj. 'What was Bryn doing out there anyway?'

She shrugged. 'Ulfa will have sent him. He is — how you say, her learner?'

'Her apprentice? The one she teaches?'

'Ah, yes. They share,' she touched her brow, 'you know. She says also you have this, yes?'

So they shared visions, or the old woman was somehow able to send messages to the boy. Of course it was how he had been able to find the two of them in Ansham. This was power indeed! And it made sense, that given Ulfa's age she would have a pupil. As he had been

Arn's. Ignoring Sonj's question he said, 'Then if someone can guide us to the spot where he was found? It would be best to catch them before they reach the king's holding.'

'Of course,' the young woman said curtly, as if the question had affronted her. The light had grown enough for the birds to wake and the first of the big black creatures planed down to strut about their feet. Her lip curled disdainfully. 'Will the Crow warriors be guides enough for you?'

23

They started with no more delay than to snatch a hurried meal, eaten standing, the reins in their hands. Marric, remembering Leris's words had warned Ramie of a possible attack on the encampment, but the Trader still insisted on accompanying the rescue party.

'I'll come. And Nebo. Ex-army so he knows his way round a weapon. But would the Appellans really come this far into the Grass?' The trader's short beard was grizzled, his hair greying, but a life on the road had kept him fit.

'If the whole thing has been planned, yes. I'm told that King Hardfar wants rid of the Crows and, it seems, a couple of the other border clans. What better way than to make an ally of their old enemy? Which also gives him a bulwark against our own alliance. Just suppose the two were to unite, wipe us out and immediately march on Ansham. Don't forget its position, surrounded as it is by Appellan land. They could fall upon it before Darien even knew we were dead, and long before the Baratans could join him to oppose them. And I for one couldn't vouch that the Meddii would join us. They were always lukewarm on the subject of mutual defence.'

Ramie pulled a hand over his beard. 'And you learned this how?'

'It's mainly conjecture,' Marric admitted. 'But there has to be a reason for the various attacks on the caravans, on Slate, on our own king and his son. We know that Appella was behind them, muddying the waters, trying to set us against each other. We know they're building their army. It makes sense that if their intention was to divide our alliance they have something sneaky in mind. So who would ever imagine them allying themselves to their traditional enemy?'

'You, obviously.' Ramie frowned. 'I can see the benefit for Morrik but what does Hardfar gain by it? An end to ceaseless warfare — well, isn't that why we're here — to make peace?'

'It's a different sort of peace he's after. The truth is the Grass has fought for so long the border clans are running short of warriors. They have been losing them for tens of years. Burran told me for instance, that both Leris's sons, her parents and siblings, all save Sonj, have fallen in the constant fighting with Appella. Multiply that more or less by all clan members and you see why their case is growing desperate. The loss falls heaviest on those nearest the border while the clans to the east, like Hardfar's own, are scarcely affected.'

Marric wiped the crumbs from his mouth and gathered the reins on his mount's neck, saying hurriedly as Ramie followed suit, 'So the king sees it as his opportunity to grab greater power not just for himself, but for his sex. Women have a much greater say here in community affairs than even we are accustomed to. The Grass is basically a matriarchal society. Well, Hardfar would change that, and what better way than by becoming a political ally of Appella where women know their place and keep it?' He mounted, reining about to face Leris who had ridden up with a short train of warriors behind her, Bryn, and Sonj with Burran beside her, among them.

'Your men are ready, Prince?' she asked curtly.

'Yes.' He glanced around at them: Nebo, Ramie, Osram and Leu. It wasn't a great force but the caravan needed protecting too and the smaller merchants attached to it would be useless in any sort of battle.

'Then let us go.' She nodded to Bryn and the boy set off through the featureless grass at a swinging trot. The rest fell in behind, followed a moment later by a long string of crows winging darkly overhead. Marric saw Osram's head lift and his mouth tighten but the big man made no comment simply letting his free hand drift down to touch the hilt of his blade.

With unerring accuracy the mute boy led his party to the area of flattened and blood-spattered grass where Sandos's body had been found. Osram, the most experienced of the Rhutan party, dismounted to crouch and study the ground before walking a large circle to cut for sign, stooping and stopping every now and then while the rest waited on him.

'Well?' The bite in his tone revealed how Marric champed at the delay.

'I make it five all right. One of 'em was here, waiting. Probably got that arrow into Sandos afore he knew anything was wrong. Didn't keep him down though or he wouldn't have got the other wounds. They overpowered the prince, then rode off with him. Yon dumb boy couldn't have seen the extra tracks in the dark. Point is, if nobody's missing where did the single ambusher come from?'

'From Glam.' Leris hissed the words. 'I will cut out that traitor's tongue when I find him.' Sonj said something to her, a quick rattle of Pampasan and Marric saw Burran wince.

'What was that?'

The other coughed. 'She said the tongue wasn't enough. They should go lower.'

'I don't disagree. Where now?' But Bryn was already leading off, eyes on the ground, running ahead of his horse. When he was sure of the direction he slowed a little and with astonishing agility leapt lightly into the saddle when the animal's longer stride brought it abreast of him. He glanced back at Leris, pointed ahead and the party settled into a faster pace.

They rode all morning alternating their horses' paces between walk, trot and canter, the clansmen frequently leaping off to run beside their mounts for a while before regaining the saddle in one lithe movement. They were superb horsemen, and women, Marric amended, watching Sonj repeat the manoeuvre. For himself he stayed on his mount, fretting at the need to conserve the animal's energy when he wished only to push it to a reckless gallop.

Around noon they slowed to a walk again and ate in the saddle, the crows that had earlier on vanished into the blue distance reappearing like magic above them. Bryn tossed up a crust which the leading bird snatched from the air, then he reined beside his foster mother and began an urgent dialogue with his hands. Leris turned to Marric answering his raised brows with a dismal look.

'He says they have too much of a lead. We will not catch them before they reach the city.'

Marric nodded. It must be the birds — Ulfa's eyes in the sky. Despite himself he felt a little frisson of disquiet at the oddity of the old woman's power. But it did explain the crows' sudden return. He said, 'Then we follow. Though for the life of me,' he said, having had all night to ponder the matter, 'I cannot see what Hardfar hopes to gain by taking the boy.'

'I have told you. Did you not listen?' Sonj asked irritably. 'It is to bring us to battle with him.'

'But the flaw to that argument is that it will also bring the wrath of three armies down upon him. Does he wish to fight the whole world? Either he is a fool or —'

'Or what?' Osram asked when he paused frowning.

'Or there is something I am not seeing. They are an insular people,' Marric murmured, 'but surely they are aware of our strength? And he already has Appella to deal with. It doesn't make sense.'

'Worry about it when we've got the boy back,' Osram said. 'That is, Light save him, if he's not already dead.'

'I can see even less sense in that,' Marric said. 'Unless somebody slipped up and his body is somewhere back behind us, and we are simply chasing his killers.'

They lost the tracks when they came to the road, itself not much more than rutted wheel tracks through the grass. Roads were few in Pampasa, those that existed formed by the simple means of vehicles repeatedly travelling the shortest distances between points until their passage inhibited growth. Earlier they had found the ash of a small fire where Sandos's killers had paused to refresh themselves and their mounts. The hour was late by then, the sun slipping away, and the birds had again deserted them. Seeking a roosting place, Marric guessed. He turned to Leris.

'How much further to the city?'

She sighed, stretching her back. 'Too far. They will be there by now for they had a full night's start on us. It is pointless to continue on, Prince, if we are not to arrive on exhausted mounts. The horses need rest.'

'And water,' he agreed. Their own waterskins were dry as well.

She turned her mount, 'Then we must follow the horse pads to a spring. This way.'

Marric looked at Burran who was nodding. 'The Grass has many spring mounds, sir. They bob up everywhere and are easy enough to find, you just follow the pads. The springs are why the herds are so widespread. As far as I know there are only a handful of rivers in the whole country so the springs are vital to the free movement of the clans.'

Leris led them along the narrow trodden paths through the grass, thick with the hoof tracks of wild horses, arriving just as the sun vanished. Marric saw a great shallow basin as if the earth had been mounded up to contain the sheet of water it held. Bubbles in the centre showed the influx from the spring beneath as the horses drank deeply then lifted dripping muzzles to blow gustily and shake weary bodies before moving off and dropping their heads to graze.

The place was well used by wildlife. They built a dung fire from the dried droppings and ate a frugal meal then lay down, booted and spurred, among the saddles to take their rest. Marric's body was weary but his brain wouldn't rest. He heard a low exchange between Osram and his son, Leu still berating himself for Tarris's predicament, then his father's assurance that his son's presence would have accomplished no more than his probable death.

'Still I should have been with him. He is my friend,' Leu insisted.

'And you are more use to him now than if you were dead. Get your rest,' Osram replied. 'We'll be riding again soon enough.'

The clansmen had already settled themselves. Somewhere an owl called and Marric wondered where, in this treeless country, they spent their days. The moon had not yet risen and the stars were very bright. He thought of the young prince they were seeking to rescue, the promise he had latterly begun to show, and of his parents' heartbreak if he perished. It would mean war again and a loss of the steady gains Darien had been making in righting Rhuta's ruined economy. And once the two nations were militarily engaged would Morrik lose the opportunity to launch an attack against Ansham, the loss of which, Marric guessed, rankled most with Appella. He doubted it. So Rhuta would end up fighting on two fronts, never mind the loss of a major trading partner, for despite their mutual history Appella was once again that. Disaster loomed every way he looked...

He took a pull at his imagination. It wouldn't, it mustn't come to that. They would recover Tarris, the clans would mete out their own justice to the transgressors and he and the Crows could get back to diplomacy and trade, and let the shadow of war fade into the might-have-been. It needn't be the disaster he feared... His eyes closed and when the owl called again, its wings a soft hush as it flew by in the darkness, he was lost to sleep.

By sunrise they were back on the road, both men and horses refreshed by the rest they had taken. Marric straightened to ease the kink in his back for it had been years since he'd slept with no more than a cloak to shield him from the bare ground, and pondered their approach once the city was reached. There were no walls, Burran had told him, so getting in wasn't a problem. Resistance would come, he guessed, the moment they were recognised. He ducked with the thought as a cloud of blackness swept towards and over him in a cacophony of sound. The birds were back. They wheeled above the cavalcade, their leader swooping down to land on Bryn's shoulder. He saw the boy put up his hand to stroke the shiny feathers before the crow lifted off again to rejoin the flock and resume a slow wingbeat overhead.

Leris reined alongside him, head angled to watch the show above them. 'Well, Prince you have ideas, yes? For when we come to arrive.'

Diplomatically he deferred to her. 'What do you suggest? A night approach?'

'It would be wise. Hardfar can call on many warriors. We should seek to take him from the city. Maybe we have to kill some of his men for this, but we do it quietly, yes?'

'But someone must survive to tell us where the boy is being kept. We cannot search the whole city for him.'

She flicked a dismissive hand. 'Hardfar will tell us.'

'Can you be sure of that? He's not going to come quietly.'

'He will come. Dead or alive,' she added, granite faced.

'No.' He reined in so suddenly that Osram's mount was forced to jerk up its head to avoid bumping into his horse's rump. 'Settling scores comes later. The whole accord between our countries will fall through if the prince is harmed. We must secure him and to do that we need the king, or somebody, capable of talking.'

Colour flooded Leris's face, she drew in a deep breath and he saw the fury flare in her dark eyes before she mastered it. Those around her stiffened and Marric sat very still exuding what calm he could. He said as gently as he could. 'He is my nephew, the heir to the throne of my country, and dear to his father's heart.'

'As Rost is my kinsman,' she grated. 'He has betrayed his blood, and his clan, and dead at my feet he will be for what he has done.'

'Then don't let his transgressions include the peace that could lie between our lands,' Marric urged. 'Let me secure the prince before you act.'

She let her breath go on a sigh and nodded grudgingly. 'Very well then. We will wait. But not for long, Prince.'

'And after?' he asked, hiding his relief. 'We'll have to fight our way out. Would taking Hardfar hostage smooth our passage?'

She shrugged. 'What good are the plans? You have fought before, Prince? Then you know how it never works like you think.'

'Dead right.' Osram nodded at her as to another veteran. 'It's a sort of law. Plans go to shit the moment you engage.'

Leris had been right in the estimation she had given the previous day. They rode till mid-afternoon and then the outskirts of the city — a ragged, desultory sprawl of buildings along a gentle swale with a greater mass behind them — appeared. There was a river whose banks they sought to the south of the place and here, within what shelter the trees offered, they lay up until dark. Marric spent the time watching what he could see, which was little enough. Only one barge passed down the river, and they were too far from the buildings to make out anything much but the smoke of numerous chimneys.

He found the lack of walls as strange as he had in Barat. It made the city appear unfinished, but it was also a strong hint that no foe had ever penetrated this far into the Grass, and he hoped that would result in a corresponding slackness in the guards. For there must be guards or wardens of some sort, he supposed. When asked however Leris shook her head.

'At the king's hall, there will be guards, for his,' she sought for a word, 'importance, yes?'

'His consequence?' Marric suggested. 'Then who keeps order in the streets and guards against thieves?'

'Oh, there are watchmen but they are nothing. Not warriors. They will not interfere with fighting men.'

Perhaps not, but still to attack the king's own hall would be like poking a nest of ants, unless city living had loosened the clan cohesion that was so evident in the border dwelling tribes. Marric shared his misgiving with Osram though he couldn't let the consideration of consequences stop him. The fighting would come now or later, for war was inevitable unless they managed to retrieve Tarris.

'Knife work,' the big man grunted. 'Me and Nebo should go in, account for the sentries if he has 'em. How big's the joint? If we can get in quiet like maybe we can handle it without an outcry and be away again with the young feller before the alarm's raised. Ideally. What're we talking? A dozen hangers on? That not too many for our crew.'

Leris, when applied to for numbers shrugged, but she did agree to let the two Appellans take care of the sentries. 'If we get that far without bringing the whole boiling of 'em down on us,' Osram observed gloomily.

They ate a frugal meal from their supplies while they waited for full dark, and then moving closer to the city, waited again for its people to douse their lights and find their beds. Finally when all was still and silent save for the occasional bark of a dog they left Bryn in charge of the horses and followed Leris silently through the streets, weapons ready in their hands.

It was absurdly easy. Nobody challenged them, here and there a dim glow behind a fretworked window showed a night light and once they heard the distressed sobbing of a child. A dog snarled at them from an alley but fled with a yelp from a low curse and accurately thrown stone. There was no sign of the Watch.

'This is bloody unreal,' Osram breathed. 'You sure they aren't all dead?'

Leris snorted briefly. 'For why should they fear?' she asked bitterly. 'It is we on the border who sleep light with our blades always ready.'

They pushed on over a small cobbled bridge, wincing as a man's sword swung wide with a clatter against the stone abutment, and then the large, dark shape of the hall was before them. A dim glow came from a guttering torch in the wide courtyard, its light showing the broad, double doors of timber closed now against the night. The party halted while Osram and Nebo, exchanging their swords for daggers, melted into the shadows. Marric strained his eyes but failed to pick out the sentries' forms. Perhaps there weren't any — or they were only daylight additions meant, as Leris had said, to enhance the king's position.

They waited for what seemed an age during which doubt suddenly shook Marric. Why had they assumed that Hardfar would sleep here in his hall? He could have a house elsewhere in the city. But no, somebody must be here, he told himself, or why the burning cresset, guttering though it was? Before he could question Leris, the shadow that was Osram was back at his side.

'Two,' he said economically. 'Both dead. Deserved it too. Bastards were sleeping on the job. The doors have a bar on the outside. You can hear snoring.'

'Good,' Leris said. She spoke low, rapid words in her own tongue and her clansmen nodded. Burran translated for the Rhutan party.

'She's saying that Rost is hers to kill. And that we must keep one of theirs alive. Also the king who will face Epona's justice.'

Osram nodded and looked at Leu. 'Stick with me and the prince. Guard his back.' Leu nodded tensely and swallowed. Osram gave him a gentle buffet on the shoulder. 'You'll be fine, son. Blade up, and here we go.'

Before entering Leris bade Sonj recharge the cresset so when the doors opened the fresh flame threw light over the murky gloom within. Starlight showed through the high windows shadowing the spaces where the men slept. The light dispelled this and also woke the closest face it fell upon. The man's eyes opened and city dweller or not it took only seconds for him to register the intruders and roll to his feet, roaring a warning as his blade flashed up. He died on the instant, Sonj's arrow taking him through the throat. Then quarters were too close and the fighting figures too confused for further bow work.

Marric, pushed forward by the rush of bodies about him, tried to estimate the number of those they faced but the fitful light made it impossible. He was aware that one of the Crows, an older man called Yerb, was guarding the door, then finding himself suddenly engaged by a man that thrust at him, his face a silent snarl and his movements frighteningly quick, was forced to concentrate, abandoning the search he'd been making for Tarris. It was not likely the boy was here in the hall anyway. He swung and missed, jabbed back on the return and felt his blade engage with his opponent's arm, then Osram turned and ran the tribesman through before they could do each other further damage. It had been very close, Marric had felt the tip of the man's sword sheer through his tunic, without touching his skin.

Beside him Leu shouted suddenly and lunged, stopping the blade of one who had aimed at Marric's back. He spun, sword angled low and took his opponent behind the knee, severing something vital for he fell with a shriek. Leu was panting and raised a bloody hand to his mouth. Marric, said, 'You all right?' and the boy nodded. A man screamed in the melee and in one of those moments where the world seemed to freeze he saw Leris swing the flat of her blade hard at the back of a man's head. He went down as if pole-axed and Ramie, who had been desperately defending himself against his roaring charge, skipped nimbly aside from his fall.

He was the last opponent. A Crow pulled a cresset from the wall and lit it from the burning one. From his post Yerb swung the doors closed then found the inner bar with which to secure them, while Leris, taking the cresset walked from corpse to corpse, then shook her head in frustration.

'Tie him,' she snapped indicating the man she had felled. 'He is not here, damn him.'

She spoke of Rost. Burran made his own inspection and said, 'None of them are. They must already have started back.'

'Idiot!' Leris rounded on him, furious. 'For why will they return, Scribe? To be killed? Either they have not yet come or —'

Marric's heart sank. 'Or they were never headed here in the first place.'

'They were,' the woman said positively. 'And now we find out where they have gone. Bring the live one here.'

This turned out to be the man whose hamstring Marric had cut. He was in a bad way for his wound had bled extensively. They tied a rough tourniquet about his thigh but he was already so weak that Yerb's effort with his fist had him quickly unconscious. He was revived again, and Yerb pulled out a knife but Leris shook her head snapping an impatient command.

'She's afraid more blood letting will kill him,' Burran murmured. The wounded man had grasped the fact as well and refused to speak.

'Kill him,' Leris said and before Marric could shout a rebuttal, Yerb leaned forward and plunged the blade into the man's throat.

'What have you done?' Marric cried. 'We had an agreement!'

'And I will keep it.' The errol's eyes were flat and hard. 'Here we cannot stay, Prince. The night grows towards the morning and we must be away before others come. Or we leave not at all. Bring him,' she said of the bound man and three clansmen seized the now stirring figure. The cressets were doused, the door opened and the whole party left. The bodies of the dead sentries were pulled into the hall, the door barred again from the outside and Leris led them back through the streets, having first taken the precaution of gagging her captive.

They made it back through the streets without meeting a soul and then downriver to the waiting horses. Bryn had heard their approach and met them, his hands full of reins. Silently they mounted, the boy going up behind Leris so that the bound captive could be tied to the saddle of Bryn's mount.

'Where are we going?' Marric asked, reluctant to leave before he had an answer to Tarris's fate.

'Away.' Leris snapped. She said something in her own tongue and he looked to Burran.

'She thinks we have a few hours, if nobody enters the hall. And that will be time enough to learn what we need. She is very angry to have missed Rost and the others, but maybe Hardfar can also tell her where they are,' he said.

Marric's eyes widened. 'The prisoner is the king?'

'Yes, my lord. I recognise him from when they brought me here.' He grimaced. 'He was going to have me torn apart by horses. You don't forget something like that. Or the man who would order it.'

Marric scarcely heard him. 'Won't that make it worse — stealing their king? The whole city will be after us, man.'

Burran shook his head. 'No. See, here a man leads until he's beaten. Errol or king it makes no difference. Sooner or later somebody will enter the hall and realise from the dead that Hardfar's been bested. So they'll choose another to follow. It's not to say they won't come after us — because we did attack them. But it won't be because of the king, so really who he was makes no difference in that sense. He has lost whatever clout that, as their leader, he once held.'

'I see.' Dawn was almost upon them. Already the trees stood out in silhouette against a lightening sky and he could glimpse the shape of his mount's head. A rustling above the treetops and a lone caw showed that their faithful shadows, the crows, were also abroad. There had been no chance yet in the rush of movement to enquire about possible injuries so he asked Burran now.

'Our lot are fine. Dodj has a slashed arm but it's nothing.'

'We got off lightly then.' They had come to a little opening, a grassy glade amid the trees and here Leris, who was leading, reined in. The light had strengthened steadily, the former grey behind the timber now touched with gold. Marric could make out the faces of their companions, see the weariness beneath tense expressions, as the closest rider reached down and grabbed Hardfar's boot. He yanked it high and the bound man gave a startled cry and fell from the saddle. Glaring, he sought to struggle to his feet, his hot gaze travelling about the faces of the riders now encircling him.

'Stay down.' Leris commanded and the crows that had flocked to the branches of the trees about them, set up a derisive chorus. Their leader flew to Bryn's shoulder to stroke its wicked beak against the boy's soft cheek.

'What is this, woman?' Hardfar blustered, but he obeyed, and remained on his knees.

'Epona's justice. You were warned. Ulfa herself came a great distance, with the pain of age upon her old bones to warn you, Hardfar. But did you listen? Did you fear our Mother's rule? Always, you think the male must know better. Well, I give you one chance, before Her justice is served. Where is the Rhutan prince, and the treasonous dogs from my own clan for whom also justice awaits?'

Marric, watching closely saw Hardfar swallow at something he glimpsed in the woman's face. Then courage, or recklessness stiffened his spine and lifted his head in defiance. He knew his death was certain. The implacable ring of warriors fencing him around must have shown him that. 'Gone,' he cried triumphantly. 'They will be aboard ship by now with their Appellan friends. He will make a fine hostage, the boy, to hobble the Outlander bastards when Morrik takes Ansham. Oh, and don't worry about trying to warn them. You'll have your hands full anyway with a little surprise that has been organised for you. I wish you joy of the discovery. The last raid you might say, for you and those other blind fools that follow your spavined old Mare who'll be out to pasture and forgotten before the blood cools in your body.'

Leris, who had paled during his outburst, gave a scream of rage that was echoed by Sonj but before either could draw a weapon the birds rose in a raucous flock and in a blur of shimmering feathers and avid beaks flung themselves at the deposed king. Hampered by his bound hands and instinctive effort to gain his feet, he hadn't a chance. They smothered his head, pecking, gouging, beaks reddening, claws tearing at skin, their bodies smothering the man's shrieks. When finally they whirled away to settle again in the trees Marric stared in horror at the ruined, eyeless face.

Hardfar, rocking on his knees was making a strange keening sound, his bound hands fumbling over his bloodied face where a pinkish, watery trickle bled from his empty sockets. Behind him Marric could hear somebody, Leu, he thought, retching. Leris dismounted as a lone bird with a bloodied beak circled down again to Bryn's shoulder. The boy, face unmoved, put up his hand to smooth its feathers.

The errol drew both sword and dagger, holding them by their blades. She said, 'You were warned but in your male pride you wished to be blind and deaf to Epona's greatness. So be it. Justice is served.' Standing behind him as he snarled and turned his head towards her voice, she raised the hilts of both weapons and smashed them against his ears. Hardfar gave a roar of rage that dwindled to nothing. He moved his head from side to side in a questing manner and Marric realised that the blow had rendered him deaf.

'Bring him,' Leris commanded remounting, and a couple of clansmen dismounted to haul the sightless man back onto his mount. Osram, looking as stunned as the rest of his group swore foully.

'What now, sir? If the Appellans have him on a ship then we are too late.'

'They may not have sailed yet. We can't be too far behind them.' Marric cast a haggard look at the newborn sun. 'A day perhaps? Surely they will have rested overnight in the city. How far to the coast?' he demanded as Leris turned her mount in beside him.

'Too far,' she said crisply. 'You will not catch them now. Your young man has gone, Prince. And we must return.'

'No! We must follow, even to the shore if they are there. While there is a chance I'll not abandon him.'

'Then I am too sorry but you will ride alone. You heard him speak of the surprise. It can mean only an attack on the clan from the city. I must go. First I will put you on the way and then we leave.'

And from this decision she would not be moved.

24

They crossed the river in the early light, tugging the captive's horse along with them, and thundered through the timber in an easterly direction until the country leveled out again into another endless vista of grass. There was a track of sorts. They followed it at a canter for a little while hoping that the hoofprints before them were made by the men they wanted, but there was no way to be certain. The land seemed deserted. Marric supposed that farming pursuits must be carried out closer to the centre of population for there didn't seem to be a soul other than themselves in the whole landscape. He was just beginning to hope that Leris had rethought her decision to leave them when she raised her hand and her troop pulled to a halt around her.

'Is far enough,' she said and pointed ahead. 'Keep on, Prince. The road will take you to the coast. But the ship will be gone. And now we return. May Epona give you the speed but I fear much you are too late.' She nodded to the man riding beside the mewling king and as before he stooped swiftly and heaved. Hardfar shouted in shock and bewilderment as he hit the ground, then the troop wheeled their mounts and rode off, back the way they had come. Sonj accompanied them. Burran, looking torn, stayed at Marric's side.

'They're leaving him to die?' Leu sounded shocked.

'And doesn't the bastard deserve it?' his father

demanded. 'Come on, we're wasting daylight. Any idea how far it is, Marric?'

'None.' Marric nudged his horse into movement and the frenzied shouting behind them was lost in the renewed thunder of hooves. Only Leu seemed bothered by Hardfar's fate. Burran however swiftly put him right.

'He brought it on himself. And you're likely to go the same way lad, if you interfere with clan justice. These people play for keeps.'

'He's right,' Osram agreed. 'And every moment wasted is one taking the prince further from us.'

The day passed to the beat of hooves and the swish of grass ploughed underfoot by the horses' legs. If they caught the party before it reached the ship, and managed to get Tarris back, Marric reasoned, the deal the king had made with whoever was acting for Morrik would be forgotten. Without a hostage they had no leverage against the three allied countries. If, on the other hand they missed the ship... Uselessly he wished that he had some way to warn Darien, but a rider, even killing his mounts, would still need the better part of a moon of days to reach Ripa from the middle of the Grass, and that if he was not hunted down first by either clansmen or Appellan. And it would take more time for Barat and Rhuta to muster their armies and cross into the Upper Land. If on the other hand the prince, by accident or design, was killed, then time had no relevance. There would be war. Darien would not stop until Appella was a charnel house if it took ten years to make it so.

The snake's strike and the ambush came together, the one foiling the other as neatly as an act from the Goddess's hand. The creature was coiled in the grass and rose in a spring the length of its own body to sink its fangs into the leather of Burran's boot. His mount reared with a mighty snort and fell again as the arrow took it cleanly through the chest. Burran fell with it, catching from the corner of his eye a glimpse of Osram charging the section of grass from which the ambush had come, only for the big man to have his mount shot from beneath him. So instantaneous was its fall that the arrow must have found the animal's heart. With no time to act his rider went down with his horse, the impact knocking him unconscious.

Struggling groggily erect, half his mind on the snake's whereabouts, Burran grabbed futilely for his sword only to find himself menaced by a familiar figure aiming an arrow at his chest.

'Rost!' the name was a curse.

The man grinned mockingly at him. 'You'd do well not to annoy me Scribe, or I could put an end to you right now. Lift your blade out and drop it. Now.'

Burran swore but did as he was bidden having instantly seen that resistance went beyond futile into madness. Osram was flat on the ground. Nebo, with an arrow in his throat, was surely dead. Ramie and Leu had been similarly unhorsed. Marric, standing beside the latter with a sheltering hand on the boy's shoulder said stiffly, 'Do as he says.' The ambush had been perfectly executed for he saw they were ringed around by six clansmen — the four Crows, and two strangers, who must be Hardfar's men. And with them two taller, fair headed men, Appellans.

Marric said calmly, 'We are not resisting, but I need to see to my man.'

'Get him up then, we'll be moving,' Rost answered and as Marric moved to squat beside his fallen bodyguard, added to Bark. 'Fetch the boy.'

Osram was groaning his way back to awareness. Marric helped him sit and Leu held him swaying in position.

'May Asher send the Black Apes to a lake of fire,' he moaned. 'My head!' But Marric made no reply. His gaze had followed the man called Bark, who had vanished into the grass. Presently two horses staggered erect from their ties and then a bound and gagged figure was thrust out of concealment to join them.

'Tarris!' the breath went out of him in relief. 'Thank the Lady for that.'

Rost overheard him and grinned again. 'Looking for him, were you? We thought we'd wait and add to the bag. Two princes for the price of one. I reckon our friends are getting a bargain.'

Leaving the recovering Osram Marric went to his nephew and wrestled the gag off while Tarris squirmed in his bonds. 'Are you hurt?' he asked tackling the tightly knotted grass ropes. The boy was dishevelled and there was caked blood in the hair above his right ear but the glare he turned on his captors had more of hate than fury in it.

'They killed Sandos.' His voice cracked on the name. 'Bastards! Shot him down like a dog from ambush.'

'I know, lad. I was with him with him when he died.' He chafed Tarris's swollen hands. 'You're not injured then?'

'No.' He looked aside, ashamed. 'He fell and they knocked me out before I could get my blade free. I would've defended him. I —'

'I know.' There was no time for more. Osram was on his feet, shakily so but standing, and the rest of their captors' horses had appeared out of the grass.

Ramie and Burran having checked the body of Nebo stood glowering as a clansman methodically searched them for concealed weapons, getting a knife from Ramie's boot and both their belt daggers. Marric, who hoping to keep his had thrust it into an inner pocket of his trousers, also had it taken. Their hands were tied then a long rope of twisted grass was threaded from one man to the next and the end of it tied to the saddle Rost occupied. Only Marric's horse still lived and him they unsaddled and turned loose, having first looted the bags of anything useful.

Osram, eyes slitted with pain from his pounding head, said, 'Where're you taking us?'

'You'll work it out, sunshine,' one of the Appellans smirked. He looked him up and down. 'Army deserter, eh? I'll warrant the general'll be pleased to see you.' Then Rost swung into the saddle, the rope jerked, and Burran at the head of their little column was yanked forward, towing the line of his companions along behind.

It was dusk when they reached the coast. The beach was a desolate looking spot with low wind-twisted scrub growing along the dunes that fronted a rocky shore. Strange, lumbering creatures that Marric alone recognised as seals humped away from the party to slide into the darkening sea, and a group of seamen taking their ease about a fire kindled near a boat drawn clear of the water rose with shouts and waves of greeting at their approach.

'Beginning to think you was lost,' their burly, grizzled-haired leader said. 'Tide's on the turn. Let's be moving afore we have to carry the bloody boat to the water.'

The boat, Marric saw, would not hold them all. The older Appellan realised it too. He said, 'Take the prisoners, then return for us.' He looked at the clansmen, 'You'll be heading back?'

'Yes,' Rost agreed. 'I've a hankering to see the errol's face when we join your lot and she realises it's over. There's an old woman needs gutting and a young one,' he smirked at Burran, 'who'll find out what she's been missing when a proper man beds her.'

'You vile, double-crossing dog!' Burran, forgetting the rope, made a leap at him that ended with his face slamming into the rocks. Ramie stumbled behind him, and only Osram's weight prevented his fall. 'You won't get away with it. Hardfar's dead — or as good as. The birds have had his eyes!' Burran raved as he was summarily hauled to his feet and thrust into the boat the men had shoved down the shingle. Its keel was already afloat as he was tumbled into it.

'Is that so?' The Appellan said.

Afterwards Marric realised that they must have discussed the matter beforehand for no word passed between the shore party, only that single look. But he was too annoyed at Burran for giving away what might have been used to their advantage to pay attention. He hissed, 'Shut it, you fool!' then jerked about at the sounds of conflict.

The Appellans had drawn their weapons and fallen upon the clansmen. Taken totally unawares two of them were cut down in moments. Rost and Bark being furthest from the boat had more chance and used it to put space between themselves and their attackers. Then the closest seaman tripped Marric deftly into the boat. With his hands tied he was unable to break his fall and by the time he clawed himself up the fight had moved behind the bushes screening the dunes, but there could be little doubt of its outcome.

Leu, falling over his father's legs, was the last prisoner aboard, by which time their abductors had returned, the leading Appellan thrusting his blade home as he came. One of the seamen was bleeding from a deep gash in his arm. He held it, swearing, and delivered a vengeful kick to the body of the nearest clansmen.

'Get that tied up,' the senior Appellan wiped his blade on a dead man's tunic and sheathed it. He glanced at the waiting horses. 'Pull the gear off 'em. We'll take that. Not that anyone's likely to come looking but if they did they'll just think they boarded with us.'

'And the bodies?' His companion asked.

'Second load for the boat. Dump them over the side.' He stroked his jaw and considered. 'Better this way. With Hardfar dead and this lot accounted for there's nobody to say different when the savages get the blame, once that pup in Ripa gets round to discovering that, oh, dear, he's lost a couple of the family. It'll keep him occupied until we've finished with Ansham.'

His words sent a thrill of horror through Marric. Faced with a threat from Appella, the last thing that Darien would consider would be that Morric had made an alliance with the Grass. Why would he? The hostility between them predated the reign of his grandfather's grandfather's time by who knew how many generations? Long before the Old Race of Ansham had been more than a collection of independent villages, and before the Horse Lords who became the Appellans, had ridden out of their hills to conquer whatever their blades could take and hold, the Appellans had fought with the wild clansmen of the Grass.

Nobody in their senses would ever imagine an alliance between the two. He breathed a desperate prayer to the Lady that Leris, unaware though she was of his present plight, would think to send a warning north to Ripa. It was, he told himself, unlikely to happen. Extremely unlikely. Compared to what Appella could raise she had a mere handful of fighters to spend against them and was unlikely to spare even one to carry a message or even to plead for help that could not possibly arrive in time. And that without the complication of hostages for Darien to reckon with.

Neither Marric nor Burran saw the disposal of the bodies of their enemies for they had been secured in the bowels of the ship before this occurred. Roped together and with their hands still bound they had made the difficult climb up the ship's side to the deck from where, turning to stare back at the shore, Marric had seen the freed horses vanishing behind the low scrub. They would join up with the wild herd he supposed, and at the opposite end of the country to them, the Crows would never see them again.

A heavyset sailor carrying a wooden club shoved them across the deck and they were herded below into darkness. It was a crowded space filled with loading of some sort, lacking light and with the sound of water slopping about below the boards. Asked where they were bound their guide lifted his club in a threatening manner and growled, 'Shut it.' Then he vanished through the hatch they'd entered by and they heard the thud of a hammer against metal as it was secured behind him.

In the dimness they settled themselves as best they could, then everybody spoke at once. Leu's, 'What happened?' cutting across Tarris's, 'How did you find me, Uncle?' and Ramie's resigned, 'So much for trading in the Grass.'

'Quiet,' Marric said, 'and keep your voices down. Information first. Tarris, any idea where they're taking us? Did they speak of it at all?'

'No — just to the general wherever he is. But Uncle, the clansmen have made an alliance with the Appellans! That man Rost couldn't stop talking about it. They've planned a combined attack, them and the Appellans, on the Crows and their neighbours, to wipe them out before they join forces with the Appellan army.'

'Leris guessed as much. And General Morrik means to take Ansham back. He thinks that holding you — holding us,' he amended, 'will stop your father from intervening.' He grimaced. 'We have made it worse by getting ourselves captured as well. When it was only you he held it was all a matter of bluff because he could only threaten your death. But now he can afford to kill any of us should Darien try to call his bluff by honouring his oath to Ansham. And he will still have you.'

Tarris bit his lip. 'I am sorry,' he said wretchedly. 'And all because I wanted to hunt! If I hadn't gone with them this would never have happened. And Sandos would still be alive.' Then remembering he looked up with sudden hope. 'But you — Uncle, you can get word to him, can't you?'

'No,' Marric said baldly. 'I am no magic worker whatever you may have heard. Anything we can do to save ourselves must be done as ordinary men.'

'How?' Osram demanded practically. 'Does anyone here have any knowledge of ships?'

Ramie, Burran and the two boys answered in the negative. 'I've travelled on one,' Marric admitted distractedly for something teased at his memory — a storm and a man shouting at a terrified seaman... He drew in a long breath and felt again the itch of salt spray on his streaming face, and the comforting touch of the Godess's hand. 'Yes!' Eyes alight with hope he said, 'We must wait our chance. There will be a storm — a bad one.'

Osram's eyes narrowed. 'You know this?' He asked baldly, but not how.

'Yes. That is when we will make our move. But first things first, we have to find a way to free our hands.'

Leu murmured apologetically, 'I can't reach it but I've got a knife.'

'Light love you, son!' Osram exclaimed. 'I'd forgotten. In your boot?'

'Yes. But it's behind my heel, and there's not enough slack in the rope.'

'Everyone budge up,' Marric said. 'Maybe Tarris can reach then. Or Ramie you could try pulling the boot off.'

Adjusting their position allowed Tarris's hand to graze his friend's heel. He said, 'I think I can reach.' His questing fingers brushed the top of the hilt but he struggled to get purchase. 'It's very tight,' he grunted. 'Can you lift your foot a bit?'

'Not really.' Leu's face was contorted with effort, and the muscles of his calf twitching. 'Hurry up. Aah! God's balls! Now I'm getting cramp.'

'Well it's a stupid place to carry it.' Tarris complained.

'It's not, numbskull, because I've still got it,' Leu snapped.

'Hah!' Tarris grinned suddenly, just the flash of his teeth visible in the dim light. 'You mean I have.' He drew out the small knife which he'd clamped between two fingers. It was only the length of his forefinger, but the blade looked to be razor sharp. He passed it to his uncle as Leu straightened his cramped leg with a groan of relief.

Marric glanced at Osram. 'Your idea, I suppose? I remember Rissak carried one too.'

The big man shrugged. 'Bodyguard's tools. So, we just going to sit here like trussed chickens or are you going to cut us free?'

'In a bit,' Marric said. 'We can't make a move until the storm, so let's be sure they don't intend to check on us before then.'

25

Not much sound penetrated below decks. The captives felt rather than heard when the the anchor was raised and the sails set. Soon an unpleasant swaying coupled with a repetitive rise and fall of their prison had Leu swallowing noisily and, had there been light enough to notice, turning a queasy shade of green. The others were unaffected, but the ship's movement seemed to stir the smell of the bilges wafting it upwards through the hold and it wasn't long before he vomited.

'Aargh!' Tarris wrinkled his nose in disgust, trying to inch back from the mess. 'Must you?'

'It is the sea illness. He cannot help it,' Marric reproved. 'Nobody seems to be coming so —' He slashed Leu's wrists free of the rope that held them together, and cut his hands loose before beginning on the others.

'Leave the rope whole,' Osram suggested. 'It might be useful.'

They had no weapons but once able to move about, and leaving Leu to his misery, the rest made a thorough search of the hold, coming up with nothing more lethal than a sturdy length of timber and an old baling hook, used as the name suggested to pull bales and bags of goods into place. With its curved, sharpened bill it would be a fearsome thing in an enemy's hand, Marric thought, but useless against a sword. It wasn't a promising start but if once they could gain the deck there might be loose implements they could get their hands on. Even an oar would help, if they could make it to the boats. And the storm would cloak their presence on deck.

The dimness in the hold changed to an unvarying blackness as time passed. Gradually the talk and speculation and the making of provisional plans died away and there was only Leu's wretchedness to keep them awake. They were all thirsty, but hunger wasn't an issue, the increasingly fetid odour of the hold and the sufferer's groans saw to that. The sea rocked the ship in long swells that, coupled with the stink of vomit and bilge, had them all feeling queasy. Leu finally succumbed to exhaustion and the rest of them also fell into fitful sleep, starting awake whenever an extra plunge of the ship rolled their slack bodies against some obstacle in the hold.

Marric dreamed but only of Darien in the palace at Ripa, and then of his daughter, alive and laughing in the sunlit waters of the Lakes where she had never had the strength to play. His heart lightened as he rejoiced in her happiness and he was smiling in his sleep when Osram shook him into wakefulness.

'What?' He sat up reluctantly, his mind still in the past, noticing belatedly that it was possible to see the big man's face, and also that their prison was creaking and swaying in a way it hadn't before.

'It's dawn, or a bit after. I think your storm's here.'

'Good. How's Leu?'

'Not well. But he's nothing left to spew. Best leave him lie, I think. It seems to help. What do you want us to do?'

'Nothing yet. The storm should get worse — much worse. Then we'll have to force the hatch. Maybe,' he cast a look around at the cargo, 'we could open some of the crates? There might be something in there that would serve as a ram. I'm pretty sure I heard that seaman bolt it after him.'

Osram looked dubious but after a word to Ramie and the others they set to with a will. The baling hook proved its worth both in its ability to rip open the canvas covering on bales and to prise up the corners of crates. In this manner they uncovered cotton and grain, slabs of salt beginning to ooze through its covering, bales of dried skins and barrels of some sloppy vegetable matter that Osram cautiously tasted then spat out in disgust. Ramie, tasting in his turn, brightened.

'Here's breakfast,' he said. 'It's pickled cabbage. They eat it in Meddia.'

'They can keep it then,' Osram declared, ripping open another box. 'Ah,' his pleased exclamation brought Marric to his side, hoping for weapons, 'dried apricots. Now that's more like it.'

All save Leu satisfied their hunger. Tarris chewing appreciatively said, 'But these must come from Rhuta. How did they get aboard this ship?'

Ramie said, 'Traded on, Prince. The original load could have been sold anywhere and then sold again to the next ship. Some trade stuff goes half way around the world before it stops.'

'Or,' Marric said thoughtfully, 'it could be that this is a pirated Rhutan ship. Or possibly, the cargo from one such. Did anyone see the name?'

'Swift something I think,' Osram said.

'The *Swift Jenny*?' Ramie looked round. 'If so it is one of ours. I've consigned wine on her before this. In which case there might be some aboard now.'

Wine always travelled by ship and the vintners had enjoyed several bountiful years in succession. It was enough to energise Burran. He turned his attention to the remaining barrels and gave a cry of triumph on finding the branded crest of a well-known vintner on one. They used the baling hook to pierce the bung but having no vessel with which to catch the flow made use of their hands. The pitching ship made this problematic but they managed to satisfy their thirst, then Leu was coaxed into swallowing a few mouthfuls but it only set him vomiting again.

'I want to die,' he moaned clutching his abused midriff.

'You'll be all right the instant you set foot on land,' Marric promised. 'I have seen this illness before.'

'Your pardon, my lord but there doesn't seem much likelihood of that,' Ramie said. He looked ghastly in the dim light, his hands, and the tunic where he'd wiped them, stained red with wine. 'If this storm's as bad as you predicted isn't it likely to sink us?'

'It is of the Lady's sending so that cannot be true,' Marric replied firmly. But, he thought, his vision had shown the ship in imminent danger. He wondered where they were and if the captain would seek shelter or run before the gale. He knew nothing of ships. Would the open sea be safer than seeking to close the land? He had no way of knowing, but though they were pitching about at present, the ship still sailed on a fairly even keel so matters were not yet desperate. Noisier than they had been certainly, for even in the hold they could hear the occasional faint shout and a high-pitched thrumming like insane keening, coupled with thunderous cracks of sound that must be the sails and rigging meeting the blast. The cold intensified, a sort of damp frigidity that settled slowly over them. He rubbed his arms to warm them.

'Best to keep busy,' he said, turning to the partly despoiled cargo. 'What else are they carrying?'

Amongst other goods both fragile and durable, there turned out to be a bolt of woollen cloth which they hacked into lengths to use as cloaks and rough bedding. It was impossible now to stand without clutching at a fixed point so violent had the pitching become. The rain roared down, possibly, judging by noise alone, mixed with hail that deepened the chill in the air. A tremendous boom and a shudder that travelled the length of the ship shook them all. It was time, Marric thought. If they waited too long and the ship did founder they would go to their deaths locked in the hold. Not that they were likely to fare much better on deck, but no man relishes the thought of being trapped.

Osram, being the strongest, and buttressed by Ramie and Burran to prevent him being thrown off, climbed the steps until he could wedge himself and batter at the hatch with the length of timber. When he tired they changed position with Burran on the steps and Marric helping to hold him there. They had to vary the pattern of their blows for fear of attracting attention with too regular thuds but they kept at it and eventually a vicious whack from a tiring Ramie jolted the sealed hatch open. It slammed down again at once, but not before a blast of icy rain had swept into their prison, dousing them all.

Shaking his head Marric started up the steps and was put aside by Osram who had retrieved the length of wood. He thrust the hatch cover up in one swift movement and stuck his head out, almost blinded by the gale and pouring rain. The deck was a scene of chaos with indistinct figures struggling over a mass of sail that kept billowing away from them. The mast had come down across a boat, stoving in its side, and the seamen seemed to be struggling to rig another in its place. Just before he ducked back into the shelter of the hold Osram heard a cut off scream as a man went overboard. The sea was a nightmare, the waves towering over the taffrail and sluicing the length of the decks. Anything loose was lost and there was as much ocean as rain in the water soaking the men.

'Well?' Marric demanded as the big man dragged a palm across his streaming face. 'How does it look?'

'Not good. Bloody awful in fact. The mast has gone, a

man just went overboard and I dunno if the captain was steering for it, or it's because of the mast, but we're mighty close to land. That's one mother of a gale out there, so the visibility's shit but there's a shadow on the off side that's gotta be the coast. If they don't get matters sorted soon we'll be finding out the hard way.'

Marric mentally converted the horseman's 'off' to the seaman's 'starboard' and nodded. 'Time to make a move then. The crew must all be on deck. Which means we can slip out and make a search of the ship for weapons. Let's meet up near the wheelhouse with what we find and take it from there.' Osram glanced back at his son, and Marric shook his head. 'Best leave him there for now. He's too weak to help himself.'

'Right. I almost forgot — the boat's smashed. The mast hit it. Not that you'd ever launch it in these seas.'

Marric shrugged. 'There must be another. But that's a seaman's job. We'll have to stick with the ship and trust we can make it to the shore if it strikes. Anyone can't swim?'

'Me,' Ramie said.

'Well, if you go into the water, grab something and hang on. May the Lady protect us all.'

The scream of the gale hit them the moment the hatch was raised. The rain was blinding and icy, sucking away body heat in an instant, and the wind ferociously strong. One after the other they crabbed their way across the open deck, hearing fragmented shouts from the men toiling on the ropes. Tarris, as the lightest, was flung across the deck as the ship heeled and only stopped by Osram's grip on his shoulder. Ramie skidded on the wet boards but saved himself by a frantic clutch at a backstay and in this fashion they struggled, unobserved by the oblivious crew, to the companionway and the comparative quiet of its shelter.

They separated; Osram still carried the timber baulk while Burran had the bale hook. Ramie, from somewhere on the deck had come up with a longhandled gaff. Seeing Tarris about to turn down through another hatch Marric stopped him. 'You're with me.' He was not of a mind having once found his nephew to let him out of his sight. They reeled along the passage they had chosen, being flung forcefully from side to side. Cabin doors banged monotonously and from somewhere deep inside the ship a grating metallic squeal sounded. The first two cabins were a shambles of wet clothing and other belongings tumbled anyhow in heaps. A leaking porthole above a bunk had drenched the bedding, and a terrified looking cat with sodden fur was crouched among it. In a larger room that Marric took to be the captain's, a chest had torn loose and smashed the legs of a chart table, spilling everything it had held to the floor. A wine flask and glasses had shattered amongst what looked like the remains of a chamber pot. Yanking open a latched door at the head of the bunk Marric found two swords, one of which he threw to Tarris.

'Here. Find anything?'

'Only this.' He held up a metal spike. 'Not as good as a dagger, but handy in a close fight.'

Marric stretched his memory back to the single boyhood voyage he had made and an old sailor who had demonstrated knots to him on a sunny deck as they sailed up the Great River to Ripa. 'It's a fid. For splicing ropes. Come on. That other cabin, it'd be an officer's. He must've have had a weapon. We'll check it again.'

There was a blade they had missed, wedged below the bunk; Marric grabbed it knowing that somewhere there had to be more. There would be times when ships needed an armed crew. There were pirate attacks, particularly around the islands of the Eastern Sea but they had no more time to search. He had begun to notice a certain sluggishness as the ship rolled as if she might be taking water. Not a healthy situation for any aboard, particularly Leu, helpless in the hold. A persistent tingle at his nape warned him that their time was running out.

26

Osram must have sensed it too, for when Marric and Tarris reached the deck again he met the big man, one arm supporting his son with Ramie and Burran bringing up the rear. The former had the rope wound about his body to free his hands.

'Any luck?' He had to half shout to make himself heard above the roar of the gale.

'Three swords.' Marric handed him one, grabbing the buckling Leu as Osram removed his arm to slip the baldric over his head. 'What about you?'

'We found a chest. Iron, probably their armoury. We couldn't open it. Nothing in the crews' quarters. Burran got a knife from the galley.'

It was a decent size and looked sharp. 'Good.' Squinting his eyes against the rain Marric nodded at the upper deck. 'That's where we want to be. Quick as you can, because she's taking water.'

In a way the fact helped them for the increasing weight of the ship had dampened the rolling effect making it easier for them to move about. But that was also true of others. A sudden shout behind them brought their heads around to see a figure rushing at them across the deck, shouting something that was instantly lost to the wind. Marric heard Osram grunt, 'Had to happen,' then the full weight of Leu fell upon him. He dumped him unceremoniously on a step, snapped, 'Guard him,' at

Tarris, then followed the other three in a headlong rush across the streaming deck.

The man who had given the alarm was armed only with a belaying pin snatched from the jury rig the crew had made for the new mast. Perhaps he was counting on numbers to overpower the escaped prisoners, or had not reckoned on them being armed. He got in one wild swing before Osram cut him down, and Burran used the gaff appropriated from Ramie to rip open the face of the man behind him. The third crewman goggled in horror. 'You killed the captain!' he blurted, and took three hasty running steps before Marric, forgetting his blade, slammed the discarded baulk of timber against his head. He went down and lay still.

There was a long moment of silence in which the rain eased then the ship creaked alarmingly, and a crewman screamed a warning almost lost in Osram's full-throated roar as he swept Ramie and Marric aside. Then the half erected jury rigged replacement for the mast came crashing down where they had stood but moments before.

It was the last straw for the crew. Marric, picking himself up glimpsed the bulk of the land through the space the smashed rail had left when the fallen timber hit it. Where the original mast had fallen three men were mindlessly trying to lift it off the stoved-in boat. Somebody, presumably the mate if the captain was dead, was threatening a man but the ship was doomed, you didn't need to be a seaman to know it. Even as he watched the vessel listed further and the make-shift mast tilted past the point of balance and slipped overboard. The seas were high, but the ship's weight in the water had dampened them in its immediate vicinity. He gauged the distance to the land. They appeared to be in a bay, though the shore, given the driving rain, was indistinct, but it was their best chance. Their only chance. He said as much.

Ramie swallowed and looked down at the surging sea. His face whitened. 'You lot go. I'll stay.'

'No you won't,' Marric said. 'That timber will carry you ashore. Burran will go with you.'

The younger man nodded. 'You'll be fine. Here, shove this in that rope.' He handed him the butcher's knife and while Ramie was securing it, he thrust the trader sharply between the shoulders, tumbling him forward. Aided by the now distinct lean of the deck, he fell straight over the side. His yell was cut off as he hit the water, and a moment later Burran's feet clove the surface beside him.

'We've not long,' Marric warned. The crew was ignoring them in favour of the remaining boat but as it was on the high side of the deck there was little hope of them getting it launched.

Osram nodded wordlessly. Tarris, told of the plan, simply nodded. 'Good thing I learned to swim.' Copying Marric he kicked off his boots, said, 'Now?' and without waiting for an answer jumped.

Osram was speaking urgently to Leu who nodded. He was swaying on his feet and Marric moved up to his other side to grip his free arm. 'We'll go together.' And then they were falling into icy heaving depths. Sound vanished and it was almost a relief to be rid of the pounding weight of the rain on his head and shoulders. His lungs started to hurt as they continued to plummet down, and down, then his feet touched the bottom and he pushed hard and kicked frantically for the surface, hauling on Leu's dead weight and fighting the overwhelming urge to open his mouth and gulp at non-existent air.

He broke through into glorious air mixed with brine and stinging rain. Gasping he grabbed Leu's head, tilting it back to get his face above water, then Osram was there, anxious and blowing. The surge was tremendous, constantly dousing them under the tugging waves. The bodyguard glanced over his shoulder, bared teeth very white in his wet face. 'Gotta — get — away!' he bellowed and Marric realised that the ship was poised on the point of turning turtle behind them. Hearts bursting with the effort they swam for their lives, dragging the unresponsive Leu, to avoid being crushed beneath the wreck or pulled under by the eddy its sinking would produce.

In the event the wave of energy created by its submersion had the effect of speeding them forward. A huge tongue of water shot over their heads and when they emerged from it, gasping and half drowned, Marric's floundering arm struck a rock. Reflexively he seized it and a moment later his knees hit the sea bed. He rose unsteadily feeling the icy rage of the sea tugging at his legs, and with his last strength staggered up the beach to collapse onto coarse wet sand.

Leu's gagging roused him. 'Oh, for Light's sake! Not again,' he groaned rolling over. But it was an excess of sea water, not the sickness, causing the problem. Osram pushed himself up and the fleeting thought crossed Marric's mind that he had never seen the big man so spent. The bodyguard cast a look at his son and his principal then squinted up the beach. 'The others?' he asked hoarsely.

'No idea.' Groaning Marric stood. 'See to him. I'll go look.'

Both Burran and Ramie had survived, the latter with a darkening bruise down the side of his face, stark against the grey of his short beard. With his wet hair and deeply lined face he suddenly looked his age as he limped through the rain, waist fattened by the wet coils of the rope he still wore, from which the handle of the butcher's knife still protruded.

'You made it then.' Marric's gaze swept beyond them. 'Tarris?'

'Sweet Bel, I'd forgotten about him!' Ramie said tiredly.

Burran shook his head. 'There was a current though, he might've been swept further along. I'll go back.' He jogged away, and Marric, sighing a little for the resilience of youth, plodded back up the shoreline, watching the wave's edge and dreading to find a body tumbled within it. When he finally came across it, his blood seemed to freeze then he was running, splashing high-kneed through the restless medium to seize the figure that floated face down and turn it, only to find himself handling a stranger.

'Oh, thank you Lady.' He gasped, dropped the anonymous crewman, only the first, he assumed that would wash ashore. Heart rate steadying he continued his grisly search until a shout from Osram brought his foraging to an end. Turning he saw the sturdy shape of Burran and a slighter, shorter figure toiling slowly towards them and as if to seal the benison of his nephew's survival the rain suddenly eased into a drizzle and then stopped altogether.

'It feels late,' Osram eyed the grey overcast tented above the dripping scrub on the wet headland and the rock-littered patch of sand behind them. It was impossible to tell whether the sun had just risen or was about to set. He looked at Ramie. 'Any idea where we are?'

'And you expect me to know because?' Crossly the trader helped himself to another handful of the dried apricots that Burran had scooped into a bundle and stuffed into his tunic before quitting the hold. They tasted soggy and salt laden but were very welcome to the hungry men.

'Doesn't your work take you all over this benighted country? I make it a night and half a day on the ship near enough, and we were headed south. Say Carj lies midway between Providence and Quade, and that we were moving faster than you'd ride —'

'But it wasn't a direct passage, not with the storm,' Marric interjected. 'More to the point, what's our next move? We need transport, and water.' They had drunk from rainwater pooled amid the rocks but that would be gone in a matter of hours, even if they could stay where they were. 'Food and weapons too.' Between them they had Ramie's butcher's knife, Leu's miniature dagger and the sword that Osram had somehow retained in their battle to the shore.

Tarris, who had sat without speaking, suddenly pointed towards the headland.

'There! Smoke. I thought it was, but with the cloud...'

Osram was on his feet, narrowed gaze following the young prince's finger. 'I don't see —'

'No, he's right.' Leu, who had improved markedly with food and a short rest, was nodding. 'A building. Has to be — no campfire would've survived the rain.' He looked at his father and hazarded, 'A fishing village?'

'Only one way to find out.' He got to his feet. 'We should get off the beach, my lord. If there's people around we want to see them before they spot us.'

The smoke was much further off than it had appeared. They plodded over the first headland, and then a second, only to find another looming far ahead. But at least the storm was over and the sky was gradually clearing. It was hard going on bare feet, for only Ramie and Osram had kept their boots. The coastline here seemed to consist of a string of shallow bays, and the foam breaking half a league out to sea in the fading light seemed to suggest a reef. If their own transport had touched the end of it, Marric thought, it would explain why the ship had taken water. The sun, glimpsed between thinning clouds was sinking over the land before they were close enough to smell the smoke which seemed to be coming from two points, quite close to the shore. Their clothes had dried on them by then but all were weary by the time they breasted the final headland and looked down into a deeper cove from which the smoke was rising.

Osram hissed 'Down!' He sank onto his haunches, staring at the three ships anchored below him and the two buildings from one of which the smoke was issuing.

Ramie peering beside him said, 'But that's — they're our missing ships! There's the *Maybelle* and *Journey Maid*. I don't recognise the other.'

'Not sunk then, but pirated,' Marric murmured. 'I wonder if their crews are down there? Because if they are, there's our passage home. Tarris, tell me what you see on shore. Anything that catches your eye.'

'Yes, Uncle.' The boy leaned forward. 'Well, two buildings then. The smoke is coming from the smaller one. The other one's bigger, made of stone or maybe clay bricks. Built for defence — a bit like the ones you see on our docks — no windows and the door is barred. I can see the timber brace holding it shut. Wait — a man's coming out of the other place — no, they're two of them — carrying something between them —'

'It's a pot, like for cooking,' Leu put in.

'Yes. A very big one,' Tarris agreed. 'Big as a tub. They're taking it to the shed. Is that someone else still inside? I thought I saw —'

'Yes,' Leu said, 'I saw it too. A third man.' He paused. 'It's not really clear but I think both the men have blades. They've put the pot down, and yes, one has drawn his sword. The other's taking the bar off the door. Now he's heaving the pot inside. It must be quite heavy. Now he's backing out and they're barring the door again. His mate has put up his sword.' He looked curiously at the men about him. 'Can't you see any of this?'

'Only the figures,' Ramie admitted, 'none of the detail. You've got young eyes, lad. That's the difference.'

'Well, it's answered my question,' Marric said. 'The

crews, or those who survived the taking of their ships, are here. All we have to do is release them.'

'Let 'em settle for the night first?' Osram suggested. 'If there's only the three of them I can't imagine they post a guard. The place looks like it could've been the outpost to a garrison, so nobody's breaking out of it in a hurry. We keep the noise down, we could be on the ship and away before they even know it.'

Marric nodded. 'Good. That's our plan then.' And catching the look of despair on Leu's face, added, 'Can't be helped. And the weather looks set fair. It will make a difference. you know.'

'Yes, sir,' Leu muttered bleakly though it was plain he didn't believe it.

They waited while the early stars pricked out and lamplight grew in the window of the smaller building. And another in the wheelhouse of one of the ships. Osram nudged Marric. 'So, more than three men. You reckon they've guards on them all?'

'Watch for lights,' Marric replied but no other appeared, and the remaining ships faded darkly into the night. The smell of woodsmoke drifted to them and a teasing aroma of cooking meat that came and went with the fitful breeze.

Ramie swallowing, muttered, 'I hope they haven't cleared the galleys and there's still food aboard. I could eat an ox.' The apricots had been finished hours before.

'You can eat all the way to Deem,' Marric said, 'supposing there're officers enough among the captured men to run the ship.'

'Why wouldn't there be, Uncle?' Tarris asked.

'Well, if it was me the first thing I'd arrange would be their removal to another spot. Surest way of avoiding what we're planning. You can't sail without a navigator.'

'Yeah, but only a twisty bastard like you would think of that,' Osram said cheerfully, to the young prince's horror. 'Don't go looking for trouble. It'll meet you halfway every time.'

Marric chuckled, 'As you say,' and was interrupted by an urgent murmur from Burran.

'But sir, we can't go to Deems! We must get back to the Crows. With the attack coming they'll need every fighting man they can muster.'

'There's not much we can do about it from here,' Marric said. 'I'm sorry but that's the truth. I'd help Leris's folk if I could but our first duty is to our own land. We must get word to the king to send men to Ansham's defence. Everything we have worked for will be lost if Appella attacks that country and we do nothing to help them.'

In an agony of dismay and frustration Burran gritted, 'But my lord, my woman is there! And anyway the Appellans won't attack now they no longer have the prince.'

'We don't know that. And they don't know they've lost their hostage. With the crew dead who's left to report our escape? And Morrik hearing nothing to the contrary might well assume the plan has been successful. In which case he could be marching on Ansham as we speak.'

Burran drew in a breath, visibly fought with himself, then nodded. 'As you say sir. Then I must go alone.'

'How? Be reasonable, man. You would need a dozen mounts if you could even find your way. Forget it. Besides, it's possible that with Hardfar dead the raid against the Crows won't happen.' Or, more likely still, they had already chosen a new leader and rode to war as he spoke. Burran would be aware of that too, he knew, but his duty was owed to his king and country first, whatever the personal cost.

Marric looked away trying to ignore the glimpse of misery etched on his man's face, recalculating for the hundredth time the days it might take to reach Deems, then find a swift boat to take them upriver. Darien might not even be in the city — he was often abroad visiting the various counties that made up the broad reach of Rhuta. There was no royal progress for him, a visit to his various governors was no different to a day's hunting, with a packed lunch and a lightly armed escort the only concession to his position. So if he wasn't at the palace factor in at least another day before he was reached and could sign the order to get troops moving in Ansham's direction. But men could neither travel nor fight without supplies, and the mountains would fatally slow the wagons.

Fast cavalry might make a dash, but to arrive too late on spent horses and with no back-up, was to invite further disaster. Marric breathed out slowly, holding himself still against the desire to pace and fidget. He should have followed Rissak's example and learned to juggle he thought, and the memory of his old mentor with his cool head in emergencies helped steady him.

Then finally it was time. The lights had vanished from ship and shore and they had seen no guards. Treading carefully behind Osram they slipped down the headland and across the open ground to the larger building. Here the big man halted them at the end of the building furthest from the guards' hut while he reconnoitred the back. While he was gone, Marric turned to Ramie.

'Keep them here. I'll be back in a moment.'

'I'll come with you, Uncle,' Tarris said.

'No. Stay and keep your eyes open.' Something about the simplicity of the bar securing the entrance bothered him, and a few moments spent with his hands exploring what he couldn't see, confirmed his suspicion.

'There's a chain locked onto it,' he murmured on his return. Osram was back by then and tutted in frustration to hear it. 'We'll not get in that way.'

'Shit! Then we'll have to move the wagon. The bloody thing is loaded too.'

'What wagon?' Ramie demanded but once around the back it needed no explanation. Perhaps the heavy wooden door there had no means of locking so the Appellans had simply driven a loaded wagon up against the outward opening door.

The bed of it contained a half dozen bales which from their odour held greasy wool. 'From Ansham. Meant for a ship's cargo.' Ramie used the butcher's knife to hack through the ropes securing the bales. 'Right, over the side with them.'

That was the easy part. They loosened the brake and cleared the ground before the wheels then working in silence save for their grunts of effort, rocked the heavy vehicle back and forth before gaining enough momentum to roll it a wheel's width forward.

'And again,' Marric gasped. They hardened their muscles, feet sliding on the soft ground and with a final gasping effort the wagon lumbered on another few paces before dragging to a stop.

'That'll do.' Osram bent forward getting his breath then straightened, pulled his blade and swung the door back. It creaked loudly and he froze before ducking inside, the others crowding his heels.

27

Inside was as black as pitch. They bumped into each other and stopped, stretching their eyes in a vain attempt to see. After a while the blackness didn't change so much as thin a little and Osram inched forward through what, Marric thought as he spread his arms, seemed to be a tunnel. If so it widened and then amazingly a soft nimbus of light appeared somewhere ahead. Osram halted again, then grunted and moved more easily forward until those following him found themselves in a wider space, humped with shadows across the floor space.

The light came from the dying embers of a fire. Osram stooped to the nearest bundle and shook it awake, the man rearing up with a smothered shout that brought an irritated groan from a nearby sleeper. 'God's balls! Don't start again, Trent!'

'Wake up! The lot of you, wake up.' Osram nudged another form. 'You want to stay here or go home?'

'Huh?

'What—?'

'Where'd you come from?'

It was impossible to count the rising men but there seemed to be above a score of them, bearded, cranky and excited once they grasped the situation.

Osram was succinct in his message. 'We want a ship and a crew to sail her. Your guards aren't stirring, so if we can sneak our way aboard can you get us out of here? And have they seamen enough to follow us?'

'No, at least not here. Their crew left a ten-day back in the *Swift Jenny*.' The speaker was a short, stocky man with a sailor's roll to his hips and a heavy beard. He squinted at the newcomers. 'Cap'n Throst of the *Maybelle*. Me and my crew was pirated by those bastards in the *Jenny*, but she ain't back yet from wherever she went. They killed some of my crew, stole the cargo and we've been locked up here ever since. Bel alone knows what my House is thinking back in Ripa. We shoulda been home long since. They'll have us sunk and all hands lost.'

'And yours is not the only ship to go missing,' Marric said quietly. 'The king and the guilds are very concerned. I will explain why later but for now we must make all speed. The vessel closest to the shore has guards aboard but the others appear deserted. I need a boatful of volunteers in case I am wrong. Then we must make a quiet and orderly departure.'

Somebody had thrown an extra billet of wood on the fire and the room had lightened. A man peering from the shadows said querulously. 'So you say. And who exactly are you, cully?'

'He is Prince Marric, own brother to your king,' hissed Osram. 'Shut it, if you've nothing useful to say.'

'All right, Osram.' A mutter of surprise passed through the huddled group then Throst, seizing an object near where he had lain stepped forward.

'I'm your man, my lord. And Beni, Lud —' He named half a dozen others who stood up to join him. 'You have weapons?'

'No, unfortunately.' A murmur of disappointment sounded. 'A sword and a knife only, so leave whatever that is,' he nodded at the object Throst carried, 'and improvise with anything you can grab.'

'It's birds,' the captain replied. 'My cabin boy grabbed

them before they cut him down. He was a quick lad. But there's been no chance to release them since.'

'Bel be thanked and the Lady also!' Marric's heart leapt. 'Guard them with your life then, man. We have greater need of them than you know.' For an instant the cavernous gloom about him splintered with light and he saw the council hall at Ripa. Light glinted on the maps and serious faces of the men about him, and the message lying slightly curled on the polished sheen of the table top... Then it was gone but his heart had lightened. 'That's the best news I've heard this night. Right, let's go.'

In the end the seizing of the *Maybelle* was something of an anti-climax. A wind had risen and the sough of it covered what seemed to Marric as the over-loud grating of the boat against the shingles as the men hauled it to the water's edge, and the splash of the oars as they rowed towards the deserted ship. And it was deserted, a quick and silent search by the barefooted volunteers confirmed it, then two seamen rowed back for the next load of sailors. In all it took three trips and then there was the further nerve stretching business of getting the anchor up and raising the sails, every clunk of the chain and flap of the canvas sounding like a thunderclap to wincing ears.

Finally with the moon long set and only the stars to show where the black sea ended and the sky began they drifted like a ghost ship from the bay and once clear of the land, with the *Maybelle's* keel running smoothly through the dark waters the helmsman set their course north for distant Deems.

The galley was still provisioned though the cargo had been stripped from the holds. The decks were stained with the blood of the dead crewman, for there had been none to swab it clean, and the door of the captain's cabin had suffered from a heavy blow that had splintered the jamb. Such weapons as the ship had carried were, of course, gone, but more concerning was that two of the huge water butts had been damaged in the melee of the taking of the ship.

Three of the crew, including the mate, Marric learned, had been killed along with the cabin boy, who had turned back to grab the cage of birds and been knifed for his pains.

'He was fond of the wee beasties, but he might've been meaning to release them. They'd have been a warning in themselves, that the ship was in trouble,' Captain Throst said. He had proved a sober individual with little to say for himself, his brooding presence a daylong fixture on the bridge. He ran a taut ship, and had re-donned the blue turban of the sea going trader though nothing was left of his current venture. He had stood aside from his chair to allow Marric to sit and pen a careful message in a minute hand, to Darien. The hollowed reeds affixed to the bird's legs were tiny so in the end he had sent two birds, reserving the third in case of further need.

The two men stood to watch their feathered hopes circle once above the ship then arrow away to the north west until they were lost in the dazzle of blue.

'If they get through the whole of Rhuta will owe a debt of gratitude to the lad,' Marric said soberly. 'His action will have made it possible for the king's forces to counter whatever General Morrik has planned. What was your cabin boy's name?'

'Roddi.' Throst's voice hitched but the lines of his weatherbeaten face were like granite in the clear morning light. 'It was his first voyage. He was my son.'

'I am sorry.' There was nothing as futile as words to cover such an occasion, Marric knew. He gripped the man's arm. 'I too have lost my child to death, and not even to save a country, which this may come to. There was no malice, no intent. She was just too ill to live.'

'Then I feel for you, Prince,' the captain said, 'for I

at least can take my vengeance as often as the chance comes.'

The shortage of water forced the *Maybelle* back to land and the laborious task of refilling the patched butts. The captain had chosen an uninhabited spot for the landing, with no sign of grazing or homesteads and though Burran had looked longingly at the hinterland he had eventually sighed in resignation and turned back to his task. He could not even be sure that he stood upon the Grass; it could as easily be Appella. The days were all the same at sea and it puzzled him how any man could know where the ship was at any given point. Trying to count the muddle of days and nights from the time they were taken he thought it must be at least a seven-day hiatus since he parted from Sonj. He tormented himself with the thought that perhaps she was already among the slain, her spirit fled to join the phantom horses, never again to lie in his arms, or call him Scribe, or laugh at his attempts to master her tongue.

The weather remained fair and they made good time, though nothing could be fast enough for the Rhutan contingent. Ramie fretted for the fate of his abandoned caravan. Leu, despite no ill effects to date, lived in dread of a return of his sea illness and haunted the deck, loath to step below. He slept in the night dew rolled in a cloak on the bare boards. He had lost weight, which made him appear even taller, and a scruffy patch of beard adorned his face. Tarris, with nothing but the shadow of a moustache on his upper lip, sniffed his disapproval, but was secretly envious. Only Osram, exercising with Burran and the two young men using makeshift wooden blades for arms, seemed unaffected, but he had always worn an imperturbable face.

Finding Marric alone on deck he came to lean against the railing beside him. 'You think they got through — the birds?'

'I hope so. If they did then by now Darien will have got word to Slate, and some sort of relief force should be on its way. Cavalry perhaps. It should be enough — I mean once Morrik sees Rhutan arms in Ansham he'll know his plot's been uncovered, which would mean he has no hostage. The only reasonable course open to him then is to withdraw. May Asher give him sense enough to see it.'

'Aye,' Osram nodded thoughtfully, 'which might just mean he'll fall on the folk in the Grass instead. Now, that ain't something I'd fret over, not normally, but it seems a pity to lose the ground we've made with Burran's lot. Never thought I'd hear myself say it,' he added honestly, 'but peace does seem the better path there. Light knows you can't beat the tricky bastards by fighting.'

Marric sighed. 'Well it's out of our hands now. May the Lady keep our people from harm. Of course Leris may have guided them out of the Grass, but that doesn't exactly make them safe either.' The ship heeled to a strengthening wind and he clutched the rail to keep his balance. Reminded, he asked, 'How's Leu faring?'

'Well enough, but he dreads another storm.' Osram glanced around at the glittering sea and cloudless sky. 'I doubt he need worry, but he'll not be at ease until he's ashore for good.'

'Aye,' Marric murmured. 'Tranche once told me the motion took some men so.' Both fell silent at that remembering old friends fallen in the war against the same enemy that threatened them now.

And so at last they came to Deems, the busy gull-screaming town at the mouth of the Great River, where the waves crashed on shingle and the sturdy cottages housing the fishing fraternity seemed welded to the rocky shores. Marric had first visited it as an apprentice trader. He remembered the awe he had felt at his first glimpse of ocean, and on another trip the girl he had bedded here and to whom he had given the wisp of silk. It would have taken time they couldn't afford to find a smaller craft heading up river so the party stayed with the *Maybelle* though their progress must necessarily be slower. Marric freed the last bird to announce their coming and when, days later, the city came into view, an escort from the palace was waiting for them. Marric added Throst to their number for the short journey to the palace.

'For the council will need your account of the piracy,' he said.

Ramie announced his intention of setting out for the Grass once his report to his guildmaster had been made, and Burran, who had prowled the slow moving deck like a caged wild creature as they had battled their way upstream against the current, said brusquely, 'Not without me.'

'The king may have need of you,' Marric reminded him. 'You are his only source of knowledge of the region.' Burran ground his teeth but made no reply.

At the palace the full council was waiting in the council chambers. Darien, looking preoccupied greeted them all, nodding curtly at the reason for Throst's inclusion, before ordering refreshments then taking Marric aside for a quick recount of events. The messages the birds had carried had, of necessity, been brief so he knew only that the party had been attacked, captured, and managed to free themselves. Marric gave him the broad strokes, ending with, 'So half of this is supposition on my part. I don't know if Morrik still intends to move against Ansham. Every man involved perished with the ship so there was none to carry the news of our escape. Once he learns the vessel is lost he can only assume that the prince died as well — but he could still mount a bluff on the fact.'

'Oh, he already has,' Darien said. 'Ling knows nothing of it, but Guildmaster Trent was slipped a note by some street lad. Addressed to me, from one of Morrik's spies I imagine. It said they had Tarris and if I wanted him back then Ansham was the price.'

Marric frowned. 'Sent when?'

'I got it a ten-day back. Of course the boy who brought it knew nothing. A handful of coppers to deliver it, and he said the man was cloaked with nothing of note about him. Slate is very worried. There are rumours of war in the wind in the Upper Land. Whispers that Morrik is set on bringing Ansham back to the Light, of cleansing the land of the Mother cult. He — Slate — is demanding our help. I have sent men with orders to show themselves but not engage the Appellans until they heard from me — which they did when I got your last message. I have since put them at Slate's disposal.'

Marric said absently, 'So, he has recovered. I am glad. What of Duko?'

'The Baratan cavalry is coming. However we've had no word from Meddia, which is no more than I expected. They were always lukewarm about the alliance.'

'Yes.' Marric sipped his wine, reviewing what he knew. 'I should alert them at the Lakes,' he said abruptly. 'We will need more men, for Morrik has made common cause with some of the Pampasan tribes. His plan is to loose them on Ansham in return for his help in disposing of the border clans who stand against Appella and the forces within their own land who would overthrow the present matriarchal traditions that give women equal status with men.'

Darien frowned. 'Should we concern ourselves with an internal squabble? The Grass has never been a friend of ours —'

'They could become so, with a little timely assistance,' Marric interrupted. 'We live by trade, Darien, and those I met are anxious to trade. Think of the advantage if we could make alliance with them! Another blade at need against Appella. Because Morrik will not be the only Appellan general to dream of conquest, you know. The Lady herself knows the men of that country imbibe war with their mothers' milk.'

'Aye, you have the right of that.' His brother stood and stretched. 'So, you would counsel we move to a war footing, get more troops through the pass, and what? A relief column to the Grass? That will go down well with the veterans,' he added wryly. 'Most of them cut their teeth fighting against them.'

'Yes. I and my man Burran will go with them.' He hesitated, 'I cannot decide whether it were best to keep Tarris's survival a secret, or wave the lad in Morrik's face. Doing so might prevent a battle in Ansham, but it won't stop the Appellans from attacking Leris's folk. And believe me, brother, should they succeed there, which they well could with the treachery of Hardfar's clan, you do not want to face the combined fighting power of those two peoples.'

'As you say. Well,' the king took a deep breath, 'let us break the news to the council that we have another war to fight.'

28

A hectic few days followed while preparations were made and the reserves called back from their trades and fields to the army. At the end of it two hundred men, with Marric at their head, set off for the high pass. Darien was in daily contact with Slate but no Appellan army had yet shown itself at Ansham's borders although he had received reports from the half dozen shepherds keeping watch outside the country, of the movement of troops. Appella's army was marshalling but the state was geographically large. It would take time Marric knew, for Morrik to move his forces into position. He was gambling on it, on getting his two hundred lightly armed mounted men unseen into the Grass before the more cumbersomely laden Appellans could arrive.

Once away from Ripa, Marric and Osram left the column (ably led by an officer called Ninnik with Burran as guide, and Ramie among the fighting men) to ride for the Lakes. Ninnik had orders to make his best pace and they would catch the column up, Marric said, in the Upper Land. Troops from the Lake Country would follow to join them, or divert to Ansham as need dictated.

The two men arrived dusty and weary from the long, hard pace of their journey to find Lake Town humming with activity, the call-up well under way. Fenny, with tiny stress lines between her brows greeted him thankfully, and for a long moment they held each other tight before he stood back, still gripping her shoulders to say regretfully, 'You know I cannot stay?'

'I know my love. But you are here now. Osram too?'

'Aye, he's gone to his family.'

'How long then?' She asked practically, calling a servant to bring food and draw a bath. 'Is it really war or just posturing? There is some absurd tale going around that young Tarris was taken hostage?'

'He was, but we got him back. Morrik doesn't know that yet and when he does — well perhaps it will be nothing but posturing after all.'

'And the barbarians — how did it go with them?'

He paused in pulling off his boots. 'Ah, they are the reason for my haste. There is not time to explain but the Mother requires that we help them. They have a female deity too. I have never known such power as Her seer channels! She is able to control the minds of men and animals. A strange people —' He kicked off the last boot and stood, swaying a little with weariness.

Fenny took his arm and led him to the table. 'Enough,' she said firmly. 'No more talk. You will eat and bathe and sleep. You are dead on your feet. The war, if it comes, can either wait while you rest or get along without you.'

A day later the two men were back in the saddle, heading for the smuggler's way up the mountain. The punishing climb saved them two days, knowledge of which Marric had counted on in leaving the column. The side trip to the Lakes had been an indulgence of sorts though he had told himself that he owed it to his people to show himself rather than simply order them into battle, if it should come to that, from afar. Darien had agreed. He was staying in Ripa until the Baratan forces reached the capital when he would ride with them. Tarris, they had decided, should stay behind.

'We cannot risk you both,' Marric had said firmly. 'Battle is chancy, and whilst I would love to parade the prince before Morrik's gaze to show him how badly he has miscalculated, there is no certainty that he would recognise him. Whereas your presence would send an unmistakable message. It could well be enough to make him withdraw.'

'And therefore the more likely to attack your friends in the Grass,' Darien observed, his features tired and careworn from days of worry and planning. 'For if he loses his chance to take Ansham then surely he has a greater reason to make an ally of the dissenting tribes there. Will your two hundred be enough?'

'If they are not then you can despatch more once Ansham is secure. We are bound first to them,' Marric reminded him. He ran distracted hands through his hair. 'Gods! It is enough to make you think our grandsire mad. He did this lifelong and seemed not to lose the taste for it. There are times when I long once again for the life of a simple trader.'

'Hah!' His brother had grinned at him then, his cares momentarily forgotten. 'Merchants and their dealings. Believe me, I know all about that, and simple they are not!'

They had parted when Osram arrived to report that the men were ready, but not before Tarris, with Leu hovering hopefully nearby, had earnestly begged both his father and uncle to allow him to ride with them. A season before, Marric reflected watching his nephew swallow his chagrin at their refusal with a stiff bow and a step back, he would have reacted quite differently. Sandos had done well by the lad. Osram had lifted a brow at his son but Leu had shaken his head.

'He is my prince, sir. I will stay to guard him.' It was plain that his loyalty cost him but Marric silently honoured his action.

'He could be in no better hands,' he said quietly, and Leu had flushed with pleasure.

'Thank you, my lord.'

It was possible Marric thought, squinting into the distance as he rode, that the Baratan forces were even now approaching Ripa. Doku would send cavalry, and this time there would be officers amongst them able to speak the Rhutan tongue. The country had blossomed under its young monarch, opening itself to trade, taking into its court embassies from other countries, and establishing learning centres where the languages and customs of those nations were taught. In less than two decades it had changed from a closed, strictly controlled society to a more cosmopolitan state — all of this made possible by its forwarding thinking king.

Osram broke into his reflections. 'Riders ahead — could be troops. Likely our lot but maybe we should get into the timber till we're sure. Could be some of Morrik's.'

A short while later they broke cover and spurred to join the column which had itself pulled into the timber for a quick meal. The horses, unbitted, were grazing while the men ate standing. Ninnik was customarily laconic in his greeting which he accompanied with a salute. 'My lord. Good to have you back.'

'You've made better time than I hoped. Any problems?'

'None. We met with a messenger from your original escort. On his way to Ripa to get further orders for his captain who was concerned about your failure to return. I sent him back with orders for them to join us.'

'Well done,' Marric said. Tarris's abduction and subsequent activities had driven away all thought of the minor detail of the escort left behind to kick its heels. 'The men are travelling well?'

'They're in good heart. That man of yours is cracking his neck to get there. Trader Ramie too. Worried about his men, and with good reason. I wouldn't be trusting any painted savage from the Grass.'

'They're tattoos, not paint, Captain,' Marric said. 'And do remember the clan we're joining are our friends. It's your countrymen at the moment, who are the enemy.'

'Yessir,' Ninnik said woodenly, plainly unconvinced.

It took another three days of hard riding during which time the neglected escort joined them, its captain plainly surprised to find some of Marric's party with the newcomers. The same day a single crow arrived winging up from the south. Unnoticed at first it circled the riders once from high above then flew lower until it was flapping above the men close enough to draw attention to its unusual behaviour. Having traversed the length of the column it dipped towards Marric's uplifted face, uttered a loud caw, then sped off back the way it had come, to where far in the distance the undulating waves of shoulder deep grass could be seen.

Ninnik frowned after it. 'That's queer. I've never seen a bird act like that. And where's its mates? You don't often see crows alone.'

'The ones in the Grass seem a little different,' Marric admitted. 'I think that may be where it came from.'

'Let's hope the men don't see it as a bad omen,' the captain grumbled. 'Crows, ravens — they're all death birds to soldiers.'

'Ignore the incident then,' Marric advised, heartened by the creature's appearance. Ulfa had sent her eyes which meant she still lived. They were in time then, but the fact that she was looking for them surely meant that an attack was imminent. Knowing that Ninnik had planned a shorter day to rest their mounts he said abruptly. 'We'll switch horses again at the noon halt and ride on. Time grows short and a guide is waiting.' Ulfa, he was positive, would send the boy. A growing sense of urgency convinced him of the fact and must have flavoured his tone for

Ninnik's eyes narrowed. He glanced once at Osram riding beside the prince and nodded.

'As you wish, my lord.'

Marric's instincts had not let him down. When their shadows lay long across the open grassland and the last of the light was splintering their vision something moved ahead. A trooper called a warning and men's hands flew to their weapons.

'No!' Marric stood in his stirrups and raised his arm. 'Hold. It is a friend. Burran.'

'Aye, my lord.' Kicking his horse into a canter the man peeled away from the column to arrow towards the single rider. Those watching saw the two meet, then both were off their horses, rushing at each other, their further actions lost in the sheltering Grass.

'What's happening?' Ninnik said uneasily. 'Asher's Light, it could be an ambush. These savages —'

Marric laughed. 'No ambush, Captain. I have a feeling he's greeting a friend. Here they come now.' So, not Bryn. Better of course to send a messenger who could speak their tongue. And who better than Sonj?

She was armed and impatient, imperious in the saddle, her dark eyes snapping as she regarded the troop. Burran sweeping up beside her looked like a man reprieved from disaster, grinning fatuously, relief and joy leaking from every pore.

'So, you are here, Prince,' she bowed briefly from the saddle. 'And you have brought the help you promised. Ho, the trader man too. And these others — they will fight? There are many who come against us, Prince. The Blood-drinkers have a new king but it takes them many days to choose. Much argument our spy reported.'

'You had somebody observing — a man?' Marric added quickly. This was an unexpected bonus.

'Of course. Naturally they will shoot the crows but a man they do not think of. And though many come many more refuse. Some fear the Great Mare's power for all have heard of Hardfar's fate. Two clans only will stand with us,' her slight breasts heaved with her indrawn breath of contempt. 'The others wait to see who will win. Perhaps we will kill them too when our enemies are dead.'

Behind Marric Ninnik whispered, 'A girl? Don't tell me she's in charge! How come she speaks Rhutan?' A low murmur ran also from man to man as the company craned to get a look at her tattooed strangeness. It was one thing to hear about female warriors, quite another to see one with a quiver and bow across her shoulders and a curved fighting blade at her hip.

'Is it far to the camp?' Marric asked.

'When the moon comes we will be there,' she announced and wheeling her horse set off at a swift trot, Burran at her side.

Ninnik shook his head briefly, then raised his arm swinging it forward in the universal signal for movement. With many a sideways glance and muttered oath the column clattered forward into the Grass.

29

The camp where the caravan had first met the Crow clan was deserted. Sonj had been less than accurate about the distance and the moon was well up, the time closer to midnight than sunset, before the weary troop rode into the settlement of Carj. Sentries had been posted and the leading horses shied violently from the shadowy figure rising out of the grass to confront them. The column was shown where to camp, the horses were led off by silent clansmen to water and graze and then Marric, with Osram and Burran in attendance, was taken to the main hall where Leris appeared from the living quarters to welcome them. She was fully dressed, her hair pulled into the single plait that her warriors wore and a curved blade riding at her hip.

A lamp burned on the table and she moved swiftly to set out food for the travellers while Sonj brought washing water and a pitcher of the sour ale they produced. When all was ready the errol seated herself and invited their attendance.

'Come eat. And then we talk, yes?'

'There is much to discuss,' Marric agreed. He was famished and content to eat in silence although Burran conversed in an undertone with Sonj throughout, hunger apparently a secondary consideration. Osram ate methodically his gaze roaming the room as if assessing it for defence. Carj like Glam had no walls; that was plain enough, even in the dark of night. They had ridden straight from the grassland into the sheltered vale with no hindrance to their journey, a situation so foreign to him that he had commented on it.

'The town is open? How do we defend it without walls?'

Sonj overhearing, had said tartly. 'When enemies come we ride to meet them, we do not hide behind walls.'

Now, the meal ended, Leris asked her most urgent question, 'So, you have your prince back, yes? And the traitors — where are they?'

'Dead,' Marric said. 'They are all dead. We had to follow them very far. Then we were captured by Rost's lot. He had two Appellans with him and they in turn killed the clansmen — Rost and the others. So the people of the Grass could be blamed for the prince's abduction. Rost and his friends were only ever a convenience to the Appellans. The ship they put us on sank in a storm and we had to find another. That is why it took so long to return. But we are here now. How much time have we before the Blood-drinkers arrive?'

'Little. Two days perhaps? Ulfa slows their coming but it is very —' she looked to Burran, firing a rapid question.

'Tiring,' he said and she nodded.

'Yes, tiring. She is old and such magic takes much power. It makes them afraid to hear Epona's children thunder in the grass, and they question what they are doing. Their hearts shake with fear, but not enough. When daylight comes again they forget to be afraid. And those who want our deaths most laugh and call them coward —'

'She is here now, Ulfa? You keep her safe?'

Leris shook her head. 'Her power is greatest at the Mounds. She will not leave them. Besides none would dare harm her.'

Marric wasn't so sure but saw no sense in saying so. However he knew that faith was in many cases, his own not excepted, its own protection.

'And my people from the caravan — what of them?'

She shrugged. 'They are as safe as anyone here now is. If we lose they will be sport for the enemy. Some say they will fight with us. I told them they should leave, that Bryn would guide them, but they would not — for fear of the Red King's men.'

Tired as he was, it took a moment for Marric to realise that she meant the Appellans, the reference pointing back to Temes, or possibly even Cyrus. He sometimes forgot how very insular the Pampasans were, and how little news made it into the Grass. Trade would change that — if they were granted the time to develop it.

He said, 'The Appellans have no king these days, he was killed in the war. General Morrik is their leader. It is he who hatched this plan with Hardfar. He thinks to use your people as a tool to conquer us because he cannot do it alone. They should know he will not deliver on his promises. Appellans worship a god of Light and fear the mysteries of the Goddess — any goddess. In Ansham they banned the teachings of my own deity for many years, and killed off Her priests. They will do the same with your Epona because to them only a male god can exist. And they hate seers and oracles like Ulfa.' He straightened his body to add urgency to the message. 'My mother was such a one, Leris. And was murdered for it. You should bring Ulfa here where your warriors are.'

Leris shook her head. 'It is as Epona wills, Prince. I doubt not Ulfa already knows the manner and time of her death. Besides I cannot interfere with those the Great Mare chooses to shepherd Her herd. That was Hardfar's folly. It shall not be mine. You are finished? Good. There are beds prepared for you here in the hall. You should rest now.' She kindled a wall cresset from her lamp then carried the latter away into the inner rooms, leaving Marric and Osram to find their rest. Burran, Marric belatedly realised, must already have his own place and had slipped away to it. It was no surprise that Sonj too had vanished.

The following morning Marric begged a bow off Leris, for his own had been lost when they were captured, and he had no other to replace it. The errol gave him the choice of the weapons hanging in the hall and he tried them for fit, settling on a right-handed bow with a decent weight to the pull. He then selected a handful of arrows and took himself off to practise. The town was crowded with tents dotting the fields beyond for the warriors from the Fox and Coney clans had come to join the Crows. Leris had sent Sonj and Burran amongst them to explain the outlanders' presence, and, he suspected, to push the argument for trade when the business of war was done.

Meanwhile Ramie, having brought his caravanners up to date organised them into a defensive force for the children, the pregnant women and the few elderly not included in the fighting band.

'It all depends on the numbers that come against us,' he said squatting on his heels, hawkish eyes endlessly scanning the grass, reminding Marric of earlier times, though he had not then walked with the slight limp he had since acquired. 'There's a chance — a very faint one — that you won't be needed,' he told Jako, whom he'd placed in charge of his goods. He sighed and scratched beneath his turban tilting it a little to one side. 'I'm getting too old for battles. I was your age before the Prince here could walk and that's got to be more than thirty odd years ago.'

"Course you're not, sir,' the young trader protested. 'Besides,' he added optimistically, 'you must have a plan to defeat these heathens.'

Ramie snorted. 'The plan at the moment seems to be that we ride out with these mad heathens to kill or be killed. So if you survive and I don't, get the caravan home. Though you might have to fight your way through Appella to do it. That will depend on what happens at Ansham. Still it's wise to be prepared so if it all goes to shit don't hang around. Forget the camels; lives are more important than goods.' He got stiffly to his feet and catching sight of his subordinate's downcast visage clapped his shoulder. 'Just do your best, lad. There'll be none left to blame you if you fail.'

Osram and Ninnik conferred on tactics but as the latter gloomily agreed the meeting between the clans was likely to come down to a screaming, free-for-all dog fight with neither plan nor orders to follow. 'No discipline. Everybody does what they want.' He shook his head disbelievingly, 'What a way to fight a battle.'

'As I recall it's worked pretty well for them. They killed enough of us,' Osram reminded him.

'Yeah, in ambushes. A full on battle is different.'

'Well, we shall see. We've got to get close fast, stop 'em using their bows or they'll slaughter us before we can land a blow on them.'

'That should be fun,' Ninnik said dourly.

In mid afternoon the crows began to arrive, first a single bird, then a pair and as Marric, seated beneath a tree beside the hall watched, a dozen more flew in to land on a bough above him, strutting its length and turning their heads to eye him boldly. It reminded him of something and he looked at Osram, never far from his side.

'Have you seen the boy?'

'The mute?' The big man thought a moment and shook his head. 'Not since we got back.' He jerked a thumb upwards. 'They're something to do with him?'

'I'd hazard a guess they are. Perhaps he's with the shaman?' But that didn't explain the birds' presence. Then a moment later a rider cantered to the hall door and flung himself from the saddle. It was Bryn. He dashed inside while the crows set up a clamour, taking wing to flap about cawing before settling again along the ridge‑capping of the hall.

'Something's happened,' Osram. 'Maybe they're coming at last?'

Leris confirmed it only seconds later, striding from the hall, eyes bright and her hand on her blade. 'They are half a day out,' she said. 'Gather your men, Prince, for we ride immediately. We will meet them in the dawn and send their souls to the barren plain where no life is.'

'How many?' Marric asked practically.

'Fewer than I feared,' she said. 'Perhaps three times our number? The new king, who will be a Blood-drinker, can have brought only his clan.'

'More than enough, by the sound of it,' Osram rumbled. He swung away, 'I'll pass the word to Ninnik, my lord.' He was always most formal when things were serious.

'Aye,' Marric replied in unconscious mimicry of Rissak. 'Tell Burran too.'

'He will ride with us,' Leris said firmly. 'Scribe is Crow now. My sister has chosen him.'

'Very well.' It was no real surprise. A young man isolated for a long period from his own people, of course he would become attached to those he lived amongst, and the girl was pretty enough if you overlooked the barbaric inking of her features. How she would take to life in Ripa was another thing — but by tomorrow's eve it could well be something neither of them would have to face. He hoped it proved otherwise for he had seen a precious tenderness between the two that Fenny would have approved. He put the thought from him. He could not think of his wife now when his duty and all his energy must be given to his goddess and his king.

30

They rode out in company shortly before dusk, the Crows led by Bryn who knew the enemy's position, with Marric's two hundred soldiers, and the warriors of the Fox and Coney clans following. These could be distinguished between Marric learned, by their facial tattoos, each clans' differing from the others. The Coney's included a cheek swirl, reminding him of the girl Leu had tarried with while Tarris was abducted. None of the newcomers spoke any but their own tongue, all eyed the strangers curiously while much of the conversation between the newcomers and the Crows obviously concerned the Rhutans. The taller Appellans amongst them were eyed askance, though Burran assured Osram and the others that their presence in the host had been fully explained to, and accepted by, their erstwhile enemies.

Bryn halted them at length and Leris announced that here they would wait for the dawn. The boy's fingers flew as he conferred with his foster-mother, then she touched his shoulder and he bowed over his mount's withers before pulling him around and vanishing into the deepening dusk. The air had turned to shadows with the sun's departure, the tiny birds that flew above the grass had vanished and most of the crows that had flown with them streamed away after Bryn. Some half dozen remained, fluttering familiarly down to perch on whatever offered as the company made camp. A saddle upended on its pommel, an upturned water bucket, a horse's back.

They posted sentries, ate a cold meal and the leaders conferred briefly under the stars. Burran with Sonj beside him came to sit with the Rhutan men. Before settling down he touched Marric's arm. 'Could I have a word, my lord?'

'Of course.' Marric stepped aside. He could barely see the other man's face for the moon had not yet risen and the starlight gave only shape not definition to faces. 'What is it?'

'Only to say — well to tell you that tomorrow I must — You see she is my woman, sir. It is different in the Grass. They don't wed like us, and it is not the man's choice. There are rules. I must fight with the clan that has taken me in, because my blood is her's now — Sonj's, I mean. She has chosen me. You do understand?'

'I do, Burran. So, it seems I shall have to find myself another spy. For you I take it, will be staying on here?'

'Yes, my lord,' he said simply. 'If we survive tomorrow.'

'Never doubt it,' Marric replied heartily. 'And my congratulations to you both.'

As full night settled over them the wisdom of their fireless camp soon became apparent for one of the clansmen, a Coney, Marric thought, appeared silently behind them to say something to Burran who immediately looked at Marric.

'A message from Leris, sir. She says come.'

He followed them both, aware of Osram padding silently behind. Leris's form, outlined by starlight, stood staring into the darkness and then as he drew level he saw it too, a distant flare of firelight like a single torch shining between the grass stems.

'They are closer than I thought,' she murmured. 'If we had not stopped here we must have ridden into them, Prince.'

He whistled soundlessly. 'Their sentries will be almost stepping on ours!'

'I have called ours back. Keep your men silent. Epona blesses the weather for if the wind were blowing the horses would scent one another and give the alarm.'

'Yes. You do not fear a night attack?'

'They do not know we are here,' she said simply.

Marric suddenly stiffened, inclining an ear to the space between them. 'Are you sure of that?' he hissed. 'Listen! I hear horses.'

'Yes,' she seemed unperturbed as a faint shout sounded from the camp. The hollow drum of hoofbeats grew slowly louder though still distant, and a torch, small as a candle flame from where they stood, was thrust aloft, then almost instantly doused.

'It is Ulfa's work,' Leris said, turning aside. 'She sends the ghost horses to unsettle our foe and remind them who rules here. It is strange,' he could feel her looking at him, 'that you, an outsider, can hear it too.'

'I also serve a goddess, even as Ulfa does,' he said. 'That will be why.'

The explanation seemed to satisfy her. 'Get some sleep, Prince. It will be tiring work tomorrow.'

In the greyness of predawn they made their preparations, settling baldrics, tightening girths, nervously unsheathing blades to test the ease with which they lifted from their sheaths. The horses sensed the tension of their riders and shifted restlessly about. Marric, who had cat-napped through the night, had thrice heard the thunder of the phantom hooves and wondered how many of the enemy were rethinking their position and wishing themselves well out of the coming battle. Clan loyalty he suspected, would hold them, but fear of the Goddess they were defying might well shred their resolve. He hoped so.

From all he had heard of the age long enmity between the denizens of the Grass and their Appellan neighbours, they were a vengeful and savage foe. Rissak, Osram and Ninnik, all had fought them during their time in Cyrus's army, and spoken of their fighting ability. He hoped he wouldn't have to kill a woman then remembering, reflected that, after all there were not likely to be any today among the ranks of men who wished to oust them from any meaningful position in the clans.

Time stretched endlessly until finally Leris was riding towards him, grimfaced in the pearly light, her bow in her hand, her hair tied back and her warriors behind her. He glimpsed Burran and Sonj, and found himself wondering how soon it would be before the former wore the Crow tattoo of his companions. If he survived the day. If any of them did. Casting the thought aside he nodded at the errol.

'Ready then?'

'We go, Prince. Follow close, our bows will give you protection.'

He nodded tightly, and gathered his reins. 'Good luck,' he said, and then they were surging forward, a dense mass of thundering horseflesh, flying through the grass, trampling it flat, with the lithe forms of the clansmen low on their mount's neck. He had meant to ask where Bryn was, for he had not seen the lad return, but perhaps Leris had sent him from harm's way. And with a jolt remembered that he had forgotten Hardfar's original plan of a twin attack with a force of Appellans to sandwich the border tribes between them and the Blood-drinkers. With Tarris removed from the equation he had dismissed the possibility of the event occurring, but what if Morrik hadn't?

There was no time to worry about it now. The first gleam of gold was in the sky and a sudden warning shout came as they were sighted. It seemed to trigger a slow motion eruption of riders bursting from the grass ahead, filling Marric's sight with the bobbing heads and wild manes of the enemies' mounts. They appeared to stretch to fill the horizon and from somewhere outside his own dismay he heard Osram exclaim, 'Light save us! There's thousands of the buggers!' It seemed as if the entire nation must be there, faces streaked with soot and ash, and like the Crows and their companions, bodies flat along their horses' necks — only the Crows were no longer so disposed.

Each rider, as if simultaneously signalled, had sat upright in the saddle, bow in hand and a flight of deadly arrows were loosed seconds before the two sides met. With no idea how long it had been there Marric found his blade in his hand and then the whole world narrowed to a focus on the nearest foe as the two sides met and he yelled in fury and terror and swung at the man trying to kill him.

Initially, surprise had given the border clans the advantage. Marric, slashing and dodging, doing his best to stay alive, tried to keep track of events but it was hopeless. It was kill or be killed and both sides hacked at each other with a will, but all too soon it became apparent that surprise alone could not save them. The numbers facing the Crows and their allies were simply too great, and slowly the tables began to turn. Their initial drive into the opposing ranks had been blunted by sheer numbers, and a static foe was the easier to kill. Bows were now useless, they were too closely joined to use them, but the curved blades were deadly and a dismounted rider was as much at risk from his enemy's mount as his blade. Marric had not realised that the ordinary looking, shaggy legged horses had been trained to kill. They kicked and struck with deadly precision and in rapid succession he saw two of the unhorsed enemy die in this fashion.

Then his own situation suddenly worsened. Ducking wildly to dodge the blade that would have split his face, what felt like a thrown boulder took him in his ribs. He sagged in the saddle gasping, peripherally aware of the blow descending on his sword arm which despite his best effort he had not the strength to counter. But Osram was there, roaring something, and the hand that held the sword went flying past Marric's bemused gaze, the fingers still clutching its hilt. Its owner howled, staring at the stump of his arm, even as Burran swept in, their mounts crashing together as the younger man seized hold of a toppling Marric, holding him in the saddle. Burran's left arm was sheeted with blood, but he spared only a glance for his master, his eyes sweeping the mass of roaring, screaming warriors and their wild eyed mounts. Looking for Sonj, Marric belatedly realised. The effects of the blow were lessening. He gasped, 'Fine. I'm fine,' and clawed himself erect. 'How are we doing?'

'Not good. They're too many of the bastards!' Osram bellowed. 'The Crows are falling like flies in a freeze.'

Then Burran was gone, cutting his way back into the fray. Marric surreptitiously felt his ribs, dreading to encounter blood but his skin seemed intact. He could now see for himself the truth of the situation. They were outnumbered, and their casualties were heavy but the Crows and his own men fought doggedly on — for what other choice had they? It was kill or be killed, and he very much feared as a Rhutan whose name he didn't know, fell beside him, and he himself slashed viciously at a tattooed warrior's thigh, opening it to the bone as the man raced past, that they faced the latter fate.

Then a face leapt out at him from the tattooed mass before him, glimpsed and gone on the instant as the man spitted a young Crow, and swept by. Marric gave an involuntary shout, 'Rost!' but the rider had vanished back into the melee and Ramie was suddenly beside him, chest heaving and blood staining the end of his unravelling turban.

'Prince,' he gasped, 'Leris said be — ready — pull your men — back.' He wiped his streaming face with a bloodied hand, streaking a scarlet stain over mouth and chin. 'Asher's balls! I'm too bloody — old— for this caper.'

'Pull back? We can't retreat! They'll slaughter us.'

'It's her order, sir. She said — you must obey.' And then he bellowed something and swung at a rider charging at him, dropping as lithe as a boy down the side of his mount to avoid the countering thrust.

A quick glance showed Marric that Leris and her warriors were disengaging, as were the remaining forces of the other border tribes. The manoeuvre showed him just how few of them remained and his heart misgave him. Retreat now was suicidal, nevertheless he yelled to Osram and saw him signal and the order slowly spread through his men. It seemed counter-productive but they would have no chance alone; a quick glance over his troops confirmed it. He estimated that less than half remained.

In the way of battles the enemy sensed their wavering and a roar of triumph arose from the Blood-drinkers. They pressed forward with renewed vigour, only to pause with lifted heads and slackened arms as a thunderous roar arose trumping even the noise of battle, and the very ground began to shake. Burran, pale and gory raced up to Marric and the hardpressed core of his men.

'Flee, now!' He yelled. 'For your life. Go!' And yanking his mount about spurred away towards the ranks of the Crows now hastening from the field. A stream of Blood-drinkers had begun to follow, but now held back, questing about for the source of the noise. Marric needed no second bidding. Whatever was happening he wanted to be elsewhere. He had heard of places where the earth shook to such an extent that mountains fell and rivers disappeared. Perhaps it was happening now. His men, clustered about him, were looking fearfully to him for a lead.

'Ride!' he shouted and put spurs to his mount.

They were just in time. Scarcely had they cleared the edges of the battle when the rumbling revealed itself in a tide, a positive sea, so wide and broad was it, of thundering horseflesh. Hundreds upon hundreds of the wild horses, mad-eyed, riderless, bolting as if from packs of slavering wolves they tore onto, through, and over the battlefield. At the very last second and hardly crediting what his eyes told him, Marric saw Bryn peel away from the lead and flog his foundering mount towards the Crows.

The mob of wild horses however held straight on. Their numberless bodies covered the whole flattened area where moments before the battle had raged, over the bodies of dead and dying men, and injured horses, and those still hale with no time left to escape. All fell victim to their furious advance. Of the Blood-drinkers gaping before their coming those close enough to the edge of the stampede could be seen frantically spurring their mounts in a bid to escape, but the wall of horseflesh mowed most of them down. Perhaps a hundred made it clear. One, quicker witted or more fortunately situated than the rest, had darted aside at the very start though it left him on the same side as the watching Crows sitting slack-jointed and amazed as the carnage unfolded.

It was Sonj who pointed him out and made to rein after him.

'Let him go. There has been death enough.' Leris said, her face grim. 'He is like to be one of the few today to escape Epona's wrath. He can spread the word to any who doubt Her power.' She looked at her foster son, drooping beside his horse whose head hung to its knees from exhaustion. 'You have done well, my son. So, Prince. We have survived the day where many haven't. Your losses are heavy?' The

Crows and those of the other two clans certainly were, a ragged remnant all that was left of the hundreds she had led onto the field.

Marric nodded, his mind pre-occupied with what he had just witnessed. The lead of the horses, still galloping, had vanished into the distant grass, as the last hundred or so ploughed their way across what had been the battlefield. 'How in the world did you —? Where did he find them? And to get them here —'

Leris drew herself up. 'The Great Mare knows Her children's need. Those who would challenge Her reign do so at their peril. It is finished. Come, let us treat the wounded and leave this place of death.'

They did so. There was no sense in going back, and none anyway had the heart, to revisit the carnage the wild herd had made. Neither friend no foe could have survived their passing. Every man of them was bone weary so they rested and ate and tended to injuries where they had first pulled up. Those with wounds, despite the pain of them, mostly fell into an exhausted sleep, and even Osram, without a scratch upon him, stumbled as he walked. Battle took men that way, Marric knew, as if their vital spirits fled once the danger had passed. Ninnik was among the wounded, his leg a bloody mess, Ramie, more fortunate, was only missing half an ear. Marric couldn't remember the names of all those missing from the ranks, but he went amongst the remaining, comforting where he could.

Leris was tireless in her efforts among the clansmen. She had taken no hurt herself and saw first to Bryn who swayed where he stood, eyes vacant and lost. The crows had returned with him and were now among the dead, their harsh cries drifting back to the living in cacophonous glee.

It was not until all that could be done was, and a rough camp set up that Marric thought to mention to the errol he had seen Rost among the enemy. She jerked upright from where she lay, hands flat on the ground as if she would spring to her feet. 'You told me he was dead, Prince!'

'I thought he was. I didn't actually see him fall but the rest were dead so I assumed... He must have escaped from the beach. Perhaps on one of the horses they loosed. But not this time. Nothing could have survived that,' he waved at the mounds of death where the crows pursued their grisly work, 'unless he was among the few survivors. In either case he is beyond our reach now.'

A dreadful suspicion was taking root in Leris, which he read easily in her gaze. She swung her head to look where the lone rider had gone. 'Or that was him.' Marric saw suspicion firm into certainty on her face. 'Who else would have cunning enough to sense the trap? And the speed and skill to evade it? And why flee this way unless —'

'Because this side was nearer?' But Marric hadn't seen from what point the racing rider had started, he had been too intent upon the sight of Bryn cutting away from the herd he had led to save them. 'Besides, why would he —?' A finger of unease traced his spine. 'What do you fear?'

'Ulfa!' She was on her feet, shouting for a horse. Bryn jerked erect as if pulled by a string and was running, the boy who but a little while before could scarcely stand, and others were rising too.

'What's going on?' Osram demanded.

'It's Rost. We think he lives still despite —' Marric waved a hand at the carnage on the flat. 'I saw him just before the horses came — Leris thinks it was he that escaped the herd.'

Leris, he saw from the corner of his eye, was in urgent conversation with her sister who nodded and released the reins she was holding to the older woman. Marris said hurriedly, wanting to be done with it, 'She may be wrong but she fears for the shaman's life. I go with her. You stay and see the men back to Carj.'

'No,' the big man settled his baldric. 'Ninnik can —'

'Ninnik is hurt. And you are too heavy. The horses are spent and we must make the best time we can. Rost — if it was Rost — has at least a two hour lead on us.'

Osram frowned. 'You haven't thought this through, Marric. For starters why would that lot,' he gestured at the clansmen, 'listen to me?'

'They don't have to,' Marric said. 'Unless I'm mistaken Leris has just left Sonj in charge.'

'Right. Still, Rost must know he'll be killed on sight in Carj. Why would he risk it to slay one old woman?'

'For revenge. Do you think the horses came without her bidding? It was Epona's doing but Ulfa made it possible.' Marric snatched up his waterskin, settled his blade and grabbed the reins Bryn handed him. 'I must go. Make what haste back you can for the Appellans may still be coming.' He reined aside, tossing the warning over his shoulder as he spurred his tired horse after the woman and the boy already streaming away from the make-shift camp.

31

There was no speed to be got from the weary horses. After the first wild dash from the impromptu camp it took no time at all for the animals to drop from a gallop into a sluggish canter and then a trot. Forcing the pace would only lead to their complete exhaustion so the three riders trotted and walked by turns, their minds ranging ahead in fear and impatience. The day had progressed past midday, but not by much, Marric judged, and marvelled that the morning's events now seemed so unreal. Many of his men were dead. He had not even checked with Osram that Leu wasn't among them — then, with an irritable shake of his head remembered that Leu was safe in Ripa with Tarris. Which brought his thoughts back to Morrik and the fate of Ansham.

They trotted and walked and Bryn, with the astonishing resilience of the young, even leapt down at times and ran beside his horse, but there was no hope, Marric judged, that the animals would make it all the way back unless they allowed them rest. He said as much, pointing out that Rost's own mount must be as knackered as theirs but Leris insisted upon pressing on. In the end he was proved right when sometime after moonrise the errol's mount stopped quite suddenly then slowly folded to its knees. It could go no further.

They unsaddled in silence. The other two horses walked a few paces and then lay down, Marric patted the neck of his, feeling remorse for the way he had pushed it and the caked rime on its neck where the sweat had dried.

'Rest then,' Leris said resignedly and spread the damp saddlecloth to make her bed. They had no food but the last spring had filled their waterskins and given drink to the horses. Their stomachs would have to wait. If the horses recovered sufficiently they would rise and graze. If not — Marric gloomily calculated the remaining distance or tried to, but he was so tired he slept instead.

At dawn Bryn's and Marric's horses were grazing. Leris's was on its feet but its head hung low and it was plainly incapable of going further. She mounted behind Bryn and they set off at a sober walk, all three knowing it was most unlikely they would beat Rost, if it was Rost, back to the Mounds. If that was where he was headed. They had assumed a great deal Marric told himself; they could have it all wrong but his nerves crawled at the hobbling pace forced upon them while every instinct clamoured at him to ride like the wind before it was too late.

Crows, only a handful, followed them again and it was by these that the scouts found them. Three of them, proceeding cautiously in search of news, they rose suddenly from amid the vegetation aiming levelled bows they lowered as recognition kicked in.

'Scop!' Leris exclaimed to the leader. 'What has happened? Why —?' Intimations of disaster made her hands clench on her weapon.

Nothing however had happened, which accounted for their presence. They were scouting for news, either of the enemy or their own men. It was the third day, the man called Scop said since the warriors had left. Had the Blood-drinkers come or not?

'Yes,' Leris dismounted and strode towards him. 'They came, most are now dead. We need your horses. Ours, as you see are spent. The clans are returning but they have wounded. Return yourselves and prepare for them.' His two companions having by this freed their hidden mounts, she seized the reins, handing one lot to Bryn and the other to Marric, then sprang into the saddle. 'We have no time,' she called back as they gaped after her, 'but it was a great victory.'

Their shouts of triumph at the news were lost as the three kicked their mounts to a gallop and left them in their dust.

Hunger forgotten they rode fast drawing a straight course that bypassed Carj as they headed directly for the Mounds. They were not far now and at first, concentrating on the path Leris was cleaving through the grass, Marric almost didn't see the smoke. Then he glanced up and his heart seemed to stop. He shouted and pointed at the roiling black column, but by then the others had seen it too. Leris's mare spurted ahead as though her spurs had abruptly been applied and Marric quickened his own mount, his heart suddenly weighted with dread.

They had come too late. He knew the moment he saw the man's figure heaving what looked like a table through the burning doorway. The thatched roof had fallen in through smouldering beams, and a tiny figure lay crumpled by a low stone wall set about a spring, with several dead crows lying nearby. Leris's mount slid to a stop, rearing a little from the pressure on its reins but before she could fling herself off Bryn gave vent to a terrible cry, the loudest sound Marric had ever heard him make. He flew from the saddle and the birds aloft above the burning hut spiralled down to him. His face was white as bone, his eyes wide and staring as he walked with deliberate steps towards the startled Rost, who dropped the rickety chair he'd been about to add to the conflagration, and drew his sword.

'Come on then, you dumb bastard,' he snarled. 'There's nothing I'd like better than spilling your useless blood. The errol's pet. Well the old witch isn't around to protect you now, sonny. First you, then her.' He nodded at Leris stalking, blade in hand behind her foster son.

Bryn might not have heard. His hand rose pointing as he continued to pace and Marric saw that he was in the grip of a furious rage. His mouth moved as though he spoke but no sound emerged and Rost, who had momentarily looked a little disconcerted by his fearless approach, for the boy hadn't even reached for his blade, laughed.

'No last words then?' He sprang suddenly forward and even as a bird flew straight into his face, swiped it from the air and laughed again as its bloodied carcass fell at Byrn's feet.

'Get behind me!' Leris shouted but Bryn stood his ground and smiled instead.

The weird action gave Rost pause. A man with slower reflexes might not have noticed, or have chosen to ignore that smile. The boy's lips moved again and Marric, advancing with his own blade out saw Rost's sudden unease. He must have sensed the danger he couldn't see for he whipped about, sword up to meet it, then cried out in baffled fury and fear as the bay horse he had ridden and left with trailing reins where he'd dismounted, flew at him with ears laid flat and murder in its eyes. Before he could move it reared and swift as a striking snake, felled him with a single stroke of one forefoot.

'God's balls!' Marric ejaculated, staring at the dead man's bloodied face. His left temple was caved in and his brain was on view, pierced with shards of white bone. The bay, its hide streaked with the white rime of its travels, snorted, shook itself then nickered to the other saddlers and wandered across to join them, reins dragging in the dust.

Bryn ignored the body. He knelt to lift the dead crow which he carried over to place reverently with its dead mates before lowering himself to sit cross-legged at Ulfa's side. He was crying soundlessly, Marric saw, the water gushing from his eyes with just an occasional hitch to his breathing as he lifted the shaman's old head onto his lap and let his tears fall on her bloodied face and scant white hair. Her clothing was soaked crimson from a sword thrust to her side. Lying there, so small and light she resembled nothing so much as a pile of discarded clothing, over which her acolyte, for surely Bryn was that, grieved.

***

For three days the clans waited war ready, with scouts out and their horses at hand but no Appellan troops appeared. The scouts riding reconnaissance continued to report in while Carj regained some semblance of normality.

The depleted army had returned by then. Those severely wounded had either died or were hovering on the edge of the road to recovery. Mourning for those who fell was a brief affair — death having become all too common an occurrence to the clans. Ulfa's passing was the exception. Her body was interred in the mound where her grandmother, one time chief of the clan, had been laid. A dozen men led by Bryn had undertaken the task of dismantling enough of the barrow to allow ingress for her remains. Burran, Marric had been surprised to learn, was among those who had participated in the task, even hampered by his slashed arm, but he was a clansman now and related, or at least attached, to the errol's family. Bryn had not returned to the hall. From the time of their arrival there he had remained at the Mounds, watching over Ulfa's body, organising her interment and then staying on.

He would build his hut there, Burran said, as Ulfa had done long ago, and live there as she had done, where the power of Epona was greatest. Already the wounded were seeking him out for help in healing, and part of Sonj's daily task was to facilitate this, interpreting his hand signs for his patients.

'So, when do we leave, my lord?' Ramie asked on a day of wind wracked clouds, when the tops of the trees shivered making dancing shade beneath them. 'Summer's passing, be autumn by the time we clear the pass. Winter comes earlier on the plateau, you know.'

'Yes, I do know,' Marric said absently, remembering snow and the heat of a shepherd's bothy with the door sealed and a fire roaring on a hearth. 'As to when — your trading is done then?'

'That it is, and if we take home more goodwill than actual goods, well that is coin in its own way. I have no complaints on that score.'

'It has been worth it, save for those whose lives were lost,' Marric agreed,' but we cannot leave until the injured can travel. How does Nimmik?'

'He cannot walk yet but he swears he can ride.'

'Then we will wait,' Marric decreed, 'for he will ride the better with a few more days rest.'

32

Several mornings later Bryn rode back into Carj to visit his foster mother. There was a new certainty about him Marric thought, watching him pass, not just gained from the respect with which he was greeted by his fellow clansmen, but something within himself. He was closeted with Leris for a short space of time, and when they emerged the errol carried a bedroll and a saddlebag of provisions.

'Something has happened?' Marric asked. It was a brisk blowy morning with a thin raftering of clouds marking the eastern sky. Ramie was right, he reflected, autumn was not far off. His eyes quartered the blue above him and yes the crows were there, wings wide spread, tossed in the wind. 'Bryn has brought news.'

'Yes. Your people come. I go to meet them. You will ride with me, Prince?'

It was sometimes hard to tell from her syntax whether she was issuing an invitation or a command, but it suited him to agree so he did.

'Willingly. Did he say how many come?'

'A war band.'

'Ah.' They would be from Ansham then, which must mean that all was well there, a battle avoided — or won. He wondered if Darien was with them. It seemed very possible. The prince who had raised an army and ridden to battle to win back his rightful throne was never far from the surface of the king, weighted now with cares for his kingdom's politics and economy.

A dozen clansmen, including Sonj and Burran, accompanied Leris, Marric and Osram. The errol led, seeming to know exactly where the two parties' paths would cross, but of course Bryn aided by his feathered friends, would have told her. And sure enough once Leris had thrown up her arm to halt them they had waited but a short time before the mixed party of Rhutans, Old Race and Baratans rode into view. Darien, as Marric had expected, was leading them. He said briefly, 'That is the king,' and spurred to meet him.

Darien's party halted at sight of the two horsemen, hands involuntarily dropping to their weapons, then their redheaded leader shouted, 'Marric!' and jumped down off his horse.

'You are well? Unhurt?' He flung an arm around him to pound his back. 'How did you know we were coming? Have the tribes fought as you feared?'

'I am fine as you see,' Marric laughed with relief. 'And yes, there has been a very bloody battle which the Crows and their allies won. I'm afraid our losses were heavy though. And you? What of Ansham? It's safe or you wouldn't be here. And you have excellent company I see.' He bowed to Doku. 'It is good to see you again, my lord. You are well?'

'Yes, I thank you.' The huge black man grinned. 'Though this time the sport failed — due mainly, as I understand it, to your efforts. Still, it has been interesting. I have never travelled these lands before. And Darien tells me we go to meet a woman who is both warrior and chief?'

'That is so, my lord. And a most able leader of men.'

'Then I would my councillors were here to see it.' Doku chuckled. 'The knowledge might kill some of the old fools.'

'Then come.' Marric swung back into his saddle. 'Let me introduce you both.'

Riding back with them he had time to see and greet both Jem, come in his father's stead, and Cran, and some of Darien's Appellan officers among the group. Slate was recovering but not yet ready for the saddle. Conflict had been avoided, but it had been a near thing. The Rhutan cavalry it seemed had arrived in the nick of time.

'We reckoned they'd over-run us in the first charge,' Cran said. 'There were thousands of the buggers, most of 'em horsed. We'd done what we could to fortify the place, but we knew it'd never hold, not against the numbers they had. Then the captain of the cavalry — it was Rissak — rode out under a flag of truce. Wouldn't take anyone with him, just sat his horse in front of them all and yelled for Morrik. Well of course he had to appear willing or be shown up in front of his army. Rissak told him King Darien was on his way and if a single soul died in Valleyford, the full weight of the King's Alliance would fall upon Appella. There wouldn't be a town standing or a man alive to mourn it when they'd finished, he said.'

Marric whistled. 'Well, he always speaks his mind.'

'Aye, he does that,' Cran nodded. 'Morrik told him he was bluffing, said he knew Darien wouldn't come. So Rissak said the only thing that wasn't coming was the *Swift Jenny*, that she had gone down with all hands and Prince Tarris was safely back in Ripa. He left him with that to think about. Is it true the prince was abducted?'

'Yes. So there was no attack?'

'We stood to arms all day and kept watch that night. They started to withdraw the following day.'

'Until next time,' Marric said.

'Ah, well,' Cran grinned. 'They'll have to find 'emselves another general first.' He nodded towards the two men riding before them, 'The king's black mate? Some of his men visited the Appellan's camp that night. Dunno how they got through the sentries but they came back with Morrik slung between 'em. When the rest woke up next morning they found their general gone — vanished. I think that's when they decided to leave.'

There was no time for more for they had reached Leris's group. Marric presented her to both kings. She nodded brusquely to Darien, offering him an armclasp, but couldn't quite disguise her astonishment at sight of Doku's shining black skin.

'My lady,' he bowed to her. 'It is a pleasure to meet a woman like yourself. In my land, unfortunately, we hide our women away and forbid them the power to be themselves. It is the custom of my country and a very bad one.'

'Then why don't you change it, King?' she asked forthrightly.

Doku grimaced. 'I am trying but that is how it has ever been and the priests support it. And many of the men would not see it change.'

She snorted. 'Men! Some of our own thought that way too. They are dead. The others learn better now. Come, I will take you to my hall where we can talk and refresh ourselves. We are honoured,' she said carefully as one suddenly remembering diplomacy and aiming it at both men, 'to have you come so far to grace us with your persons.'

'That is what allies are for, to speed to the aid of their friends,' Darien said smoothly. 'And both our countries would be happy to count you amongst them.'

Later, after a meal and the meeting that followed with several clansmen including Burran and Yerb in attendance, Marric slipped away to find Cran. Bryn had not come to the gathering, but he had no need, Marric thought spotting the crow perched silently above them in the hall. When he judged his own presence was no longer necessary he left, finding Cran swapping stories with the wounded Nimmik who struggled to his feet to greet him.

'So, what has been decided, my lord? Are we for home now?'

'Sit down, man,' Marric said. 'Yes, your lot will return immediately. However a light force, a mixture of our men and some Baratans will stay for a while at Valleyford, in case the Appellans change their mind, though it's not likely with Morrik in custody. It will serve too as a reminder that the Appellans have debts to pay.'

'Debts?' Cran asked.

'The pirated ships and their missing cargoes. The ships they can return, save for the *Swift Jenny*. But her owners must be compensated for her loss, and the others for the value of what they carried.'

'And if they refuse?' Cran raised his brows.

'Then the alliance will place an embargo on their wool. The troops will see that it does not leave the country. It is their major export and much of it leaves from Valleyford for the wider world. I think whoever fills Morrik's shoes will find it cheaper to pay up.'

'And what of Morrik himself?' Nimmik said. 'Cran tells me the Baratans stole him away in the night. What has become of him?'

Marric smiled. 'He'll be making an enforced stay in the Black Country. They don't keep slaves there but their landholders have indentured workers, mostly debtors and criminals who have committed lesser crimes. They are tied to their place of work for certain periods. Doku seems to think that five years might provide a fitting sentence for one who organised theft, murder and insurrection against friendly governments.'

'Fitting indeed. It should serve as a warning to future troublemakers,' Cran observed.

'And a vast deal easier than the sentences handed out here.' Nimmik had plainly heard of Hardfar's fate.

'Aye.' The word reminded Marric of something. 'Rissak did not ride with the king?'

'He stayed at Valleyford with the troops,' Cran said. 'Darien's left him in charge there.'

'Of course. Well, he'll be right at home.' Rissak had been born in Ansham, on one of the big Appellan holdings when the country was a vassal state of its larger neighbour. He and Cran had been boyhood friends in the days when the Old Race was seen by their overlords as little better than slaves. 'It is odd, is it not, how life so often seems to return us to our beginnings?'

A shadow crossed his heart then and for a moment the world seemed to stop. Cran said. 'What is it?'

Marric shook his head, schooling his features. 'Nothing. A stray thought.' He could see he wasn't believed but the other man knew better than to pry. Arn had said it first, that a man's unmaking should come to him unannounced. And a gentle death in sleep, he thought, was surely better than one in the maelstrom of battle. 'We must all take the crow road in the end,' he murmured.

Cran looked enquiringly but did not ask for he too had, on occasion, walked in the thin space between the worlds, which Marric sometimes forgot. He waved a dismissive hand. 'Just a saying they have here, when someone leaves.' A harsh cry brought his gaze up to where two black shapes winged their way above them. 'The clans all have totem beasts and the crow is Leris's. And if I'm not mistaken in the direction those two are flying, they indicate our way home.'

'Very likely,' Cran pursued it no further. He nodded towards the opening hall door. 'Seems the meeting is over. The kings look happy enough.'

'They do.' A sudden feeling of wellbeing suffused Marric. He said, 'We have changed the world a little this day, my friend.' The words found a faint echo in his memory. 'Do you know Arn said that same phrase to me when we met to ratify the agreement between our own two countries? Let us hope that this will be as beneficial. So much hatred and death over so many years — who would have thought today could ever happen?'

'Who indeed?' Nimmik, who had completely missed the earlier interplay between his companions, grunted. 'The only thing less likely is that a people could make and actually drink the swill these barbarians call beer. It's a crime against a man's stomach.'

'Tell Ramie,' Marric advised, rising. 'Perhaps he can bring grape cuttings on his next trip.' There was a flash of light and for an instant he saw them, the long caravans throughout the unfolding years, bringing ever more trade and converse and curiosities to nourish the growing sophistication of the peoples of the Grass. He saw buildings rise where the camel trains passed, roads bringing greater ease of travel, a polyglot population increasing in wealth and diversity. And behind it all, ghosts in the grass, phantom hoofbeats thundered, fading to silence as he blinked away the vision. Epona would still rule and all would be well with Her people.

Overhead a crow cawed hoarsely. The bird from the hall. It dipped above him in its flight, white ringed eyes knowing, before the wind lifted it up to circle into the cloud-tattered sky above the endless leagues of grass, following where the earlier pair had gone.

***

Printed in the USA
CPSIA information can be obtained
at www.ICGtesting.com
LVHW050049021123
762565LV00010B/940